Strike the Bell Boldly

By the Author

FICTION

Strike the Bell Boldly

The General

The Pedlocks

Man of Montmartre

Geisha

Lion at Morning

Beach House

NONFICTION

War Cries on Horseback

Treasury of the World's Great Prints

Salute to American Cooking

The Real Jazz, Old and New

PLAYS

High Button Shoes

Strike the Bell Boldly

A NOVEL

BY *Stephen Longstreet*

"The principle of political necessity is
a rich source of strong emotions, a fertile
germ of the most dramatic situations."

—NAPOLEON TO GOETHE

G. P. Putnam's Sons   NEW YORK

SBN: 399-11916-7

Library of Congress Cataloging in Publication Data

Longstreet, Stephen, 1907-
    Strike the bell boldly.

    I.   Title.
PZ3.L8662Sw   [PS3523.0486]   813'.5'4   76-51426

To the unknown man at a 1976 national political convention who offered me a drink of bourbon and the words, "No matter who you vote for, the government gets in anyway."

BOOK I

The Apprentice

Chapter 1

Some folk who lived among the mule deer and the long-tailed cur-lews when Jason Crockett first emerged on the northwestern scene—modestly as a state's treasurer—assumed he was one of the Crocketts decended from the fabulous Davy Crockett. Every television viewer in the state knew that Davy had died at the Alamo. In actual fact there were several Crockett families who could have made the same claim: the Killamook Slope Crocketts, who were rich timber-cutters, and the Reed Flats Crocketts on the Cumpqua River, fish-canners and bankers—not related, they hoped, to the Star Bay Crocketts. The opposition newspapers pointed out some Crocketts were a shift-less lot; part Indian, Klamath and Mountain Sioux. The men drunk-ards, the women whores; which was not fully true of people following Rousseau-like natural patterns, on welfare.

Jason was one of the High Sky Crocketts, his grandfather, Horace, having taught mathematics at the High Sky State University there. The High Sky Crocketts, caustic, Episcopalian, hardworking, had be-gun as orchard-growers, timber-cutters, and supporters of education at various small colleges until the grandfather, the math professor Horace Crockett, had managed to work his way through the Vista City College and establish his family in High Sky, where he taught for forty years and never got over the fact that his son, J. (for Jasper and never used) Willard Crockett had left off getting a solid educa-tion to establish at first a sawmill, then a supply company, then a lumber-exporting business.

J. Willard Crockett was a hard-driving man, full of rippling op-timism and prejudices. A short man who shaved off his beard and splendid moustache at twenty-two, married Hilda Harris, a missionary's daughter of Scottish piousness, unquiet and garrulous. J. Willard entered politics not as a candidate but as a leader of the party in Clargmore, Blue River and Pioneer counties before he became chairman for the entire state and a great deal of the Northwest. To his friends he was a man with an infinite yearning; to his enemies, "One smart sonofabitch."

J. Willard had a rarely shown terrible temper, a sweet disposition when he got his own way, which was often. He always ate hot oatmeal with cold milk at breakfast and four stewed prunes, and he drank buttermilk. His activities had produced four reappearing ulcers by his dedication to his business, political activities and an inexhaustible vitality. When his son Jason was a small boy, his father would lecture him and his younger brother Theo and his sister Ida Mae over the hot oatmeal and cold milk.

"I don't expect you to work the way I did, the son of a patch pants college professor with his bare ass sticking out. But just remember you're a Crockett, and start the day with hot oatmeal. There's nothing like it. Never mind that crispy messed-up crap in the cornflake boxes with that pissed-on trash sweetening."

"Language, language," J. Willard's wife Hilda would say, smiling. For a missionary's daughter Hilda Harris Crockett wasn't shocked by her husband's language, but she still retained enough of the old-time religion her parents had preached in China and India to hope "Mr. Crockett," as she addressed him, wouldn't burn in hell when he died. She took an interest in his business dealings and the political shenanigans the party indulged in to deliver the votes of the coastal counties for the candidates it backed.

Hilda Crockett was a cheerful woman, loved her children and felt J. Willard was a natural anarchist. Rather shy in company, she enjoyed herself in bed with "Mr. Crockett," as she continued to call him not only in public and in front of the children but also in the sweet ferment of a vocal, fully appraised orgasm.

"Now Mr. Crockett, hot oatmeal is fine but a bit of eggs and bacon and some good cured country smoked ham gives muscles, and Jay is too thin. Needs blood thickener—red meat."

"Wararwarra wararra," J. Willard Crockett would reply, his only form of protest when his wife got his dander up. He himself was a vegetarian then, a follower of the long departed Dr. Graham who invented graham crackers. As long as Jason could remember, his father ate a great deal of fruit for his habitual constipation; he also suffered from hemorrhoids and would only eat fish during the spring salmon season when he and Jason went trout-casting in the Blue River country.

J. Willard was a moral man sexually. He never joined his fellow political cronies in cavorting with the call girls and whores at the state or national conventions. He had never been unfaithful to his wife. In his youth in the lumber camps J. Willard had learned to drink hard, but he gave it up with the appearance of his first ulcer. But he was not cured, for every two or three years he went on a bender, "a real toot" as the family doctor, Homer Mitchell, called it; usually resulting in a bleeding ulcer. J. Willard would come back after three or four weeks at Doctor Welp's Sanitarium in Ocean Grove, "dried out" and aware drink could kill him. J. Willard spaced his bats, as he called them, usually about every four years, mostly after a hard-fought national election. Hilda would explain his being away: "A touch of his old rheumatic fever."

J. Willard should have been a very wealthy man, but he spent too much time shoring up the political work to be done. "Goddamn drones and piss-ants, failed lawyers and fat cats always ready to exploit the party. There are times I wonder if we wouldn't be better off with a stupid king and some walleyed prince."

He eyed Jason, Theo and Ida Mae spooning up their hot oatmeal and cold milk with no great enjoyment. "Just grouching as usual."

"You'll grouch yourself into another ulcer, Mr. Crockett," said his wife.

Jason grew up wondering why his father was not like other fathers, who owned trotting horses with sulkies, drove Packards, Caddies (the Crocketts had a beat-up Buick and a Ford station wagon).

When Jason was eight he went off in the station wagon with his father, headed for Blue River for the salmon fishing. It was fine living under the big pine trees, in a real log cabin motel, and casting his own line over the side of the bobbing boat, insects skating on the water, and watching the leaps of metallic-scaled salmon as they came on board with a swirling ballet of agony to lie on a bed of moss, gills flapping, drowning in air. Sometimes Jason got a bite himself, and his father would help him reel it in.

The fish, split open on shore under the madrone trees and broiled over hot hickory embers, was even better than ice cream, served out of doors. Um! Um!

J. Willard smiled and wiped his mouth on a paper napkin. "Now you understand, don't you, what we have here? A damn fine country wilderness, and we have to save it from the piss-ants."

"What's a piss-ant, Pop?"

"It's some goddamn lawyers usually who can't make it in real life so they run for public office and set to sucking on the national tit. It's the eastern bankers and la-di-da Wall Street pirates and Washington junket-takers. It's everything bad against what's so good out here." He turned to the waitress. "No stewed figs? How about stewed prunes? This state grows some of the best, you know. No? Well, a dish of bran. Not the damn doctored stuff. *Plain* bran." He smiled at his son. "Keep your bowels open and your mind clear and you'll have the world by the short hair." Jason for many years thought his father was a great philosopher.

Jason liked the summers they spent in various timber lands where J. Willard Enterprises was cutting, thinning out timber in the national parks. Being state chairman and high in the party did have some clout. Jason collected quartz diorite, agate, veined boulder conglomerate, saw a brown bear eating toyon berries.

"I love the damn trees, Jay boy. But you have to clear the underbrush, take out the culls, the diseased stock, and replant. Hell, I put in two seedlings for every tree I cut down. Some day you and Theo and Ida Mae will camp under trees your old man's crews planted today. Trees a hundred feet tall, maybe two thousand feet of timber in every one. While they stand, *that* will be our monument, not some half-assed gravestone. No, Jay, when I go, I want to be cremated and my ashes just spilled down over the fall of the Klamath. You promise your old man that."

"Aw, Pop, that's nutsy talk."

At ten Jason would ride the tug pulling the great rafts of logs, bark falling away, the smell of wild parsley in the air, down to where they would load the logs on ships with Japanese markings and smiling little men with gold-rimmed teeth would serve him some funny food while Pop joked with the officers.

J. Willard Crockett had served in the Pacific Theater as a major in World War II, supervising the building of airstrips in the Marshalls, at Kwajalein and in the Marianas. He'd been wounded in Okinawa, and when showering with Jason and Theo he'd let them touch the angry red scar tissue over his left shoulder. It was hard and rigid and Jason would feel his scrotum tighten. "Got hit on the out-skirts of Jima, bringing in the aircraft gasoline tankers."

Theo was a year younger than Jason, a sleepy kid who wore thick glasses and part of the time a patch on his right eye; his left one was lazy and so to encourage it to try, the good one was covered up most of the time. Jason was the wild one, and Pop would cuff him when he got into trouble, thump his head as if it were a croquet ball. Pop didn't believe in leather-whipping you, but he could give you a solid shot to the head, or when real angry kick you in the ass. Jason ap-proved—it was a kind of male way of doing things. Charlie Peckin-paw, Jason's friend, got whacked with a length of mule harness. Hilda would frown. "Just remember, Mr. Crockett, you keep hitting them in the head and you'll get a first-class idiot son."

"Aw, Ma, it don't hurt."

"Doesn't, *not* don't."

Ma had taught in a Presbyterian mission school in China before marrying Pop, so she insisted on grammar and no baby talk when they learned to speak.

By the time he was twelve, Jason ran with a country gang of wild-talking but decent boys; High Sky town youths who drank Cokes, ate greasy hamburgers, listened to early Sinatra, Red Nichols and Russ Columbo and explained sex to each other, usually in foul terms that thrilled them. There was as yet a hazy contradiction of relationships in their world. Jay was a good student, liked history and art, gazed in an emotional quandary at the naked dark girl in Gauguin reproduc-tions of his friends, Hank Wales and the part Indian Mose Hawker. They often went off to the woods with packs of franks and potato chips, or gathered in Main Street bookshops to look over motion-picture magazines of pictures of Joan Crawford and Ginger Rogers, leading to bull sessions in someone's room, beating their meat to see who could get it up first and get it off before the others. Real high life was smoking cigarettes, stealing pippins from an orchard, hooting at the movie shows at the Gem or Bijou and groaning at the love scenes and offering advice—"Grab her!"—and adding kissing sounds —"Um! Um!" Jason, when alone, felt their activities had scope but little breadth.

In high school Jason was known as Ginger Jake and Hank Wales as Pony Express. Jason was the star of the football team, played second base on the team that won the county baseball championship. He and Hank had the contract for class rings from a San Francisco firm, did a thriving business. He and his brother got to running a bicycle repair shop in his senior year now and then in the Crockett Enterprises warehouses. Jason was good-natured, got good marks in subjects he liked, poor ones in math, biology, Latin. He was a whiz at history, won an American Legion essay contest ($50) for his "Whigs and Federalists Revisited." He and Hank led the debating team against Blue River High and Mark Twain High School, taking the affirmative: *Resolved*, That the electoral-college system is obsolete. The year before they had taken the *other* side and won. He sensed the power and some of the danger of being able to talk competently on his feet, at times glibly.

Jason was elected class president, but missed out as valedictorian to Hank Wales; Hank so lean, a cheerful wit with buck teeth and taffy-colored hair. Hank was studying to be a Baptist preacher. He already had a hell-fire delivery and was a fiend for facts, with quotations from the King James version and the poems of Walt Whitman. "We're going to be great men, Jay." (Hank drowned that summer in a storm on Lake Spruce trying to save a dog.)

Jason never forgot his friend, and in heavy sadness at seventeen worked that summer at timber-cutting in one of J. Willard's stands of pine. He learned to handle a sixty-pound power-saw, drive a caterpillar tractor, and became aware you never used the term *lumberjack;* logger was the proper title. He went into Coquilleville in Pioneer County after the last payday, got high on beer and was laid in a Polish whorehouse, the timber crew insisting it was time Jason lost his cherry. He wished Hank Wales could have been there. For a few weeks he worried; he thought he had the clap or the old rale—what the loggers called Big Casino. He was spared.

He entered Stanford. J. Willard had insisted he go to college out of the state. "Go see the world and don't become a drunk or get a decent girl into trouble. Eat lots of fruit and keep your bowels open, your fly closed."

The four years passed so quickly, delightful summer backpacking trips into the High Sierras. In his junior year there was a trip to Europe on a freighter. God! To walk the streets Balzac did—Hogarth, Casanova. In Rome he got drunk, in London had an affair with a rich bitch from Vassar who brushed him off when they got back to the states. Class president, football star—two letters for that and baseball. Phi Beta Kappa; also a real case of clap this time. J. Willard insisted on a law course at the University of Pennsylvania.

"For protection against lawyers, the shitheads, and you'll see the eastern legal hotshots close up. And you'll get you a law degree. Greatest scum on earth, lawyers, but to lick 'em you have to know 'em. They control politics and the courts; they're shiny with deceit. And you'll be fighting them all your life. You want to come into the business, or you want politics?"

"I don't know, Pop, I really don't."

So he went east to study law and hunt for a stability of purpose.

One night when the snow, bone-white, covered the earth, there was a telegram. Ma was dead suddenly. A bad heart Hilda knew she had but had not told them. It was sad to see J. Willard look so old, so busted up at the graveside. Theo blinking behind his thick glasses and Ida Mae leaning on Aunt Millie. Way off in the mountains a cloud was moving across a rock face he had climbed once with Hank Wales.

The minister was chilly, and he read quickly:

> In thy presence in fullness of joy,
> At thy right hand there are pleasures evermore.

Jason remembered a line from English Lit: "Death hath taken down so many." And he felt more alone, lonely.

Maybe that was why he got married when he went into the law firm of Welton, Bixby and Rosegold in Vista City. He was healthy enough and feisty, too; and had slept with the wife of his professor of international law, also conducted an "affair" (made out, was more honest) with an Italian-American girl, Gina, who worked on the *Pottsville Journal* and was a chain smoker. She was divorced and had a three-year-old child, a little chatterbox of a girl. They made love in Gina's flat while the place smelled of baby pee and the bourbon highballs they drank, and she gave him his first face job. Gina wanted to be a novelist and Jason sent her a portable electric typewriter when he left law school. One night they met John O'Hara in the Coachman's Bar in Scranton and got looped together and talked of Faulkner and Chinese food.

Jason first saw Sheila Ann Mallory at the Talltree Country Club at the Thanksgiving party and they danced to Hoagy's "Stardust." The Mallorys were Scotch-Irish but Protestants. The club had an unprovocative quota: two Catholic families, one Jewish (Dr. Rosen-sweig, the best surgeon in the state). But so far no Negroes. Jason and Sheila danced well; and she looked beautiful to him, ripe and ready, not like any girl he had ever met. He told himself it was Nature's trick to make fertile girls so alluring, ready for the mating ritual. They were at the mercy of their perceptions of each other, slept together twice before they decided they wanted to get married. J. Willard didn't object. Her family was powerful politically, backers of the right candidates. The Mallorys ran savings and loan companies and the Mallory House motels, rivals in the state of the Holiday House setups. They served better coffee, they claimed, and occupied better sites. Sheila liked Jason's humor, the shape of his head. She suspected she wasn't particularly sexy and he insisted she was.

The wedding at the Mallory estate at Star Bay was like a political convention. Senator Paul Ormsbee came out from Washington and the President sent a telegram of good wishes. Buster Miller, the state house majority leader, was there. The ceremony was properly High Episcopalian, and J. Willard gave them a house in the best suburb of Vista City—Garland Grove—and the Mallorys filled it with antiques, some of them genuine; "the ugly ones," Sheila always claimed. She had fine perceptions, a sharp sense of social conduct, tenacity and ingenuity. They had a daughter, Laura Belle, and Jason ran for state treasurer the year their son, Teddy Willard, was born. Three years later Jason was lieutenant governor.

Jason was a remarkable speaker, crowd-pleasing, with a total recall for facts and figures. He was earnest and had backed the governor in a failed attempt to clean out the civil service rackets, tame the influence of the lumber and oil and fishing lobbies; had seen to it that the union lobbyists—the Wheelmen and Drovers Union, the WDU—didn't get all their demands. Also to keep the ranchers and farmers from getting things all their way against the needs of the cities, he and the governor had to compromise all along the line. Jason didn't sell out, but he saw that to get things done one had to deal. One had to give, permit a new dam in return for free school lunches and old age aid; permit Bingo in churches in a trade for relaxing film censorship by a bigoted bishop.

Jason learned to become a skilled political opportunist, to be liked and hated, to be seen as a coming man. The governor, Ben Brownson, began to fear Jason as a rival in the next election.

Old Ben, known as Elephant Breath, had been twice governor and wanted to make it once more before he retired on a good-sized pension and into the figurehead position in the law firm of Hayes, Kaminsky and Wheeler. He was a cheerful, lazy man, rather indefinable, with a liberal image, but always being quoted on the need for tradition, manners, morality and the northwestern way of life. As J. Willard put it to Jason while they lunched at the country club: "Ben's for the tall trees, the salmon leaping, blue skies, low taxes for big business, old-fashioned education. He's a generation out of date. Want to take him on? Run for governor? Speak up."

"Old Ben's a loyal party man."

J. Willard looked up from his bowl of stewed figs. He twisted around in his seat—his hemorrhoids were bothering him. "Hell, remember—only the party matters, usually, not the man. We've pushed some fatheads into some high places. But what counts is the party. Whatever else Jefferson and Washington and Adams and all the others in silk knee pants did, they gave us a goddamn fine foundation. On it we set little actors in motion. But it's only as boarders in the state capitol, or into the White House. Sometimes they forget themselves and are ungrateful."

Jason grinned and cut into his small steak. "The White House?"

"Look, we haven't had a great man there since FDR, the sonofabitch. Truman, he's just a fake folk hero, built up by the press. Come on. How bad do you want to be governor? Can you taste it, Jay?"

"Maybe I do."

Chapter 2

Jason Crockett was his grandfather's favorite grandchild, and Horace Crockett was a scholar and an intellectual. ("Almost a sin out here," he would say with a stentorian guffaw, "the whole damn state is dedicated to the false legend that the nation was mostly built with muscle, not brains. And that the man who chopped a tree down the fastest was superior to a man who could read Latin and enjoy Homer.")

So Horace Crockett was perhaps nearly the only one person in Vista City able to gauge Jason Crockett beyond his skill in the political field, and his abilities to present himself as a deserving candidate. Horace had enjoyed walking with Jason past the green pools of April, the water all frog spawn, and explaining to the boy the charm of his house with its porte cochere, cupolas, dormers and Ionic columns over the legendary log cabin; so much spoken of but no longer used except in some wilderness part of the state as a hunting camp. As Jason progressed into manhood the old man charted in his mind the assets and the faults of this his favorite grandchild.

Jason grew up to be a handsome man with deep-pigmented blue eyes. "Well, we do judge by appearance too much still." Jason was honest, he kept his word, he respected his father, and his grandfather moving into the slow depletions of age. He didn't drink too much, he appeared faithful to Sheila.

Jason admittedly could overpower inertia at a political gathering. At worst he would at times, when in a brooding mood, linger at some precarious emotional peak; he kept his inner thoughts to himself too much. On the other hand, one had to admit Jason was a thinker, but not a deep thinker. Well read in college, he had done little serious reading since. For all his years at Stanford, and in the eastern school, he remained an unspoiled provincial, some—the opposition—even said a hick. Which did him no harm with the voters. In Jason the old man felt the Protestant ethic had not gone sour but had however become somewhat ambiguous.

"A good man, our Jay," Horace told J. Willard. "He has fine qualities. But he's lacking that which will come with maturity, I hope. An awareness of the corrosive side of life, of the tragedy of just existing on this strange planet. There's no austerity to his moral base."

"Well, Father, that calls for a little whiskey." J. Willard never permitted himself any doubts about his children. Hot oatmeal and cold milk had made them solid in body, and his own decent and ironic, aware view of men and conditions had, he hoped, given them a better view of the truths of the world than the over-pious, the lazy, the dishonest or the fanatical.

Horace Crockett also felt it was downright farcical the way Jason at the moment of some victory—in the debating society, at a major championship football game, before winning some election by an easy majority—would begin to sweat and have doubts, even, in some cases, vomit. J. Willard would just explain, "He's a finely tuned violin, string wound up a bit too tight."

"Well, he has to work to get a stable equilibrium."

"Don't be a wet blanket. You'll have dinner in the Governor's Mansion yet, Father."

The old man smiled, "You better see to it. It's the only thing besides your whiskey that keeps me alive and kicking."

"Now, if you ate the right breakfast—"

"Shut up and pour us a round to the next governor, Jason Crockett."

Wanting to be governor and getting to be governor were two different things. One must define oneself by obligations and risks. First of all there was Sheila. The night he couldn't sleep and went downstairs to mix himself a drink. He came back to find one of the night table lights on and his wife in her powder-blue dressing gown sitting up in the big double brass bed.

"All right," he said, "you don't have to stay up because I can't sleep."

"You used to sleep with no trouble at all. Used to hate you for it."

"Want a sip?"

"No, look, Jay, why be governor?"

"Hold it. I have to be nominated, have to run to be governor. I'm not so sure I'll make it."

She looked at him with that half-hooded glance, that wide pretty Mallory mouth. He knew the look; the married woman's look of staring a man down, a dumb husband. Yes, the married woman's look of *Why don't you grow up?*

"I haven't made up my mind, Sheila."

"Make it up, say no."

He sipped the drink. He drank a bit too much when under tension. The Mallorys, now *they* were the drinkers. That's why Sheila watched him at parties, at political clambakes. Her old man was a boozer, two uncles had died of the sauce, and she had a sister who kept getting arrested while under the influence and driving a car. Funny girl, Sheila. All that character and that little solid core of female dark impulses, a wariness of humanity, and given to rational conclusions. A good mother but a bit on the cold side, a splendid lover but no nonsense once the act was done. Yet at times she surprised him. There was in her a delicacy crossed with an intensity of purpose.

"I'd rather you left politics."

He swallowed the last of the drink and got into the big brass bed. They had bought it at auction the first year of marriage in San Francisco, and it was supposed to have belonged to a famous Clark Street madame, Nell Kimball, at the turn of the century. The first year of their marriage they had called the bed Whoring Acres, later The Baby Farm.

Jason sat in the bed by Sheila's side, bodies not touching. "A little late, isn't it, to change my trade?"

"You have a good law practice. A fine firm, solid contacts. You'll be a judge when you're forty."

"It's all right, the law. But it's just a dirty game mostly. Not really justice. It's just what references one side can bring up against the other side's references. A game for the sliest, the best voices."

"Isn't politics?"

"Hell, it can be so much more. Besides, Honey, I think I have something to offer. I guess I want excitement and the spotlight. All right, I admit it—there is a fat streak of ham in me."

"Unrealizable fantasies, Jay. Your father has them. Your grandfather, Old Horace the schoolteacher, he had them."

"Oh balls," he said, "let's get some sleep. Maybe they, me, I'm hunting for some truth."

Sheila snapped off the night table light, "Do you put truth in the first *or* second place?"

What the hell, he thought in the darkness. What kind of a crack was that? First or second place? He remembered he had written at Stanford in an essay: *Truth is a permanent force for persisting through change.* Not bad, not bad at all. He was sure he had permitted himself no false assumptions in his college years. But looking back in fact, he'd been a square kind of creep with his sense of moral profundity. Only his popularity in football had saved him from being someone looked down as an overserious drip, a country jake.

He yawned, felt the drink warm his entrails—and Sheila so alive and close, the odor of her, so personal and sensual. It was real: the warmness, the movement of a prone body; slight, but there as she breathed. He wanted to reach for her, engulf her, rope her to him with his limbs all over her. He felt his vulnerability—his drinking, gambling, desire for public notice.

But goddamnit, a sexual urge just now couldn't change his decision; yes, palpitating doubts, vulnerability or not, he was going to try for the governorship. I'm no college innocent anymore, confirmed in hope by a coercive church upbringing, placidly accepting that all is right with the world if one worships with the right people. I have learned the techniques of politics, the handling of public controversies, the charm of smoothing fools, setting siege to money sources and using my skill of voter-bedazzling. For their own good, of course.

He heard Sheila in a half-sleeping mutter speak: "Jay—can't you sleep?"

He was on her, over her, and in her, to her surprised but non-resisting reaction, but carried away. When they were first married, before the children came, he had been a bit ashamed of using her body to calm himself, of using her as a kind of prescription, a needed treatment for his nerve ends, his pent-up tensions. But these assumptions no longer pressed down so heavily on him in these moments of frenzy, actions that could not be called pure love actions. Rather the barbarian within, banging at the gates. One accepted the need, one did the act: now, now, *now.* Sheila responded, moving in those little body gestures and giving off throat sounds and mutters of pleasure.

She was Sheila, he was Jason, and they were at this, had been, would be.

For some reason, as he came, Jason thought of Stravinsky's ballet *L'Oiseau de feu*, which they had seen in Washington, D.C.—he a delegate at the last convention of a commission on rivers and harbors, a convention that had accomplished nothing. He was not a ballet fan, but Sheila and their daughter, Laura Belle, had insisted—and at the new Kennedy Center for the Performing Arts—and—

"You bastard." It was Sheila speaking in a low and amused voice. His sudden primordial impulses countered her fear she wasn't sexy enough.

He kissed her cheek. She said, "Go to sleep, Governor."

Jason did not fall asleep very quickly. He always suffered when he had no sure stability or sureness of purpose when he vacillated. Had he in this sexual assault on his wife made his decision? There was nothing to do but to be nominated and get elected. Ideals need not be true—merely plausible.

Those who know only Jason Crockett the public figure, the speaker, he thought, don't know my self-doubts, the battles I fight with myself. The demoralizing periods when I wonder if it wasn't better to be some greedy, overpriced lawyer, like so many I know; the Scotch-guzzling, client-screwing attorneys at the club. But what of my crackbrained idea that I could help, could offer something special as governor to the helpless voters manipulated by timeservers, windbags, fat cats, fart sacks—not forgetting the few humorless bleeding hearts. Also there is in me this public need for applause, a need of approval from the faceless mob; the standing to take an ovation, the clasping of my two hands held high over my head at their approval, vocal applause. Politics is the ability to confront whatever can be imagined. Something in his childhood was to blame for his doubts. That Freudian crap about being put on the potty too soon? Seeing J. Willard, J. W., as a monster he wanted to unconsciously topple from his perch? Nonsense. As someone had once said, "Anybody who goes to a psychiatrist ought to have his head examined." Take me as I am, he thought, falling into a deep sleep . . .

There was a dream, just before morning. He was standing on a very high platform and there was a deep chanting from thousands of people someplace below him—also guffaws: "Throw the bum out!" "Take me as I am," he called out, willing to serve, willing to suffer, able and honest, knowing the ropes, aware, oh *so* aware, "folks, that I have your interests at heart while they play 'Swanee,' and keep me high on your shoulders and feed me steak and get my picture on the cover of *Newsweek,* and I promise on my sacred oath I will kiss your ass at high noon on the steps of the Capitol Building." Now he was barefooted and walking over the heads of the crowd quickly, almost flying, stepping on head after head, and Alice (who?) said, "Jam yesterday, jam tomorrow, but never jam today" . . .

That was the time to wake. It was a new dream with apricot-colored scenery. Not at all like his recurring dreams of being suddenly put down in a strange place and no one willing to tell him where he was.

He opened his eyes carefully as if caught in an indiscretion. Sheila was gone, the smell of her, the concave pattern of her head still on the pillow. He smelled coffee brewing. Sheila the coffee fiend, up at dawn before the arrival of their maid.

Jason put on a robe and went into the breakfast nook (it was a nook, *not* a room). The Sony television set on a cabinet shelf was on, and Snow Williams, troubled by the letter *r,* was interviewing a scarred Arab with a hawk's face, very good teeth and a Charlie Chan moustache.

". . . it's wealy true you Arabs want only peace, are weady for a settlement of all the problems in the Middle East."

"Only de peace is on are minds. We haft for de Jews only the luff of brudders. Racists Zionists even them we will welcum once they gives up the Jew country—I mean de Zion state und let us becum again brudders . . ."

"Your actions sound weasonable—but your terrorists don't wealy bear this out."

Sheila poured a cup of coffee. "I suppose, if you go for governor, thee and me will have to get up in public and smile like Snow Williams."

"I hope not—all those capped fangs." He added a spoon of sugar, a dollop of noncream, and sipped the mixture. Somehow the noncream suggested goat pee. "You'll accept, Honey."

"Like hell I accept, Jay. I *just* go along. But if it's what you want—okay, okay. But no funny hats like Pussy Brown, when her husband was running for judge."

He took hold of her hand and pressed it. "Thanks. I know you feel I'm a nut about this—but anyway you'll help. I need you, I need you and the kids and the sense of us being a unit. Oh hell, I'm making a speech."

Sheila stood up and pulled tight on the belt of her robe. "I better go get dressed before you get horny again." She laughed. "Remember the McCallen party when you announced for state treasurer?"

"On the floor of their bathroom."

"I got lint in my hair. A lousy housekeeper, Mrs. Rita McCallen."

Jason watched his wife leave the kitchen, still slim, sassy, and was pleased he had been faithful to her (but for a few lapses under rather strange conditions). The back door opened with a zing of the spring and Fran Colter, their live-out maid, came in, a large black girl, carrying a bundle wrapped in a blue cloth under one long arm. Fran did the housecleaning from eight to twelve, prepared lunch if anyone was at home, put on the dinner and then was off to her college classes at the state university at Vista Boulevard. Fran was hard-eyed, rather clumsy—she'd never be a tap dancer, J. Willard had said when she dropped chicken à la king on his sleeve. She was working for her master's and had told the Black Union at the college she didn't give a fiddler's fuck for any white person.

"Morning, Fran."

"Morning, Mr. Crockett."

"How did the school exam go?"

"Like fair."

She nodded and turned on the tap over the soiled dishes in the sink, pulled on pink plastic gloves, raised up a dust storm of Ajax powder.

"I'm going to try for governor."

She poured more Ajax over last night's dishes, took an apron off a hook, tied it on. "You expect us blacks to vote for you, Mr. Crockett?"

"Why the hell not? I'm no Archie Bunker."

Fran Colter began to scrub the dishes with a small sink mop. "No niggers on the board of Crockett Enterprises. Only burrheads at your country club are waiters and caddies."

"I'm not two hundred years of history, Miss Colter."

"You home for lunch? A cheese omelette?"

"Look what's been done—ask your mother. She knows of the changes. They've been there, or your grandmother."

"Uh-huh. You be here for lunch, Mr. Crockett?"

He shook his head. He better leave before Fran brought up bussing. Today he had to get a group together to work for the nomination and for the election. J. Willard would have some ideas—and he had to be held down. He almost, as he passed, slapped Fran's bony beige-skirted ass. Only she'd think it was sex.

The party felt they owed the governorship to the old crock of a Judge Bensinger who had been in the national media for a month over some Indian fishing rights he had defended. *A hero for salving the wrongs we had done our red brothers.* It hadn't amounted to much—the higher courts decided against the Indians as usual—but it gave the old crock a self-importance that could only be rewarded by appointing him dean of the Blue River Law School—to step aside for Jason.

The real test for Jason's nomination had been in the meeting at a ski lodge below Mount Lincoln. "No smoke-filled room," J. Willard had said when assembling the group over the phone. "Lots of snow, booze for toasts of victory—and *no* broads."

There were present—as a cold wind stirred the trees and rattled awnings—Senator Paul Ormsbee from Washington (white hair, the well-fed look of a pink-skinned baby); Bascom Rice, the state wheeler and dealer; Buster Miller, the party's leader at the statehouse; Barney Binsky, the lobbyist for the lumber and cannery people; Wallace Klamath of the Wheelmen and Drovers Union, with his thick black hair, his Indian grandmother's cheekbones. He was president, dictator, boss of the WDU, the tough associate of longshoremen, cannery workers, loggers, machinists, the plywood and newspaper-print mills' rank and file. And Sarah Doggens, the only woman present, chairperson of the Women's Division of the party—big, old, still able to shout.

The lodge was set among Douglas pines and pitch pole firs. The room paneled in some dark wood, the big stone fireplace burning two huge logs while below the lake was an indigo blue. It all set an atmosphere of some drama about to be performed in a mood of delicately balanced stability, yet in risk of being ruptured. There were drinks, but only two cigars lit. Most of the men had given up tobacco, and were on diets in fear of coronaries. The fat paunches, the smell of good Havana leaf were missing. Sarah Doggens smoked unfiltered English cigarettes ("Live dangerously").

Senator Paul Ormsbee, sipping a hot toddy, lifted the glass, a ruby finger-ring flashing in reflection of the fireplace. "There are no better stock than the Crocketts. Jay has the quality essential to a fine candidate." Senator Ormsbee had been in the Senate for twenty-eight years, and would retire soon and take up bookbinding, his hobby. He was the utilities', the lumber interests' man, clever and only now and then touched with senility. He honestly felt that free-swinging corporations "within reason" made prosperity.

"Thanks, Senator," said Jason. "I wouldn't think of trying for it unless you were in agreement, Senator."

"Damn right," said J. Willard. "We'll need a big war chest to win the governor's chair. Everybody helps, industries *and* the unions."

Wallace Klamath was one of the cigar smokers (a Cuban cigar brought down from Canada). He dropped ash on the polished pine floor. "You're clean with us, Jay, and we'll dip into the election support fund. All legal and aboveboard. But, Christ, no more of this crap about the Mafia and the WDU playing footsie."

Jason shook his head. "Come on, Wally, you know it doesn't matter what is hinted. The unions don't give a damn one way or other; you're all too solidly entrenched. I need your backing and all I ask, Wally, is no strikes just to show your muscle."

"We only strike when the welfare of the people is shit on, pardon me, Sarah."

It was a close-knit, discursive two hours. No one recorded the talk. No one would mention it. There would be no notice of it in the newspapers.

Bascom Rice told the story of the Chinese girl and the parrot, and Sarah the one of the onion ring and the husband. Buster Miller rose and stretched and added there was no worry about certain districts in Kinglet County. "We've got this gerrymandering thing going to pocket the opposition so they couldn't elect a jackrabbit to a carrot festival. Now there are some jolly girls down at the Badger Inn if anybody wants to dance and raise a roof a bit. The Bay Power and Utilities is having a sales convention."

Jason felt no touch of reality as he and his father walked back to their cabin. These people, he thought, they aren't bad or evil. They're power brokers. They have their special interests: the workers, Sarah's women's rights, the pulp mill owners, the lumber corporations. There were state problems: costly services, roads, schools, prisons, coastal pollution, rising city and suburban crime. The party men were alert, aware and able, but demanding. Some were greedy, one or two dishonest, but they were a machine, skilled in politics, and they had produced in the last fifty years the party that existed. It stood by honest government (in theory).

J. Willard said, as they trod the frozen earth, "They'll back you, they'll raise the money, and with God and the weather, the PR people busting a gut, you'll be governor."

"How come, Pop, you never went for it?"

"I've been tempted. Ooh, I've been tempted. But I've a stronger character."

Chapter 3

The posters and billboards for JASON CROCKETT FOR GOVERNOR didn't feature the Davy Crockett coonskin hat or his Kentucky rifle, but they did carry a suggestion of a frontier America with a background of a tall grove of native pine trees, lofty snowcapped Mount Lincoln, and this carried over to television commercials of hunters, fishermen, waitresses, loggers, and married citizens in trailers. All looking directly into the cameras admitting Jason Crockett was part of our history and was "like the rest of us, interested in keeping us green." Or some flycaster of a senior citizen looking over his glasses and reeling in a rainbow trout: "Well now, I've got the time, and he's helped make it good time. I don't see how we kin do better than Jason Crockett."

There were some who said the folks in the commercials were actors brought up from Hollywood. Or players from the university's School Playhouse in High Sky. But that was mainly not true: only two ringers were hired by an advertising agency looking for oldster types, and while they might have been professional actors, they were genuine senior citizens drawing the state's old age aid and needing it. It was also pointed out the rival candidate wore monogrammed shirts and even had a French cook.

Wally Klamath of the WDU got the unions to back Jason, the Wheelmen and Drovers shop stewards seeing to it that the Crockett posters stayed up and that the rival candidate's—accused of nonunion printing—had trouble getting their sheets up on the billboards. Two weeks before election the polls showed that Jason would carry the state with 62 percent of the votes. But Buster Miller, the party's floor leader in the legislature, saw a cloud forming on the horizon.

It was not just that it was raining the usually hard seasonal winter rain. The fifth floor of the Lewis and Clark Building, the Crockett election headquarters, at nine o'clock at night was at a slack moment. No coffee breaks taking place and the photocopy machines only turning out some porno verse for a few friends, written by the head of the typing pool. The huge photographs of Jason on the wall were beginning to curl on the edges and the sweeper, an old black man, was slowly making his way, pushing a wide broom, through empty cigarette packs, Mr. Goodbar wrappers, crumpled press flimsies and handouts. A small radio played some Rolling Stones. The TV was dead.

Buster Miller came in, stomach well forward, waved to a few people and moved toward the walled-off offices where J. Willard at a rolltop desk was eating a Bartlett pear, slicing it carefully.

"Jesus, J. W., there's a hell of a hassle going on at the statehouse."

"Isn't there always? Who stole a red-hot stove lid? Have a pear."

"No thanks. I'm off my feed. Listen, it's the damn Wheaten-Ruiz Bill, 902A." Buster Miller unbuttoned his top shirt button, loosened his tie. "Damn 902A."

"Hell, Buster, it's just the usual bill for investigation; legal checking on certain funds held in trust. Comes up every few years in some form or other."

"This one has the clout behind it to pass."

J. W. shrugged, chewed pear, wiped his mouth with the back of a hand. "We're a pretty honest state, nothing much comes of these things. Of course there's always some shithead who yells about the violation of innocence."

Buster Miller walked about, inspected a badly stuffed raccoon on a shelf. "It's Wally Klamath, the Wheelmen and Drovers. They're obnoxious as usual."

"Jay has been real cozy with the WDU. What's their beef?"

"They want Jay to come out strong—both feet stomping on 902A."

"Aw, come on, people like the idea the state accounting and fund checking is doing a good job; well, going through the gestures."

Buster Miller sweated a lot, was reaching a finger under his shirt collar as if to release himself from being garroted. He twisted his neck and grimaced. "The afternoon *Vista Banner* had some fink list with its editorial as to salaries and investments of WDU pension funds."

"What are unions for but to put some extra butter on some folks' bread?"

"Nine-oh-two-A would take the union leaders to court, and it has clauses some sonofabitch snuck in, making certain investment and bonus payments illegal."

"Oh, that must rile Klamath and his boys." J. W. put the pear core carefully into a paper bag and put the bag into a wastebasket. "We better have it out at ten tomorrow at my house. Jay's coming in from Boiler Bay, so have Wally Klamath come on over and we'll comb him out happy."

"It's a damn crisis."

"Now, Buster, *never* call a crisis a crisis. Call it a situation. You can figure out a situation, but a goddamn crisis, that's dangerous." He put a pear in each pocket. "The polls are holding up fine, so no bleak desolation on your mug. We're going to win this—a walkaway."

"Not if the union foremen start withdrawing the support of their men and women."

"Buster, I never believed that crap that what union leaders decide on politics ever really gets down to the rank-and-file dues-payer. They think more of their bowling balls than the polls."

"Maybe so, maybe not; but if WDU gets to coming out officially against Jay—"

"Wash your mouth out with Scotch, Buster."

J. Willard Crockett wasn't really as calm as he appeared. He had been through union wars and election battles, and always claimed he had the scars to prove it. Jay needed the unions to win. The entrenched WASP minorities of inherited wealth, lumbering, paper mill empires, fishing and canning interests would vote the party ticket, but they were and remained a minority at the ballot box. Good to milk for funds, but in numbers for a solid majority it was the cities' and towns' workers and ranches and farms and factory hands who were the majority; and Wally Klamath was a sort of folk hero, a man of furious resentments studded with grudges.

A good part of him was Indian, the rest was said to be Polish or German. He had come far from trucking logs on twelve-wheel rigs in his own beat-up trucks, committing furious sabotage on mill machinery, to leading the big strike against the Wilamot Paper Corporation. He had been able to push the WDU to aid in electing working union-backed mayors in three cities, and defeated three right-to-work laws presented by certain groups. He had busted (it was no secret) with goons a rival union of leftist idealists for child care centers, flush toilets in outlying crop pickers' shacks. He and J. Willard walked wary of each other—Willard Enterprises was fully unionized, with fat fringe benefits.

Wally Klamath represented power and it was no idle remark he made in Chicago at a union convention meeting: "I can stop every wheel from turning on the West Coast, in the factory and on the road, and don't let any of the fat bellies forget it."

As with the Auto Workers' Union, the other AFL-CIO hardfisted collections of power, no one really wanted to test the strength of the WDU. The WDU used whatever method got it what it wanted. Goons, boycotts, some said sabotage, and there was gossip of arson and Mafia connections, the disappearance of several too nosy or rambunctious minor union leaders.

Jason was for unions, workers' rights, and was not as ironic as J. W., who would shrug it all off. "You give power to any bunch of people with doubts and irritability and they produce a leader, a real, solid troublemaker from the ground up, yes? But in the end he likes the dollar cigars, the hundred-dollar call girls, the big houses, the expense accounts, just like the heads of du Pont and General Motors. Then the hazy implications of relationships move in. Who are they really for?"

"There are boundaries of the powers of leaders, Pop."

"On paper, sure, like in the morals mottoes on church signboards."

"Wally, sure he's a role-player. The big shaggy labor leader all for the boys. But he's honest in his demands for the WDU."

"More or less we all are honest, eh, Jay? I never blew a bank safe, or peddled dope. And didn't someone note it's just as illegal for the rich as the poor to sleep under bridges?"

The meeting at ten the next day in J. Willard's parlor (he never called it a living room) in his old house in High Sky was attended by just a few key men. The parlor was a large room with heavy rafters, a wallpaper pattern of the 1940s favored by Hilda, J. W.'s dead wife. The furniture was good, solid stuff. "Not a goddamn antique among 'em." The lighting fixtures were from a movie palace gone to rubble twenty years ago.

Jason had arrived first, damp and cold, hungry, and had eaten a roast beef sandwich while his father explained the situation, as Jason nodded, chewed and sipped beer.

"Pop—I understand."

"Close to the vest, Jay, play it like a poker hand. Subtle, even preposterous, no wavering. But keep them on your side."

"Wally's boys have been *very* bad boys. He, too."

"Now don't go religious, not right now. After the election you can crack the whip. You want my advice?"

"Nope. I'll play it by ear."

Buster Miller and Bascom Rice arrived carrying two briefcases. There were greetings, some small talk. They accepted some drink, served by J. W. himself as he turned the servants off for the night.

Bascom, hardly looking the campaign manager he was, set down the briefcases on an end table. "Slice it anyway you want, 902A has a good chance of passing in the assembly."

"Or," added Buster Miller, "knocked in the head."

Jason grinned. "That divided?"

Bascom Rice nodded. "You speak up in favor for it, Jay—it's in. You say no to it—loud—and it's dead this session."

"So you double-talk, Jay," said his father. He showed first the palm of his hand and then the back of it in a slow gesture.

"Thanks."

Jason watched the rain fall. It had been falling for hours, sliding down the windowpanes of the parlor, the puddles throwing up shards of highlights outside. J. W. began to pull down the shades.

Wally Klamath appeared with the WDU treasurer, Artie Glasser; a thin, too thin man with a slight touch of Parkinson's palsy, pale gray eyes and a habit of answering most questions with "Well, now—" And not getting much further. Wallace Klamath used him as an echo rather than an important union official.

There were greetings, some attempt by J. W. at a jest, followed by ritual drinks as all sat facing each other in overstuffed, handsome club chairs. Buster Miller was smoking a cigar too quickly and coughing.

Wally Klamath hadn't smiled; he presented a tenacious stubbornness as he folded heavy arms over his bulky torso. He was acting out his stance of a union powerhouse, a man of the people in a good tailoring that didn't fit his big body; a size 18¼ shirt, collar open, tie badly knotted. His jacket lapel had a small enameled American flag, a gold marine sergeant's chevron from his days as a war hero. Pinned on his vest was the blue and gold WDU button. Just an ordinary button, no jewels or gold backing.

He slapped a large hand—well manicured—on the table. "So, it's *tochis offen tish,* right?" Wally Klamath liked to use Yiddish jargon, Spanish, Indian phrases to show he liked all laboring men no matter what their ethnic background. "Jay, we stand behind *you* when you stand behind *us.* We only want one tit, you can hand out the other three any way you feel like."

"I'll need union backing, Wally. I want your backing, but the WDU isn't the whole state. I know you feel you can stop everything moving. But you're no damn fool to start a civil war. Now you want my views on 902A?"

"You bet your sweet ass we do, the rank and file do."

"You feel, don't you, the organization can't stand an investigation this bill calls for?"

The union treasurer pursed his lips. "Well, now—"

"Stifle, Artie. Nobody can stand any Peeping Tom in business *or* politics. Even Jesus Christ, didn't he get the deep six? Right now the bleeding hearts, the pinko freaks, the union-busting corporations can make trouble. Jay, all we ask is you just say 902A is a hasty, unfair bill, see? And needs deep revisions. A fairer appraisal on both sides. That's all we ask."

"That all you ask?"

"Reasonable, very reasonable, Wally," said Bascom Rice.

"I don't give a damn what the Assembly does after election, reasonable or not. We have time to— to— well, cool them down."

Jason took an envelope from the inside pocket of his jacket. He sniffed, sneezed. He was getting a cold and knew it. His throat felt raspy. He needed sleep after a good long soak in a very hot bath. He needed to lie close to Sheila and maybe get up by morning the strength to make love. Maybe he'd even throw off the cold if he didn't have to face the next hour or so. He gave Wally a thin smile and thought why the hell did people run for public office, take the crap, get their lumps, be poor-mouthed. Why? He knew why—he knew the gut feeling of doing and being in a political campaign, the lure of having one's say, maybe even power in the fortuitous play of chance. Face it—it was an insatiable, clamorous delight.

"Wally, I've been going over polls and private data and counting noses. It's a close one. Without your endorsement, I don't know. And I'm not bullshitting you. I need labor votes—lots of them."

"You're damn right. You'll not be sitting in the catbird seat."

J. Willard snorted. "Back off, Wally, an endorsement doesn't deliver rank and file for sure."

Buster Miller grimaced. "Nothing's for sure."

"Try it without us."

Jason fingered some sheet of paper folded twice. "I have here an official petition given me in Reedport. By the New United WDU Committee."

"Back off, Jay. They're some leftist bastards, Local 630 troublemakers. No fuckin' official standing in the unions."

"Artie, you as treasurer can tell me if the figures I'm going to read are close."

"Well now—no one officially gets to—"

"Go ahead, Jay, let's hear what lies those commies have suggested. I'll cold-cock 'em—I swear it."

"They claim it can all be proved. There are photocopies, too":

The rank and file pay $120–$300 a year in dues the leadership enjoys, the benefits unmatched in any other union and in few corporations today.

The top WDU appear as executives with six-figure salaries, including free vacations, French chefs at headquarters in Washington, and three jets and turboprops. In the air force of the WDU is one of the largest private fleets in the country.

Last year ten officials received $100,000 a year, with some getting more than $150,000.

"Wally, you get two hundred twenty-five thousand plus expenses, and multiple salaries are common. Artie there holds ten posts, including General Organizer, a title you give out at will. It brings few duties and carries a forty-thousand-dollar salary."

"Well, look here—that's dirty pool."

"J. Willard said, "And big numbers."

"So what. Look at Meany, Woodcock, and what Jimmy Hoffa ran off with. Or Henry Ford, David Rockefeller, or the ITT brass,—it's just what's being paid for good men. And goddamnit—see, *I'm* good!"

"Good enough so Local 788 gave seventy-two thousand in bonuses to three of your officials, including the president and his son, the secretary-treasurer, and deals on cars—nine officials bought late-model autos from the union for a total of twelve thousand? Top officials' fully paid vacations with expenses for wives, secretaries, aides and dogs?"

"That's the national WDUA convention."

"Unlike colleagues in unions belonging to AFL-CIO, which prohibits salaried officials from being paid for running pension funds, WDU officials have set up these funds into another source of bounty. For managing the fund at Local 267, Boss Charles Ott got nearly twenty thousand dollars over and above his regular salary of forty-six thou and the thirty thousand he got as a general organizer. And non-WDU people share the pension riches. The administrator of the Utra Welfare Fund, Lawyer Vlad Polski, was paid eight hundred seventy-eight thousand and nine hundred dollars—about five point five percent of the fund's assets. That's for last year."

Wally didn't change his expression. "Every cop-out socialist rag on the West Coast has been making claims like that."

"These are official figures from reports you've had to make to account to Internal Revenue. Listen—'Ten million on loan to Las Vegas enterprises by the WDU pension fund brokered by what could be Mafia figures.' "

"Are you going to come out against 902A in your next speeches? That's the issue tonight. *Not* bookkeeping."

Jay refolded the sheets of paper as he stood up. Buster's cigar flared up and he choked; Bascom Rice handed him a glass of water. Buster sipped and stared at Jason. J. Willard's features seemed shaped in a kind of skull-like grin. "I don't like this feeling I have of alienation and isolation among old friends, Jay; give a little."

"I'll go this far, Wally," said Jason. "I'll not mention it. And if I'm questioned about it, I'll say I'm studying it."

"Nope. Not good enough."

Jason permitted himself a mocking smile. "I *am* studying it. Anyway it's a federal matter—you know the state can only go so far."

"No dice. You're putting half your ass on each side of the fence. Hell, man, we're partners—the old political infighters. I like you, Jay. I admire your old man. We're doing great things for the whole West Coast, for the state. I don't like to go from push to shove."

Jason shook his head. "That's it, Wally, take it or leave it."

Buster Miller said, "Please, no ultimatums."

Wally rose, elbowed Artie to rise with him. "In twenty-four hours I suggest you have a press conference knocking hell out of 902A. I wouldn't be happy to have the whole Wheelmen and Drovers Union withdraw its endorsement of you. Like an old sweetheart returning the engagement ring. *Capisce?*"

J. Willard said, "You sonofa—"

Jason stopped his father with a gesture. "You do that, Mr. Klamath, maybe I'll come out for the bill if I still like it on rereading."

"You're not as smart a gazabo as I figured."

"Your own rebels are going to give these figures and facts to the press tomorrow."

Wally and Artie went out slowly, not stalking out as was later reported; just moved out of the parlor. Buster Miller, a dead cigar in his mouth, said, "I wouldn't start my car any morning from now on, Jay, not without looking under the hood."

Chapter 4

Jason Crockett's race for the governorship is still remembered in the state as a provocative, razzle-dazzle affair in which the image of a young man emerged, one who appeared to be in harmony with himself, his party and his state. Not always in that order. But one of no public egocentricity and some introspection. He was a good speaker, often off the cuff. His prepared speeches had a tendency to get a bit confused in their delivery when he attempted to move away from the text and explain a bit clearer what he meant. Sheila was often at his side, smiling, cutting cake and lifting up some soggy, drooling infant for him to make eyes at: he refused to handle them himself. He was at his best with late-hour drinkers calling for "a little toddy for the body."

He had a good knowledge of issues and had ready answers, perhaps too ready answers, not a destructive quality in an election. He became aware, as the campaign moved on, of the obligations and the risks of the political atmosphere. There were audiences in for the kill, to hoot and heckle. Also there were expectant faces in the misty dawn under old trees by already bypassed rail lines; the whistle stops, the depots, the people that came in bib overalls, in pickup trucks to cheer, if only the name Crockett. There were also banquet rooms hideously modern. When tired, Jason's smile had a slow congealment.

Jason had come out for Bill 902A and the WDU made no move to withdraw its support of him. The wiser heads of the union felt it was best to support the young progressive rat rather than his conservative rival—an old war-horse who had little to offer but contemplative nostalgia and stories of how in his youth he had ridden the great log-rafts down the roaring forked rivers and once owned a horse, a pacer, that he drove in a sulky just over the two-minute mile.

Jason, after a day of hurried breakfast with the Catholic school board, a meeting at the Elks to get a plaque, a lunch with Rotary of Bibb lettuce, half a chicken, nearly iron peas, hot breads, ice cream in the form of the Rotary insignia (vanilla and strawberry), was bushed. There was the afternoon with Sheila at the Indian Penny Hotel facing a meeting of the Daughters of the Pioneers, some in hats, half in pantsuits, to whom both he and Sheila spoke of the need of bronze historic markers on the projected Pioneer Freeway.

No rest, but a five o'clock cocktail gathering at the Cresthill Country Club. Jason showing affection and equanimity to the golfers, the town banker, the town's law firms, a grain elevator manager, some tweedy college professors. Usually also the town's society, all of whom suggested money and some of whom would contribute to the governor's race. Here he knew they looked askance at levity and he held back his best jokes.

Dinner had to be crowded in with the party's higher-ups in Pineknot County; wise-looking oldsters with remaining hair plastered over bald brows, hawk-eyed young lawyers on the make, attorneys Jason always felt were idealists undecided between taking up malpractice insurance work or running for some public office to attract attention. It was cigars and Scotch, or hotel martinis out of Beefeater bottles that didn't contain Beefeater's. Old ladies with blue-rinsed hair, a lot of them remembering grandfathers who had made it big after many hardships; some even mentioned Davy Crockett and the Alamo.

If there was not a party powwow, then the candidate was at some formal $100-a-plate dinner—a repeat of the lunch menu with (Sheila noticed) hors d'oeuvres added, and steak or roast beef instead of half a chicken. There would be radio and television reporters present if the town was big enough; if not, some young earnest girl journalist with a camera ("I hope you are someone who doesn't think women's libbers are all dogs or dikes").

Usually he and Sheila begged off dropping in at someone's home for drinks and meeting the local minister or rabbi, the self-made county millionaire, the mother superior of a local convent. The highway contractor Jason could handle, but the regional novelist working on a trilogy of the pioneer settlement of the state was a problem. ("Have you heard the old expression: shiddle-cone-shite?")

Good people, earnest people, status-seeking or job-hopeful people. Some a bit cracked, eccentric, one or two mad enough to certify.

By midnight, unless Jason had to talk long-distance with the state capitol or with Buster Miller or the campaign managers of various counties, he and Sheila would relax in robes at the Big Pine Motel or the Holiday or Ramada Inn or the Bear Trail Hotel, the television on to some late-late show (Bogart, Cagney, Bette Davis), the sound way down and Sheila wondering if she had enough nylons for the trip, or to make a quick trip to Sears in the morning.

"How many more days till election, Jay?"

"Six, Honey. I promise after that it's the kids and fireside for you. And sixteen hours sleep for me."

"No, then comes judging pickles and pies at the state fair."

"They take elections seriously in this neck of the woods."

"Yes, Dear."

Sheila mashed out her last cigarette of the day in the hotel ashtray, sighed, closed her eyes and sank back on the bed.

"I wouldn't do it for all the hairdressers in Hollywood."

"Do what?"

"Be a politician."

"Thanks for not asking me 'Why do you do it?' "

"Well, I know." She beat her pillow into a more comfortable shape, without opening her eyes. "I know. You're earnest, you're a show-off, you're a sweet guy who really thinks he can make things work better, and you're a crowd-lover."

He set his watch and his little phone book on the night stand. "A lopsided image, Honey. Can't you add a desire to serve, a feeling if I don't do it the party hacks, the lobby bad boys would take over? Huh? Don't you—"

But Sheila was already asleep or faking sleep. He moved on bare feet—he hated slippers—over to the windows looking down on a night Main Street of traffic lights, the same chains: J. C. Penney, Ward's, K-Mart, Thrifty Drug, Rexall, Safeway supermarket, Exxon gas stations, a Xerox copy of every town its size he had passed through. Sometimes, as here across the street, a big red building with a tin cornice and the letters *1910 McCreedy Block* but mostly the same facades, the same wax window figures mincing and primping: COTTON SALE, also displaying the same blue jeans or organdy gowns, summer ending, back-to-school bargains. The same motion-picture front advertising Robert Redford and Steve McQueen films and, if it were a larger town, a city, a Bergman or Fellini picture. He disliked the enigmatic Bergman gloom, the smudged photography, and enjoyed the Fellinis, or did when he had time before running for the state's highest office.

He stood by the window, unwinding, wondering if the WDU would knife him at the last minute, or were they going to save their best efforts for defeating 902A in the legislature?

The night was turning chilly; the moon had a distant, icy fragility, but he did not close the half-open window. Rain was moored in the trees. It would shower in the morning. The traffic lights began to blink their late-hour reds and greens. There were no train whistles anymore, Jason thought, the way there had been when he was very young, or if there were still train whistles, he was no longer alert for them. There had been so many, a disconcerting abundance of whistles.

Tomorrow he and the staff would move on to Morriston, the next night Timber City, Wednesday the county fair at Mission River, hearing his two formula speeches, honest enough, but he was tired of glazing over what he really felt deeply about certain issues. ("Leave 'em no apprehension," Buster had said as he read over the first text of Jason's speeches. "No admonitory finger, just keep 'em happy, feeling they are thinking right and the opposition is an exploiting set of bastards.")

Jason felt the night air good on his face, his robe tight-buttoned around his neck . . . Here I am and what I am I know. No dark misanthropy—but no orgy of sweetness and light. A husband, a father, a candidate. Also in speeches I present a pastiche of sentimental epitaphs, bland assertions and oracular flaptrap. All so I may have an office to serve, do my duty, show I have brains and ideas and ideals. I'm not unctuous, and I've taken no payoffs, bribes, gifts, pocketed no funds, make no dishonorable promises. I am not cruel. I don't screw boys or sheep; not a sadist (as far as I know), and the only bad habit I have is gambling; I've cut down on poker anyway, and yet I have a wild streak of putting money on horses from time to time that don't win too often. I drink a bit too much, but I'm not an alcoholic (not so far); I watch the glasses, stop after the third martini. And I'm aware sophistication does not mean true experiences.

I'm in a trade that destroys modesty. I'm not humble, not Uriah Heep. I can't kiss ass, I flatter a bit, but good-naturedly. Jesus, do

I understand the political game; so much of it unscrupulous, and I shake the greasy hand, return the smile on the dishonest face that gets out the vote; I must watch out that my sense of being superior doesn't grow into an ego I dislike in others. Sometimes I practice complacency. I'm no seer prophesying doom or glory. I don't have all the answers. But I agree with Cicero: *When one's hour has come, don't miss it.*

All in all I'm a human item—a fallen-away Presbyterian who believes in the Sermon on the Mount, and as a lawyer, I do not like lawyers with their outrageous fees, their perverting of the political scene. I have a jaundiced view of American jurisprudence. It's available if you can afford huge legal fees . . . *And* it's going to rain, not wait for morning.

He was tired enough now, ready for sleep, relaxed—events of the day drained off. He went to his big suitcase, took out a bottle of Old Forester from a leather case holding it and a fifth of Haig and Haig. He poured a small silver cupful, swallowed and sighed with a somber expression. He hadn't meant to have that nightcap.

He got into the twin bed, the one facing the door; Sheila liked the one facing the windows. Jason felt his limbs relaxing, his chest feeling less heavy, his breath coming and going with ease. The vague ideas that preceded sleep ran through his numbing mind . . . protocol honors the man's office, not the man . . . *if monarchs were the hand of God, gentlemen were the fingers of the king* (English Lit, senior year) . . . there was this girl when I was sixteen, seventeen, and she had a feisty laugh and the beguiling look and I had the time and the place. Yes . . . on the sea grass between the rocks, both jaybird naked and the seagulls *gawk gawk,* and the salty smell of kelp and her hair and that's one way one finds one's center of gravity . . . sea sand in one's crotch and . . . Jason slept, undreaming.

Jason Crockett was elected governor of the state by a fairly good majority, but no landslide. The unions had not attacked him, but had not raised hurrahs either. The oil and timber and dairy companies had poured money into the efforts of the man Jason was running against. Jason got a majority of blacks, the Indians who voted. For reasons never too clear, he didn't get a majority of support from the Catholics or the Jews. But he was governor. He took the oath of office on the steps of the old, historical state capitol, with its copper goose-turd green dome, a sea of faces on the lawn patterned below it. Sheila and the children, young Teddy and Laura Belle, very perky in blue and old rose organdy. J. Willard himself with a few bourbons in him, very pleased, and Buster Miller and the rest of the party strong boys in freshly dry cleaned formal morning dress, all thin smiles.

The second time Jason ran for governor it was a true landslide. He had performed well, knocked heads together. The greed of utilities, the phone companies had been held in line, the oil corporations hadn't been too grabby after a few hints there could be price-fixing investigations—also of certain money passed. The WDU defeated 902A during Jason's first term. There were some hints of favors done, some members of both houses of the assembly changing their votes at the last moment; 902A joined so many other good bills that died the second time around. The Catholics and the Jews, the big timber-cutters, paper mills, the cannery companies, the "Women For" or-ganization had all felt Jason Crockett was worth reelecting. Some be-cause he had done good, others who felt he was a better choice only because Charlie Ringel, the reactionary he ran against, had strange ideas far to the right of the late New Liberty party or the Birchers. The only problem Jason ran into in his second term was the opposi-tion to his hope for a wild-land and coastal control bill, designed to save the still untouched mountain forests, the shoreline where seals basked on rocks and otters cracked clams on their furry chests with stones held in their paws. Jason feared for the state's coastline; how to keep it from getting into the blueprints of speculators and devel-opers who were encouraging a sweep northward of people fleeing the smog and congestions of California. When Jason favored the Snath-Chasum Bill to discourage the growth of the state's population be-yond a capacity that would have disfigured and polluted the state, turned valleys into thousands of ranch-style half-acre estates, the oil, paper mill and timber interests retaliated with a law prohibiting a third-term governor.

"Goddamn zealots," said J. Willard, "you'll have to make the move to Washington. You're elected senator or you're through. In politics there is no benevolent providence—you make your own miracles."

They were in J. Willard's garden, watching the Japanese gardener replace late-blooming pansies with beds of African violets.

J. Willard was getting old. Jason figured the old boy was deep in his seventies, yes, seventy-seven. Hadn't slowed up much, but limped a bit from stiff joints, and his face was wrinkled and freckled with liver spots. His voice was registering more pronounced treble and bass.

"There's Senator Paul Ormsbee. We need him, Pop. And there's Senator Decker, and he's Buster's nephew, so it's no dice there."

"Well now—Paulie is getting on. Maybe we can convince him this could be his last term."

Jay watched the gardener press a plant into the earth. "Paul, he's too good a man and the state needs him in Washington. And I don't want to be Ambassador to Bajokooko or something like that. Anyway, being too long in politics, I've noticed, creates induced paranoia."

"You could sneak back to law. It pays. You're not rich, and the trusts I have to leave four kids and grandchildren, well, it's not peanuts, but—"

"No law office. Think I'll ranch. Get some cattle. I own a chunk of the Pancoda Valley. I'll try it with a big mortgage, and borrowing from Sheila's folks."

"Balls," said his father. He shouted at the gardener, "Hey, Hokusai, why so many snails? . . . Raising beef, unless you know the angles, is a losing proposition. You'll get back into politics. Hell, I can just look at you and *know*. You've smelled battle smoke and have the yen."

"Sheila says it's in my horoscope. She reads it daily in the newspapers. Had my chart cast by a Madame Nina Tracktenberg."

J. Willard winked. "God will find a sinner, my grandfather used to say—when sober—even behind a thousand doors."

A month later the door Senator Joel Decker was behind was on H Street in Washington, D.C. It belonged to a foreman in the Government Printing Office, Sam Hansen, and when he found his wife, Florrie, and the senator copulating on his unexpected return to get his raincoat—the skies were threatening—the foreman fired a .45 Navy Colt at Senator Decker's lurching naked ass. He missed, but by evening the newspapers had the story and someone presented them with a batch of misspelled love letters of an erotic content in the senator's handwriting. Senator Decker said someone had copied his writing, a clear case of forgery. As for Mrs. Hansen, she came from the senator's state and the husband had misunderstood a meeting no more intimate than trying to get her Aunt Ernestine's World War II pension claims reinvestigated. Mrs. Decker said she'd stand by her husband's side.

Most of the state's newspapers indicated Senator Decker was merely following in the sexual patterns that in Washington had taken over the best of superior men: FDR, the Kennedys, Ike, others—up to the present resident in the White House. But the perfidy of politicians was well known and the small-town preachers took to the air to talk of sin: they were against it. Senator Decker announced he regretted he would not be running for a new term as senator; there were family matters, business, the Decker plywood mills that needed his full attentions. His wife, it was rumored, forgave him and forgave him *and* forgave him.

As a popular governor, Jason Crockett easily won the nomination for the seat in the United States Senate. The timber and real estate interests were happy to assist him to leave the state. He was elected by a fairly large majority.

He ran against a turkey farmer, Waldo Fullenkendorf. On election night, he and Sheila and J. Willard were watching the predictions of the TV networks and incredibly verbose comments of local and network national experts and soothsayers. Sheila said, "Well, there we go again."

They were on the tenth floor of the Bison-Hilton in Vista City. Jay said, "You'll like Washington. You enjoyed it, didn't you?"

"That was as a visitor."

Their son came from the next room. Teddy at fourteen was a handsome boy with a rather sullen expression, which was merely an expression, his parents said. He was a rather likable young man, they insisted, a shortwave radio freak, facetious about baths, free of acne.

"I'd rather finish school here," he said.

His grandfather switched channels. "Yakadee, Yakadee. Severeid, Cronkite and God."

"Just this year anyway," said Sheila. "We'll see about an Ivy League prep school next year."

"All faggots," the boy said. He went over to the table with the bottles, the soda, gingerale and an ice bucket. He poured himself a small Scotch. Jason and Sheila said nothing. They were readers of child and adolescent psychology books. Jason sensed Teddy smoked pot. Was it really a generation gap? Sheila wondered. ("It's just a lousy set of events, and a time all out of whack. But he'll be all right. All right.")

J. Willard said, "Get away from that likker, boy. It costs twelve eighty a fifth, wasted on Seven-Up drinkers."

The door of the suite banged open and three happy men and two women, party workers, came in. Someone tried to sing "For He's a Jolly Good Fellow" and someone else "Hail to the Chief."

J. Willard stood. "Saddle up, Jay. They're waiting in the ballroom. Fullenkendorf has conceded."

Chapter 5

As J. Willard put it of his son's chances, "It's a pushover. A slice of pie now Jay has the nomination." The opposition didn't amount to anything. Carter Oppenheim was always running for public office and his two speeches, with no frivolous irrelevance, were too well known. One speech was for the workers, the other for the business interests. The first spoke of the glory of the muscles that built this mighty state in extreme exhilaration and honest sweat; the second, of the brilliance that created the industry and progress of a splendid state.

The Socialist Workers' Party, as usual, put up an intelligent, too-smooth-talking man with a contempt of compromise—also a woman social worker as lieutenant governor. They were the only two candidates that seriously used charts, figures, passed out booklets, *The Devouring State,* pasted up posters, UNION LEADERS NEVER VOTE FOR YOUR UNION'S INTERESTS. They were humorless, often dull, and they got 5 percent fewer votes than usual.

It was in some ways a passive election. Jason made two or three speeches a day, wore orange makeup to do television appearances. The newspapers all over the state got their added amount of advertising. Even the opposition media were given political advertising. There were good clear photographs of Jason, and of him with Sheila, Teddy and Laura Belle on the lawn of their house, with Pop and their half-collie named Dog (cute?) and Red Prince, the tiger-striped cat from next door.

Jason's speeches were good ones, his delivery fine. If sometimes he felt he was too much the actor in a play and was playing for laughs, for applause, he'd go back to being a speaker running for public office. It was heady stuff, being on stage, he told J. Willard in the town of Ten Pines, the last speaking stop before returning to Vista City to make a final television appearance.

"Very heady stuff, Pop. You want to play the audience like a trout on a line, let out some sure-fire phrase that will get them clapping, and you toss in some little one-liner of a joke and milk the laughs."

"Well, Jay, there's no such thing as abstract politics. Or the best minds getting into office on only their intellect. Naturalness and amiability win elections, not nobility and pious hopes."

They were at the Blue River Hotel, a ramshackle old ruin with bathtubs bound in oak and standing on brass lions' legs, the rooms lit by turn-of-the-century gas fixtures converted to electric light bulbs. They still had napkin rings in the dining room, and a stuffed brown bear in the lobby. Both Jason and J. Willard hoped the place would survive as a historical site.

The two men were waiting in the hotel lobby for Jason's office assistant, Andy Wolensky, to pick them up in a state car; the small airport at Ten Pines was hemmed in by fog. The main street of the town had long since given up the necessity to struggle. This was called "solid virtues based in the past."

"Jesus, I envy you, Jay. I never had the savvy to run myself. I got to playing the eccentric and it took over. There's no confidence in anybody like me for the voters."

"Pop, you don't play roles, you *are* an eccentric, with some kind of built-in subtlety of introspection."

"Yeah, yeah, but if I had a better digestive system, I'd maybe have tried to show them how to run a state."

Jason watched the old hotel clerk clean a pen point. "You do in a way, Pop—run things—like the men behind the ballot box. You are the party man with the incisiveness and the comprehensiveness to get things to roll and add up."

"Cut the crap, Jay. You know what I want to really see? You president." J. Willard looked around the hotel lobby, its red-globed table lamps, the clerk examining his inky fingers. "Yes, I'd hate to say this in front of witnesses, but that would be a joy for me before they plant me in the family plot in All Grace graveyard by the side of your grandfather Horace."

"You always said you wanted to be cremated."

"Okay, I'll buy that, ashes to ashes. Hell, I'm no Joe Kennedy, the bastard and his litter. It's not on my part wanting to rub people's noses in the dog shit to show we made it. It's just, well, I'd like to see us kick the ass of the way things are permitted to run. Watergate didn't really create much self-scrutiny and the unions and big business are steering a cockeyed course."

Jay looked at his watch. "You forgot to curse Wall Street and the eastern establishment."

J. Willard smiled and raised a fist and held it close to Jason's nose. "Well, yes, maybe I did. But it's a white bread world, and any nation that sticks to white bread, trash hamburgers and store-fried chicken needs all the help it can get."

"You're a dreamer, Pop. For all your perceptibility and your hard edges. I'm going to be realistic about the state of the nation. I'll feel my way, keep my eyes wide open. I'm your son—sure, I see the main chance, and if I get within reach of it, I'll grab hold of it—but right now I just want to be a senator. I'm a fairly honest man, I think. I'm no cynic, and if I can keep my ego in a cage, I can do things. If not . . ."

"No *ifs* tonight. That if-shit, Kipling wrote it, didn't he? Where the hell is your car?"

"It's foggy—traffic is slow. You get to thinking about *ifs,* alternatives, and some folk end up making a hole in the river."

They drove back to High Sky with an escort of two state troopers on their cycles, Andy Wolensky driving the big state car, the radio turned on to Nashville sound doing "Your Cheatin' Heart."

Two days later as Jason was cleaning out his desk, taking down his signed photographs of various people, with the aid of his secretary, Clair Brooks, Buster Miller came in and Jason shared with him the last four inches of Old Forester in the bottle. They sat at the emptied desk, drinking. It was a marvelous old desk and Jason wished he could take it to Washington. Solid golden oak, carved with figures of Indians, fur trappers, and a buffalo head in each corner. But it was a state treasure.

Buster Miller poured himself a refill, swished it around in his mouth, swallowed. "Don't be so goddamn starry-eyed about being a U.S. Senator. I want you to get up to the top of the greased pole and do good, be big. But there are practical advantages. The pay will run over sixty thousand dollars a year. You'll be getting a big federal pension if you stay in over five years."

"I could make more money if I stayed in law and stooged for corporations or bled last wills and testament estates."

"Now, now, you'll be meeting lots of lawyers."

"Too many lawyers," said Jason, taking a sip.

"Two spacious offices in Vista City and one in High Sky, an office in Washington; spacious, located in the House Office Building just across the street from the Capitol. You'll have an allowance to hire a big staff, and the House provides furniture, office machinery and a stationery allowance. You'll send letters to constituents and press releases, too, with a congressional frank. All your trips back home are paid for and those junkets are opportunities for foreign travel. It's a pretty good job."

"I'm there to do things."

"Well, don't strain or get a hernia. You know damn well there's that seniority system. The seniority system reigns supreme. Everything is determined by the length of time you put down in your record; your committee assignment, your permission to offer an amendment to speak, even your parking space. You move up only when those in front of you die, retire, are defeated. It's the old pecking order. Don't try and get around it."

"I don't know if I'll play ball, all the way, I mean."

"You will. You're smart and feel this is the big chance. When you first get to the Senate, you'll see the longer you stay the more you'll like the seniority system. You become part of the institution, attitudes change; become protective of the system and perhaps even reverent. Being in Congress becomes very comfortable and with seniority comes power, power deserved because you have waited out the system."

"Christ, Buster, you make it sound like a club."

"That's what it is—a *very* exclusive one, too."

"Damn it, it's a commitment to deal with complex issues; energy, housing, the budget, the environment, the world coming apart at the seams." Jason threw the empty bottle in the wastebasket.

"You'll do fine."

"I'm already getting the pressures from outside groups whose intentions are honorable, but who view your principles as either good or bad with nothing in between. Whether it be oil, timber, Common Cause, Americans for Constitutional Action, Americans for Democratic Action, the AFL-CIO or the WDU, their positions are rigid. Now I figure my constituents sent me to the U.S. Senate to study the issues and then to use my best judgment. I'm not to surrender my judgment to any group, no matter how high its motives, in deciding what I feel to be the best course of action as a senator. Does that sound too much like a speech?"

"It does—keep it for reelection."

Jason wondered would he ever be as cynical and practical as Buster Miller. The day before he, Sheila, Teddy and his secretary, Clair Brooks, were to fly to Washington Jason went for a walk down Main Street in High Sky. He had grown up here, lived here and had for it, he thought, the same feeling that perhaps Mark Twain had for the Mississippi. Walking that night, he wondered about taking old loyalties with him.

He'd have to get together an office staff—a dozen at least for a senator. Clair, who had been with him two years, was good at her work, a country girl with a University of Michigan education and a sense of fun, an impulse to generosity, but wary—a bit of a wit. She got along with Sheila and called her "Mrs. Crockett." Best of all, he never felt sexually interested in Clair; whatever her personal life was he didn't care to know. He didn't want to penetrate beyond her spontaneous gaiety.

He'd take Andy Wolensky as office manager. Andy had been Jason's clerk in the governor's office. A short, hard little Polish-American, suspicious of all popular values, his family were farmers up at Star Bay. Andy had played halfback for some cow college and had gone into Crockett Enterprises' publicity office, where Jason had found him writing about the 200 practical uses of wood around the house.

He'd think about someone to run his home office in Vista City later. A senator certainly had a lot of fat jobs to offer.

Walking to Main Street after ten at night, he felt already like an expatriate. The store windows still lit, but doors locked, steel grilles now across many of them. High Sky also was feeling pensive and worried about its crime rate. But the street was still partly paved with those mottled yellow bricks first laid down in 1903, and where trolley tracks had once been, blacktop existed. Almost all the fronts of the business buildings had been modernized with plastic, chrome and shaped plate glass. But Jason, looking up, still found some old vast iron overhangs and stone cornices and remains of legends—raised letters, chipped out or painted over. WALT & IRA IRONMONGER, GRAINS AND CATTLE BROKERS EST. 1872, SAMUEL SPITZ & SONS FINE WEARING APPAREL. As a boy his favorite sport was tracing the old letters: STUTZ CAR SALES & SERVICE, and he passed before stucco pillars between which had hung a sign from his adolescence, ATHENS SODA FOUNTAIN AND LUNCH, *Biggest Banana Split in Town.* (In sheer show-off spirit he had once won a race against Hank Wales to eat three Jumbo Giant Splits. *Ugh!*)

The Ironmongers and Spitz's were gone (so was Hank) and the only Stutz Bearcat car in town belonged to a high school teacher, a car nut. Yes, Plato Spiropoulous did pile up the biggest banana splits in town at his marble soda counter and you sat on twisted wire chairs with Serena Cody, who gave you your best blow job; overhead the big ceiling fans stirred the air. And your head was full of Gary Cooper that night at the movies saying "Yep" as he kicked up some horseshit with the point of one of his cowboy boots. Serena Cody now? She runs Milady's Millinery, raises chow dogs.

Well, Jason thought, let's skip the Thomas Wolfe perceptions of the delight of losing innocence. It's a good town and a lousy town. It's a fine place to grow up in and a rotten place to be from the wrong side of the tracks; to have Indian or black genes or to be a mudsill or redneck in exile from Dixie. It's a healthy place, lots of green landscape around it. And a town run by Bascom Rice, County Chairman, and his gang, stealing a bit here, paving unneeded streets, owning the Pioneer Gas and Power, and the Killamook Brick Works. Not a bad school system, either, but they pay "Pooper" Jackson, the football coach, more than the principal. That's what's so magnificently illogical about American life.

It was a town he loved, and the kind of a place the poet wrote about as a place to hang your childhood. It had an easy indolence and the ricochet of its gossip was often deadly.

Jason went into the Farmer's Daughter Bar. The neon beer signs were celebrating COORS and MILLER'S. Inside, the familiar smells of malt, spilled whiskey and just a faint whisper of piss from the john in the back. The television was tuned to a hockey game. A half dozen men and two women were sipping drinks and munching chips or holding a fistful of salted peanuts. Jason felt part of the homogeneity of the scene.

"Hi," said Jake Bishop from behind the bar.

Two people waved to Jason, the rest watched the swirl of men on ice, the sweep of murderous hockey sticks, and gave a howl of delight at a slam of a player against the barrier and a lifting of sticks.

At the Farmer's Daughter the patrons had a deluded belief that violence was strength.

Jason wanted to order a Carlsberg. American beer was too sweet, too doctored with chemicals, but he ordered a Miller's, a bit angry he was playing politics by ordering an American brew in front of the natives.

"Bust his nuts!" shouted a middle-aged woman at the television, a little woman with silver gray-blued hair, cut short. "Hit 'em, hit 'em in the nuts."

"Toronto four, the LA punks goose egg," said the bartender. "They start as kids on ice up there, them Canucks."

"Maybe so." Jason sipped his beer, gassy bubbles breaking in his nose. "Been up to Blue Lake, Jake?" He and Jake Bishop had gone through grammer school together before Jake ran off to join the navy.

"Naw, tied down to this dump. My fucken kid he decided to go and is in marine boot camp out in California. They'll bat the fucken ass off him. Want a bowl of red?"

Jason nodded. Jake's chili, always steaming there behind the bar in a big hot pot, was famous in three counties. Jake claimed he never cleaned the electric three-gallon heated pot, just dumped in more onions, more red beans, more ground grade A. "My old man began this chili in nineteen forty-five the day he come out of the fucken army, and I'm not breaking the tradition. Only now I gotta charge four bits since the fucken inflation."

It was good chili and there was a very good fight on the hockey rink. Jason ate slowly, spooning up carefully, savoring the spicy mixture. A man with a paunch, a twisted nose, and a scarred cheekbone got off his bar stool and came up to Jason.

"You stink," he said. "You stink, Governor."

"Put it in writing, Chuck, and I'll frame it."

The man turned and went out.

"One of them pinko radicals," said the bar man. "I'll give him a bung starter on his fucken head next time he comes in."

"He's just feeling big, Jake, telling off the new senator . . ."

"Yeah, senator now, eh? We all voted for you. All but my wife's old man. He's not got all his marbles since the highway department tore down his fucken house for the highway exit over by Bear Crick."

"A fucking shame [it's catching], Jake."

"Remember we used to go there, you, me and Hank Wales, catching frogs."

"Sure."

"A sweet guy, Hank," said Jake, "a real sweet guy. The good go young, huh?"

The hockey game ended and on the screen a crowd pushed its way onto the ice. Security men were rushing out to keep the players from being mobbed. A very serious fight resulted. But the television screen changed images and a pale man with thin hands held up a can of dog food. "This sports special brought to you by man's best friend and his best healthy diet, Doggie Dindin Dinner."

Jake switched channels to an old black-and-white Western. One of the women got off her barstool, a young woman in a white nurse's uniform, white stockings, white shoes, a perky little cap pinned to her amber-colored hair. She came over to Jason.

"You're a good man, Senator. From rind to seed, as my old grandmother used to say. Jessica Snyder from up Star Bay."

"Thank Granny for me."

"I will. She's ninety-two and sharp, I mean real sharp. Still plays poker, just for matchsticks now. Used to deal for Soapy Smith up on the Yukon. Well, I gotta go on duty."

Jason pointed to the small gold-and-blue WDU pin pinned to her cape. "Since when? Miss—?"

"Nora—Nora Nilson. We affiliated. What the hell, you pay more dues, you get more health benefits, Wally Klamath says."

"Tell me, he put the pressure on?"

"Maybe. I gotta get rollin'. I got this old man conking out at the hospital. God got no respect for money. Worth sixty million dollars, this old fart—and as Doc Satenstein says, 'he's dying poor as anybody.'"

"You're a philosopher, Nora," said Jason.

She went out.

On the TV screen there was the stock shot of the Indian attack on the stagecoach crossing the desert—footage from a John Ford movie cut into so many films. Jake took up the empty bowl. "A nice hunka ass that. I don't know but a broad all in white, those fucken white stockings, they send me. Nora now—I don't suppose you'd care to tear off a—"

"Thanks, Jake, no."

John Wayne was on the roof of the stagecoach picking off Indians as if shooting tin ducks in a gallery. Jason laid down a dollar with an encompassing smile for the bar's patrons.

BOOK II

On the Hill

Chapter 6

Goddamn, thought Jason Crockett, it's not rational. Here I am on this road of slush with soft snow falling lightly and melting when it hits the black surface. I can't get through to anyone—there's no exchange of pleasantries—no one to stop for me to ask directions—why this manic indifference? The cars go by throwing up icy muck, splashing through the potholes. I'm cold, I can't understand why I'm barefooted, and I'm walking toward the vague shapes of low buildings. I'm someplace in the Middle West, I don't know why I know it, and I expect an empty taxi to pass, but nothing like that happens and in the deep ambivalence the sky is clearing. I take a bus and the people pay no attention to me. I keep asking, asking, we are going to *where?* Where do I want to go? The city is strange, yet I know it but I can't communicate, I can't get answers even purely illusively. I get off and go walking through a neighborhood of black faces, lounging shapes burning tobacco. A dangerous thing to do; run-down houses and strange smelling of red beans and rice, trash in battered cans, and I keep turning, turning down other streets. I smile. To be liked for one's virtues is to be loved for one's faults. At last there is a pier and it stands over water dimpled by a rippling of little waves wind-pushed. I have no way to go and people are pressing closer, closer. It's a sonofabitch of a situation and—

He came awake to find he was sweating, mouth-breathing. The hotel suite was overheated and the drapes smelled of dry cleaning. There was daylight out there, a yolky sunlight that here and there managed to creep into the ($50 a day) room. Sheila slept in deep placidity on the next bed, face distorted like a pouting child's, pressed against the double pillows she always used. He remembered they had brought their own down pillows to Washington. Damn the dream, his first in the capital. He'd had it or one much like it recurring from time to time for over twenty years. His mouth felt dry. The little traveling clock in its red morocco case with a grave face noted 7:42.

His evening clothes had slipped off the back of the chair he had hung them on, coming in late in the overcheerful turbulence of too much party booze. Sheila's gown was just where she had stepped out of it the night before. He itemized, shifting position on the bed: pale panties, cobwebby stockings, silver-toned slippers toe to toe. They had come back late and a bit crocked from India Kingston's party. What a brawl; all those famous faces of sensitivity, temperament, cruelty, power. Faces you saw yammering on "Meet the Press" and "State of the Nation." Or who got mentioned by Susie Knickerbocker or Jack Anderson in their columns. Arrogant officials, dominating congressmen, mongoloids from the dark Soviet secret sides. *Streng verboten* to talk.

What a head. Hangovers weren't getting any better as he grew older. He reached for one of the Winterman's cigarillos he had taken up smoking when he gave up cigarettes. He lit one with his old army lighter. The hand was fairly steady. He inhaled deeply, the smoke helped create an orientation toward reality. Sheila would sleep for another hour or so. She had a lunch date with Congresswoman Shirley Lippman and Alice Ormsbee. And he? Jason looked at his day's event card that Clair had prepared. He winced. First day as a United States Senator in Washington. At least ten things he had to attend to, people to meet, settle into his suite of offices. He had to be braced against error, inconsistency, know whose ass to kiss, whose to kick.

The phone gave that snotty, high-priced hotel tingle. He let it ring three times, then saw Sheila stir. He picked it up and looked at his wife. She continued to move about, frowned and turned, but didn't awaken. She'd worn well. Twenty years full of wearing well, two kids, holding of the Women's Tennis Singles big, ugly and precious silver cup from the Willabee Country Club. He almost leaned over and spanked her naked ass. She had been so tired or looped from the partying she hadn't even got into a nightgown. A behind curved like the cello he'd once played in high school.

"Senator Crockett?"

"Yes." Jason savored old intimacies, body games, felt his genitalia go on the alert.

"Will you take a call from Mr. Boylan O'Rahilly?"

"O'Reilly?"

"O'Rahilly, sir, *r a h i l l y*."

"Oh, yes." He closed his eyes, brought up an image of a short stocky man with a polished, tanned bald head, wise blue eyes, a mouth like a string purse over small barracuda teeth, a very jolly man with a laying on of hands while he half whispered to you with a faint chortle.

"Hello, Senator, get home okay?"

"All in one part. A hell of a party."

"India gives the best. AAA all the way. Grand to have met you and the missus. A beaut, a real beaut. They really raise up swell women out on the coast."

"We studs always felt so." The cigarillo tasted sour, his head ached, Boylan O'Rahilly with a voice like a macaw? The word *bread* seemed attached to it. Yes. "Bread" O'Rahilly, airline lobbyist; bread, meaning money in jive talk. Bread O'Rahilly always ready to hand out a legal contribution for a good cause for any public official or elected representative.

("I don't expect nothing. Not asking a thing. No siree. Just remember the airlines, they tie this nation together.")

". . . so, Senator, we're picking this Miss Airline Hostess at the Press Club next Thursday, and the Western Section winner is from California, who else but you to present her the award and prize?"

"Contact my secretary, Clair Brooks, O'Rahilly."

"Bread, Bread Boylan, my friends call me."

"Bread," said Jason Crockett and hung up. A guy with a calculated impudence yet friendly as a puppy. He called room service, ordered two breakfasts in half an hour: bran, whole wheat toast, buckwheat pancakes and bacon, strong coffee, real, *not* the decaf. He went into the bathroom. After the morning indecencies, a quick shower, a hurried but careful shave with his electric razor, he felt ready to face the day. His—repeated to himself—you lug, your first in Washington D.C. as a United States Senator.

The face set in a half grin in the mirror was his own. Good lines, only one good chin—no need for masseurs to attack corpulence. Forty-six years old, not bad, lot of light brown hair but thinning too fast, it would do. The scar on the right cheekbone adding something very macho to the long head, jawline well defined, chest sagging a bit. Need more handball. Jog more, cut the Scotch down, the Beefeater martinis, push away the blueberry pie and the vanilla ice-cream scoops dumped on it.

No sign of indulged ostentation—no, he'd lived simply, honestly, decently—fairly decently. He had existed at times for so many years in hotel rooms on political tours, first as a young legislator, a state official, then as nominee for governor and as governor, during the hard-fought campaign just this year against that sonofabitch for the U.S. Senate. So he felt at ease in the hotel suite. Damn expensive suite, but J. Willard had insisted it was his treat, and the old man usually had his way. ("Hell, Jay, there's a period of gestation. You have all those shitheads in Washington to figure out. So spend money.")

Jason dressed in the dark blue suit over the pale blue shirt; he wound up the black tie with the bird design on it, pulled the knot into place. He hunted up his English shoes, a bit too pointed, but they took a very high gloss.

He walked to the bedside and covered Sheila with a sheet. She looked appetizing there, the smell of an always ready woman, half asleep, a good odor, and her own special skin scent.

He could wake her for a quickie, like a hasty gratuity—but a glance at Uncle Wilbur's gold watch (left to him in W. W. Crockett's last will and testament), snapping open the double lids to show time was fleeing and the room service knock was about due, if the service was all it was cracked up to be—forget it, he told his hard-on.

He called down for Miss Brooks' room.

"Morning, Senator." The country girl drawl, veneered with the best college accent skillfully applied.

"Morning yourself, Clair. I didn't wake you?"

"Wake me? I was up at six, took a walk. It's a great big place just like the history book pictures and the postal cards. Greek-Roman and up to its navel in history."

"Breakfast?"

"Had it. Senator Ormsbee is picking you up at ten-thirty. You have my list?"

"Right here in front of me. Print it out bigger next time so I don't have to do the bifocals bit."

"You made the *Post,* page three, the *Star* set you among the society folk. Has last night's party picture of you and Mrs. Crockett, with Mrs. Kingston, Paul and Alice Ormsbee, Valentine Engelberger escorting Esme Lowell. Even spells your name right."

"Has Bremont called back?"

There was a pause and Clair's voice grew in firmness. She was twenty-four and raised on a tree farm in a rain forest and never covered up her country voice even with her college education. She was crisp and stern. "He's our first crisis. Gave it to us with bucolic simplicity."

"I knew he was pressing for something. What?"

"Wants you to take on a press gal, PR stuff, for your office, one he favors, and not to talk about the Lippman-Walters bill until this gal fills you in. Her name is Stacy Decker."

"Who the hell does Grover Asa Bremont think he is?"

He heard the hoot of Clair's laugh. "Congressman Bremont thinks he's the millionaire party leader of the House, and, you know, he *is*."

"No dice on the Decker dame, unless she's really good, and I haven't read the Lippman-Walters Bill yet. Get me a copy. Now see if that Georgetown house is ready to move in."

"Kitchen items missing—that's holding it up. You know unions."

"None of that talk."

"It's Teddy's birthday. He's fifteen."

"Thanks, I knew. Get him that shortwave radio set he asked for. I'll write a card from me and Mrs. Crockett."

Sheila had turned and opened her eyes. She muttered, "Who's playing the drums?"

Jason hung up. "Good morning, Honey."

"Not so early," she protested, smiling. "It's blasphemous to say it's a grand day before my eyelids get unstuck."

Sheila had a good silvery voice and was a low-key waker. She was hardly ever herself, she would say, until after a shower and a good workout on her gums with her WaterPic. There was a knock on the door and room service came in, a wagon with a built-in metal compartment and much white linen and pots of coffee. The waiter produced plates of pancakes and bacon and toast, all from a flame in the belly of the metal table. He also passed over two newspapers.

Sheila said, "Just pour me the coffee." She gulped, yelped it was scalding and disappeared into the bathroom.

In ten minutes she was out in a robe, and had two black hot coffees very quickly. She bit into toast and sighed watching Jason finish the bacon. "I hope this isn't every night in Washington, Senator."

He looked up from the copy of the *Washington Post*. "We overdid it, Honey. Got to learn to take it easy, take it slow."

The petulant thing about Sheila (he always marveled) was her quick recovery for the twenty years they were partygoers, not hell-raisers, but full-lived. The fact remained she never looked a fright in the morning. Even with hair undone and no makeup she was more than presentable. Still slim, no sag, maybe a bit overmuscled, arms freckled from all that tennis in the summer sun. Never the morning horror like some wives of our friends. Just curt and solemn until after the shower. The country club called them "a settled happy couple"; those that had any opinion of the Crocketts. There had been times in the first years of the marriage when Sheila could be a flibbertigibbet. Well, never mind, Jason thought; gone with the past.

A good-looking, middle-aged wife who still liked lovemaking and had a querulous attitude when he was away from her. A son who wrote folk music, and Laura, a daughter of eighteen at the University of Michigan. On her own, and lord knew what kind of way-out life she'd been leading since she was sixteen. But living perhaps with that professor of modern art. Not as bad luck as the governor before Jason, whose son had died with a needle in his arm in a Chicago YMCA toilet. Jason thought of the Crocketts as a self-sufficient island —invaded at times, true, by a public life demanding they dance to the public's tunes, mostly at election time.

"We should have rented the house, Jay, not bought it."

"Like hell. We're here to stay. Besides, I hate rented houses. They always smell of Black Flag and something dead in the walls."

There was a knock on the door, and the voice of Clair Brooks. "Good morning. Hello, good morning."

"Come in."

Clair Brooks was a bit too tall for a girl, some might have said, and had a quivering alertness and a good smile. She had corn-colored hair naturally, long legs and a handsome face without it's being that of a great beauty. Rather large feet, Jason felt, long-fingered hands, the left one now grasping a new attaché case of brown leather.

"It's a fine day, sun out and the traffic thick. Morning, Mrs. Crockett. Your hair appointment eleven-twenty downstairs. Ask for Josh— lobby rumor he's the best pixie there."

"Thanks, Clair. Oh, Jay, that's the new briefcase I had your name put on."

"Attaché case," said the secretary, rubbing its surface, "not briefcase. And just the letters J. C."

"Never use them," said Jason. "Carry everything in a brown paper bag. J. W. always said that gives the folks the idea you're not a snob."

"Now, Senator, you know that's just election gossip. I'll scuff it up a bit, bang it about."

"Never mind. I'll not carry it today."

Clair looked at her wristwatch, a man's Seiko design with a stop-latch attachment and other mysterious dials. "Snow Williams is on, the Wicked Witch of the East. You're on her noontime show soon."

She flipped on the television set. "I could do her Washington midday show as good as her and for a third of the money. This is just her morning five minutes."

The screen filled to reveal a heavily made up, hazel-eyed woman with rhinestone-rimmed glasses and a shiny mouth facing a beautifully dressed young woman. The hazel-eyed woman was holding a box of paper tissues and having trouble pronouncing the letter R. ". . . wight here. Only these have the strength in time of need, only these are scented without offending. Weally strong and scented. Now my guest this morning is Esme Lowell, a Washington wenting agent who has helped make Washington suburbs what they are. She is also the niece of Senator Austin Ames Barraclough, the philosopher leader of his party in Congress. Esme, dear, why are prices so outwageous for houses around Washington?"

The young woman gave a searching glance at her questioner, as if trying to keep the amenities on a banal level. "Because everything is overpriced outrageously these days."

"Esme, perhaps I mean why?"

Esme Lowell smiled. "Would you say, Miss Williams, you were overpriced?"

("Snow Williams is going to gore her," said Sheila.)

But Snow Williams merely smiled, showing a splendid set of capped teeth. "Ah, yes, I'm sure I am. But would you turn down a fortune for just gabbing? There is talk your uncle is weady to accept the nomination for the presidency at the next convention."

"I doubt it. The media gossips need names as news."

"How is his health? Fully wecovered I hope."

The woman laughed, hunted a cigarette in a handbag. "I hear he swims the Potomac daily, lengthwise."

Snow Williams had the skilled instinctiveness, alertness when not to carry an interview much further. She gave an understanding grin and held up a box of Klean Kitty Litter. "Now for a message . . ."

Jason said, "She's the best of three overpaid witches on the air. Numero Uno maybe." He pulled out the heavy butter-gold watch from his vest on its heavy gold chain and looked at the time again. The uncle's watch. The uncle, Uncle Wilbur Crockett, once a well-known professional gambler and a bon vivant. Jason felt with the watch ticking away on his body no harm could come to him, not with the ace of spades set in small diamonds on the outer lid.

He kissed Sheila's cheek and tapped Clair on the arm, "Don't overload my appointments."

"Wear a hat, Senator."

"Can't get used to them." He went out.

Sheila said, "Got a cigarette, Clair?"

"Sorry, Mrs. Crockett. Gave them up months ago. When you did."

"Don't remind me."

Chapter 7

The gleaming black Lincoln limousine of Senator Paul Ormsbee stood several yards away from the curb, blocking part of the street in front of the Sheraton Park Hotel. The motor purring, a thin cloud of blue exhaust escaping. The doorman of the hotel knew better than to ask a senator's car to move closer to the curb. It was a good clear day and the ten o'clock traffic was moving both ways, the federal civil service employees having already been at work for two hours or at their first coffee break at the Interior Department, Census Bureau, Smithsonian, or other giant bureaucratic beehives.

Jason Crockett came out of the hotel lobby buttoning his topcoat, hatless, carrying the attaché case. Senator Ormsbee's chauffeur, a sullen-looking black, opened the car door with a "Mornin', suh." Jason slipped in beside Senator Ormsbee, who, fresh-shaved, pink-skinned, had his hair combed up (so Jason thought) like a white curl of whipped cream. The older man sat well back, arms folded on his lap.

Jason caught the scent of the morning's tot of bourbon on his fellow senator's breath. ("Some drink to feel happy in Washington without feeling guilty"—Buster Miller.)

"Good morning, sir."

"Never mind the formality, Jay. I'm just the senior senator. Settled in?"

"So far. We've been getting a house ready in Georgetown."

"Good boy," said Senator Ormsbee. He beamed benevolently, slapping Jason's left knee. "You plan to stay. Good, good."

The car was moving with a mass of converging traffic. The tourists were out heading for 1600 Pennsylvania Avenue and several busloads of Japanese, some Africans in long robes and fezzes went past. Lines were forming in front of marble Greek and Roman facades.

"I'll get you set in your offices, Jay. Get you a corner one when one turns up. I've had my office manager pencil in a staff for you."

"I'm keeping Andy Wolensky as my office assistant and Clair Brooks as my private secretary."

"Good, the sooner you attach them to the public feed bag the better."

"I don't think of it in those terms."

"Yes, well, you will. You'll need them, over a dozen." The senator reached into a small door pocket and took out a flask, swallowed a drink. He handed the flask to Jay. "Not what you've heard. I'm not a drunk. I drink a lot, that's all. I'm getting you on the Senate Agriculture Committee. Care for the Bureau of Ethnology?"

"You tell me."

Jason took a polite nip. Senator Paul Ormsbee replaced the flask in its pocket. "Booze and women are needed here by many of the boys on the Hill. I don't fuck around, otherwise I'm like some of the rest. Doing my best. Working hard. I've been here eighteen years and once more around some of the park and I'm retiring. I'll get you set in the best Senate Office Building and I'll take you around to the Senate Chamber and introduce you to the right people. *Our* people. It's a club, sure, but also a jungle. You'll meet the speaker, the majority leader. Good Joes. You'll also need to know the doormen, the cloakroom folk, the messenger service. I'll see you get a good table in the dining room, a parking space that isn't in Virginia. Those are the important things we'll do today. Oh hell, I'm not cynical, but I've seen so many young whelps come here with high-hanging hopes and a briefcase full of worthy bills they hope to introduce."

"It's an attaché case, Sheila tells me, not a briefcase."

"What's in it?"

"A list of county chairmen back home, also women's clubs officers and six guidebooks to Washington. I now know the Pentagon has six hundred and thirty-two committees to take care of its interests."

"That all? You'll get free copies of the Constitution, the Bill of Rights, and the Senatorial Procedure for Introducing Bills."

"I'm not planning to introduce anything, no bills. Just at first observing."

"Smart, *very* smart. I'll alert you to a listing of what bills we support and what groups we favor."

"I've a pretty good idea." Jason was observing the activity in the morning traffic. "A hell of a lot of ginkgo trees."

"When you've been around long enough, you'll know all good deeds have a price you pay God. I wanted to remake the federal union, clear up the stables of overstaffed, loafing civil service, jail all lobbyists, refuse all payoffs listed as campaign funds. I was a naked, innocent young prick."

"You're respected, Paul. You've gotten some fine bills through with your name on them."

They were passing a park with several bronze statues of men in bird-soiled period costumes, also a group of pigeon-occupied soldier figures in turn-of-the-century uniform, all charging.

"What's that one for?"

"Bird shit. You'll find more monuments here to people and to forgotten events than any place on earth. You know something, Jay, the first day I got here old Senator Henry Blattner from Killamook Slope drove me to the Senate Building and I told him I'd be president some day. I was a goddamn young fool in those days."

"I don't think so. You almost had it a couple years ago, the nomination. And you still may."

Senator Ormsbee beat on Jason's knee again. *"Almost* gets you a cup of coffee in this town, with thirty cents. First thing I had printed in the *Congressional Record* said, 'Don't work to make men equal, work to make them superior.' You can publish anything you want in the *Congressional Record* at free rates. Folks back home are impressed."

"Paul, you didn't try hard enough for the nomination. If Austin Barraclough had gotten the New York and California delegates up against the wall, banged their heads to unpledge themselves—"

Senator Paul Ormsbee sighed, made a sucking sound with his tongue against his teeth. "Austin wasn't himself that convention. Hasn't been himself since. Greatest man the Senate has had in three generations, but—"

"Getting old."

"Old? He's years younger than I am. He's, let's see, Austin, he's fifty-eight. No, it's not age, it's a lot more. But it's personal. The goddamndest things happen to people. Austin, he's gone to the edge—and looked over into the abyss."

They rode the rest of the way to the Senate Office Buildings in silence, Jason remembering he had a scrapbook someplace, begun in high school, with clippings of FDR, Eisenhower, Lyndon Johnson. As for Senator Barraclough—there had been a lot of clippings, a *Newsweek* cover of Senator Austin Ames Barraclough, kingmaker, Senate leader, co-author of the Winston-Barraclough bill, the Barraclough-Skinsky bill, the man who had made the nominating speech for a president (who unfortunately—he said later—had been elected). Austin Barraclough had even committed the crime of writing a fine book explaining the failure of bureaucrats in power. It had become required reading in some college courses. Senator Barraclough, for all the rumors and gossip, still stood high in the power that ran the party, that controlled the senators in certain vital votes. But the whispers were many concerning his mental and physical decline. Just to recall him had depressed Paul Ormsbee to silence.

The Lincoln came to a stop on Capitol Hill among a herd of high-priced Detroit models. Senator Ormsbee recovered his smile as they got out. "Notice, Jay, no Mercedes, Rolls or Jags. That's unAmerican, but some of the fat cats have them as a second or third car back in their garages. Now I know this one is an ugly building and overcostly, full of error and inconsistency, and furnished like a Denver whorehouse in the nineties—*but* it's ours."

Once inside Jason was impressed. He liked the overornate quality in woods and marbles; he knew he lacked the aesthetic sense of current chic taste—he left that to Sheila. In styles he had a vague idea of Regency and Art Nouveau, but beyond that he liked comfort and not too much color.

His suite of offices was of several rooms. The inner one was in mahogany, the yellow drapes smelling of cigar smoke. The Persian rug, obviously a copy, had several big stains; a dog, he suspected. The bookcases had leaded glass doors but contained only some Duz and Mars Bars cartons and government publications on beetles.

Senator Ormsbee sniffed, looked about. "Old Sam Getchoff had these offices. Sam chewed tobacco, kept a fox terrier, as you can see, a dog with a weak bladder. And Sam took his desk with him. I think they buried him in it. It sure was big enough."

"He was a good senator."

"Self-reliant but not steadfast. And he'd have taken the Washington Monument home if he could have figured out how to ship it. But you have a furniture and decorator's allowance, so use it. I'll see you at noon and we'll have lunch in the Senate Dining Room and then go to the Senate Chamber."

A young man appeared. "Oh, this is Tony Burgess, my office manager." The young man, with prominent teeth, balding head, nodded. "Tony, you take care of Senator Crockett till his own people get settled. Gotta run, Jay. See you."

Tony spoke through a partly blocked sinus. "Sure thing. Happy to meet you, Senator. I got you two typists to start, a messenger, mail clerk, and you can have up to eighteen hired hands if you want 'em. Plus a staff back home, all on the taxpayers, and—"

Jason waved Tony to stop. "Yes, yes. Thanks, Tony, I know. My secretary, Miss Brooks, will be here soon and my office manager, Andy Wolensky."

"You got G4 as a parking space. Real Good. I'll wangle something also for some of your staff. Good parking spots." He held out a small black notebook. "Senator Ormsbee asked me to give you this."

"What is it—call girls?"

Tony looked shocked, his scalp turned pink.

"No, of course *not,* Senator. He doesn't go for that. But it's a listing of people on various committees, organizations, lobbyists, embassy numbers, who can give you—give you *that* information. There are CIA and FBI contacts. Nothing hush-hush—just for contact in case you want contact."

"In case. Thanks, Tony."

Tony looked over the room, opened and closed a glass door. "Anytime, Senator. Anytime at all." He handed over a card. "If you want to stock up on likker or anything in other items close to wholesale, just call this number. Raoul Cortez, Cuban anti-Castro. Get you anything."

"I don't think so."

"It's legit." Tony smiled. "No strings. It's a sort of discount cutrate house, congressmen senators use. Even the faggots at State."

"Thanks."

After Tony was gone, Jason sat down in an overstuffed club chair, its ancient springs protesting. He felt a sense of triumph in having these offices, touched with a bit of the preposterous, the ludicrous. He could look out through the big double windows (very clean—they must have been washed that morning) and *there* was Washington, D.C. A patch of blue sky with one cotton wool cloud, a corner of some stained marble building. Below the hum of traffic the putt-putt of some motor bikes. Nothing could spoil his subtle feeling: I'm here to help run this great nation.

"So this is Washington!" He was unaware he had spoken out loud.

There was a knock on the door and a thin girl with glasses and long, brown uncurled hair came in, followed by two porters pushing a desk on a dolly.

"Senator, I'm Ruth Munday, head of your typists' section. I felt you could use a desk till you picked out one of your own. This is one we call General Grant style."

"Thanks. It will do. But I need a clean rug and drapes."

"I don't blame you. You want the desk where?"

"More to the right, and take out the sofa."

One of the porters grimaced, scratched an arm. "We got no assignment slip to pick up a sofa."

Jason said, "Well then, just take it out and throw it into the street."

The porters looked at one another. The black one said, "We'll find a place for it, Senator."

After they were gone, Munday grinned. "You'll do, Senator. You have to show you don't scare at the working man. You'll do."

"So will you, Miss—"

"Munday, Ruth Munday. You want any information, just yell. I've been here eight years. Two before that in the Indian B section."

"Thanks. Miss Brooks, my own secretary, will be here soon. Fill her in. Don't make her cynical."

"No sir, Senator. I'm Science of Mind Church. There's Coke and soda water in your dressing room fridg. Soap, towels, all fresh. What else would you want?"

"Clair, Miss Brooks, will get to hustling. Thanks, Miss Munday."

"Any time, Senator."

There was, he noticed, an old-fashioned tin alarm clock on one of the bookcases. He went over and wound it. Somehow it seemed to make the late senator, Old Sam the dog lover, alive and real. This tin alarm clock must have once cost a dollar, and now, forgotten in packing whatever was at hand at the time of the senator's departing forever, it was left behind. Jason set it on the scarred desk and listened to its loud steady tick. He sank back in the lopsided club chair and closed his eyes. He hadn't felt fully rested for some time in all the pervading activities. His sleep was troubled by the recurring dream, his waking hours full of getting ready for Washington. With some fears, some exaltations. But all in all a kind of wonder, and sometimes a bit of doubt. The old grade school lesson: the big frog in a small pond, or a tadpole in a big lake.

And Washington was frightening, no doubt of that even from the little he'd experienced. Could he get a guest card to the Chevy Chase Club? Could he avoid the entrenched freeloaders, the cranks and fanatics, the honest strivers? The habitual office servers who just held on to their ironic way of life. Would he be lost among the hundreds of thousands of civil servants, the clerks, typists and computer hands, the museum staffs? He was already aware of the black faces, so full of amusement, indifference or hate; set high in the crime rates of the city. Still there was a marvelous exhilaration in so much history crowded together—and the Capitol Building with its German World I helmet used as a dome. It was too much to consume all at once.

He relaxed, limb by limb, he nodded off a bit, dozing and waking, brooding over Senator Ormsbee's confession of *his* first day in Washington and thinking of becoming president. An old man now, boozy, timeserving, glad-handing. Senator Paul Ormsbee, set on safe committees, making popular decisions, doing the lobbies' bidding. Lazy, careless, well-liked, loyal to wife Alice, but not one of the Senate's sterling noblemen. Would Jason Crockett be that in twenty years? Christ, he, too, had been thinking of being president some day. Why not? Look at all the nonentities raised to power.

The presidency? He had to admit to be thinking of it; alone but for the comforting sound of the old alarm clock, he *could* think of it. The idea had come to him, the thought had been lurking there someplace in him since he first saw a political convention when he was ten and J. Willard had taken him to Chicago. A vivid memory of the warm atmosphere, the smell, the dust and the stomping and cheering. It had awakened in the boy an emotion that here anybody (male) could have a chance (if native born) and sit in the White House (if not a Jew, Negro or a Commie). As he grew older and watched J. Willard and the gang run the state and the West Coast, it was clear it wasn't that simple. You had to have an organization, funds, and listen to the right people, the political savants, support certain things. Turn one's irrational dreams to rational facts.

(Pop was good at explaining. Pop knew who could be president and who couldn't. "Brains, wisdom alone, abilities don't mean a thing. You have to be able to charm the tail off the devil, have that stuff, charisma, so every yahoo in the crowd thinks you love him, are aware of him. And it's gotten us some fine men into the White House —and some awful duds, too. Now me, Jay, I couldn't be president, Stevenson couldn't, Uncle Wilbur couldn't. But you could, Jay. Don't ask me why. All you need is a little more gall and to brush the star-dust out of your eyes, and—")

Jason was aware Clair was shaking him awake. "Hey, Chief, you were conking off. You have a lunch appointment in the Senate Dining Room."

"Yes, must have dozed off."

The rest of the day and evening Jason remembered only as a series of faces, hands shaken, remarks made to him and banal words he answered with, words as nebulous as he could make them. There were people smiling and people being serious. An objective weariness overcame him. And several people asking him how he stood on the Indian Land Bill. He said he would be studying it. He would ask Clair what the hell the Indian Land Bill was. His most vivid memory was of a drunken general singing "Got Gonorrhea in Ole Korea."

That night as he and Sheila prepared for bed he had a sense of not being very much in touch with reality, but feeling fine. *Fine,* a word Hemingway used to use a lot. Fine. Fine. He was a bit high himself.

Tired, too, but wound up, needing release and thinking of rolling over onto Sheila. But he was too damn bone-tired, and as he began the first gesture toward physical contact (a kiss on the neck) he fell back and said, "A full day."

Sheila muttered into her pillow, "All those people, so sure of themselves."

"Or acting like they were. Drinking Dom Pérignon and talking of the Chevy Chase Country Club and how you have to wait ten years on a list to become a member."

"We'll never be here that long, Jay."

"Why the hell not?" He rolled toward her again. "Don't we live on K Street in Georgetown? Aren't we getting into the *Green Book?*"

"What's that?" Her voice was muffled, uninterested.

"The real *Social Register* of this town. I got trapped into talking at the Gridiron Club next week. That shitty reporter at dinner, the one with the rabbit teeth—the syndicate big shot—him saying 'The only way to look at a politician is down.' I'd like to kick his—"

He yawned and fell back absorbing shattered images and was soon asleep.

In the next week he and Sheila felt their way through social ameni-ties and dinners. Lunched, met more people. Teddy went back to school, Fran, their maid, brought back from a trip to relatives a black cook, Daisy, who smiled at lot and had a great way with frying fish and baking special spice cake. They planned a dinner in their own house, as soon as the rewired light fixtures in the dining room were put up. Sheila had found them in an antique shop off New Jersey Avenue—bronze and crystal with eagle motif; from the home of Rutherford B. Hayes, the dealer swore.

They attended a soiree musicale (German lieder) at the Foxhill Road home of the widow of a former "most powerful man in Congress." They attended services Sunday at St. John's Episcopal Church on Lafayette Square. They took Senator and Mrs. Paul Ormsbee to the Sans Souci restaurant, just a block from the White House, and met such important people as Art Buchwald, Sri Jha Lakshma and the head of the Bureau of Indian Affairs, Matthew Wilson, a sharp little man who spoke softly in a hardly perceptible voice.

"Want to talk to you, Crockett, about the Wyler-Oyle Indian Land Bill."

"Certainly, I'm studying it."

Wilson patted Jason's shoulder with a well-cared-for hand. "Good man . . . You look charming, Mrs. Crockett, an asset to our society here. You're not one of the Cave Dwellers."

Paul Ormsbee explained: "Cave Dwellers are old, established Washington families who think too highly of themselves."

After the Indian Bureau chief had left, Alice Ormsbee said, "Old Matt hasn't changed his line since Eisenhower took him out of an army tank and a major's uniform."

Sheila, looking over the place, the slow-breathing waiters, the feeders, said, "The Indian Land Bill, what is it?"

"Very important," said Paul Ormsbee. "Must talk to you, Jay, seriously about it. Coming up for a vote soon."

Jason had read the bill once and said he wanted time to look up some detail in its contents with the aid of a map.

The next week Bread O'Rahilly asked Jason to lunch at the Metropolitan Club. He was not at all the ruddy-faced mick Jason had expected, not a man with a fat handshake or the look of a Tammany ward heeler or bartender. Not at all. O'Rahilly was a well-groomed man, almost of an obsessive refinement. The only ornate detail was a red silk waistcoat. His pale blue eyes, long shapely nose suggested to Jason a film actor of the 1930s (Edmund Lowe?).

"They talked of the city, of national events at first.

"Now, Senator, I'll never lie to you and I'll never ask for a naked favor for the airlines I represent."

"What's a clothed favor?"

"One that's good for the country."

"And airlines."

"Among other things, yes. I'm not one to go stepping on the Constitution. Paul has asked me to get you a guest card at the Burning Tree Golf Club. You play golf?"

"Not well, have no time to study its finer points."

Bread O'Rahilly motioned the waiter for another round of drinks. "Was that Beefeater, Wilmont?"

"Oh, yes, Mr. O'Rahilly. You always ask for Beefeater martinis."

Bread O'Rahilly turned back to Jason. "You can trust the bar here. Some places refill the bottles with horse piss."

"Boylan, let me ask you something."

"Bread. Boylan is for my priest when I go to confession. Oh, yes, I go. As my father—God rest his soul—used to say: 'I feel time's incessant passage, bleeding away.' "

"What's behind the Indian Land Bill? It looks good on the surface. We're at last living up to a series of 1854 treaties with the Sioux, the Shoshoni, the Nez Perce, to pay them for the land we seized and never did pay for."

"And it's a bill long overdue. The red brothers are going to get, you know, forty-nine million dollars. They'll be riding around in Porsches and Rolls, eating high off the hog till they spend it. You hear about the Iranian ambassador's wife? Last Halloween she handed out caviar to kids coming for trick or treat."

Jason looked at his plate of crab à la Maryland. "I can't seem to get it clear just how much land is involved in the bill."

"There are political ramifications and cockeyed land surveys. Paul given you the facts?"

"He seems not to be too sure as to *which* survey maps are being used. Level with me, Bread—I'm a new boy here—and you want me as a friend."

The lobbyist seemed about to whistle. "There's the Library of Congress."

"I've got three sets of maps from them."

"Ah." Bread nodded as the fresh drinks were set down. He looked directly at Jason as they lifted their glasses, frosted, chilly to the touch. "Don't ever quote me, but certain ranching and mining interests are about to give our red brothers the fucking of their lives."

Jason slowly sipped his martini. "How?"

"The actual price when the smoke clears will be seventy-five cents an acre."

Jason smiled. "Thanks for the figure. I'm paying for these drinks "

Chapter 8

Our Colonial Ruin
Georgetown, Dist. of Col.

Dear Pop,

Mark Twain is said to have remarked in the Willard Hotel saloon (they didn't call them bars or grills when Mark Twain was a reporter in Washington) "It's a great place to live, but I wouldn't want to visit here." At the moment Sheila and myself we don't know how we'll ever get used to the amorphous social atmosphere. But sane people like Paul and Alice Ormsbee assure us we'll be real gung ho natives at all the popular water holes, as they call the cocktail parties, in a few weeks. We are being introduced to embassy receptions, and certain eating places and clubs. Do we enjoy it? Maybe, as the Blue River man said when he saw his dog screwing a skunk.

First day on the job after a really good, cheap-priced lunch, a gourmet's delight which the Senate dining room keeps to a very low cost, Paul took me to the Senate and introduced me to the members in the cloakroom (really a club of easy chairs and rockers) and to some handshaking from both parties. I had my seat and in the Senate Chamber Paul just in front of me, to keep me informed as to what was going on. There is a reciprocal tolerance mostly among the members. It's damn impressive, and you meet all kinds. Some senators look like harem girls too ripe on the vine, some are folksy as Minnie Pearl, and then the "snowtops" (as the older incumbents are called) sit with such a kind of staid dignity you wonder if they're stuffed. There are half a dozen special men, greatly talented I think, and I hope to know them better. The mandates and mores of the U.S. Senate are very interesting and often sly.

Senator Barraclough, whom I wanted to meet, wasn't there. The gossip in the cloakroom was he had a few too many martinis at lunch and stepped into a phone booth and said, "Up. Third Floor." And so he was assisted to his car and driven home a couple weeks ago. If true, a very great man and political powerhouse must be ready to retire.

It was ten minutes to two when we got to the Senate Chamber. Session was about to begin and the place was humming like a violin. There it was, the brown marble oval that I stood in awe of, with the page boys—white *and* black these days—distributing bills and legislative calendars to the historic desks, and here and there a polished spittoon, a tradition from the days when most men chawed and had amber-stained moustaches. The parliamentarian came in—a bit petulant—he and the clerk of the Senate and the sergeant at arms were in a huddle, most likely cutting up a basketball pool, Paul said. We had a good showing. The sound now reached the obsessive haunting of a tuned orchestra.

I looked up at the public gallery; some Boy Scouts, a bland Oriental face, bearded Arabs—not much of a crowd. In the family gallery were two senators' wives and a nanny with a child eating cookies. The diplomatic gallery was empty but as I looked, two British types took their seats.

The Vice-President, a defrocked liberal, rapped his gavel. The Senate chaplain rose in dusty black robes and went into a pious twang based on some prose style from the King James Version, asking His good and fervent help in this hour of meditation and the cries of our Jeremiahs as the nation faced grave problems—might now the Divine aid look down on this splendid body of lawmakers and inspire to complete victory the high hopes and visions of peace, kindness and charity we held for all the world. And take unto His cherished haven those dead in far places destroyed on sea and land, symbolized in the past by our desires for eternal peace, without ourselves demanding any gratitude or thanks for our crusades to set up order in far corners of this planet, and soon in outer space.

Paul smiled, turned to me as I rearranged some papers, whispered "I have a bet he ends with something from the Book of Psalms today."

I shook my head. "How much you have on it?"

"Two tickets to the next tryout of a Broadway play in town."

"I read he's best in the Book of Job."

"Ah!"

> And behold, there came a great wind from the wilderness
> And smote the four corners of the house,
> And it fell upon the young men and they are dead.

Still and all, Pop, it's a great gutsy feeling to sit and watch the procedures. Even your iron-hard hide would soften a bit when you see here the men who help keep the nation on a kind of cockeyed even keel. The fact that they are timeservers and some are loafers, vulnerable to diverse influences and maybe worse, doesn't matter. As a body I think they stand for something vital. And if the voters kick our asses hard enough, I think we shall survive and do fairly well.

So Paul rubbed his brows and repeated, "And it fell upon the young men, and they are dead." Didn't his son die in Vietnam?

It needed fifty-one senators for a quorum. The clerk began to call the roll. A senator asked for unanimous consent to have the quorum call dispensed with, but there were two rings for a quorum and it turned out that a quorum was present. Looking on the balding heads, the graying locks of hair, the dye jobs, the few toupees, these bodies looked like a cross-section of the people in the streets—more portly perhaps, a bit more of a twitch or a tic here and there. But solid enough men, and human enough, too; human often, I knew, within the peripheries of their own personalities, prejudices, desires.

Someone cheered in the visitors' gallery, someone started a cough, but it was going to be a quiet day—unless, said Paul, unless someone brought up the Senate Ethics Bill before the Chamber and out of committee. I reinspected the galleries again. A four-star general, columnists' legmen, National Science Foundation people, staff officers from the Joint Chiefs of Staff. And behind them some faces.

The special interests are always present, their lobbyists there in rank. This season they have pretty much castrated the Fair Packaging act, the Revised Auto Safety bills, beaten down the policing of loan sharks and shady savings and loan companies. I hear a small group feels hope for the disciplining of the three major television networks for their low standards and cynical disregard for the free air they use and often pollute. Forget it.

Paul clued me in at who waved to him—Tim of the life insurance lobby and auto claims association, adamantly working to see no one insists on the whole truth on costs and claims in policies. At his side a fine black-eyed beaut of forty-odd who lobbies for department stores, perfume and cosmetics (selling 2¢ of lard for $10 an ounce). Solly, who entertains congressmen on weekend flights to Acapulco for winegrowers. Conrad, lobbyist for six trade unions, half of whose leaders are in prison or out on appeal. Matt for the auto and steel unions; old Crowly Seldon, watchdog for the Civil Liberties Union; bread, airlines and oil. O.R. of the Freemen's Rights Guild. Paul said, "They are fighting for the right to put live rattlesnakes with poisoned fangs in every child's crib. A noble cause. I would miss them if lobbyists were abolished."

I went to phone to see if there was anything new at the office. Just four people who wanted to get to the visitors' gallery. I said see to it. I went into the Senate washroom to have my shoes shined.

Paul joined me. "A short session among the earnest strivers and the mediocrities. My grandfather had a mansion on N Street as the representative of the Huntingtons, and as a boy I remember the senators coming hat in hand to take their tainted money—as it was called then—and make their promises to be good boys. Those simple times are gone and now, I suppose, one bribes computers, makes false charts and endows foundations to warp the image."

The only fun in the chamber today (the real work starts next week) was a tangle of Senator Monti Chad from Oklahoma (and typecast for a John Wayne movie) and Senator Maurice Silver from Ohio, a big-city boss type. Both by reputation sterling corn-pone performers. They had a sharp debate going on, the kind the press likes for its small talk and heavy jests.

"I ask the respected senator from Ohio to yield so I may answer some preposterous rumors," said Monti in his county chairman's drawl; he had been a medicine show professor in his youth, peddling a cure-all for man or beast. He, an office holder with tact, forbearance, was adored by the poor whites and the old and cattle barons alike. "I ask to speak to refute those items of incredibility that have appeared in some northern papers hinting that I am in league with the opposition party in my native state to infiltrate the . . ."

Senator Silver, at ease, said, "I do not yield. The item before this sitting of the Senate is the matter of the Silver report on the Senate Ethics Bill—morals and procedures in acceptance of lecture fees."

"I ask you to yield."

"I will not yield on matters not directly pertaining to the measure."

An opposition member, Senator Hamilton, rose. "Now we make a little cash, sure, lecturing. But if the opposition is in conflict among itself, I would like the gentlemen to yield to me. I have here some figures . . . on junkets and gifts . . ."

Senator Monti said, "If the gentleman from Indiana is referring to certain trips to India to investigate the pineapple crops of that country with a party of forty-two that used blocked funds at the U.S. Embassy in Paris . . . or for that clearing of the Old Keystone Canal by the army engineers . . . a bill of great merit; I'm sure no senator here has not aided his . . ."

Hamilton smiled. "No, I'm not using even the cost of the Cactus Park Historical Monuments Funding along U.S. highways, or the reconversion of land spoiled by strip mining. Bill A-four-oh-six-five-dash-nine-oh-eight-three, which is in process of consideration . . ."

Silver said, "I do not yield the floor, Senator."

Paul said it was all a ritual. They would trade off a canal against some historical stretch of highway—your bill for mine. Some dam for a fish hatchery, some park for a dying town played off against a federal celebration of a major Indian defeat. I sensed there was an undercurrent of drama in the Senate that I was missing. This surface bickering could cover some major shift, some blast from the White House escalating some major policy or a stand against some "must" budget.

The talk in the Senate as to future business was that the matter of CIA interference in Latin-American elections would be talked over with a new investigation committee formed. It would tie in with defense appropriations (too high but set to pass) and someone would bring up post offices and the flood control bill coming out of committee. The Mississippi and the Missouri and Red rivers were tearing hell out of the Middle West again as usual. The Senate had to ask approval of a medal struck to recall Tanacharisson, half-king of the Senecas (1728–1801). There was a cocktail party for some United Nations delegates at the Soviet Embassy on 16th Street. I said no—I had had a full day.

That's the first day, Pop. Mostly high-level tête-à-tête. If you like these details, I'll try to keep you informed. Clair and Sheila and myself, we went out to the house we bought in Georgetown. Paul thinks I should have rented. But I'm not the type. Sheila is excited about some wormy old furniture she saw over in Virginia across the river (the Potomac!) at one of those Jesse James antique shops, stuff to fill out what we're shipping from home. All I want is a room with wall space for books, room for files and a radio, a small Jap radio (I guess they're "Japanese" now: only Japs when we're at war with them, huh?).

The house, in the rim of a rigid social stratification, is of the original red colonial brick, such is the claim. New slate roof. A stone-walled cellar. I'll have to have it air-conditioned, I know. Good hand-hewed rafters in the dining room. Too narrow a staircase, where I'll hang my Winslow Homer and Remington woodcut prints. Big bedroom, but low-ceilinged as all these houses were built to save heat. There is a sleeping porch off it, screened, and a hell of a view of a bit of garden, a former privy now a potting shed. The old carriage house is a two-car garage. No bargain I suppose. But nobody loses money in real estate as you sell for at least a third or more after a few years. The former owner, a State Department man in hush-hush work (a master of the double cross as Paul insists), put the house in a kind of order. Some Arab gangsters killed him in the Rome airport, and Esme Lowell, niece of Senator Barraclough—she runs a real estate firm on Wisconsin Avenue—found it for us on our first trip to Washington after the election to get to look over the city. The house had been a slum ruin for a hundred years like all its neighbors, until Georgetown became fashionable and restorations took over. Never skillfully restored—the State Department man was always low in funds—and while it has charm and warmth, there are ominous cracks, and trouble opening and closing some of the warped doors and windows. The kitchen has its original rough, smoky rafters and the brick fireplace now has a modern gas range alongside of it. The house is certainly historic; I can guess hard to heat in winter, squeaky and with a perverse groaning of dry-rot timbers. The refrigerator is set in a knotty pine recess.

Besides letters to you I'm keeping a notebook of what I find out. No, not a journal—just jottings. I am pecking this out with two fingers on my cranky portable in what Sheila calls my den—as yet unfinished. It's a small room with sloping ceiling, faded yellow wallpaper and risky wiring; Thomas Edison himself may have done the job. I'll get some bookcases, a bit of rug, a side table for glasses and bottles and some curtains for the small double windows overlooking the next-door driveway. And I'll be snug. It's nearly one o'clock, and the night is blue-black. The city seems very still, and I'm getting used to being a senator and being in Washington. The night sounds grow a bit, but it's only some cars passing. Sheila has just come in to say better get to bed. Tomorrow, she insists, is another day, a very good observation. I'm meeting Senator Barraclough soon. Goodnight. Sheila says she too.

JAY

Jason liked a well-run but easygoing office atmosphere. He set up Andy Wolensky as his administrative assistant and office manager, moved Clair Brooks into a private office next to his and set up Miss Munday as captain of the outer offices. He had an office staff of eighteen various people he was still trying to recognize by face or name; typists, file clerks, messengers. And as to what they did, that too was often a problem.

Andy, solid and chunky, had hired a driver, a wide-shouldered black man with a face scar and one gold-rimmed tooth, to chauffeur the Senator's Lincoln. J. Willard had also shipped out a tan roadster —"So Sheila can go marketing."

"Now Chief," said Andy, "you have no worries from the office. We'll keep it running. As a senator you get a heated garage, use of the 'members only' elevator, free flowers from the Botanical Gardens, haircuts, shoeshines, a gym, and—" Andy picked up a fresh list of government privileges.

"Shut up, Andy. Get me some background information on Senator Barraclough."

"I'll get cracking on it." He again consulted the list. "You, all the family, get free medical attention and hospital rooms at Walter Reed or Bethesda. Listen, Chief, would you believe half a million free envelopes and fifty trips home, all on the cuff."

"Andy, I don't need an accountant. Have my notes on the Gridiron Club speech typed up."

"Okay, okay."

Jason wasn't too impressed by what a senator got "on the cuff." The Senate was classed as The Club by many, and rightly so; from its famous bean soup to the $500,000 a year each senator was permitted to spend on staff salaries, and—as Paul Ormsbee added—if he got on a few top committees he could run his staff up to seventy-five, "And have a million and a half to spend on them. Jay, it's size that counts here. And if you work hard at it—as some don't—it leads someplace."

No, Jason swore to himself, he'd be damned if he'd get trapped as so many were in figuring out how to fatten an office staff, get hold of the extra allowances for stamps and a bigger home office. Back in Vista City he'd keep the staff at a minimum. He was more concerned to be making the right contacts, and the one he wanted most to make was with the head of the party for over twenty years; Senator Austin Ames Barraclough, once the ruler of important political ramifications.

It had been Buster Miller who had said to Jason on his first day as an elected U.S. Senator, "Skip the bowers and wavers-in, go right to the head men—the *man*. You get him to like you and you've saved a lot of wear and tear. Kiss the right ass is the national sport in politics—kicking the right ass, go easy there."

Austin Ames Barraclough had not been seen too often in the Senate Office Buildings, or on the Hill, in the Senate Chamber at the Capitol. There were rumors—and Washington was, as Jason soon saw, a rumor mill—that Barraclough was dying of cancer, that he was in an alcoholic drying-out sanitarium in Maryland, that he had suffered a series of heart attacks, that he had swallowed sleeping pills and—the most heard story—"He's so damn senile they have to have him wear diapers. Feed him with a spoon."

Jason was long enough in politics to ignore all this. The drinking problem was most likely true. The Congress and the Senate had its many lushes, its dazed glassy-eyed members who sat and were unaware of the business at hand. Or those who drank heavily at lunch and, far from any center of gravity, were not with it the rest of the afternoon. The speaker was known to be tanked at times while he fondled his gavel, and certain key chairmen of committees that favored the Pentagon were known and respected as men who "could walk a straight line even while pie-eyed."

Some text in Jason's notebook:

At fifty-eight, Senator Austin Barraclough had joined the names of those much gossiped about. After twenty years of great success, some even said genius in running the party on the Hill, the Senate, he appeared to be in full decline. He had a huge house on Dupont Circle, but was now in the Barracloughs' Georgian estate across the river in Virginia. He was related to the Baracloughs (with a single *r*) who ran the eastern shore of Maryland and had much of the southeastern seaboard under their political influence.

The Barracloughs (two *r*'s) had been here early, and proud they had not come as most Virginians had, as bonded indentured servants, freed from Newgate Prison under threat of the hangman's rope at Tyburn, or from debtors' gaol on condition they be transported to the New World to make their own way. The Barracloughs had on the other hand been exiled for rebellion against a king: picking the wrong side and feeling it was better to grow tobacco, indigo and rice in the wilderness than be hanged, drawn and quartered, the head exhibited on a spike at the Tower of London.

Such anyway, I read in certain histories borrowed from the Library of Congress by Clair, were the semi-gentry beginnings of the Barracloughs. Most in 1776 had remained Tories, loyal to King George III in the American Revolution. But Cyrus Barraclough, who sang "Yankee Doodle," had lost an eye at Brandywine. Cyrus bought up land grants from unpaid soldiers in no condition or hopes of holding on to them. Cyrus ran for the Congress under Jefferson, got elected, was involved in a parentcy suit, became Governor of Virginia under Madison, was wounded in a duel over a horse race, and died rich—and disliked as an honest man who said slavery was foolish and uneconomical, *and* called dishonest for agreeing with Alexander Hamilton that the common man was too common and that to give him the vote and rights of the squires and the landowners and the lawyers would wreck any ideal government he hoped the American (limited) democracy would produce.

His son, Silas Winston Barraclough, supported Andrew Jackson, dealt in slaves, but imported Irish paddies to work his fever-ridden rice swamps; a good black cost $900 and "as with a good horse, one doesn't risk valuable property." So the Irish died of malaria, yellow jack and assorted ills, survivors getting drunk on moonshine by their smoky fires smoldering to drive off the night-biting insects, and dying cursing Silas Winston Barraclough who built the foundation of the Barraclough fortunes.

From then on the Barracloughs were lawyers, sat in Congress, one was a vice-president, one nearly a president between Hayes and Cleveland. Almost didn't count, Austin was told as a boy. He learned early to look with pride on the walls of Potomac House across from Washington on the Virginia side, to study the portraits in good oils of a Captain, of a Major Barraclough, two more state governors, a secretary of state, two ambassadors, one to the Court of St. James's and the other to die of native rum and the old rale in a tropical nation. Also there were whispers of a Barraclough, a friend of Oscar Wilde's, and who was the Sam Barraclough hanged in Wyoming? ("every family has its failures").

Potomac House was a grand old Georgian pile of whitewashed brick and tall columns, gardens of rare shrubs and plants. A good library. Benton Barraclough had subscribed to Audubon's elephant folio, *Birds of America*, and his collection of classical pornography included a dozen erotic watercolors of Thomas Rowlandson's. There were Barracloughs painted by Gilbert Stuart and Copley, by Sargent, by Whistler, and a strange one of Mona, Austin Barraclough's second wife, done by Dali: she leaning on a broken statue dotted with crawling ants—and in the background, a giraffe on fire.

Austin Barraclough, son of Governor Clifford Ames Barraclough, had stroked the varsity crew at Princeton, married a society beauty who divorced him to marry a Polish prince ("everybody is a prince in Poland but sheepherders and Jews"). Austin's second wife, Mona, was a distant relative of both the du Ponts and the Bancrofts of Boston. A strange combination, some said, but a striking beauty, a splendid horsewoman, a collector of primitive American art, hand-sewed colonial quilts and Pennsylvania Dutch pottery. After a serious fall from her favorite gelding, Tar Baby, at the Richmond horse show and a bad spine injury, Mona retired to a Barraclough estate in South Carolina, and the Washington rumor mill hinted she was addicted to drugs because of the constant pain of her injuries.

Austin Barraclough never talked of her to his friends. He seemed more reserved than ever, lost his temper often and it was clear he was drinking much more than usual, and he had been a solid drinker since his youth. The Barracloughs were not only collectors of fine wine cellars, but had reputations as boozers—"Gentlemen, suh, who could hold their likker, suh."

It was clear Austin Barraclough was losing that claim. He had actually walked into a phone booth mistaking it for an elevator and twice the Washington police had picked him up wandering along near the Chain Bridge and seen him safely to his townhouse on Dupont Circle. After a Christmas party near the Shoreham Hotel he had been mugged by three black youths and, refusing to give up his wallet, his grandfather's watch-and-chain, had been stabbed in the right arm but held on to two of the muggers until help came. He was a big man, six foot three, and still had the shoulders and arms of a Princeton letterman, had never gone to fat. In the last year his face had grown puffy and the skin color gone to a putty tone instead of its former ruddy tan. It was clear the party's leader in the Chamber was suffering from more than personal idiosyncrasy. Two marriages had produced no children. His closest relative was his niece Esme Lowell, daughter of his late sister, Amanda, who had married the wrong Lowell, it seemed ("Worcester, not Boston"), who had a passion for Washington's late night poker games and who died happy as a grig over a card table on H Street while holding three aces in a $600 jackpot. Just dropped dead smiling across his winnings, still holding his winning hand as his heart gave a skip and a bump and burst.

Esme was bright, handsome as a teen-ager. Someday she'd be a great beauty, people said, or gawky; she was neither, but very attractive at twenty-eight. First came Vassar, a session on *Vogue* as a third assistant caption writer, a marriage with a charming man who wrote for a newsmagazine—a marriage of tedious unsensibility that ended after four years when he insisted there was nothing wrong in being bisexual, or bringing a male friend home for a session of six legs in a bed.

Esme was bright enough to sense she was not shocked, just revolted. After her divorce she went to Europe to write press copy for an Italian company that used second-rate American actors to make preposterous Western films with Italian peasants as cowboys and villains. Esme lived with the director, Emilio Abbatutus, which resulted in a daughter, Bianca (or Betty) whom she brought back when the film company was taken over because of its success by some huge collection of Texan corporations, which quickly ran it into the ground for the tax losses it needed.

Esme moved in with her uncle and aunt. Austin Barraclough was having problems with Mona, his second wife, even before the riding accident. Esme took to running the household at Potomac House and Bianca, aged six, going to the Alexandria second-grade public school. Esme moved out six months after Mona Barraclough left for treatment for injuries, or was it drug addiction?—no one was sure for which. Esme Lowell opened a small real estate office first in the Chevy Chase district, and as she knew so many people, "everyone," was invited to embassy dinners and balls. She had played in the halls of the Capitol as a child, tossed jacks and rolled hoops (actually) by the Japanese cherry trees; she was successful, stuck to a limited clientele, or newly elected politicians seeking living space. She housed embassy staffs needing country houses or some discreet adultery needing a posh flat. When a failed hero had to leave town after defeat at home she would sublet his flat, sell his house, even get rid of his cars or dogs (she disliked cats). Most people who knew her felt her cold, reserved, witty.

Esme usually dined with her uncle twice a week. They were both movie fans of ancient pictures and went at least once a week to the Recall Cinema to see scratchy versions of Garbo and Gary Cooper films, and delighted at Buster Keaton, and Laurel and Hardy, Charlie Chaplin and the Keystone Cops. When Uncle Austin was "ill" she had been renting 16-mm films to project at Potomac House. Senator Barraclough used to sleep through most of the showings of early Cagney, Errol Flynns, Bette Davises, and William Powells and Myrna Loys.

End of Jason's notes on the Barracloughs.

Esme had sold the Crocketts the old colonial house from an ad they saw in the Washington Post (*original Geo.Twn. col., fully renov. modern appl. . . . 3 baths, serv. qtrs. 50 fr. frontage. orig. timbers, rafters . . . coach hse., gar.*).

Jason phoned Esme when Senator Barraclough had not appeared in the Chamber at all for the first week of that session. Jason had sat in his seat and looked at the senator's empty place.

Esme was pleased to hear from Senator Crockett. She hoped he was enjoying his delightful Georgetown Colonial.

"Well, it's quaint, and Mrs. Crockett is having a field day furnishing it. The ceiling's a little low for me, and it moans and groans at night like someone were kicking it."

Chapter 9

The party last night had been faceless people gossiping at dusk, punctuated by glowing cigarette ends. As the day heated up, it was clear to Jason it would be one of those humid periods when the Washington basin, never the most healthy kind of landscape, produced a miserable kind of weather. He shaved damply with his warm electric razor. Sheila was sleeping late. She had been making order in their house with Fran Colter, who had come along from Vista City as housekeeper and maid and, it was hoped, as part-time cook. ("It's a black town, Washington, isn't it? *That's* for me.")

Jason put on his gray linen suit and a short-sleeved shirt and decided to add a tie. Esme Lowell yesterday had arranged his meeting with Austin Barraclough, and it was best to present himself with a necktie. He had a breakfast of some damn cereal fortified with God knew what chemical goodies and tasting of straw and too much sugar. He sipped iced coffee. Fran kept asking, "Some eggs, bacon, ham? You need something on your stomach for the day, Senator." He found her disquieting persistence distracting.

He said "No, this will do, Fran." His neck was already itching with prickly heat; the damn electric razor had pressed too hard on his sensitive neck.

"This is sure a black town, Senator, blacker than black. Of course mostly field hands for grandfathers."

Jason sucked a bit of ice in the coffee and heard the peep-peep of Esme Lowell's car. He decided to wear a cloth tweed hat bought on a trip to Ireland years ago—home-woven and shaggy; then decided no. "Take some coffee and a toasted English muffin up to Mrs. Crockett."

*　　*　　*

Esme Lowell's battered Caddy was out front. She prided herself on using the old pale blue car so in need of paint and some fender work; actually enjoyed driving some embassy secretary or well-heeled senator's wife around in what she called The Heap to view some house or flat. In time the gossip columnists had made the battered car a kind of social status symbol.

Esme herself, for all the humid heat, looked cool in pale lime-green linen, her amber-colored hair brushed back in a boyish hairdo, just a hint of dime-sized jade at each earlobe. He thought she looked hard, self-contained as an egg.

"A bitch of a day, Senator." She had a firm voice, deep toned. Esme Lowell reminded Jason of old films with Jean Arthur. But she didn't look like Jean Arthur: being tall, long-legged with a rather classic nose, as seen on Greek statues. A hard woman, Jason felt, as he got in and they drove off into the heated air. Heat undulated off the street's surface like an out-of-focus photograph.

"Close the windows. The air conditioning might work."

It did as she headed The Heap for the Chain Bridge across the Potamic, passing grandiose marble columns and sprinklers revolving in small parks.

"I want to thank you, Miss Lowell."

"Nothing to thank for. How's Mrs. Crockett coming with the house?"

"Howling at the plumbing, cursing the window-washing crew. The usual games of moving into a new house. Well, not a *new* house."

"You can always sell it at a gain, you know. Those old crocks in Georgetown are in demand. Values going up."

He watched her extract a cigarette from a handbag and shake her head at an offer of his lighter. "I don't light them. Just need the feel of them in my yap. I smoke one a day—at bedtime."

She didn't seem to want to carry on a conversation.

"I've wanted to meet Senator Barraclough. And this seeing him at his home will give me, I hope, some better understanding of processes and protocol here. I'm green as goose—as—"

She looked at him—"Goose turd?"—as they got onto the bridge. The sun was glaring lime-white. People and cars were moving slowly on the Virginia side. The reflection of windows and traffic burned into his vision. Esme opened a glove compartment and took out a pair of sunglasses.

"Here, try these. Look, Senator, you've been hearing rumors about my uncle. Who hasn't in this fucking town."

Jason tried to show he didn't mind a woman using such language.

She went on, "Who said 'Hearts that are delicate and kind and tongues that are neither—these make the finest company in the . . . world'?"

"No idea."

"Anyway, the hearts aren't kind here, and I don't know what your ideas on fine company are. Uncle Austin has been through several crises, and as you've heard, he hits the booze."

"There are lot of folks in Washington who do. Or anyplace."

"But not with his brains, his skills, his damn obligations. Anyway, he didn't bite my head off when I mentioned your name. He has shown an interest in you; some law you pushed when governor."

"I'm flattered." Jason rubbed his raw neck.

"Bread O'Rahilly keeps his posted. You've met Bread . . . ?

"Just on the run, and telephone. Isn't he a rather mysterious figure?"

"You mean loaded with money to hand around?" Esme smiled, took the unlit cigarette from her mouth, opened a window, tossed it out, closed the window. "He's a lobbyist for certain special interest groups. Oh, perfectly legal. He's a sonofabitch, sure, and corrupts people maybe. But as Uncle Austin says, or said once, 'When you break bread with the enemy at your own table, sit facing him so he can't get you behind your back.' Actually they're old friends." She looked out on clumps of gas stations, trash-food frontage, super-markets with kids out front sucking ice-cream cones. "Uncle's a has-been, you know. Why would you bother with him, Senator Crockett?"

"Do I look like such an ass-kisser?"

"Lots of you first-time characters come here with that gleam in your eye that you'll change things, and get pointers from Uncle Austin, find the Holy Grail of power. Want to be president?"

He was learning to counter-punch with her. "It hasn't been offered."

She laughed, a deep throaty laugh. You damn cynical bitch, he thought. Maybe she had his number, maybe he did have ideas for change, his name on famous bills, amendments—in some future con-ventions his name and image could be carried on banners at the deci-sive moment as history turned the page. He felt cross, the car's air conditioning was breaking down. Esme fiddled with some dashboard levels. "It's dying. Always does after a while."

They had turned off the main highway and were on a narrow side road among heat-scorched dusty trees, a meadow run wild, in the distance some horses were in a fenced-in area. There was still some green world left, he thought, smelling of horse manure. He felt his armpits, crotch, get damp, his neck-rash burn. God, he'd like to tell this dame off. "I don't think Senator Barraclough is a has-been. He may not be active at the moment, but his track record is goddamn good. And he's still the party leader in the Chamber."

"Just a title. Your Senator Ormsbee is acting leader. I think you're barking up the wrong oak tree. Uncle Austin, he can't do a thing for you, Senator."

He pulled the necktie loose, opened his shirt collar. "All right, Miss Lowell, so I've come to pay my respects to a ruin. Go ahead and enjoy ribbing me. There are some splendid ruins all over the world. Better than the new shapes they're putting up."

"Try cleaning up after a ruin." The car moved off on to a blue stone drive that needed raking and ran for a quarter of a mile past shrubs and old trees. It was all very impressive but in need of care. The gray-white house appeared as the drive curved to the left. Potomac House in early nineteenth-century aesthetics was impressive. Its paint had held up well under some tawny and fruit-green lace of vines. The steps up to the tall columns—Jason counted six of them— the tall windows had a grace and composition that seemed to mock the glass and plastic of piano box modern structures. Form follows function, my ass, Jason thought as she brought the car to a stop. "I'm impressed," he said.

"Six layers of wallpaper in the hall," she said as they got out of the car into a blistering damp heat. "Slave quarters empty but for three families of refugees from Vietnam. Uncle Austin was a sinner, a war hawk. And they'll never leave. They run roadside stands: stuff from Uncle Austin's vegetable gardens of course." She kicked at a cast iron hitching post standing on a block lettered BARRACLOUGH.

The double doors with the fanlights held brass work (or bronze in need of polishing); the green turtle-colored patina on them seemed somehow proper. Jason tugged at the bell pull, but Esme let herself in with a key in a Yale lock.

"Champ doesn't answer the bell if he doesn't feel like it." The hall was cool, the grand staircase spiraling up like the curves on a snail's shell. There were heavy gold-framed pictures all the way up, but it was too dark to see details. Jason made out a Chinese umbrella stand, a fumed oak coatrack with a mirrored center and metal hooks, one holding a tweed jacket with leather elbows and shoulder patches, a linen hat with trout flies on the brim band. Canes overfilled the Ming umbrella stand. He made out an old tavern sign.

> Drink the punch.
> Fire the gun.
> Beat the British.
> Very good fun.

A big hulk of a black man with a flattened nose, wearing a white jacket, came out from a room on the left.

"That you, Miss Esme? You bring the lamb chops?"

"They'll deliver, Champ. Where's Uncle?"

"He's in the book room." Jason was aware that the house had been air-conditioned. The dining room to the right, its chandeliers tied up in linen bags, seemed unused: shrouds covered chairs and tables, crystal globes overhead tinkled as the air conditioning stirred them from some vents in a panel. Esme led past a wall of Chinese tapestry of storks on long legs and waterlily ponds, with a philosopher in a small boat fishing, set against a world of high mountain ridges and a pale moon.

The library windows had their shades drawn, but Jason made out three walls of books, mostly in rare leather bindings, a yellowed globe of the world in a black teak stand, a heavy table three feet across, two Tiffany lamps on it—as he faced the gleam of tiles on a carved fireplace.

"Uncle?"

Jason became aware of a wide-winged red leather chair and a figure deeply seated in it, a tall broad figure, long narrow head, bare feet, no slippers. The man wearing a Japanese kimono robe. Mostly Jason was struck by the head; a comatose apparition. It also reminded Jason of some Roman busts in the Vista County Museum of Art. The waxy color helped, but the broad hinge of the nose, the eyes half-hooded in the crowfeet in which they sat were not that of a statue—they suggested life voluble and proud. Yes, pride was there in the skeptical thin slit of a large mouth held closed.

At fifty-eight, Senator Austin Barraclough looked ten to fifteen years older. Not so much disintegration, Jason decided, it was the lighting. Rembrandt lighting they had called it in the college art class. Features picked out by suggestive highlights. There was a reality to the scene, to the setting, the figure in the chair. Jason felt some human inconsistency or secret set out before him. The spell was broken when the figure spoke, "Goddamn it Esme, you broke my train of thought."

It was a good solid voice; crisp, with just a suggestion of southern theater.

"Never mind the train, Uncle Austin, Senator Crockett is here." She pulled back a drape, slid up a shade. The room leaped into detail. The room of a man who indulged himself, or his forefathers had, with Rowlandson watercolors (rather bawdy), a Hokusai courtesan sketch, framed Audubon prints of the Great American Turkey and the California Condor.

"Cut the light, damn you, girl."

Esme lowered the shade, but did not replace the drape. She seemed immune to the older man's tone or manner. The head of Austin Barraclough turned quickly, "Sit down, Crockett." Jason took the hand offered, a big hand, warm, with a pulse in it, hard. Not much pressure, but a good handshake. "Esme, ring to get us something cool. Tom Collins, yes, Tom Collins. Champ! Champ, you bastard you, where you standing? Tom Collins!"

He smiled at Jason. It was a good smile. "Haven't been well." He cleared his throat as if rattling soft pebbles. "Yes. Well Senator, I like our conservation bill, that bit of trickery too to get it passed." Esme went toward the hall. Austin Barraclough said, "The Collins!"

Esme said without turning around, "Easy does it."

"My father, J. Willard Crockett," said Jason, "admires you."

"J. Willard? Oh, yes. Faces, people, they fade in memory, you know, after awhile. Now, I'll be back in a few days as party leader. No matter what the doctor says. I need good young men with balls, cojones they call it, eh, out your way? Yes. Got to slap the Senate into shape. All ends loose ends now." He seemed to drop his interest and stare at a T'ang horse on the fireplace. "Yes, Crockett, I'm tired —ass-dragging tired. You ever—never mind."

Jason could see Esme had been right. There wasn't much left of
the great man of twenty, of ten years ago, but his reputation. He was
still the symbol, the defender of the Constitution, hero of partisan
victories. Or at least the use of his name applied to so much of the
party business, the Senate's procedures.

Champ, the butler, or whatever he was, in his white jacket came in
with two tall glasses sweating coolness.

Austin Barraclough took one, Jason the other. Esme had not come
back. Austin took a sip, frowned. "You black bastard, it's lemonade!"

"You bet, Senator." The big Negro was grinning. He spelled it out,
"*l e m o n a i d*. Lemonaid."

He went out chuckling. Austin Barraclough sipped, grimaced.
"Champ used to be a hell of a boxer. Once knocked Cassius Clay on
his duff, he claims. Air Force captain—oh yes—brusque, aggressive.
Spent six years in a North Vietnam prison. Mean, *very* mean. And
they did some things to him."

"I hope to be able to work with you in the Senate, sir. I hope you
will depend on me."

"Depend? Depend? Oh . . . you intend to stay in Washington. Esme
said she sold you a house. Mean, very mean girl. She's all that's left
of this branch of the Barracloughs. She, and my wife . . . who's off
someplace . . . else." He flung the glass of lemonade against the fireplace tiles. It shattered over the blue Delft surfaces. "Whiskey!"

Jason looked around. He felt too alone.

Austin Barraclough said, "I used to drink a lot, you know. I mean
I really hung one on when I was going good. You know William
Faulkner used to be a houseguest here. Once . . . yes . . . we two used
to really booze it up. Never said much, Bill—just drank and stared at
you. But now . . . they watch me. Yes."

"I look forward to seeing you in the Senate Chamber, sir."

Austin Barraclough seemed to recover. "Next two years a convention. A national convention. Been paying any attention to it?"

"Studying the prospects of the party. It's a toss-up. Reputations are
made overnight. A week on television and some people get ideas they
are presidential timber."

"Dispassionate professionalism wins elections. But move with the
times—never fall back to entrenched positions. Now tell me . . . get
me a cigar from that box, take one yourself . . . I want your candid
opinion."

They sat smoking. "Crockett, tell me about Zack Boone. He's making big noise in the West. You see him as presidential timber?"

"He's in good shape. In the West, we drift too much, dream too often."

"Now, don't play the road-company Marcus Aurelius. But the opposition is in worse shape. Our major problem: the rich western boys still have us by the balls. But the moderate groups are growing. Not rotten with anti-Semites, Turks, and Birchers."

"But in the main the omens are good, and if we have a national ticket that's more exciting than the old Tarzan movies on television, we can have a grand ride of it—and win, close, *but* win."

Austin Barraclough asked, "How's the private poll on the President's rating?"

"The President is falling in popularity in the party, overseas on the world scene, nationally. Vice-President is a millstone, a defrocked liberal, a born target for picket lines, and the average citizen thinks he looks like death warmed over on television. But the President will still beat any ticket we've talked over so far. He may smell like skunk oil with his folksy manner, but the big handout programs of the city machines, defense orders to his pals, are still in his fists. He can still take us *unless*."

"Unless?"

"Unless we don't make our usual mistake of letting the mush-mouthed windbags and the Stone Age types panic the convention? Seize the convention."

Austin nodded. "We must help also to widen the rift between the liberal and the segregationist barons of the Confederacy."

Jason shrugged. "From the South it doesn't smell too good. Well, that's what the private poll shows. If we have the men, I'd say we can win. It'll take a firmly run convention, good governors, a lot of young bright people organizing the party away from the horses asses of retired admirals and generals talking out of turn. We can put the party in the White House in two years if we deserve it."

"Crockett, you're a young man with a mind and wary eye. I can tell. Give me the name of a winner."

"The ideal candidate? Well, here are the survey themes. Association with national issues is far down among the qualifications for eligibility. Talk on controversial issues counts against a possible candidate's eligibility. That's why governors are preferred as candidates. Their public service, unlike senators', has been limited to state and local affairs. Eligibility involves matters little related to qualifications for office, such as religion, business connections. Age may be a factor, sometimes health. Since the advent of television, photogenic image is injected."

"And? Name names. Ormsbee?"

"Maybe he's speaking too soon, but we have a front runner—and he's no surprise. If a payoff scandal doesn't kick up too much of a fuss. I don't think it will. People don't really care about international kickbacks."

"Suppose it has to be someone else?"

"Well now—" Jason was suddenly aware he had lost Austin Barraclough. The older man had lowered his head, his arms began to twitch and he made mumbling sounds that grew to meaningless vowels. The ability to communicate seemed lost. Champ came in followed by Esme. Champ was carrying a shotglass half full of whiskey in his hand. He managed to get it to Austin's mouth, who swallowed quickly, spilling some down his chin and neck. He became calm, his eyes remained closed. He muttered, "Keep this SOB. We might get a worse SOB."

Jason looked at Esme and then at the man in the chair. Champ wiped Austin's mouth and chin with a tissue he took from a pocket of his white jacket. Jason felt the scene part farcical, part revulsion.

Esme said, "I think we better be going. Uncle Austin, he'll be alright now."

"Till the next shakes," said the butler, looking at the empty glass in his hand.

Austin Barraclough opened his eyes, glanced up at Jason. "Oh, yes, been expecting you. Don't tell me, I know your name. Yes, of course, Grover Asa Bremont."

"Jason Crockett, and I want to say meeting you—" He held out his hand, but Austin had closed his eyes again. The rank smell of raw whiskey and old leather from the many books in the room mixed with something else. It was clear Senator Austin Barraclough had peed himself wet.

Out in the heated day Jason looked over the rolling green country, the sky like brass, and followed Esme into the car. (*The Holy of Holies in the Temple contained absolutely nothing.*) The prickly heat on his neck was inflamed and tormented him.

As they drove down the blue stone drive, Esme put an unlit cigarette in her mouth. "I felt you had to see for yourself. He has been fighting the drinking, but then he has these shaking spells, and the shrinks and the docs try things, turning him from one distraction to another, but he's too strong a character as a drunk to get anyplace near to coming out of it."

"He spoke damn well there for awhile, really logical and to the point."

"Yes, for a minute or two he fooled you, didn't he? Uncle was a great ad lib speaker."

Jason, without being aware of it, was scratching his prickly heat. "You mind if I drop in on him anyway from time to time? I mean, he might like to know how things are going on the Hill?"

Esme looked at him, shook her head and smiled. "You really feel for the poor bastard?"

"I sensed . . . I mean, do you know what he meant. . . . He said something about his wife being away."

Esme's mouth went into a frown. "No comment, Senator."

BOOK III

From the Past

Chapter 10

Driving away from Potomac House, Jason remained silent. Esme gave him some searching glances as they began to merge into the thick traffic moving toward the District of Columbia. He thought of a man who preferred to drown in whiskey and not in water.

"You look in shock, Senator."

"Not shock, Miss Lowell."

"Esme will do, Jack."

"Jay, never Jack. Not shock—it's always sad to see change in people. Fine good people. Or just a beautiful woman twenty years after you first saw her. Nature is a bastard."

Esme laughed. "I was taught Nature doesn't give a good goddamn—it's indifferent to us. Just wants us to reproduce and then tosses us away. As for Uncle Austin, I admit it's a shame. God, I need a drink myself. The Coach House just ahead, Jay—okay?"

Jason said it was as they passed the inertia of an old burying ground. He was damp again and his neck on fire; the car's air conditioning had come back only part way.

The Coach House was a modern copy of a colonial inn with old apothecary bottles as lamp bases, a dark bar and grill, plastic copies of antiques. But the Tom Collins they were served was good and tart and very cold. Someplace canned music played "Climb Every Mountain." Esme and Jason sat among potted plants and hanging flowers, enjoying the cool darkness and their drinks. A man in a tweed jacket at the next table was reading a Christie paperback, the barman stood figuring a racing sheet with a short pencil stub. All, Jason felt, a million light years away from Austin Barraclough at Potomac House.

"I don't think you'll get much help from Uncle Austin. It's not that he's lost his marbles. The doctors don't think that. It's just he doesn't seem to care, and when he doesn't drink for a few days, then he starts on a big one, and it's a *bad* one."

"I don't want to pry," he said. Jason was a bit upset by his reaction to Esme Lowell. There seemed no female warmth for all her good looks, no letdown of an ironic quality for all her clearly defined intellect. "There was a hint of something—of—"

"Oh, about Mona, his wife. His second wife. Don't go imagine any soap opera. There has been a disagreement between them over things none of your business. There was something climactic, and she's in South Carolina. She hasn't been well after she took an asser off a horse."

"Another Collins?"

Esme looked at the heavy man's wristwatch she was wearing. "Just one is all I take in daylight. I've got a business appointment. Yes, life is a kick in the rump. But if you don't bend over too often as a target, it's bearable. Uncle Austin, he never had to bend over being a Barraclough, and nobody dared boot his tail. Oh, the Barracloughs, they had it fine, had it big. History, land, money, social position— and power. They loved power."

"Nothing wrong in the way they used it." He fumbled for his wallet.

"Nothing, *if* you were on their side. But if something goes wrong, they end up one busted-up drunken old crock like Uncle Austin. I bet he never read Kafka: 'In your battles against the world, always bet on the world.' "

"I never read Kafka either." He raised a finger to the barman. "Check."

Esme stood to adjust her clothes, the way Jason had noticed for some time women did with a charming human consistency.

"This is a popular place for taking somebody out for an afternoon. There's a motel set up out back. Lots of congressmen and senators come here for hanky-panky with some of their staff."

"I'm married."

"Cheat?" Was it levity or interest?

He took her arm, "As you said about Uncle Austin, there are things we don't talk about."

*   *   *

Jason decided he'd have Andy Wolensky nose around a bit more and see what the Washington gossip world thought about Senator Barraclough, his private life. No use trying to get anything from Esme Lowell. She was what they called in college "cold tittie." Attractive enough, clever, but a balls-crusher right from the start. Been married, had a child, but not by the husband. What else, what? Damn the Barracloughs, he decided as Esme dropped him in front of the Senate Building. He could forget the Barracloughs. He was a senator, had bills to read, people to meet, work to do in a welter of rampant bureaucracy.

"Thank you." He opened the car door to get out.

"Part of the tour, Jason."

"You wouldn't mind if I keep in contact with your uncle?"

"Why should I? No, not at all. He needs some human voice besides that growl of Champ's. He thinks, if strong enough, he's going to appear in the Chamber next week. They're propping him up to get the Amtex gasoline bill to break up the big oil companies shoved through."

"I hope he makes it. Thanks for your help."

He went up to his office. The Amtex Company control bill to break up a swindle, the screwing of the public by huge combines to raise the price to consumers by a billion dollars a year. He'd have to study it carefully, the idea being to force the Big Six to either import, refine *or* sell gas—not do all three.

Eighteen people, Jason figured, now were working in his office. He waved to Miss Munday, and spoke to Clair Brooks who was hanging pictures—colored photographs of the Blue River country, the scenic heights and Mount Lincoln—on his office walls. He recalled the reverent cadence of the wind in the trees on its lower slopes.

"J. Willard sent these," said Clair.

"If he sends a stuffed elk's head, return it."

"You had calls from a Mr. O'Rahilly. He's airline and big oil lobby. David Slopper, he's welfare and mental health—no, sorry, education. Welfare is Ramon Ortega, he's also mental health." She smiled as she recited. "Senator Ormsbee wants you and Mrs. C. for dinner tomorrow night. British ambassador and a junta president-general from South America are the other guests. It's pronounced *h*unta."

"I know. Is Andy in?"

Clair stepped back to straighten a picture of a fisherman pulling in at least a four-pound trout from a Killamook stream."

"Yes, and I've alerted Mrs. C. about the Ormsbee dinner."

"Short notice," he said, studying his appointment pad.

"I gather lots of these dinners give you short notice. It's about some kind of fishing rights. An international conference coming up, and you're a senator from a West Coast state."

"Like Washington, D.C., Clair?"

"Love it. Got a room in Munday's mother's house. Old, grand, run-down."

Andy Wolensky, when he came in, looked already going Washington. For all the heat he wore a vest with some kind of gold insignia on a chain, from his days as a football star at High Sky State University. Andy's heavy, broad features could lead one to expect a taller man, but perhaps, Jason thought, it was his overwide shoulders and large chest. While he appeared rough, he had depths of subtle skills in handling people.

"Everything going fine, Chief. Who you want to run your home office in Vista City? It pays twenty gees a year. He keeps the home folks informed and stirred up in your interests."

"I'll think about it. I want you to get me a report on Senator Barraclough, his bills, records, who he runs with. And also a rundown on what's behind the bill to break up the big oil companies."

"Will do. I've hired Monte Dolf as your official chauffeur. I also applied to keep Miss Munday on our staff." Andy adjusted a picture, and his voice went lower. "Anybody *you* want to appoint special? Deserving and able."

Jason grinned and looked over the stack of letters placed just so on the center of the desk blotter in its hand-tooled leather decor (a gift from Sheila on his last birthday). "You mean some deserving needy party worker?"

"You name it, not me."

"Come on, Andy—you have lists."

"I made no promises, Chief. But Buster Miller has a bright nephew who led some protests in college a few years ago, trying to keep the timber-cutting boys off state land. If he'll trim his hair and not smoke pot in public, you'd maybe like to appoint him for the home office in Vista City to get up a series of studies on the state's forests and fishing problems."

"What's his name?"

Andy was writing on a folded sheet of stiff paper he had taken from a pocket. "Charlie Keefe. He's a risk, but Buster will keep him in line. Now there's Bascom Rice's daughter, Matilda."

"Matilda? Do they still name girls Matilda?"

"Seems so. She's fourteen and wants this summer to be a Senate page boy, or I guess page person."

"It's being done, hiring girls. Check with Senator Ormsbee's office and if you can do it, do it."

"Now, Chief, you better be thinking of allowed living expenses, free trips home and back, junkets, and honorariums for speaking which used to come to fifty thousand a year for lots of senators. But lecture fees are trimmed a bit. You get fifty paid trips a year home. The late Senator used to stay in town here and charge the government thirty thousand a year. Said he went by car, so *no* records."

"The bastard. Damn it, Andy, *you* work out these things. And any lectures—pay goes to the state education fund."

"So—you want to go to Europe this spring? Or the Greek islands? Africa is open, and Hong Kong, all on defense investigation junkets, of course."

"Up yours, Andy."

"Senators get about fourteen thousand dollars free for a junket and no public inspection of how or why. It's all just lumped together in the semiannual report."

Jason lifted an arm and made a mock gesture of hitting his office director on the chin. "I only play angles when they serve the public. And sure, maybe polish my ego a bit. No junkets just for jollies. Oh, get me some more facts on Esme Lowell. I want to know how she relates with her uncle. I think she's giving me some wrong steers about Senator Barraclough. Potomac House is creepy—a sense of dry leaves drifting across the floor of a long emptied swimming pool."

The intercom buzzed. Jason pressed a lever and Clair's voice had that office finish to it; very clear vowels. "Senator Ormsbee would like to speak to you. Valid." *Valid* was a private code word between the two of them, meaning important.

"Hello, Paul." It wasn't easy to get used to calling the much older man by his first name. "Yes?"

"Been to see the great white whale, I hear."

"Yes, I have. He seems beached and ready to boil down to his spare parts."

"So I hear. Sorry to rush you into dinner tomorrow night. State wants us to smile and listen. Promising nothing. But it's important we kiss the *tochis* of the junta presidente-general—he spells tin and rubber. And we need tin and tires."

"I understand, Paul."

"Sure you do. Seven-thirty at my house." There was a pause and Jason could hear Paul Ormsbee's breathing. "Oh, if the CIA is recording this call, please fellas, send me a clear copy." Another pause and the senator was laughing at the other end. "The cocksuckers are taping, I'm sure—I can hear the clicks. See you, Jay."

"Paul, before I forget. Miss Matilda Rice of Blue River would make a good page boy or page person this summer if there is an opening."

"Bascom's kid? Why not. I'll get it worked out."

Jay placed his phone back on its cradle. His "white princess phone" as the billing read. He was phone rich. He had phones direct to the Pentagon, one to the majority leader of Congress and the party whip in the Senate; he forgot what the other two were for. But they glowed when he was to pick them up. He wondered if the CIA or the FBI or the IRS was really tape-recording? That late ego with the guttural growl, the boss of State, had passed on a list for bugging. Maybe Paul Ormsbee was getting paranoid. Could be. And the visit to Senator Barraclough had been a kind of Hitchcock movie, a trip very entertaining, certainly shocking . . .

Senator Barraclough could have been president, been nominated anyway, with his tenacity, skills, ingenious charm. And yet he had failed at the right moment to be in position. Was it the man, the kind with the languid gentility who somehow always manages to fail? Was it Freudian, all that shrink crap about the death wish, the desire to be punished?

Jason began to look over the letters already with slit envelopes clipped to the opened letters. Letters mostly with the tacit assumption he cared. Nut letters, letters of complaining at taxes, lost pensions, cranks with inventions, coy respect from oil, timber and steel, blunt demands from union organizations.

He quickly penciled in red some for Clair to answer, with formula replies, and two: *Will dictate and give answers. J.C.*

Always the casual reply. Never point the finger at the wrong person; a career could easily go kerplunk, as J. Willard used to say when Jason was a little boy and his toy boats sank in the goldfish fountain at High Sky. "Never be mealymouthed or mushy, but an insult lasts forever."

Jason thought of all Austin Barraclough could have been. Hell, a governor's seat, a senator's desk could be a springboard up, up a big arc into national heights.

Jason had these unquiet brooding moods, a penchant for disassembling his dreams to sample them. Contradictory impulses in his nature would be revealed. Could I be president? Forget it. All those people who said "Who would want that damn burden?" Still it was there and he admitted a furtive ambiguity, like an illicit passion, a desire for the idea of the White House. "The corridors of power lead to hopes of becoming a boarder on Pennsylvania Avenue." Who had said that? Yes, Austin Barraclough in some interview years ago. He had also said something about "the malice and stupidity in picking presidents."

Jason was aware something had happened to him this day. Viewing the wreck of Austin Barraclough had broken open some secret personal to himself, some hidden desire loosened within. He thought: why not? why not?

From Jason's notebook:

I must have always thought of being president. Most kids do. I can perhaps now see clearly how it can be done. First admit you're no more a passive participant. No more a psychic refugee in a fantasy world, no more given to incoherent thoughts on the subject. Cultivate Austin Barraclough. Use what residue of knowledge and skill left in him. He was damn impressive there for a few moments. And there is Esme Lowell. She knows a great deal, and could help me get into the confidence of the old man. There is no such things as abstract politics. At its best some may say politics is intellectual dishonesty. But they don't know the excitement, the power of the game, a series of rituals and rules, some of which you must break at the right moment. Use one's perceptions and sensations to take the moment and use it. Mostly I have had an aversion for open conflict. Compromise, conciliation, *but* up to a point. Now Paul Ormsbee, I think, still hopes for a thunderbolt to hit him. A dream too?

The day was more than just a turning point. It was—admit it—like a saint getting a vision. Maybe that's too strong. I have served time as a public official, been the apprentice, the loyal party man, the elected representative of the people, the party loyalist. Haven't faltered all along the line, not fallen or tripped. So far.

Clair, coming in with a new batch of mail, found Jason Crockett seated at his desk writing in a notebook and fingering a paperweight bearing the design of the seal of the Senate. He was staring at the notebook as if in a trance, his skin flushed, mouth slightly open as if listening to that tin alarm ticking on the bookcase.

"You all right, Senator?"

"Huh, huh?" He blinked and nodded, put away the notebook. "Got a little overheated. This damn weather, what they say about Washington climate is true. I've this bitch of a heat rash on my neck. Itches!"

"You sure have, Senator. I have some zinc ointment. I'll get it. The *New York Times* man called. They're doing some kind of gathering of statements from what they call the Freshmen. Can you give them eight hundred words of what you think of senators, as a new senator?"

He nodded and put down the letter opener. "Oh, you'll find stuff in the files, Clair, on what I said when I was nominated. The part where I see my only duty is to serve the people of the state, the whole country, and if any higher office ever came along, etc., etc. Add I have no other philosophy than that of service, but I think I have great knowledge of the problems we all face in the twentieth century. I have no dreams of glory, nor see myself seeking out honors or offices . . . Sound too much like self-praise? Well, reword it; add 'I am humble enough to know my duty, and proud enough to know what I represent . . .' Something like that, Clair."

"Yes, you've improved it."

"Type it up and let me see it."

She laid down the letters on his desk blotter. When she was gone, he wondered why he had said what he said in just that way ("humble enough . . . proud enough")? He was sounding like a politician, that was *too* clear. Well, he was one, wasn't he?

Chapter 11

On the floor of the House of Representatives there was a gathering of congressmen and Jason knew that in the three House Office Buildings bells were ringing in all the halls and offices; two loud bells, a signal that a vote was about to be taken on the floor. Bells for a quorum vote, a recorded vote. Three now rang for a quorum. Jason was learning the signals.

He had come to the House Gallery looking for Paul Ormsbee, who was visiting the House. Paul wanted to show him the House at work. So Jason had gone through the Capitol Building to the spiral staircase where the British as grenadiers and light infantry (was it in 1814?) had come into the Capitol, and that night burned it. Well, that was in the past, Jason thought, and he came to Statuary Hall: it had once been the House Chamber. He read a brass plate: HERE IN THE 30TH CONGRESS ABRAHAM LINCOLN HAD HIS DESK. Jason wondered what Lincoln would have felt about the Indian Land Bill.

And that other brass marker. Oh, yes, HERE JOHN QUINCY ADAMS, MASTER OF CONCILIATION AND FAMILY PRIDE, HAD HIS HEART ATTACK. His last one, it seemed.

Jason felt his own heart's beating. It seemed strong enough as he looked up at the bronze statue of Will Rogers.

J. Willard had never been much of an admirer of Rogers. ("Hell, I never trust a man who claimed he *never* met a man he didn't like. Rogers must have known a lot of shitheels in his time; what he do, put on rose-colored glasses?")

From the gallery of the House, Jason saw a vote was about to be taken on a amendment to a railroad aid act. The congressmen were holding their voting cards. About the size of a credit card, it contained their photograph and a punch-hole code. The goddamn age of the IBM, Jason thought. The congressmen were voting yes or no, he saw, by inserting the cards in voting terminals attached to seats in front of them. Some were pressing the button labeled yea, others the one lettered nay. The big tote board over the press gallery registered the yesses and noes in different-colored lights. An old man eating a candy bar by Jason's side said, "Too damn lazy to raise their hand."

The amended matter won by a lopsided vote. Jason made his way over to the press gallery where Paul Ormsbee was talking to two middle-aged people, the man with a hearing aid, the woman under the wrong kind of hat for Washington. Paul beamed at Jason, seized his arm.

"Ah, here is Senator Crockett. Jay, here are two good folk from our own state, Mr. and Mrs. Mandell."

"Martin," corrected the man, "Joe and Ellie Martin," as he offered Jason a thin dry hand. "From Blue River. Know your pa, ol' J. Willard."

They were the kind of people Jason liked. Whatever opinions they held, they didn't vacillate.

"I'll write my father I met you."

Paul Ormsbee put a hand on the man's shoulder. "Duty calls. Mr. Martin, my dear, we're due in the Senate Chamber. Anything either of us can do, why you just write."

"We will."

"I answer every letter I get from Blue River County."

After they were clear of the couple and were moving across to the Senate Chamber, Paul Ormsbee said, "Never show them you don't remember them if they say they've met you. He's some kind of county chairman. Here to press for federal aid for a school lunch funding. Glad to help. Salt of the earth, these people."

"He's not an Indian." Jason spoke softly, watched Paul Ormsbee's face as the reaction showed on it.

The elder senator stopped, just by the brass plate announcing the spot where John Quincy's life had begun to ebb. "Indian? What the hell?"

"The Indian Land Bill is a rip-off. You know that."

"Who the devil you been talking to?" Paul's noted stability of temperament seemed dented.

"Never mind. All that valuable land, a disregarded, busted treaty and you approve giving the tribes seventy-five cents an acre?"

Paul Ormsbee looked closely at Jason and began the shoulder-grasping gesture, but decided against it. "That's a damn lie, Jay. There's no one fixed price in the bill. Why, certain sections will get as high as twenty dollars an acre."

"I've looked into it. Only a couple hundred acres get that window dressing, twenty-dollars-an-acre price. The average price for the entire payment comes to seventy-five cents an acre."

The elder senator stared at the brass plate. He read it out loud: "John Quincy Adams." He seemed to be in some deep introspection as he turned to Jason. "We're living up to the treaty."

"But how? The bill will only pay at the guessed at land value in 1854. No interest payments. No taking into consideration the present value of the land."

"Jay, Jay, don't arch your back up. We're the first Senate that even made an attempt to consider that treaty with the Sioux and Shoshoni valid. No, look, I'm not giving you a snow job. That land exists in three states, long settled. It has timber, it has signs of minerals, copper, silver, coal. But of commercial value—who knows? The Indian councils will be getting fifty-two million dollars. Why, each adult member will have around twenty-eight thousand bucks' credit in the tribal fund."

"Why not a couple hundred thousand?"

"Because if we had an Indian Land Bill to pay out a couple billion dollars to some reservation bucks and squaws, there would be a hell of an uproar and—"

"And you and me, Paul, would maybe be blown out of office?"

The older senator smiled, as if on a small boy. "Oh, wouldn't be anything that dangerous for us. You see, Jay, it's wheel-and-deal. I support this bill because it will bring big parklands to our state. And there will be the timber and mineral rights, new taxes, and, well, there are certain other bills we want favorably considered by senators on committees, men from other parts of the country and so it's—"

"We kiss their ass, they kiss ours?"

Paul Ormsbee tried to sound reasonable, but hurt. "No use talking to you just now, Jay. You think on it. We have constituents, we have a loyalty due to our state. I'll send over a final breakdown of the treaty areas to your administrative assistant, Andy Wolensky. He's part Sioux, isn't he?"

"He's what the High Sky Country Club set call a Polack."

"Yes, bigotry everywhere—Jay, I'll have you meet the Land Survey Committee and maybe they'll make all this clear. Legally, statute of limitations, they're breaking out of the reservations in the eighties —hell, we don't owe them a thing. We've done this as a goodwill gesture."

Jason wanted to yell "Balls!" after the broad back of the departing senior senator, but didn't. Maybe he *was* too hotheaded. Perhaps he was stepping out of line as a freshman senator. Paul meant well, but was he dreaming of the White House—what senator didn't? Paul was wily, wise and, even if lazy and cynical—no, not cynical, easy-living—yes, and ironic. Senator Ormsbee was a man who had survived, been honored, once had tenacious enthusiasms. Perhaps he lacked the qualities essential to a great man, but he was a good one. Christ, this place changed people. Was all this marble and bronze just a shell for eager young beavers to act preposterous, and a roof over aging men sitting on their prostates making easy deals? Congress was perhaps a bigger swindle than the Indian Land Bill. The House and Senate combined staffs numbering over 18,000 people, swollen with added hired hands. The budget for it all had gone over half a billion dollars for the last year. And each member had two or three fully staffed offices back home; some Jason knew had four offices, even if one might be only an enclosed porch for a relative.

He also brooded over the damn camaraderie of the members, the club mentality, and such silly rules. Andy had impressed on him that House members are forbidden to refer to each other by name when speaking on the floor. ("The gentleman from New Jersey, or the distinguished gentleman from Utah. That's the lingo.")

But it worked. That was the miracle. Somehow, outmoded, creaking, the Hill was valid and active with the nation; a world too big perhaps to be run by these much too human groups. Yet it worked, fairly well. No junta, no coup d'état was in sight. No police state being advocated. And the grafting and deal-making had been there all the time, even when senators wrote with a feather. He knew of the Grant Administration, the stealing and pork-barreling, the days of Harding and Coolidge. No matter, one held one's nose and saw the good of the system, despite Nixon's revolting years. Overlooked the exhibitionists, the abrasive, the inordinately ambitious. One was part of the innate folly of the human condition, the handling of strong challenges. But the damn Indian Land Bill? It was a bare-faced swindle, and those few who raised any public comment were labeled pinkos, bleeding hearts.

He asked Bread O'Rahilly to lunch, and Jason had continued to expand his objections.

"Look, Jay, it's Indians. If it were blacks, now, you'd have the roof raised. They are loud, have muscle and they scare Whitey. But Indians, Mexican Americans, Chinese or Japanese Americans, no one really gets very excited. But you step on a Negro toe and you've put your foot on a land mine. Even being white is a handicap in Civil Service in Washington, in the federal jobs. But mum's the word there."

"That's why somebody today should be Indian conscious."

"Well, we were at Wounded Knee—didn't we send the FBI in for a little gunnery practice?"

Jason saw it was no use talking to the lobbyist. "Yes, I remember."

"Jason Crockett, you've got troubles; you believe in fairness, in order, legal justice. Hell, by now you ought to have been blooded and know it's a world of rogues and dupes."

"You sound like my father when he's cursing the universe for not being like him."

"If you can connect this Indian affair with the black revolution, you'd have easy sailing. Think it over."

"Where you from, Bread?"

The neat, almost dude lobbyist made an amused grimace. "Not from Dixie, and I'm not a bigot. I'm from Ohio, and my old man is a doctor—a surgeon. I'm a realist. When I step in dog shit, I don't say it's chewing gum. Recognize your responsibilities but walk slow. You raise up this Indian thing into a congressional ruckus as a part of the black issue, and you've got yourself headlines. Maybe a cover of *Newsweek* . . . Another Beefeater?"

"No, and I'm paying for this lunch. How come you're so helpful to me?"

"You mean, why I'm not a lobbyist all the time? My main job is seeing airlines get a square shake. It's the timber and mineral resources boys who whacked out that Indian bill."

"I gathered that."

"Also, I may ask you for a favor someday. Oh, a proper legal favor, from my side of the fence. And I know you'll take kindly, but fairly to them. Bread O'Rahilly always keeps his hands above the table."

Jason motioned the waiter for the check.

"I need advice from somebody who hasn't got strings to his friendship."

Bread O'Rahilly moved the salt shaker to one side, put the pepper shaker alongside it, as if playing some intricate chess game. He looked directly at Jason, serious, no smile, no good-natured ironic stare. "Talk to Austin Barraclough if he's sober, or has any control of his senses left."

"I was thinking of him. He'd see it my way, I'm sure."

"No, you fuzzy SOB! He'd explain to you why and how it's all happening. How bills are traded, how they're passed. And why the system works."

"It does, doesn't it, for all its preposterous assertions?"

"It seems to creep along, yes—even if it leaks at the seams. It's dishonest in part, and yet things get done—it does manage to keep the country running. Of course we have too many lawyers on the Hill. But they're like smelly feet. You get to live with them and they get you about, walk you around. Yes, you see Austin; if he's got any of his marbles left, he'll tell you why this bill is going to pass. There was a lot of know-how in him, and he had the savvy of FDR, the stance of a Kennedy without the phony Camelot dreck. But at the right time, no drive, no wild hair up his ass, and so—"

The lobbyist made a gesture of futility.

"What happened? I mean there's some private problem, tragedy."

"Now, Jason, no to that can of worms. I'll gossip about the Senate and the House, *who's* stabbing *who* in committees. But a man's private life, no. You'll find out plenty by those whores called gossip columnists. You know Snow Williams?"

"Just over cocktails at some party. She wants me for a pre-noon roundup show."

"Do you good. Just one word of advice. Don't get into the kip with her. She'd use you as a pipeline into the Senate's secrets."

"I don't think I'd care to hear her version of Barraclough anyway."

The two men parted liking each other.

*   *   *

Jason knew he had faced Paul Ormsbee, and he felt the heat had gone from his anger. There was a jejune bathos about Paul—so Jason decided that a talk with Austin Barraclough would be of help.

Jason called Esme Lowell's office and was told she was in New Orleans for a convention of real estate brokers. He thought, bit on a badly chewed thumb, heard the friendly ticking of the salvaged alarm clock. He had Clair ask Andy Wolensky to get him Austin Barraclough's unlisted phone number. Just using it gave him an emotional expansiveness. Champ answered and after Jason had explained who he was, and could he speak to the senator, Champ seemed to be thinking, and making gravel sounds in his throat. After a long pause, Champ said with that broken-nosed tone of men who were mouth-breathers. "I know you suh, Senator Crockett. You were here with Miss Esme. Yeah. The senator, he was talking about you, yeah. Well, he's got this office feller to set up meetings—know what I mean."

"Yes, I know, Champ. But he hasn't been to his office of late."

"Yes . . . that's for a fact."

"Could I speak to the senator direct?"

"Well, he's sleeping on the sun porch right now. But in about an hour, that's his best time of the day. He's in the rose garden, you see?"

"And if I were passing by . . ."

"And dropped in? Yeah, he used to like company. The old bastard drives me up the wall when I'm alone with him."

(There goes the image of the loyal old respectful family retainer, Jason thought.)

"What kind of cigars you smoke, Champ?"

"Hard for my wind. I dip snuff. Copenhagen."

Jason looked at his watch. 3:34. He'd get out across the river into Virginia and be "just passing by" in an hour. Jason grinned and listened to the alarm clock on the top of a bookcase. He had warned Andy, Clair and Miss Munday—who had a sister working in the Embassy in Rome—not to get rid of that old clock, a relic as sacred as St. Brigid's thighbone, he said.

Chapter 12

In the days of Austin Barraclough's grandmother, Druscilla, the rose gardens at Potomac House had produced a prizewinning flower, the Druscilla Barraclough Rose. A resilient strain under all its delicacy; pale yellow, with a dark tawny edge, a flower that until 1949 was one of the three most popular roses among rose fanciers.

"Never call them rose-lovers or rose-growers. Always rose fanciers," said Austin Barraclough.

He stood in the middle of the east bed of the Barraclough rose gardens, talking to Jason. The senator, a pair of pruning clippers in one cotton-gloved hand, looked too pale to be outdoors, uncared-for in a gray pullover sweater and unpressed flannels.

"Rose fancier," said Jason. "Not rose-lover."

"Yes."

"It's like calling a logger a lumberjack back home."

"Yes. I didn't know I had an appointment."

"You don't. I just took a chance driving over."

"Cabot? Connors? Oh, yes, Crockett."

"Senator Jason Crockett."

"Damn it, I know you're a senator. I haven't lost all my senses." He touched his brow with a gloved hand. "Day turning sultry. Will you join me for what our southern friends call a libation?"

Jason nodded. Now that he had run the old lion down to his lair—if a neglected rose garden could be called a lair—he wondered if he had made a mistake in coming out. The man looked ill, his unshaved face had a gray stubble, and he walked slowly, as if searching for the center of gravity, humming to himself as they walked back to the house and went up marble steps into a sun-room. Half-drawn bamboo blinds kept out most of the direct sunlight.

There were comfortable wickerwork chairs, a wicker table, a small radio, a bookcase and a scattering of books, newspapers. Also a batch of unopened mail overflowing what might once have been a sewing basket. From inside the house came the whirl and chimes of a hall clock suddenly aware of the hour.

"Yes." Austin struck a Chinese gong with his knuckles. "Paul Ormsbee thinks a lot of you. More than a perfunctory appreciation."

"He's been a big help to me."

Champ appeared, wearing a tan apron and carrying a feather duster. Austin acted out with hand gestures two tall glasses of something being poured into them, then turned to Jason. "Champ is the only live-in help here now. I have a cleaning couple come in twice a week, I think, to keep the walls standing. Eh, yes, Crockett. I like Paul. Not too comprehensible up here," he touched his forehead, "but a man you can trust, and he keeps his word. Keeps good company too." Austin laughed. It gave him, Jason thought, the look of a down-at-heels Silenus.

"Senator, I'm new as a shiny penny just been stamped out here. I've been governor, but state politics, well they're not big league."

"You came to me for advice? Hell, I've been out of things a little while and you know," he leaned over, "I drink. Oh, yes, I drink. Emerson said: 'The world is nothing, the man is all, in yourself is the law of all nature.' Emerson. Good, eh?"

"I didn't come just for advice. Call this apple-polishing, the fact is I've admired you. Your way of doing things. Of being able to control a system that was made for colonial riders with no modern means of communicating, and you're aware of the real guts of what we started this country with."

The older man smiled and held a hand against his chin. "I'll be a sonofabitch if you don't state it just right. I mean about the system being made for another time, but still able to sustain its hold. Oh, yes. Yes, they knew the expediencies of the world. Champ!"

Champ was back with a tray and two tall glasses, frosted. He set them down. Austin asked as he lifted up a glass, "My niece call?"

"No sir, Miss Esme, she's down in New Orleans, remember?"

"No, I don't remember." He turned to Jason. "I don't remember. Freud, you know, said you don't remember what you don't want to remember. Here's to the first today."

Jason lifted his glass and took a sip. A good Scotch highball. Austin seemed to relax with his first long sip, settled back in his chair. Sighed with satisfaction. "Truth is, not the first today. That's a polite lie. The old joke: I'm not drinking more, but I'm not drinking less either. Yes. Too bad about the neglect in the rose gardens. They need a woman's touch. Roses do. To oversee the damn gardeners. The whole shebang haven't really amounted to much since Mona was here."

Jason decided to risk a bold question. "How is Mrs. Barraclough? I hear she . . ."

The older man waved a hand at him. "Stick to politics, Crockett. How's the Senate shaping up?"

"It's all new to me, but—"

The two men talked, sipped their drinks. Or rather Jason talked on bills in progress, on generalities. By the second highball, Austin Barraclough seemed to be playing a role rather than being a failed man—an old role, of the party leader in the Senate Chamber. He was making good logical comments on the Indian Land Bill.

"Moral obligations get crowded out in a struggle to rule. Now, Jason, you call me Austin, agreed? Now, Jason, you keep worrying yourself over the Indian Land Bill."

"It's cheating the three major tribes of those districts out of their claims. *Just* claims."

"Oh, such a self-righteous young man . . . Yes, I'm sure they're just claims. But there are other really important matters, amendments, international items on the congressional slate. We have to trade and deal with others. And we can sweeten the Indian Bill a little, maybe even a lot. But to get done what we have to do this session, there has to be this damn bill passed."

"I can't support it Sen—Austin. We have two big Indian reservations in my state. Besides, it's an unfair bill."

The older man leaned back in his chair. "I love the word *unfair*. It means nothing in politics or in life, my young friend. As Einstein said, it's all relative from where you are seeing things. To a cannibal, not eating a brave enemy's heart and brain to gain his strength is unfair. To a Hindu once, not to burn a live widow with a dead husband was not only unfair but against the gods. You want to amount to something in Washington's greased pole-climbing contest, you'll have to support certain things that are good for the party and good for the country even if you have to hold your nose. Like *this*." He pinched his long shapely nose between a thumb and a forefinger.

"I don't see how I can and . . ."

"Look, you go to Senator Randell, isn't he leading the fight for the Indian bill?"

"Yes."

"Yes, tell him you can't come out publicly for it, but tell Mel Randell that you'll join a block of I think ten others—now listen, don't bug your eyes at me—who feel they can't come out for the bill either but who will *if* the bill looks as if it's going down to defeat come out and vote for it. But *only* if their vote is needed."

Jason whistled. "That's pussyfooting."

"Don't name it—use it. I don't think they'll need the block of voters I spoke of. The bill will pass without you. But you haven't offended the party, and you've shown your party loyalty. You haven't appeared in the open as supporting the bill, just stood with the secret reserved votes *if* needed. Folks back home will never know. And you've faced facts with equanimity."

Jason closely studied Austin's face. It held a thin smile or an ironic comment, he couldn't decide which. "Could I swallow that?"

"You'll swallow a hell of a lot more, Senator, until you understand how we hold the whole one-horse shay that is the country together. And you're ambitious. I smell ambition on you. Some people smell of money, sex; I smell ambition." He reached for a book, tossed it aside, picked up one from the sun-room floor. "Ever read James Madison's *Federalist Papers*? Don't lie. Most senators say they did."

"I've dipped into them. Not much."

"Dipped, eh? Like a trout in cornmeal for frying? Dipped! Listen." He hung a pair of silver-rimmed glasses on his nose, one lens cracked, and began to turn pages. "Ah, Paper Fifty-five. Where the hell is the damn passage that fits what we just talked about? Yes. 'As there is a degree of depravity in mankind which requires a certain degree of circumspection and distrust: so there are other qualities in human nature, which justify a certain portion of esteem and confidence. Republican government presupposes the existence of these qualities in a higher degree than any other form.' "

Jason said, "I used to think in those days they just drank tea and chased foxes, those boys."

"Take you out to Mount Vernon some day. Show you how practical they were. They were damn smart politicians. People forget that for all the funny clothes and shoe buckles they had marvelous minds. They knew human nature. Man isn't born corrupt, they knew, but *could* be corrupted. That's why they separated church and state. Only now some smart bastards have broken that law down, haven't they? We're going to pour billions into church colleges. Hardmouthed men with no values bring such things on. Oh, I don't mean you, Jason. Present company and all—ah, here is where Madison makes it clear he doesn't expect any of the finer qualities in human beings to always come forward when they are seeking personal ways to better themselves. Listen: 'Ambition must be made to counteract ambition. This policy of supplying by opposite and rival interests, the defect of better motives, might be traced through the whole system of human affairs, private as well as public.' "

Austin let the book fall from his hands. He leaned back and closed his eyes. "Primordial impulses, the shitheads . . . You ever meet Judge Amos Fowler?"

"I think I'd better be going," said Jason. "I wonder if you would like me to pick you up some morning, Austin, and take you out to Mount Vernon? I've been invited to dinner at Judge Fowler's."

The older man didn't open his eyes. "What? Huh? Oh, Foxy Fowler. Retired now, the old bastard, but still thinks he's a kingmaker."

"Well . . ."

"It's good talking and—someday, I'll tell you of the Amos Fowler type of man."

Jason stood up. He looked down at Austin Barraclough, sunk now into a kind of torpid condition or some dimension beyond reason and experience. Mouth open, one corner moist. Champ came out, changed into his white house jacket. "The old man, he's been talking too much, a blue streak."

"He seemed very animated."

"That's good. He needs something to chew on to cheer him up."

"Will he be alright?"

"Oh, he'll manage. He'll sleep the afternoon. Get high tonight, fire me, curse me for a mean-tusked nigger, and then he'll sleep like a baby."

"Is he being treated . . . I mean is anyone . . ."

Champ scowled, showed rancor. "I think you better go now, Senator. He wakes up mean sometimes. And swings a cane."

Jason looked at the big inert figure in the chair and left, feeling the sun on his spine as he walked to his car, wondering.

From Jason's notebook:

How much of the old wisdom, the political skill still remains some-place in the old boozer? Austin Barraclough certainly still has patches of wide political wisdom. That Machiavellian idea of how I could stand by if needed to pass the party's bill, and yet *not* come out for it publicly, directly; FDR couldn't have figured it out better. Had the old boy been ironic in reading me Madison's "degree of depravity" on the need for "circumspection"? I can learn from Austin Barraclough that political savvy, wisdom. Yes, it would be worthwhile staying close to him. I laughed as I drove off. Ambition, you bitch!

To see the world whole and see it constantly—that is Austin's secret. Things in the Senate worked out as Austin Barraclough had predicted. The Indian Land Bill was passed with the price for the land increased. It was still a swindle, but it was less so than before. I saw injustice done, didn't support the bill publicly, but was loyal to party plans secretly. Senator Randell was pleased. "Paul said you were dependable."

It left a sour taste, but only for a few days. He was active, busy on two minor but valuable committees, and was beginning with Sheila to move about in the Washington social scene. He felt no need for self-justification as to his party loyalty. He did find an old volume in a bookshop near the Smithsonian and marked a section from some of the writings of George Washington before sending it to Austin Barraclough. Between certain pages, he inserted a note.

Dear A. B.

Tit for tat, to return one quotation from those old boys in wigs for the two you gave me.

JASON C.

He had marked in red ink:

The foundation of our empire was not laid in the gloomy age of ig-norance and superstition, but an epoch when the rights of mankind were better understood and more clearly defined, than at any former period. ... At this auspicious period, the United States came into existence as a nation, and if their citizens should not be completely free and happy, the fault will be entirely their own.

He remembered Austin's remarks on Judge Amos Fowler the night he went to the dinner with Sheila that the old man was giving at the Protocol Club. There were lots of people there in the big dining room. Jason did shake the hand of a brisk little old man with the very witty eyes, the smile of ironic appraisal of the guests, but that was about it. Amos Fowler was a retired judge from some high court seat. He just held Jason's hand for a moment on introductions by Paul Ormsbee, and said in a crisp, amused voice, "Ah, one of our new ones, welcome sir."

The dinner was good. The Protocol Club was supported by the party, although it tried not to admit this. In its meeting rooms a great deal of party politics business was done, bills and amendments decided on, or if not decided on, at least actions planned on how to face problems in the House or the Senate Chamber.

Two days later there was an invitation for Jason from Amos Fowler to join a weekend party on the Fowler yacht, for a sail down the Potomac to the bay. But Jason had to excuse himself; he was involved in some very tangled pension matters for two widows (so they claimed) of long dead ex-soldiers of World War I.

And he hadn't heard from Potomac House. He wondered if the older man was too far gone on whiskey or hadn't remembered him. He left a message with Champ, just that he'd called. Champ said, "I put the messages in the basket by his breakfast tray . . . Oh, yes, most times he reads them if he has his glasses."

There was no answer from Potomac House. He sent an invitation to visit Mount Vernon. No answer.

Jason grew to enjoy the long, narrow Senate cloakroom where so much of the Senate purpose was done or mulled over, deals made, tales told during the business in the huge washroom urinals ("while shaking hands with an old friend"—Sam Rayburn). Jason grew to feel at ease on the dark leather sofas, at the writing tables, to take refreshments and soda, to overstock his private locker. He moved past the frosted glass doors to the Senate Chamber as through his own front gate in High Sky. With the Vice-President in the chair, he enjoyed the pomposity of some procedures moving often in aimless direction, so like the starlings in the Capitol portico.

He learned direction, marking in his mind the hallways, the stair-

cases. Like a mole he knew his way around the Capitol's subter-
ranean corridors, the basement where the private subway car carried
Congress to its proper destination. He learned the checks and bal-
ances in casting his vote. He even made a few speeches of no great
content. Played the waiting game as a freshman senator. Studied the
gestures and improvisations of the older men. He got some items into
the *Congressional Record*, even one of J. Willard's lines: "Who loves
his fellowman plants trees."

The day after that appeared Esme Lowell phoned. "Hello, thanks
for cheering up Uncle Austin while I was away."

"Was it cheering?"

"He seems to think so. How are things moving for you?"

"Slowly. I'm still wearing my learning wheels."

"That's not good. You promised to take Uncle Austin to Mount
Vernon."

"I wrote, no answer. I phoned, Champ said he wasn't answering
the phone."

"It's corny, but fun. I love the place myself. Look, let's have lunch.
Uncle wants you to do something for him. You like Chinese food?"

"If it's not in an arty place."

"Jade Palace at one. Meet me there. I'm showing some Arab
degenerates a house near Rock Creek Park."

"One it is."

"Oh, Uncle thanks you for the book. He gave me a message. Wait
a minute. Christ, what a woman carries in a handbag."

"How's New Orleans?"

"I ate like famine tomorrow. Shrimp gumbo, and—ah, here. I
copied out Uncle's message. Ready? 'Every age had preferred the
previous one to its own.' Sounds like he got it from a bubble gum
wrapper."

Later Jason copied it into one of his notebooks. He called it the
Going Down Nostalgia Road. "Maybe [he added] the past in some
ways had been a less crowded world. But it too had its calamities,
its own bad ways; J. Willard once said, 'About the only good thing
about the past your grandfather remembered was that they used
to play tennis on grass, not clay.'"

Chapter 13

They ate *t'im shun chow yu* and *lung ha fu yung*. The first, to Jason's surprise, turned out to be sweet and pungent fish, the second a lobster omelette. As they were still hungry, they added *yi mai kai*, barley- and nut-stuffed chicken.

"You know, we don't have this type of food in Vista City. It's the old chow mein and chop suey there."

Esme, using her chopsticks with skill, nodded. "Gertrude Stein would say: 'There's no there there.' "

Jason was using a fork. But Esme showed him how to handle chopsticks. He tried, failed and he said he'd need more lessons.

Esme said, "Next time you try the *ap chen*."

"Sounds interesting." He felt he was lacking something critical to become a gourmet.

"It's cooked duck gizzards." Her laughter at his expression created attention from other diners.

"No thanks."

They were drinking hot rice wine, but gave it up and ordered martinis. Esme said, "You've kind of brought Uncle Austin out of himself a bit—he's been so suspicious of all values—and you've taken a hell of a load off my shoulders."

"You don't like your uncle?"

She looked up at Jason, tapping her chopsticks on the edge of the table. "I don't dislike him. But he was such a god, a damn speeded-up clock of a god to Mother, his sister. And he took care of the bills after my father left the scene. You know how you get to resent the people you are beholden to? It's hell now to see him impotent as a shadow. I admired him—but I don't like him."

"You knew him in the great days."

"You mean when he had all and was top dog? He was human. He held grudges. He broke men and had tenacious drive. I see what's around to run for high office today and I wonder where all the giants went." She fed her mouth with the chopsticks—very skillfully. "No giants left."

"J. Willard, that's my father, he says it's a lot of crap, that line from Genesis: 'There were giants in the earth in those days.' He claims old times, the old times in our country, were just like times now. Only we had some scatterings of a few great men and they made it look like it was a better time."

She motioned for Jason to pour tea into the little dragon-decorated cups. "That's what Uncle Austin wants me to talk to you about, the malice and stupidity in politics today."

"Be happy to talk to him about it."

"He's taking a drying-out period at Rosemead Sanitarium. And he's not seeing anyone. It's a mean and nasty process. Ever take a cold turkey cure?"

"Not so far. I'm happy to hear he's taking a cure."

Esme laughed and sipped tea. "Don't look so mournful. Uncle, he's done the drying-out twice before—and always went back to the stuff. Anyway, he wants you to feel out how serious Paul Ormsbee is about getting nominated at the convention in two years."

"You mean for the presidency?"

"Not for dogcatcher."

He didn't care for the way she said that. "He told me that he might just retire to trout fishing and the sweet life."

"Dear Mr. Crockett, that's the dream of retiring on the good fat pension you fellows stick taxpayers with. Look at that prick who got us kicked out of the White House. He's costing us at least a half a million a year. For all that, in the mind of every man in Congress is printed an image of him, or even her, labeled *The President of the United States.* Hot dog!"

"Paul had kind of hinted around it. You think he could get the nomination?"

She seemed to think of it as she ate a kumquat. "If the party starts building him. The western big shot is dead as yesterday's newspaper, politically speaking; the southern meeting boys haven't anything for our party; eastern bureaucrats and eggheads, zeroes. You prefer Ormsbee to Boone or Bremont?"

Jason sat back and picked at some flakes of rice on the table. He felt, no use putting out a line with the woman seated across from him. She was a splendid feeder, could drink, and he supposed some men would like to take her to bed. She was *too* formidable; could she in private have some tender female moments? He brushed aside the image forming of her on a bed, stripped. Were the boobies real, was her skin under the clothes so tanned, or were there white areas and— he moved back to the question of Paul Ormsbee.

"Paul's a good man."

"He's sixty-five, isn't that a bit over the hill? Bremont is fifty-eight, fifty-nine."

"Rational, reasonable reactionary, rich and a way with serious talks in the cloakroom. Big, impressive to the older voters. Yes, I'd see Paul as the better man. A careerist, sure—aren't we all?"

"What about Dudley C. Giron? A Cajun, that against him?"

"I don't know." Jason shrugged. "There's Julius Kohnbloom, Assistant Secretary of State, but a Jew. Maggie Gary, but a female person. Laramie Scudder, the party boss, pet of the WDU and the AFL-CIO. You like any of them, Lady?"

She took a cigarette from her handbag and put it between her lips, waved off a waiter offering a light.

Jason said, "Still not lighting up? Miss it?"

"God, yes. The craving's still there strong as ever. Uncle Austin isn't too sure about Ormsbee but admits maybe he's the best we've got. See if you can chart how deep Ormsbee's presidential bite is, and Uncle would like to know if he's got big money promised. Timber, oil, fish, mining; can he get WD union funds."

"I'll do what I can. One thing Paul has—a reciprocated loyalty."

"Uh huh." They parted, she into the beat-up Caddy she called The Heap. He said, "Tell your uncle I wish him well, and I'd be pleased to see him anytime he wants."

Esme put on white gloves and held out a hand and he took it. It was clear he hadn't impressed her.

"Don't go putting too high hopes on Uncle Austin making it back," she said.

A cold, hard bitch, he thought all the way back to the Hill. Her own close relative, and she saw him as a case history. She was certainly different from most women in Washington—not that he knew too many. Certainly not like the lion-hunting hostesses, or the town's social prima donnas, widows or daughters of presidents, hard-working representatives like Shirley Lippman, who spoke like Jimmy Cagney and wore as a personal trademark a high hairdo, and earrings made of small watch movements, gold-plated. Esme also was not like the thousands of typists, file clerks, girl pages (Bascom Rice's daughter) or the female journalists and gossip-dishers on the *Post* or the *Washingtonian*. Gals, Paul said, who "love or loathe with equal strength." The brittle, over-made-up girls and women on television. (God, I'm due on Snow Williams' noontime show tomorrow.) It seemed clear that from Esme he'd never get the secret of Potomac House, the mysterious second wife, Mona, the reason behind the ruin of the Austin Barraclough. Jason knew what an alcoholic went through drying out at a sanitarium. Uncle Roy had been through it and talked of it. The withdrawal agony, drinking that dreadful, stinking white liquid, the cold water tub wrapped in cold linen, strapped down when violence came. The vomiting spasms, being given a bathrobe and slippers. And yourself to face and tame.

Uncle Roy, when Jason was a boy, had been very graphic about his cures. Reading old magazines, the drone of radio. Bland food, what you could swallow of it, with plastic forks and knives; and the bully boys, the interns, dropouts from pro football to see you didn't act up. For therapy, making little clay figures, weaving baskets. Worst of all, Uncle Roy had insisted, was seeing the other wrecks; deep-lined faces, bloodshot eyes, reeking mouths, "and knowing you didn't look any better." Somehow, Jason felt, for Austin Barraclough it must be worse. Knowing he could go back again and again, and each time think the cure would take.

Jason decided not to have more than two martinis (doubles) for lunch from that day forward. The last time he saw Uncle Roy, he looked like a loose hound dog receding inside his skin.

On his desk pad Jason lettered *Ormsbee for President* and stared at it, then scribbled over it with a heavy pencil when Clair came in with the afternoon papers.

"Snow Williams' people called . . . to remind you you're on tomorrow noon. To be there at eleven for makeup, and a run through of questions, spontaneous, of course."

On The Hill
1 AM

Dear Pop,

It's late at night and I'm here in my private office, just the security men roaming around the place, the television eyes watching hallways. I'm going over my notes for some damn TV show at noon tomorrow, that Snow Williams harpy. The things I do for my constituents. An old tin clock ticks. Remember you saying no woman winds a clock properly?

I'm unwinding after a hard day, so I'll just let my mind and thoughts wander onto the paper. Around me night sounds and street noises mingle, fading down now to mutterings. I picture the late poker games on H Street, the lobbyists' call girls slowly undressing, and I can even name a half a dozen public figures for whom they are pulling dresses over their heads, popping out nubile titties to be bitten by bad midwestern dentistry. I see Senator Wesley, our oldest, smoking his last fine cigar, the brandy in his balloon glass down to its half inch, a volume of Gibbon's *History* on his lap. A wise, hard-shelled old gentleman, aware death already has him in its teeth like a mother cat carrying her whelp . . . And some of them, I'm sure, a bit soggy at a fine bar with a lot of Madison Avenue tramps, right at home in a strange world of expense accounts, martinis, ulcers, faked audience polls and false sales charts. And our Miss Munday in the office? In some shoddy apartment house in Maryland reading Dickens to her old witch of a mother who smells like a wet dog. I had recommended *Vanity Fair,* but the old lady devoured only Dickens . . . In the Pentagon and the State Department bored men at hot lines watching ticker messages being decoded, and someplace somebody being bribed by flesh or money to supply some items of secret value, someone feeling his way in the dark to a strange rustling bed, someone on the river watching the moon scud through moored trees, someone dying at Walter Reed, maybe a dozen worn-out beings or the remains of a young soldier frayed apart, or the barely alive nerve ends of an old man trying to swallow life through tubes in arms, rectum. . . Birth: Negro babies, fatherless, popping out from between black thighs on relief in slums that smell of laundry, bad plumbing, highly spiced food. That's my night game, my X-ray vision of Washington. Not, Pop, where several big parties someplace are ended, the hostess scratching her girdle-scarred belly, the host a bit looped getting out of his pants, the overshined cars of diplomats sliding away.

I am really trying to figure out the political scene as it may look at the next national convention. Paul Ormsbee can be serious in trying for the nomination. Senator Barraclough has asked me to look into Paul's real plans. I don't know how I feel about him. Paul is a good man, but (don't tell anyone) a bit lightweight, and a man who is influenced by people he likes or who like him and show it. He's honest, I'm sure of that. However, I'd rather not make a final judgment just yet.

When I work late like this before going home to clear my head, I drive around Washington after dark, the safe parts. For this is a city under seige; bigots say a Zulu seige. Last night I drove past the rough-cornered doughnut shape of the Pentagon, where the high brass ply their indignities against the world, close-wound brains under crew haircuts placidly plan massive losses, overkills, percentages, civilian losses, death rate from jungle yaws, fail-safe and fallout. Also the relative effectiveness of germ as compared to chemical warfare, fire bombings. It's a cold, adding-machine, slide-rule, doomsday world, where Senator Redmond says, "Everything is as yet on paper, in triplicate, of course."

The radio was playing "Mexicali Rose" with some good below-the-border brass notes. I thought of the young men they've sent abroad— Moscow, London and Bonn, Paris and Peking, doing the same dance steps, or as much of them as they can afford. The Virginia countryside looked good. Too many rows of new houses, of course, too much traffic, naturally. But I was feeling free of Washington's embrace, its anesthetized faces, only eyes alive. Weekends I had gone with Sheila up to Fairfax and Fauquier and beyond. I traced Civil War battles on green-grass horse pastures where her grandfather's uncle had led raids against Washington and been a major under Jubal Early, who raided the capital with his barefoot, scarecrow soldiers and could have seized the city, maybe captured Lincoln, but didn't.

Passing Arlington (*I* was alive!), once Robert E. Lee's plantation, I had to remind myself; now it was too neat and parklike; young death should never be so orderable, with its crosses and few stars of David. So many dead, so many outside waiting for the honor of being planted here. I peered past the budding branches, at the gentle slopes, seeing the squares of turf and marble and bronze that cover some latter-day hero. I've never understood this serious yet picnic spirit of visiting clay and turf and eternal flame; nothing but undertaking skill remains. No mind, no voice, no deeds, no surprises.

Oustide Alexandria I stopped at a shopping center and bought a whole roast chicken right off the revolving electric spit, some good French cheese and an Italian loaf. Then, in the liquor store, two fifths of Jack Daniels. It was the cook's night out.

I feel lucky. Unlike so many males on the loose in the town, I haven't become involved with the tacky, tearful government girls letching for a husband to get them away from the computers and IBMs. There is much repression in Washington, and much easy behavior. The young suffer most: the clerks, typists, apprentice journalists who are not big shots; agency employees, secretaries, all those who can't afford the posh dinners at the Coach Wheel Inn; who sit in dingy bars and drink too much, smoke too much, clutched at each others' limbs in too tiny flats, boardinghouses, made-over slave quarters and garages. I feel blessed and fortunate.

I *know* this is more of a mood letter than a newsletter. You like solid facts, brass tacks you used to say. But after some months here, I'm still feeling my way, listening and trying to keep my yap shut. I blew my cork on the Indian Land Bill, but the party was committed to it. It's still in the lower house being revised. We did get the land values up, and the President will sign it. It's for his kind of people, the big interests he's palsy with and has been all his life in politics.

I still feel guilty as hell I didn't fight it harder, but it was made clear to me it was part of the setup for the good programs the rest of the session. And the Indian question had to be settled before we went on to conservation of those lands. Also, of all the Indian bills on those treaties it was the closest to being fair. As your old favorite, Cicero, put it: "Guilt is present in hesitation, even though the deed is not committed." For I was ready to support the party with a yes vote, *if* they needed me to pass it. Sheila always says "Send my regards." We expect you in Washington for the holidays in our own crumbling national monument in Georgetown. Sometimes when I get low, I feel like that artist who reduced all art to one line—and then mislaid it.

With love,
J.

Chapter 14

From the Peggy Adell Marsh column, *Washington Star Eavesdropper:*

Daisy Rio Tries Again

Senator and Mrs. Jason Crockett represented their state at the wedding of one of their best-known constituents, Daisy Astrid Rio, who inherited millions from her late husband, paper mill tycoon Bruster Carlen Rio. Daisy married Warren Blains McBride, president and chairman of the board of Mason & Dixon Transport International. The event took place at the Washington Grace Episcopal Church, followed by a reception for 300 at Daisy's elegant town house.

The former Mrs. Rio's grandfather, James W. Wexley, owned Maigold Farms (thoroughbred horses) in Lexington, Ky. Before she became Mrs. Rio, Daisy had been married to James Randolf, son of the Alfred Randolfs of Wilmington, Del. McBride, who retired as a director and vice president of Joseph E. Bose & Sons, was married to Randolf's sister, Beth, who died two years ago.

Daisy has lived practically all over the world—Buenos Aires, Beirut, Madrid, and so on. Warren at one time lived in Southern California and had been married to Frances Renson of Los Angeles. They've decided to make Washington their home—after a honeymoon in Cuernavaca and a stop-off in Florida to pick up some of the bridegroom's belongings. India Kingston, the bride's mother, is delighted they'll be near her.

Senator and Mrs. Crockett stayed for the lunch at Daisy's house, De Bon Augure, joined by the Vice-President and Ivar Hallstrom of the United Nations.

Nason Smith brought a few of the guests in her snappy red car and realized the place is a breeze to reach if you go over Chain Bridge. Mrs. Chass Irmgrid kept wishing "we had a place like this at home" because in the treillage and greenery she kept thinking she was out of town.

Everybody wore something cool and pretty—Mrs. John Woloski in blue stripes, Mrs. Sookie Rogers in a white dress with small print. Mrs. Hans Kringle, who had to leave right after the coffee to keep a date at NBC, cooling down her print dress with turquoise and silver jewelry. Denise Dale wore a quilted brown silk coat over her shoulders, covering her yellow T-shirt and canary linen pants.

Lunch included mushroom and watercress salad and poached whitefish on a bed of caviar and truffles. Wild boar ribs, game bird pâté and chocolate mousse were passed up by most of this fashionably slim bunch.

After lunch, Daisy ran across her old buddy and one time ardent date, Reggie Dalton of the British Embassy, who's such a regular they keep a metal nameplate on his table.

The bride's gift to the groom is a rebuilt 1923 Rolls Royce—priceless. The whole affair *élan vital.*

From The Washington Window (AP):

The education of Jason Crockett and the rise of Senator Jason Crockett all point to an effective, even important member of the U.S. Senate. It was not a bull-like rush, but rather a steady climb of sagacious, careful procedure, never brash, never in any way offending the party. It was a slow but sure progress with certain graceful leaps. His work on the Housing and Health Committee attracted the attention of the *New York Times* which did a story on him and the family, even the pregnant daughter living in some western commune; pictures in their Sunday Magazine section. He was appointed to the National Aeronautics Space Council. His summing up of the Joshua Mills Labor Appropriation bill helped, some felt, get it a presidential veto. (Special text to the Vista City News)

He feared that Snow Williams appearance. "It's a monster, television," he told Sheila at breakfast. "It can lick your cheek, or kick your butt, or make you look like another Lincoln or stomp you like Nixon into the ground."

They were eating breakfast in the low-ceilinged dining room. Overhead a crew of three men were replacing roof slates. A sudden rainstorm had produced water stains on the copies of copies of an old wallpaper. It was proving costly to live in a Georgetown colonial with incompetent craftsmen at $20 an hour.

"You're going to do great on Snow Williams' noon show."

"I can't get out of it. But I put it off till Friday."

"Watch yourself that she doesn't grope you."

"I'll cross my legs."

"That item, Jay, in the *News* about Laura living in a commune. Really!"

"Well, she did run off with some damn trumpet player, didn't she?"

"Oh, Sam Banner. A bit wild, but he's from Sky High. They were children together."

"Damn it. Sheila, he's still a jazz band bum. And that commune, where the hell is it? On the Columbia River; it's all dropouts and hippies."

"Now, Jay, there are no more hippies or beatniks. It's all nature now, health food, no preservatives—and they *are* married."

Jay studied some text Snow Williams had sent over. "How do they live? There's no work for a horn player on a commune. What an image: a senator's daughter, *our* daughter in beads and leather fringes."

"It's your daughter's happiness you should worry over, *not* what she wears."

He pushed the notes aside. "I worry."

"Of course, Sam isn't playing in a band now. Laura wrote us. He's farming. They raise their own food, build their own huts, I mean housing. I have some snapshots someplace."

"Never mind. I thought she was shacked up with this art professor, and now it's a music freak."

Sheila put on her sternest look of hurt disapproval, a look that he knew so well. "The conversation is closed, Senator. Go to your damn Snow Williams and I hope she *does* grope you."

"She doesn't grope her guests."

Sheila bit into low-cal toast. "I didn't mean she reaches for your fly. I mean mentally she grabs for your fig leaf." She lisped in a parody voice, "Senator, weally is yo' wife in the menapauce? Do you think it wight or wong fo' a girl under five to have sex wif a married man?"

Jason recovered his good humor, laughed and kissed Sheila's cheek —that was a good takeoff on Snow Williams. Sheila was blossoming out in Washington: working for the Society of Women's Pioneers of the West, appearing at meetings to plant trees, giving minority children vitamin-enriched milk. Sheila also was popular with hostesses entertaining wives of Arab oil men, or a black woman congressman. ("My deah Mrs. Crockett, she *knew* what a fish fork was!") Jason was often away at committee meetings late at night, or rushing down to some cornerstone laying in a southern city, inspecting an atomic power plant. Sheila had tea (which usually meant cocktails) with certain senators' and congressmens' wives. She saw a female Washington of golf, bridge, charity work at Junior League gift shops, posing for the media in white nurse's frocks, offering magazines and candy bars at certain clinics. She felt these wives did good work, but were looked upon by some as publicity seekers. They drank a bit too much. Sheila would sometimes join "the girls" drinking daiquiris or bloody marys in some fashionable eating place or at a fashion show. A congressional wife could be as busy publicly as any mate.

"You'll be working on the Hill late?" Sheila sipped black coffee. She ate a baked half of grapefruit for breakfast; she felt she had to stay slim and attractive. Washington was such a sexual jungle of mischievous hysteria, ungracious catastrophe. She, like nearly every wife of a man on the Hill, suspected that all those long-legged girls on their high heels, too much bosom showing in inappropriate costumes and their hair set just so were exciting to the middle-aged men they worked for. Alice Ormsbee put it to six of "the girls" at the Burning Tree Club after three bullshots: "Exciting those aging stags to a hard-on while *we* join the Menopause Club."

Sheila felt sure Jason couldn't be having it, making it, balling (others of Alice Ormsbee's expressions). Not with Clair, who was dating a naval officer doing hush-hush work at the Pentagon. Nor Miss Munday, who wasn't Jason's type. He had a pathological aversion to over-large gums. Still, that young stuff, dewy-eyed; eager huntresses living six to a flat someplace in a Virginia semi-slum, at the YWCA or with some busted southern family (*Board for Ladies*) with pictures of Robert E. Lee or a brass sword on their walls. Refined girls, but often stalking the male in the political deer park that was the House and the Chamber.

Sheila felt Jason was a sensual man, but well taken care of by her. Certainly they didn't neglect their sex life, and Jason, if keyed up by some debate in the House or outraged at some amendment by the wrong people, could almost assault her in his desires, even in front of Fran, their slack housekeeper, who would roll her eyes around when Jason in some haste led Sheila upstairs, once even making it in the living room with a light drizzle falling and Fran's vacuum cleaner going upstairs; they had copulated that time on the sofa, clothes flung off, garments unzipped. Rather good, as she remembered it; jubilant and earnest.

She pushed away the grapefruit rind. "I hear Senator Barraclough is coming back strong to the Hill as party leader in the Chamber."

Jason looked up from studying the Conrad cartoon in the *Washington Post* (very funny: it was against the Opposition). "There are no fixed orders of truth in this town. Yes, no, maybe he's taking over again."

"He still drinking?"

"Aren't we all drinking? Yes, he's been drinking, but it's under treatment. He's eating better. Now don't go blabbering this about the treatment to the girls."

Sheila exhaled, rubbed her rib section (just two more pounds to take off). "Esme Lowell says you're a good influence on her uncle."

"Jason looked up over the edge of the newspaper. "Where she say that?"

"We goils—as they say in Brooklyn—ran into her at the Kennedy Center at that dreadful modern music matinee. It's revolting the way tourists are cutting bits out of the drapes there, even taking ladies' room fixtures—just unscrewing them. Oh, we met Esme Lowell on the way out and she said the younger men were doing great work in Congress bringing the old hands into the modern world."

"What? Give me text, quotes."

Sheila laughed. "She said to me—alone for a minute, of course—you've been real helpful in taking Uncle Artie . . ."

"Austin."

"Uncle Austin, yes, off her hands at times when she really would have been dragged away from her business to attend to him. Direct quote."

"I've taken him out riding along the back roads, went to a dog show, made some irrelevant observations."

"Miss Lowell said he needed somebody to bounce talk off of, and is really in better health. Would you believe, Honey, she asked me if we wanted to sell the house? Someone has asked if it's for sale. She can find us a bigger one."

"I bet. More repairs, more bills."

The roof crew seemed to have stopped work. Jason picked up his attaché case as he heard the car backing out of the remodeled coach house; Dolf was on time to drive him to the Hill. He'd have to talk to Esme about not putting ideas into Sheila's head about a bigger house.

"Do you like lunching with her?"

"What? Oh. Not lunching—one lunch. Her uncle wanted me to do some work for him. Didn't want to meet on the Hill."

"Ahah."

Riding to the Hill this morning (what the hell did that "Ahah" mean?), Jason felt that Washington was a city of black limousines, congressmen, chiefs of bureaus, Cabinet faces, panjandrums from State; men grown old in small meeting rooms redolent of cigars that had died damply. Newer faces, some of them with features of pure mischief and with radical ideas to renew the mixture. Decrepit senators, with their senile drool over the virtues of the American heartland, while so many padded their expense accounts and loaded their relatives onto the public rolls. The Senate is a lot more, or should be; Jason felt himself draw into The Club, suspecting Austin Barraclough at their last meeting had not been wrong to detect something in Jason himself: "The ambition of Caesar is in you, Jason. You take politics as seriously as food, drink, sex."

Now driving to the Hill (how did Sheila know of the Esme lunch?), Dolf said, "You bet the Rams this week, Senator?"

"Rams?"

"The office football pool?"

"That's gambling on federal land, Dolf. Forbidden. Yes, I put a sawbuck on a spread of points."

"Will you be needing the car before three?"

"No, I have to go through a National Security Council report. And there's a vote coming up on 290-04 M."

"Car needs a grease and wax job."

"Yes—get it done."

When Jason got to his suite of offices the daily progress had begun. Waiting were six people from back home, whose hands he shook; letters to read, delivered by one of them; a promise to find a son's grave in Vietnam; and a shaking sadly of Jason's head on hearing the Post Office at Salmon Bend had been phased out after 154 years in existence—what if only sixteen letters a day (on the average) passed through it?

"History is history, isn't it, Senator?"

"It sure is, Mr. Grierson. How's the potato crop? Good."

Miss Munday was checking her shorthand book and Clair Brooks was sorting letters at his desk into the proper trays: *Top Attention, Answer These, Nut Stuff, Dangerous, Send to FBI.* There were, of course, no such words lettered on his desk trays, but Clair knew in what order they should be set out. She usually carried off a pile that went into the shredder in her office. It was a magnificent shredder. As it gobbled and destroyed, data, addled history were being permanently wiped out. ("Am 87 years old, blind, fought World War I as soldier. Need support for wife and six children.") There were so many to answer and file. Clair's note on this one had said: *Fraud, not on any records.* Then there were violet-inked letters from people who were forming Davy Crockett clubs and offering him the honorary presidency, and the right to send a donation for the clubhouse.

He ruffled through the surviving mail load—to be answered with forms A, B, or C. To Clair he dictated two important letters. One to his party chairman in Vista City, the other to Wantanka College accepting the honor of being next June's commencement speaker, and taking up the honorary degree of Doctor of Political Science.

He rather enjoyed these June college exercises at college town universities on green lawns set with a few bronze figures. He already had three other honorary degrees, one even presented the same day at the same college to Bob Hope and to a former Cabinet member in a disgraced administration, balanced by a great humanitarian doctor with a miracle serum.

(Next time I lunch with Esme Lowell, I'll have Andy along) (*Why?*) Clair, wearing her Indian jewelry of silver and blue stones, was writing something in Jason's attention pad. "There's going to be a debate of what bills will come up this week out of committee. Senator Ormsbee wants you to badger the Opposition leader to get a good working load of the proper bills out of committee."

"Give me the list of bills. Joe Kelly is the target."

Clair handed him six sheets of flimsy paper.

"You made the following points already, Senator, written in pencil."

He wished he could remember in detail points he had made. He put the sheets in his dispatch case. He was becoming a very good speaker on his feet. Ideas, phrases, facts, figures came to him when he needed them (if not, he could ad lib in exuberant vigor without going into details).

From the *Congressional Record:*

Mr. Crockett: Mr. Speaker, I take this time to inquire of the distinguished leader as to the program for the balance of the day and the week, and any other information on this subject which he can make available.

Mr. Kelly: Mr. Speaker, if the distinguished senator will be kind enough to yield, I will be happy to respond to him and give the program for the remainder of this week.

Mr. Crockett: I yield to the distinguished majority leader.

Mr. Kelly: Mr. Speaker, the program for the rest of the day is as follows:

The next item is HR-2702, Research and Development Planning. That is RDP.

We would hope that we would be able to finish this legislation today, but I understand there is an amendment of controversy in the RDP bill. Consequently, it is the intent of the committee to rise at six thirty. If we do not finish today, we will have it first on the schedule for tomorrow.

The next item we had scheduled was B.R. G9, petroleum reserves, Gila Hills. That will be put over until Monday. B.R. 8500, State Department authorization, will be put over until Tuesday. B.R. 4884, World Economic Policy Act, will be scheduled for tomorrow.

Mr. Crockett: Mr. Speaker, it is my understanding that the Gila Hills bill would come up on Tuesday rather than Monday.

Mr. Kelly: As I understand, there has been an agreement by all parties concerned. The only one I have spoken to on the other side is the gentleman from Oklahoma, and it is my understanding that both the Armed Services Committee and the committee chaired by the gentleman from Wyoming were in agreement to bring it up on Monday.

Mr. Crockett: My understanding from members of the Committee on Interior and Insular Affairs is that they desire the matter to come up on Tuesday.

Mr. Kelly: That has been discussed, but it seems an agreement on Tuesday has been reached.

Mr. Crockett: Could the distinguished gentleman tell the House approximately how long the session will be tomorrow?

Mr. Kelly: I would ask unanimous consent that when the Senate adjourn tonight it adjourn to meet tomorrow at ten o'clock.

Mr. Crockett: With what understanding?

Mr. Kelly: Then we would follow the will of the Members of the Senate as to what time they want to finish the business tomorrow. We do not intend to set a specific hour.

Mr. Crockett: I had conversations with several of the leadership on the gentleman's side of the aisle, and I am a little amazed, because the conversation led me to believe that it was fairly firm that the Senate would adjourn tomorrow some time between four or four-thirty. Is that not the situation?

Mr. Kelly: No; that is not so. But the gentleman knows that is the way things are. I hear that the White House is very much interested in the C.B. 43 bill, but Members on the other side voted against it.

Mr. Crockett: It just shows that one can get a bill so loused up that even people who are for it have to vote against it.

This kind of palaver went on for ten minutes more. Jason by this time—he had been a senator nearly eight months—could speak what appeared on the surface to be nonsense, but if handled properly could be a face-off and effective in getting some bills out of committee and placed on the Senate's order of business. He sparred with Kelly, a large, wide red-faced man from Chicago, with enjoyment. It was known Kelly was a man one could deal with. Facetious, nut-hard, pious, corrupted, Kelly was helpful and often wise in dealing with bills in committee, like the Gila Oil reserves measure, which Exxon, Mobil were hoping to get hold of.

Jason had hoped some sign of approval would show as he sat down, but there was a hush followed by a buzzing of members whispering to each other. All heads were turned to the entrance used by members to the Chamber. A tall figure stood there, a figure of gravity and a certain affirmation. It was Austin Barraclough. He was dressed neatly in dark blue, a suit with a suggestion of Edwardian grace and seriousness. (Jason thought, like Disraeli or Churchill?) The features were expressionless.

There was a wave of applause in the Chamber and everyone stood and turned in Barraclough's direction. The applause grew and there were heads turned, craned from the visitors' balcony, and activity in the press section among the two-dimensional shapes up there. Austin was appearing for the third time that session.

The applause continued, and some voices were raised in a cheer. Austin Barraclough raised his right arm and made a gesture of greeting.

Chapter 15

The way to Mount Vernon from the Capitol is out of Washington over the Memorial Bridge, skirting the Potomac and passing Arlington ("Hardly burying room for any more Kennedys"—Paul Ormsbee) past the irregular doughnut of the Pentagon. The ride to Alexandria, Jason observed to Austin, was crowded by buses and heavy traffic in a near hysteria. The golden day was rimmed in auto fumes, Howard Johnson's bilious shades of orange and trash food facades.

The big black Lincoln, with Dolf at the wheel wearing (after protest) his chauffeur's cap, was comfortable, the air conditioning isolating the interior with an atmosphere of its own as if that of another planet.

Austin Barraclough sat well back, looking leaner; his face held a good sunlamp tan. He wore a gray linen suit, most likely freshly pressed by Champ, for there was a scorch mark on the left shoulder. He viewed the landscape with an admonitory eye.

"Mount Vernon isn't the same as it was thirty years ago, Crockett. It's become ritual ridden, but I like it. All Americans should see it at least every ten years."

Jason could only nod in agreement. It had been very simple to just call Potomac House and ask would the senator like to come along to the George Washington Plantation? That simple—and there they were at ten in the morning fighting the chaos of traffic but paying it no mind.

"It was a surprise seeing you in the Chamber."

Austin grinned. "Stirred the animals up, didn't it? Of course it could have been an actor I hired."

"You look fit."

"A hollow shell, Crockett, a hollow shell. I'm on this medical mixture that makes taking a drink turn you sick as all get-out. *If* you drink on top of it, it can kill you. Once it made my heart feel like a bird striking a wall. I don't know if death isn't a welcome friend at a certain time. 'The skull beneath the skin,' the Elizabethans called their view of life. Always they saw it plain. We don't. We are carried to our death like painted dolls, but with Astro-turf all around to hide the raw grave. And costly—the price of a Lincoln to bury you in rare woods and silver handles." He smiled. "But hardly a topic on such a fine day. You ever get drag-ass?"

"As often as the next guy, Senator."

"You ever read Kafka?"

"Your niece asked me that too. No, never read him."

" 'What does it all matter, as long as the wounds fit the arrows.' Good bit, that?"

Jason laughed, "I don't think I'll read Kafka."

The rest of the journey to Mount Vernon was made in cheerful silence. Austin seemed to have had that art of taking enjoyment in bringing up grim topics this morning.

As they neared their destination traffic thickened, but Dolf at last wheeled the car toward the special parking space reserved for them by an early phone call. Austin looked about him with satisfaction. "You know it was actually called Little Hunting Plantation, the original five-thousand-acre tract. George's brother Lawrence built it and George took over from the widow. He was a land nut. They all were, and he expanded the place to over eight thousand acres. Worked hard, but the place was no great success. He was happy to make about twenty-seven hundred dollars a year out of it. In a good year."

"Well, he called himself the first farmer of his country. And there were no federal handouts from Washington not to plant crops."

"Come this way—I used to visit here as a kid." Austin took Jason's arm and led him to view the Potomac from the bluff. "Fine, eh? I think here was the center of George's being."

Cameramen discovered them, which roused the milling tourists to bring up their own Kodaks and Polaroids. Jason and Austin escaped to those sections not at the moment open to the public. Austin took out a cigar in the west parlor, the music room (Nellie Custis chamber) and offered one to Jason. They sat on the porch of a wing in an outbuilding, free of the visitors, smoked, watching the blue haze of their tobacco drift up into the warm air against a background of green lawns and robin-blue sky.

Austin seemed to be satisfied to sit and not speak. Jason tried to imagine the place as it must have been with earth paths swept by slaves and a gravel drive scarred by carriage wheels. He tried to hear the sound of blacksmiths hammering iron to the jong-jong sound he remembered from visits to country fairs. There would be slaves and plenty of slave quarters, farm animals and breeding of sporting dogs. Washington liked to breed his dogs. ("I lined up my bitch Betsy today with Tige.") When not riding to fox hunts, Washington would be playing whist in one of those varnished rooms, recording his winnings and losses ("rain today—2 pounds six shilling lost at play"). But Jason felt it didn't come clearly, this Irving Stone-ing of the historic past. What came between the past and the present?

It was well past the Bicentennial. Was that it? Or was it the visitors asking someone to pose closer to their Polaroid's instant, the grind of buses bringing more Americans to see the site of one of the republic's founders? ("Transportation," announced a bullhorn, "leaving from the Seventh Street Wharves on the hour.") For Jason, it all made the past seem too far gone to grasp. It was only pegged-oak floor and crystal chandeliers—perhaps the originals—and very fine furniture donated by the Mount Vernon Ladies' Association. Jason glanced at Austin. He seemed held in some brooding mood.

"Let's go pay our respects to George and Martha," said Austin, tossing away his cigar.

They walked to the burial spot; it was too simple to be called a sarcophagus. An enclosure with iron railings. Jason stood, touched as he had rarely been, and yet he could not fully explain why. Austin said, "The whole goddamn superpatriotic gushing never appealed to me. The extra special Americans who claim all the virtues in their love of country. But *here* I get a grand serenity."

Jason felt a Ping-Pong ball in his throat, a phantom Ping-Pong ball, true, but real enough at the moment to make him choke up a bit with emotion. Below on the Potomac a naval vessel was passing, the flag lowered to half mast in respect. A bell began to toll. The crew were assembling on deck facing the Mount Vernon gardens and the tomb, the men soon at attention.

Austin said, "It's a tradition. Every naval vessel passing here does the flag doffing, the bell ringing, the crew at attention."

"It's a good tradition," Jason said."

"A damn good tradition, but we only seem to keep the public ones, the showy stuff on television. Say, Crockett, I'm hungry."

"We could go to the Burning Tree for lunch."

"Too exposed. I'll get a million greetings while being told I'm looking great. And it's all just me being baked under a sunlamp a half hour a day."

"Senator, you talk fine, you take interest and make comments."

"Jason." (It was the first time he had called him Jason, not Crockett, and Jason felt good even if abashed about that.) "I may drop dead on the way out, but it's tonic to see this place again. Forget the show business side of it, and the glory games they play here. George was a different man from the storybook doll. He was a cocksman, a drinker, a fortune hunter. Martha was a bitch: crab-apple sour. But he made her a good husband. Richest widow in the colonies when he went after her. But most of all he was a hell of a great man. His image has been ruined by schoolbooks and that goddamn portrait by Gilbert Stuart. George was six feet four, had a face so marked by smallpox you could throw peas at him and they'd stick in his cheeks. Had TB as a young man, and big hands like hams. And a lousy dentist . . . Let's go to the O'Donnells' Sea Grill. I feel like soft-shell crabs. Christ, Miller's in Baltimore, Jason, it really had the best seafood. Closed now. Everything good seems to be fading, or am I just an old miserable sonofabitch?"

They had the soft-shell crabs after a marvelous clam chowder with tomatoes. They didn't order drinks, and after black coffee they sat back and Austin seemed sleepy but contented.

"Want to talk to you, Jason, about my plans for the Senate. But not today. Overdid it. Feel fatigued, senescent. I'll take some pills and rest, rest. I sleep a lot, you know."

Jason saw the older man seemed to have suddenly lost the vitality he had shown at Mount Vernon. The ride back was silent. At Potomac House, Dolf and Jason helped Austin up the steps and Champ, opening the door, looked at them with accusing eyes as they made their way into the grand hallway.

"Now you overdone it. I knew you would."

Austin looked about him as if searching for some known setting. "Damn it, what do you know? I need a little shuteye. See you, Crockett, in the Senate . . . in a few days. Great day. Jefferson's home wasn't it?"

"Mount Vernon."

"Jesus, so it was."

Champ put an arm around Austin Barraclough. "And you'll undress, no sleeping in your clothes."

The older man leaned heavily on Champ. "I ever tell you you're a mean-tushed buck, Champ?"

"Thousands of times."

Jason felt depressed; the grotesque was back. It had seemed a great day, and Austin what he had been, or close to it. And now? Just cantankerous mumblings. He followed Dolf down and out to the car. A black man mounted on a power lawnmower was slowly cutting grass along the edge of the gravel drive beyond a row of hollyhocks. A redlegged hawk swooped low over a pine tree, fluttering some small birds sheltered there. The day was heating up, the humidity made Jason feel soggy. He scratched his neck. It itched. He decided against going back to the Senate.

"Georgetown, Dolf."

Jason enjoyed the physical side of the city. Leaving early mornings, to visit a branch of the government to pick up some report rather than have Andy or Clair do it, and to meet staff people—the personal touch. It was good to be driving through the streets where so much had happened; Jason recalled old photographs by Matthew Brady, or his helpers, of men all whiskers and unpressed trousers, of the early flickering films of McKinley, Teddy Roosevelt, or Woodrow Wilson. Ghosts now jerking about on silent film footage unreeling at the wrong speeds on modern projectors. While *he* was here, alive and kicking, carrying on some of their work.

The traffic was heavy; cabs and private cars (Jags, Lincolns) headed for the Hill, coming from Chevy Chase just inside the Maryland line, and going past the Woodner on 16th, the apartment house gleaming in the morning light and the heavy butt of Senator Grady Hokom of Alabama getting into a cab. The hum of the day getting louder. The packed buses heading for Constitution Avenue, for already the visitors were out. Jason enjoyed the serene majestic monuments of the city offering honors to the great dead, the often banal heroes, philosophers forgotten. Passing the Washington Monument, the senator looked up as he always did and flipped two fingers at the granite shaft for luck, past the Bureau of Engraving, and then the car slid into the traffic across 14th Street, went by the Agriculture Department and followed the buildings to where they linked over Independence Ave. The Botanical Gardens had a few loafers and old soldiers in slippers sunning in front of it. Beyond was the New House Building, a monstrous disgrace to design, cost and to the beauty of the immense, luminous sky. The Capitol Plaza cops gave a one-finger salute on the peak of their caps. As Dolf parked the car in the reserved space, Jason almost vaulted out of the car with two briefcases, a brown folder of press clippings and a thermos of hot tea and lemon.

As he moved along the halls, he could hear the news tickers banging away, smell the government floor wax (once cause of a costs scandal) and the historic dust already at home in the drapes.

"Morning."

The girl at the outer desk looked up smiling. "Morning."

Then to Clair's desk.

"You made the society columns, danced with the Duchess of Congrove, it says in Bedee's *Post* column."

"Oh? Get me all the out-of-town reports you can on reaction to the speech yesterday."

Clair sat in an office clutter of newsweeklies, two-sheet posters, a wall of framed pictures; Jason playing a violin at the age of ten, at seventeen with a crewcut boxing a very lean black, at the Vatican with a Pope, holding a smile with slack jaw muscles.

"A very nice head of hair."

"Runs in the family."

"Most people by your time of life are already showing a bit too much of the brow, and showing lots of skin up the sides of the head."

"Do I have to have that muck on my face?"

"Pancake Number Three, Senator, gives you that nice healthy look."

"Of a stiff in a five-thousand-dollar funeral. I usually did television back home wth just a light dusting of face powder."

"Well, *there*, yes. But this is Washington, isn't it?"

There was no answer to that and Jason didn't make one. He sat in the tilted-back barber chair in the makeup room of the television studio, tissues pushed under his shirt collar so it wouldn't get soiled by makeup. The slender young man brushed on some eye shadow on Jason's lids, stepped back and nodded approval of his work. He removed the tissues. "Room C, the Dragon Lady is waiting."

It was his second appearance with Snow Williams. Jason tried not to look amused, and caught a glimpse of himself in the mirror, all yellowish, unshiny skin, sprayed hair. Certainly looked like someone like him, but with a veneer of makeup, touched-up eyebrows, brown highlights, character lines matted out. He seemed like an actor who played shady lawyers or scientists in movies. What surprised him was the hot, evangelical stare of his eyes.

Room C was spacious, draped in grays with pale blues. There was a large couch of what looked like pink leather, a low table set with coffee cups and a coffeepot. Overhead a sound mike on a thin carrying pole hovered, and two men were standing behind bulky television cameras: men who looked bored with their work and as if their feet hurt. Faintly someplace there was the whisper of the Peggy Lee song, "What Are You Doing the Rest of Your Life?"

A middle-aged woman painted to appear younger—a retouched cosmetic poster—sat on the couch, a fistful of typed sheets in one hand, a cup of coffee in the other. It was a plump body but seemed under restraint, the exaggerated décolletage shown by the crayon-blue dress. The legs were out of sight; Snow Williams was rather shy about their thickness and lack of grace.

"Ah, wight on time." Snow Williams was having a little more trouble than usual with the letter r this noon. "How handsome you look, Senator. A hero from ouah last frontier." She turned to a little man with thin brown hair and a head that kept nodding sadly, as if expecting no mercy.

"Now, for Chrissakes, get the effing sound in focus and I don't want any of those ghastly side shots. If you can't control the camera shots I'll get someone who *can*." She beamed at the two cameramen. "These boys are fine craftsmen and splendid artists, so don't smudge their work. Wight, boys?"

"Um."

"Oh, Senator Crockett, how nice to have you back."

Jason said, "Where do you want me?" The song said "The East and West of your life."

Snow Williams patted the sofa by her Rubenesque hips. "Here, close to Snow." She tossed away the papers, put down the coffee cup. "Now, I don't believe too much in this crap of going through what we'll be saying on the air. Takes the naturalness out of the whole smear. We'll skip the Harbors and Wivers Bill, chatter, and get to the party secrets wumored for the next convention. What an attractive man you are."

"I don't know any secrets."

The little abashed man had slipped away and stood between the two cameras, one of which revealed a red eye. The little man looked at the face of a wall clock, adjusted an earphone set. "Twenty seconds to air time, Miss Williams. Camera One."

"Thank you, darling."

Jason said, "I sit here?"

"You'll do fine, just fine, Senator. Like on our last show."

The song faded, and a voice of a man with an oiled throat announced "The Snow William's Noon Show," and added that its sponsors were several national products.

Snow Williams was doing some breathing exercises, expanding those breasts, with a smile attached. Millions were waiting, Jason thought, for this woman to speak, to badger people who wanted attention. He remembered that her name could be Susie, not Snow. At least that's what some said. But that was not true, Clair had informed Jason. Snow's mother, a pregnant widow from Buffalo, New York, had moved to Arizona to run an employment agency, and missed the winter she loved in upper New York State; so she had named her newborn daughter Snow in a post-birth bit of nostalgia. The Dragon Lady, as so many called her, now turned to Jason. "Welcome again, welcome Senator Jason Crockett, who—" Jason's attention was distracted by a blonde girl wheeling out two live cats and some green cardboard boxes on a small table, and he missed part of the opening question. "And so Senator, level with Snow, isn't there a plot to defuse the national nomination drive at the next convention for Senator Balbac of New Jersey, and give it to whom?"

"As the convention is two years away, Miss Williams, I hardly think there is what you call a plot."

She gave him a smirk proclaiming privileged information. "Come clean, come, there is weason to think your senior senator, Paul Ormsbee, is being prepped for the nomination."

Jason suddenly was amused. "If he's being waxed and polished, new tires, his wheels aligned—he doesn't show it."

Snow Williams laughed, and brushed Jason's arm with the cue sheet she was holding. "You are a wit, Senator. Of course your party is weady to produce a president?"

"It's up to the voters. Politics isn't a simple game played in the open, like tennis."

"What is politics?" She lifted the tone of her voice.

"Politics is all made up of persuasive theory, of eye-gouging. Some think it's played to subvert reality."

Snow Williams felt it better to change the subject. "Would you like to hear a newly discovered Lincoln letter one of my viewers sent in?"

"*Abraham* Lincoln?"

She looked at him for a moment as if annoyed at his bad taste, then she said, "*This* is a photocopy. The original is just too precious. Mrs. Marion Goldwasser of Green Springs, Ohio, owns the original. Would you care to read it, Senator?"

"No, no, it was sent to you, Miss Williams."

"Very well. Snow will read it: Dear Leander Kutz, I do find you still owe the store one dollar twenty cents on for that mule collar and would be pleased to be paid. YOURS (spelled yrs. and signed [bring the camera in close] signed) *A. Lincoln*."

She turned to Jason with a rapturous smile: "Just think, Senator, Lincoln himself wrote this, showing his humanity, his touch of humor set in the edge of moral issues, and yet a direct friendliness with people, *all* people."

"Also it indicates he wanted to be paid for that mule collar."

"A man with a pilgrim's progress to greatness growing to stature in the wilderness. Never vindictive . . . never petty . . ." she sighed. "Senator, you once said you could build a high fence around Washington and produce a perfect madhouse."

"Not me, Miss Williams. No, Senator Barraclough said that some years ago on 'Meet the Press.' "

The slur of her vowel sounds deepened. "Somebody naughty has been feeding me wong notes. Speaking of Senator Barraclough, there are stories that he is much wecovered—I am so happy for that—I mean, was it a true mental breakdown as *Time* magazine hinted?"

"Miss Williams, I didn't come here to talk of media rancor or refute gossip. I'd like to discuss the new Senate bills coming up."

Her bow lips pursed (J. Willard insisted such mouths indicated heavy thighs). The little man was cutting his throat with a finger and pointing to the two cats and green boxes. Snow Williams laid a hand with the overlong fingernails and very beautiful rings on Jason's arm again.

"We'll return to that in a moment, Senator. But now, a word for No Smell Kleen Kitty Litter, which is the joy and wealy healthy needs of all cat life, to keep odors from your pussy. So use No Smell Kleen Kitty Litter. Here are my two darlings, Mae West and Cary Grant, who grew up on No Smell Kleen Kitty Litter and . . ."

Jason had lost interest. He couldn't even try being facetious. There would be two more minutes of this, if the time sheet was right, and already the blonde girl was leading in a fattish housewife turned novelist, who had produced a best seller about a housewife who makes it sexually (as Alice Ormsbee had reported to Sheila) with various men, from the mailman to the town flasher, and as a bar hostess, a go-go dancer, and yet finds her faith again in God and a return to decency as the result of a crippling auto accident to her pot-smoking daughter. Miss Munday had discussed the book in Jason's office on the Hill as "a sign of the times."

One of the cats, as the commercial proceeded with a male voice, scratched Snow Williams' hand and she turned away from the mike to mutter "goddamn!" She adjusted her smile.

"And now back to Senator Jason Crockett, who shared with us the inner secret of his party's shenanigans planned for the next national elections. I have a surprise for you, Senator. As all my millions of viewers may not know, you are a direct descendent of the great American hero who died at the Alamo, Davy Crockett."

"Not a direct descen—"

"No modesty, Senator." She reached behind the sofa and brought up an adobe brick set into a metal plaque.

"I have been authorized to present you with this actual adobe memento taken from the sacred walls of the original Alamo, inscribed and set in a genuine silver plaque by Morris Weiner, jeweler of Dallas, weading: 'We hereby appoint Senator Jason Crockett, descended from the hero of the Alamo, Davy Crockett, a cherished member of the Alamo Texas Society, and honorary Colonel in the Pioneer Texas Legion.' And, are we looking here today at the next presidential nominee of his party?"

Jason smiled. (Oh, you bitch!) "I didn't know, Miss Williams, your show was a fantasy."

"No modesty, *please*."

Jason stood up and took the plaque (oh, you goddamn bitch). "Honors, honors," he said. The cats were watching him, the best-

FROM THE PAST 151

selling housewife novelist was watching him. For a moment there he had the desire to fling the plaque at the camera with the red eye, or better still bop it over the head of Snow Williams, who was sucking her scratched thumb. But he knew enough to never show public anger at the media. He said instead, "There is a wall for this. Thank you."

Snow Williams smiled, the shine of lip salve outlining a mouth that covered territory colored ruby red. "I can only make my own predictions and one is that if the party were smart, their candidate in two years would be, will be, Senator Jason Crockett. You've got my vote sewed up, Senator. And you've got the good simple folk, I'm sure, and all lovers of the wight-thinking ideals."

She turned away before he could tell her to stop doing the party's thinking. "And now my next guest, Susie Wallis, author of *Where Am I Here,* just sold to Avon for seven hundred thousand and to Twentieth Century-Fox for one million even. Welcome, Susie Wallis. I'm always amazed how you writers get your ideas . . ."

The blonde girl led Jason out of range of the lights. He still held the plaque, the brick, pressed against his rib section. He needed a drink. The blonde girl asked, "Don't you want to take your face off?"

"My *what*?"

"Shhh—we're on the air." The girl touched his mouth and cheeks. "The goop."

Chapter 16

The Snow Williams broadcasts seemed to aid Jason, to project him into the national scene more than anything he had actually done in the Senate. Up to then, the local press had been stolidly indifferent. Paul Ormsbee said wryly, "I'll have to keep my weather eye on you, you scene-stealer." And he laughed off Jason's answer that the damn bitch was always looking for something sensational to perk up her rating and sell her revolting pussy odor killer. Bread O'Rahilly sent Jason a huge button with the letters: FOR PRESIDENT "DAVY" JASON CROCKETT. To be followed by a phone call: "I must say, Senator, you're the first man to appear smart enough to get an early start. Oh, I know it was a kind of a gag, but two hundred television stations carry Snow's daffy show. She's a troublemaker, but don't ever overlook the clout the bitchy biddy has. Lunch? Well, you call me and I'll fill you in on some hanky-panky deals in the selling and buying of potato futures. Some smart hombres from your own state may be in trouble."

"I hope they get reamed real hard."

It was at home that the ribbing was heavy at first. Sheila, with a felicity of expression, asking "Mr. President, how will you have your eggs this morning, FDR style sunny side up, or haute gout John F. Kennedy with rum jubilee?"

Clair at the office somehow got some publicity stills of Jason and Snow Williams and the two cats—he was unaware pictures were being taken. Clair had them framed and hung over her desk; the cats looking worried, Jason wary, Snow showing pertness and insistence.

When Jason walked into the Senate Chamber, wits continued to call him "Mr. President" for awhile. He began to respect the mind-less, ambiguous power of television.

He had expected some reaction from Austin Barraclough, but when he drove out to see the older man, he found him sitting on the sun deck of Potomac House and he merely grunted, pointing to an old elm tree propped up by lengths of iron pipe.

"There are a set of robins building a nest in that old tree. I've been trying to warn them off by waving my arms and having Champ try to reach them with a pole. But they go right on, slave to Nature's coercive plans for reproducing."

"You don't like robins?"

"It's the damn cats. Up to our ass in cats hereabouts. Mona kind of turned a randy pair loose in the shrubbery, and they breed and run wild, climb after birds' nests and gobble up the nestlings like bonbons."

"I've been talking to Paul Ormsbee."

"Who?"

"Senator Ormsbee. Esme, Miss Lowell, said you wanted me to feel out his plans."

"Did I? You know, if you nail a bit of tin around a tree trunk, say a foot or so, the cats can't climb it. Slip right off."

"I think Paul is seriously thinking of making a run for the presidency. We've got a good solid organization back home, and in the Northwest, and he's liked on the coast, and—"

"I know all about that. I keep up. I try."

"Years ago you sponsored a bill of his for control of strip mining methods that destroy the land permanently."

"I recall. Ormsbee? Yes, yes. Sorry. I've got this rectitude of mind as I'm not drinking, but taking some kind of chemical mess to cut the desire." He leaned over and beat a fist on Jason's knee. "You know, the vicarious booze urge is *still* there. It's all I think about." He laughed and added, "That and those stupid robins. You spoke about the national convention. Well, that's two years off. Conventions are a conspicuous absurdity since television."

"I know it's two years away, but Paul seems to feel he's the best prospect."

Austin pursed his lips, put his fingertips against his mouth and stared at the elm tree. Champ came out with a glass of milk on a tray.

"Take it away!"

Champ set the glass down on the low table. "I don't like it any better than you do A. B., but there it is and I stay till you drink."

Austin Barraclough lifted the glass and sipped from it. He wiped his lips with a finger, smiled. "I never liked the stuff. Maybe I did when I was hanging on my mother to get at it. You know, Jason, my mother won sixteen golf championships as a young girl, and of course everything was nonprofessional in those days. Yes, the house is still cluttered with the cups she won. Tennis too. Beat the pants off Helen Wills and that French woman, Suzanne Something-or-other."

He handed the empty glass to Champ. "Don't let me see your face till dinner."

"You get another half pint in one, *O N E* hour."

Austin Barraclough rewiped his lips with a handkerchief he took from a pocket. "I recall asking for information on Ormsbee. Thank you. I have some ideas on who the party can elect. Notes someplace on the subject. Care to look them over one day?"

Jason said he would, anytime. The old boy was clearer, recovering fast. Esme had seemed indifferent—just that he didn't drink. He wasn't, at the moment, drinking.

When Jason said he had to go, Austin just waved a hand. "Yes, good of you to come to see me. You young bastards—I like your sureness. I may drop up to the Hill again. Remember, life is most interesting when slightly edged with prejudice."

Jason left him there, sitting deep in a wicker chair watching the robins coming with stray bit of cord, a few twigs, for nest building.

Champ was in the hall listening to a baseball game on a small radio, in his white housecoat, a feather duster under his arm.

"He seems in good shape, Champ."

"Well, he isn't throwing nothing at me. That's when he's in his prime, throwing things." There was a crowd roar from the radio. Champ smiled, "That's Vita Blue, he can hit 'em. I got a bet, a fin riding on this game. It's those robins A. B.'s got on his mind."

"Cats really after them?"

"Oh sure—those are smart cats. Mrs. Barraclough, she brung them from Italy, I think. Big mean fellows. Yellow eyes."

"Mrs. Barraclough, what was she like?"

Champ gave Jason an amused glance and got up to open the front door for him.

"Have a good day, Senator."

"I'll try."

Jason decided he'd have to get Esme to open up about the second Mrs. Barraclough. Mona Barraclough; as yet to him a disembodied state; he remembered her picture in a magazine, *Town and Country*, jumping a horse at some posh show. Very stylish, snooty in hard hat, trim riding pants, the tails of her jacket fluttering behind. He didn't remember the face, half turned away, but J. Willard saying, "Now that's a woman who would be a credit to the White House."

That was the year Austin Barraclough came closest to the nomination . . .

Jason came awake suddenly, jarred loose from a dream he had been having. He was hunting ducks with J. Willard and his father had been explaining something to him, not one word of which Jason understood, but he had been nodding oh yes, for it was all very clear in the dream what his father had been talking about, and then Austin Barraclough came up out of a duck blind half way across the lake, and began firing a small brass cannon, and the sky filled with the black bodies of falling ducks—then Jason came awake, staring up at Sheila, who was smiling down at him and held him by the shoulders, shaking him.

"Wake up, wake up, Grandfather."

"What, what?" He struggled up into fuller wakefulness, swallowing the heavy unpleasant moisture of sleep that filled his mouth and throat. "What the hell . . ."

"A telegram, eight and a half pounds."

"Whatever for?"

"A girl. Eight and a half pounds. Born an hour ago."

"Oh, yeah?" He sat up and listened to Sheila—and the glare of the night table lamp was too strong. He was a grandfather. Sheila was a grandmother. Their daughter Laura had given birth to a grandchild.

He said, "I understand."

"Mother and child doing fine. Oh, Jay!"

He let himself be hugged and kissed on the cheek, and he put his arm around his wife, pressing her to him. "Well, we were expecting it, weren't we?"

"A girl."

"Fine, fine. A girl." He was still half in a dream.

She looked at him, her face clear of makeup, eyelashes colorless, a shine of some cream on her no longer young skin. She said, "*You*, I bet, would have wanted a grandson."

"I never said so. A grandchild is a grandchild."

Sheila seemed spooked with joy. She recited, "A grandchild is a grandchild is a grandchild, said Gertrude Stein. We ought to open a bottle, Jay."

He looked at the little traveling clock indifferently ticking on the night table. "At three twenty-four in the morning?"

"They phoned the message. You didn't hear it, the phone. I thought maybe it was something important politically and . . ."

He was wrassling himself into his robe. "What are Laura and that creep Sam going to name it?"

"It? It's a human being, a child. Didn't say. Libby would be nice, after my mother."

Jason was fumbling for his slippers, his eyes still not in full focus. He went to a closet. Should be a bottle of champagne there; someone had sent them a half case from somebody connected with a lumbering firm. "Nobody is named Libby," he said. "Is it short for Liberty?"

"Nobody is named Liberty. Well, yes, there was a girl at school, Liberty Monasoki, her father was the junkyard king of Ohio or someplace. What you looking for?"

"A bottle of champagne."

"I moved everything downstairs."

They looked at each other and realized they were acting odd. Jason laughed. "Come on down to the living room and we'll have a drink."

He led her, two steps below, down the narrow creaky stairs of the old house; no room to come comfortably downstairs abreast. The old house seemed to know it was an event, its timbers seemed to shift and there were settling sounds—also the musty smell of the old wallpaper under the not-so-old layers.

They sat in their robes by the small teak bar drinking brandies— the champagne seemed mislaid—lifting their glasses to each other and smiling foolishly.

They had neither of them been very fond of their daughter since Laura had been fifteen—when something strange had happened to the delightful (even if moody) child, and she had become secretive, foul-mouthed, a rather nasty adolescent; attached to adoring worthless youths, she was given to the overuse of nail polish and facial makeup. And had filled out alarmingly, been sent home from school several times for smoking in the john, once for cursing out a school nurse when certain items were found in her handbag.

It was clear Laura was having "sexual relationships," as the nurse put it, with common boys. J. Willard shouted, "The little bitch needs a clout in the ear!" one day when he was handed traffic violations after she had used his car at sixteen without his permission, and been clocked at seventy miles an hour. Certainly they had had a problem in Laura. She lied, she stole small sums (not so small), she took to going out nights and calling up to say she was staying with her best friend, Deedee. A check with Deedee's mother proved neither of them was telling the truth.

Then, after a crisis in their cabin at Blue Lake when Jason and Sheila had been away at a convention in Kansas City, they had come back to find the cabin in a fearful mess, lamps broken, the deep-freeze pilfered, a gold watch missing and signs in the bedrooms that several people had been in habitation. A reel of porno film was in the 16-mm projector.

Laura had turned sullen when accused of having held open house and permitted orgies. She cursed them out and called her mother and father a couple of fucking shitheads, squares, and they could go and piss up a rope. She just short of seventeen.

They could have had some of the youths arrested, but Jason, as governor, didn't want any scandal; there was always politics to think of, the damn public image. The state police recovered the gold watch in a pawnshop and Jason sent Laura away to a strict kind of upper-class reform school near Portland.

The reports from the resident school shrink were good. Laura only ran away once and was found living with a young Mexican gardener in Brentwood. It was a year later she went off to the commune with Sam, and wired home they were married and wanted to live with Nature, and Sam, a dropout from a "Dixieland" band, insisted they live on food that had not been sprayed with chemicals.

It seemed best to settle for that. And now their rebel daughter had produced a child and they were grandparents.

"I suppose, Jay, we can phone in the morning and talk to her or Sam."

"If they have a phone?" Jason said. "Sam's against civilization."

"I'll call the hospital."

"What hospital? They don't have one. Greenfield County, isn't it. She's in no hospital, those kooks go in for natural birth. Like a cow."

"Oh, Jason . . . I'll fly out in the morning."

"You'll only get her into some psychotic state. Laura doesn't really want to have anything to do with us."

"Jason," she wept, "she *can't* hate us." He let her weep. Family life wasn't all the coy stuff of popular tradition. Not in this fouled-up twentieth century. He had so admired, liked his children. A girl, a boy; the popular set. Had felt proud and made little dreams—rose-colored dramas—of them growing up. Pals, no "generation gap." Teddy Willard Crockett, someday an All-American at State University, and maybe some post-grad work at Yale or Harvard. Laura Belle, her father's favorite, someday he'd be walking with her down the aisle at St. Martins, the best church in the state; a daughter on his arm, moving toward a handsome son-in-law of one of the best families, in a mist of Mendelssohn's music. This beautiful virgin trembling on his arm, to surrender her jewel to that sun-god with three generations of good solid family who would call him Dad. Instead, the vision had turned into a crock of shit. Or was he too bitter?

He poured them another brandy. "Last time round and back to bed. The family marches on."

"You've never forgiven her, have you, Jay?"

"I suppose not. Not fully. I never talked to my father like that—never mind—give them some money when you get there, even if in theory they scorn the stuff."

There was a brisk tapping on the front door, then a use of the antique brass knocker ("the original Colonial cast brass," Esme Lowell had exclaimed when showing Jason the house).

Jason went to the door and looked out through the square of plate glass set shoulder high. A burly policeman stood there, a black, with a flashlight in his hand. Jason opened the door, saw the prowl car at the curb. The officer touched his wide forehead with a finger of his right hand. Jason noticed the pistol holster pulled around to be handy.

"Up late, Senator? Everything okay?"

"Any reason why it shouldn't be?"

"Saw all your lights on downstairs. Lots of light. Just checking."

"Oh, sorry, Officer. My wife and me, we just heard we're grand-parents. Celebrating. Our first."

"Is it? Well, the best to you both, Senator, and the baby. Sorry to knock you up but, well, some of the goddamn gangs are out stripping cars and pilfering." He saluted Jason with his flashlight. "The best of everything, Senator."

"You'll have a drink, Officer?"

"Not on duty, thanks. By the way, you ought to have a night-light on over your side door. And if you stay out very late, call the station house and we'll send somebody to escort you home."

"Not necessary."

The officer showed annoyance. "Congressman Weise got mugged just two streets over tonight."

"Congressman Weise?" He'd raise hell on the Hill in the morning if he could make it. Jason closed the door and heard the prowl car move off. Sheila looked up from an airline timetable she was studying. "The police?"

"Our lights of celebration attracted them. Morrie Weise got mugged tonight."

"And Morrie is always defending them, asking for more handouts for them."

"He didn't say they were blacks."

Chapter 17

Sheila felt she had become another person after her visit to Laura, or rather regressed to what she had been after their own children were born; her entire interest seemed to turn toward her grandchild Libby, even if the newborn infant was a continent away. She would phone Laura twice a week and spend half an hour giving advice as to feeding formulas, diaper rash, recite the dangers of careless bathing, choking, and was almost a scientist on the varied color of bowel content and what it signified.

"All right, Jay. I'm a crazy grandmother. But a baby is a delicate, precious thing. And these commune-livers are barbarians, unsanitary too. No baths—they swim in a creek."

"Surprised they have a phone."

Sheila didn't inform him she had paid to have a phone installed there. She had learned to use acumen and tact with Jason. He was rather disconcerted about the children now that Laura and Teddy were grown, and in a way Sheila resented it. He had been a good enough father when the children were growing up, only stern when, as children get at times, they were shrieking wraiths. Then he'd lock himself away from them in his study. It was clear he had no tormented conscience about not being a jolly dad.

Truth was, is, she had come around to thinking Jason was a decent man, but also perhaps not a perfect husband. She was aware of the inconsistencies of men and women, and was becoming convinced the values of a politician for domestic life had damaged her innate self-esteem. With the birth of Libby, Sheila was admitting to herself that she had given in too often to the demands of a public life; the smiling wife of a political figure, and it could be she had not been as contented as she had imagined. (The shattered face of Pat Nixon on television, those long dry teeth, at the side of the hulking disaster.) Sheila, too, had been the good political wife on the platforms, at those dreadful $100-a-plate dinners to raise funds. Poses of overingenuous impulses, with gestures, in greeting stuffed shirts, the notorious, the important, the high poobahs herding up at state capitol functions. She would have liked a simpler life, so she now felt. She didn't know if she was honest about this; for she liked the Washington country club afternoons with a good stiff drink, looking over green tailored grounds, among the wives of men on the Hill, or the mates of higher public officials. She enjoyed, too, the awe when she was introduced to tourists as "the wife of our popular senator." She did like the little favors of a auto license plate that did away with most traffic violations; a respect that got her to the head of the line at times.

Jason was headed toward power, she knew that. He had always been pointed that way from their first days together, dedicated to doing something better than the next man, and with an eye on the main chance. He had brains and the disciplines to achieve. There had been, of course, defeats when he had kicked at the rug, howled at injustice and fools, and come to her for comfort and intimate physical satisfaction; the sexual act was his medicine. She had early discovered that, and it had amused her to see him return to tranquility after lovemaking.

She had enjoyed their bed play, their satisfactory relationship as man and woman, but the spice, the fun, the *umm* no longer—how could she confess it to herself?—was not the highest pitch of domestic existence. It was the inner flaw that haunts us all. We each must have that secret inner flaw, she decided, and hers was that the high pitch of passion with which once she faced the sexual act, had blunted. It was not, of course, as Alice Ormsbee had confessed after three martinis: "Well, it's all grunt and slobber and the sooner done, the better. I sometimes wish Paul would get himself some tootsie and get it out of his system, and not act the letch at his age at home. God knows, you'd think they'd get tired of it—the animals."

Sheila could not understand such a condition, such an attitude. For all the years of her moving among people who had morals as wily as their politics, seeing existence among what passed for higher society (with the morality of a mink farm), she still retained a sense of sin, of feeling guilt at breaking the codes of her old-style Protestant upbringing.

Jason merely thought she was too involved with the new grandchild, distracted to specific female efforts. He was working hard, even harder now that Congress was on summer vacation, bringing to order reports, polls, the results of conferences of the various county chairmen all around the nation. The party he hoped would come to the next session of the opening of Congress committed to some candidates for nomination at the next convention, or at least with some favorite sons who looked promising as vote-getters when thrown to the lions in the primaries, there to test their toughness on platforms and before television cameras. Much of Congress had flown off on junkets to Europe, to Africa, to various parts of Asia.

Austin Barraclough was not very shocked at these junkets when Jason brought out a list of men, mostly city and party chairmen, who would support Paul Ormsbee.

They were walking in the rose garden at Potomac House, the last blooms losing their petals like molting fowls, and from beyond a small wood came the whirr of pheasants in stubble. The land was posted *Private, No Hunting,* but already guns were heard far off.

"Junketing is polite stealing from the taxpayers," Jason said. "It's something some congressmen do five or six times a year. The excuse is usually some invented need to look at jute cultivation in India, or to attend a meeting in Italy on how to make cheaper ice cream."

"Why not?"

"Mostly it's hogwash to take the wife or the girl friend to nightclubs, to get drunk in Paris, laid in Berlin, and ride around in big hired cars and run up expense accounts with special embassy funds laid out for them."

Austin was inspecting the glaucous clouds in the sky. "I suppose it will never be stopped, Jason, and there's no real public bookkeeping or accounting, it's so buried under false headings."

"And the military spend millions hauling these moochers around in Air Force planes."

"Jason, Jason, it's only a few million dollars a year, four or six, and there are good honest men who don't junket. Don't look for dry rot in the trees, look at the fruit they produce. Politics has no simplicity, no honor system. A nation is made up of political parties doing the best they can with the obstinate imbeciles and thieves the voters elect. Of course we pick who they should be voting for; that's the system and it works fairly well. Better without brutality and evil than systems anyplace else, I think. God, this season's roses are going."

Austin didn't seem to be interested in the lists and Jason didn't force his attention. It seemed to him Austin Barraclough was at times showing more interest in other things, in the toads in the garden that snapped long thread tongues at the insects, at Champ's idea of a beef Wellington which Austin insisted Jason join him in eating at dinner.

"I've dined alone too often, too much, and Esme doesn't like me."

"Oh nonsense, Senator. She's alone with her own problems."

"You will stay for dinner, and don't dissect Esme for me. Cold tittie we used to call women like her."

Jason said he could stay as Sheila had flown out that afternoon to the commune. Libby had developed breathing problems, had turned blue the night before and had only been saved by being held up by the heels over a steaming tub of hot water, the vapors causing the baby to start breathing normally again. Sheila had departed from Dulles, determined to move Laura and Sam and the baby into a decent flat in Vista City and have the baby cared for by specialists.

Champ in a fresh white jacket expressed pride in his cooking. "I was the best cook they ever had at Leavenworth. Fed the hinchy warden and the grunts the best chow they ever ate. I was doing five to ten, the brass thinking I had helped frag some captain in Vietnam."

Austin laughed as they sat down to a table. "The bastard *did* frag an officer's tent. Blew up a body count that sadist General Abrams sent out to goose up the killing of more of the little people. Somebody did roll two hand grenades, pins out, under the captain's bunk. What wine do you have, Champ?"

"One bottle of the good Burgundy. *One* bottle."

Austin seemed to ignore Champ's point that only one bottle would be served. There was a fine Bibb salad, warm with bits of bacon in it. The beef Wellington was really a special dish as Champ had made it. Followed by a hot blueberry pie. Jason managed to get one glass of the wine, and Austin seemed to enjoy being the host.

Over the black coffee in the library, he sat well back in his chair, nodded indulgently at Champ. "Almost like old times at Potomac House. Maybe I've been in some crass stagnation."

"You've been soused to the gills most of the time."

"You sassy buck."

"You can send me back to the slave quarters, Colonel."

When Champ had departed, grinning, carrying off the coffee cups, Jason asked, "Aren't you fearful Champ will frag you, toss a live grenade under your ancestral four-poster?"

"Christ, Jason, don't be ashamed of liking a man. There are relationships between men that women never understood. It's not buggery or going limp-wristed. It's knowing when you have what Ernest called 'black dog has you by the ass.' And there is somebody you can turn to, like Champ who isn't contemptuous of consequences. It's only with rare women you find this combination of friendship *and* reasonableness. No impasse to exchange of ideas, of knowing one human being is out of their shell and you are out of yours, and so what if you're nothing to the damn big empty universe in its infinity. So you're just two specks of dust in real contact."

"Have you known such a woman?"

"One thinks so, once in one's lifetime, I suppose, if lucky. They're rare and they're fine, or they're a pain in the diaphragm."

"I gather you've had such pain, Austin?"

It was the first time Jason had hinted at the mysterious Mona, and also the first time he had called the older man Austin. It had been Senator and Sir, but tonight as they lit up Cuban claros, a box which Champ had set on an antique desk, Jason felt he had penetrated into unknown territory, become closer to this man, one who had once held so much party power; why not admit to an intimacy?

Austin Barraclough seemed to notice neither the indiscreet question nor the dubious familiarity.

He rose, inhaling the cigar. He went to the big French doors that looked over the river. The drapes were pulled back and the night was heavy and seemed pressed down on the earth. There was a white flash, like a crack in an egg, or lightning, and then the bass rumble of thunder like iron balls, Jason thought, rolling down wooden stairs.

"Some of us, Jason, choose a bad conscience, some of us seek a life of patient sweetness. A few exist on the hard periphery of existence because we foolishly feel we have a duty. You ever read La Bruyère?"

"No. I don't think so. I don't read much anymore."

Without turning from the windows, Austin recited, " 'Everything is said, and we come too late.' "

It was the first of many intimate talks. When the mood was on him, Austin Barraclough liked to walk along the banks of the Potomac and talk of whatever was on his mind. With Jason at his side he would point out the nesting places of birds, the pollution of certain areas, and remember the river as it had been in his father's day, and even as recorded by his grandfather in an old journal. Jason tried to come out to Potomac House at least once a week, and when Austin began to attend the Senate, would sometimes drive back with him after a session. It was on the riverbanks behind Potomac House that Jason liked best to listen to the older man, hoping he would hear those things that would make clearer the ways of politics, and remember the rules that seemed to be needed to win any action on the Hill, or at least point a way to assist or lead to a winning point.

Smoking a pipe, wearing a hunting jacket, walking bent over a bit into the breeze of a crisp day, Austin was at his best.

"What do you think, Jason, of yesterday's session?"

"I guessed at some of the motives and who was behind them."

"Don't guess. Study how men relate to each other in the Senate as in everyday life. There are ties and there are affections. It isn't all taking cash or favors from Bread O'Rahilly. No, there are responsibilities to each other, the need of knowing there is order and degrees of authority. Think of the Hill as a social unit, a family. Hell, you can speculate, be skeptical, radical or daring. But also you have to relate to other men, or you're up shit creek and no paddle. Not to be too brave and too foolish, or to say everything you think."

"That I learned as a governor."

"Most beliefs have no meaning if you follow them to the final study, and most convictions of the average politicians lack inner authority; just obeying and delivering. They, we, roam the margin of society, but we should be aware of what has to be done to keep the society in existence, or you'll have something like a goddamn Latin American junta of generals and a batch of church faces taking over, or some African sadist depopulating his nation. Authority best presented keeps a country in order and in respect for itself, ideals; without them, you have no deep ranging social sense. We need loyalties, obligations."

"That goes for parties as well as the country."

Austin stopped to revitalize his pipe with a big brass lighter that shot a spear of orange flame into the bowl. He puffed out a column of smoke. "Both parties are fully corrupt. Look at the men who control the big city votes, the union chiefs, special interests; all work on the average guy on the Hill. Oh, it doesn't have to be money. It can be quiff, as we used to call sex; or power, or glory, or just being invited to the right parties."

"The party-giving, I'm discovering."

"Have you, Jason? We have to have political parties. Should have four, of course. Liberal GOP, Conservative GOP, Liberal Demo, and a Conservative Demo. Just to have a little more honesty in party rule. But it's no go. You can only support your party."

"I wonder sometimes why we do?"

"Because your set of louts and dreamers, grafters and honest men, present a world you grew into and became a part of. Slogans, platforms, promises, add up to nothing much but farting in the face of the voter. The real hard work of politics is using what you have to keep the nation afloat. In spite of ten million endowed loafers in federal service, or the failure of justice, or overtaxing the middle class, the backbone of any nation."

"So?"

"You tell me."

Jason picked up a stone and threw it to go skimming, skipping across the river's surface. "We're taxing them out of their homes by insisting on high value of houses they bought with their savings at lower cost. The insurance companies rip them off by higher rates and, well, the prices they pay for things for no real reason or sense. But can the Hill do anything about it?"

"The Hill does it to them." The older man laughed and puffed on his pipe. "We vote ourselves fancy raises, pensions, don't we? We vote loopholes in taxes, don't we, to favor the buddies of the Pentagon in huge wasteful outlays, overruns?"

"You sound radical, Senator Barraclough."

"No, I sound damn conservative. I read Gibbon. You read Gibbon?"

"Yes, but—"

"Not lately?"

"No."

"His *Decline and Fall* history of the Roman Empire is the story of us today."

"My father said something like that. The bread and circuses of which Gibbon wrote as helping the fall and decline of Rome are our welfare state and television. A bit farfetched, I think."

"Is it? Come on, let's walk faster, it's going to rain."

They got back to Potomac House just as the summer storm broke.

Chapter 18

All the way driving to Georgetown, Jason's mind raced back and forth like the windshield wipers moving in their frantic pattern, pushing back the heavy rain, revealing the landscape now in an aspic of tea-green wetness, a landscape of which he was becoming a part. This was the territory of the main chance, this was the place of power, of wheeling and dealing. Within a radius of fifty miles there existed, in apartments, country estates and rented places, the men who controlled the nation. Gave it its international sound, its coloration.

There was forming in Jason's mind a kind of plan, no, not a plan, he decided, more like a pattern still not fully articulated, but its major design showing some kind of hovering shape of what it could one day be. The way to becoming important was using whatever steps there were at hand. A brilliant mind like Austin's, once brilliant anyway, and still showing from time to time, like today, how great and realistic it had been. Yes, Austin could be such a step. Austin Barraclough; what he could have been but had struck out, as J. Willard had put it. Austin could be studied, really studied, analyzed. For the good of the party . . . Oh yes, are you fooling yourself that is all it is—for the party? The rain had let up some, the roadside was shiny with the washing and the little streams of short lives sailed into runoff channels.

The traffic had not slowed much and it took all his skill to move past a bevy of huge twelve-wheel rigs bringing in crates, sacks; cargoes of food with which to feed the capital.

He could savor the shellfish, soft-shell crabs, lobsters and sea bass from the eastern shore, the suckling pigs and white veal sides, great cadavers of steers in those refrigerated trucks. And up from the South the last of the sweet corn and the pink-hearted melons, the Florida tomatoes, the sacks of wheat and rye flour which would be tomorrow's bread and cakes.

Jason skidded, passing a stainless steel milk or cream carrier, and decided never mind the poetry, the Carl Sandburg visions. Stay alive, man, he thought—stay close to Austin Barraclough. You're doing the old crock a favor keeping him alert and interested. He is likable in his harsh way. Through him you could impress the men who really run the party; the big wide-assed tycoons from the auto world, the big three in Detroit; the suntanned oil and natural gas wheeler-dealers of the Panhandle and the Far West; rigs pumping a hundred million barrels a day. You had to know the secret corners where the political funds came from, cash on the barrelhead, or it was no dice. There were also the city bosses in Boston, Chicago, other metropolitan heartlands that delivered, had delivered the votes when Austin Barraclough called the bosses to Washington before an election.

Yes, in a way he could *become* Austin Barraclough, a kind of copy but with more sense to him, more hard-nosed practical clarity of how one held on to the main chance. And learn by Austin's mistakes. There was something inbred, *too* much inbreeding in the older families like the Barracloughs, that had been too long the eastern establishment in both parties. Saltonstalls, Roosevelts, Rockefellers, Harrisons, Lodges, du Ponts, Mellons, Depews. Could one cozy up to them and watch for an opening, and retain one's integrity?

Jason laughed out loud. Was he really serious? Could he be that way? Could he be so cold-blooded, direct? Follow a plan that some might think of as not fully ethical? Or fair to men who had waited and worked a long time for the big chance, men like Paul Ormsbee? In politics as in baseball, coming in second didn't mean much. With Sheila gone, staying on with Laura over some baby problems that had developed, he'd be free to go on the town more, and observe—play it all by a sense of touch. Test just how far he could go with the pattern now half formed in his mind since leaving Potomac House.

He skidded the car, moving around a load of chicken crates animated by a thousand inmates under canvas. He felt his right rear fender just touch and bounce off the cargo of white Leghorns. He yelled out loud, "Watch it!" All this daffy fantasy could end here with a busted neck!

Jason brooded for the next three days. He knew from his years of running for office back home, achieving governorship, that the voters had almost nothing to do with the selection of candidates who could run for public office with any chance of winning an election. Even the tenacious primaries, which had become so important, were manipulated as to who would be presented with enough clout and cash to make an impression. Ignored as rivals were the overimpetuous and the radical fringe of vegetarians, anti-alcoholists and other fanatics; crotchety casual debris, obstreperous, but mostly incomprehensible to the republic's progress.

Now both parties were preparing for their next national conventions, and Jason found himself the man who was to promote the hopes of the western groups behind Paul Ormsbee.

It was conspiratorial up to a point, and he had to proceed with exemplary patience, work out adjustments and compensations. He was vulnerable to irony, and had to rise above malicious gossip. He did his work well and was told little scabrous secrets of all other candidates and offered ignoble expediencies. He was aware that the final calculated risk on Paul Ormsbee as the man to bring to the convention with enough delegates to nominate, would be made at a meeting of about twenty men who were the party's leaders.

Not in a smoke-filled room, not with any cynical collection of men unconscious of their responsibilities, but by hard-nut politicians, battle-scarred individuals in the enviable position of having the friendship of the various corporations, unions, banking interests, and the backing of those who produced the huge arsenals of weapons, planes, machines that were exported for sale to most any nation with the price to pay for them. The party, *both* parties, were nourished from feeding tubes inserted into the giant corporations.

And all the time Jason was aware of the power of the old man, Judge Amos Fowler, still behind a great deal of the party's political jockeying, dominating certain meetings. Not that even his presence was needed—he having at his call so many of the men on the Hill. There were legends of what Amos Fowler had been in his youth and at his maturity as a party mover and doer—when he had been a federal judge, and for some short period of time head of the Justice Department. Those unaware of still active interests now felt him part of a historic past, no longer vital or powerful. Not so, Jason decided.

Jason felt the man seemed to be often at important meetings, sliding in, smiling, bright-eyed, searching out faces, and he was still spoken of by some of the older members of the House and the Senate Chamber with respect and regard for his skills in reconciling differences. Jason found it rather surprising that Austin Barraclough had once been one of his young followers, his bright stars. But if Jason mentioned Judge Fowler's name, Austin brushed it off with distaste, even disdain. Jason decided not to inquire further as to why the two men had parted in an unfriendly manner. He came around to acting coolly, but not disrespectfully to Amos Fowler when they met. "Never make enemies unless you have something to gain by it," was J. Willard's philosophy.

Meanwhile, Jason studied in more detail how funds were gotten by the party from the men who controlled gas and oil combines. He noted the aid from the multi-billion-dollar drug industries in a nation of pill and laxative takers. Party chairman asserted it was still possible to get campaign funds from them, as from the milk co-ops, grain growers, beef raisers, fruit canners, all of whom laid it on the line in ways *perhaps* legal.

For the time being there were seemingly casual meetings of Jason with Laramie Scudder, the party boss down from New York, Senator Dudley Giron, the Cajun from Louisiana, Congresswoman Shirley Lippman, publisher James Jerome, "Big Jim" Houston of the Washington law firm of Wollen, Leadbeater, Huston & Starkweather, the "legal eagle" of the party, and India Kingston, public relations adviser to three presidents, aging but still sharp, with a pipeline into the editorial rooms of the great newspapers ("what is left of them"): The *New York Times*, The *Washington Post*, two big circulation rags in Chicago, the *Denver Post*, the L.A. *Times*.

From time to time Jason would find others at the party movers' informal gatherings at his house, or at some private club. He spent a weekend with Sheila at a country estate on Chesapeake Bay, again at Hawleytown on the eastern shore. Here was Val Engelberger, who perhaps spoke for "the Jewish bloc"—at least he knew the inner circle of Warburgs, Pedlocks, Strausses and Guggenheims—aided by Senator Joel Silverthorn, who could collect campaign funds as long as the Pentagon supported the democracy of Israel.

His notes filled with names like Senator Roland Redmond, Congressman Cheu Chin Lee of Hawaii (which called for large blondes and the best Scotch), banker Asa Clement from Security-Starkweather Bank and Trust, the second largest bank on Wall Street. Also Sarah Pearl Adams, head of Adams, Faust & Dobbin's, the most talked-of Madison Avenue advertising agency. Pearl was black and comely, and Harlem-raised. Who could forget her television commercials that addicted the nation to Seltzotak limericks with a comic actor reciting the entire text in belches and burps? The agency had been able to defeat the other party's major candidate once, creating him in shadowy images as a bleeding heart, a fuddy-duddy, a failed umbrella-maker, and as favoring the destruction of one giant industry because it caused cancer in mice, "so abolishing the jobs of twenty-two thousand workers, *all* members of the WDU."

Pearl had twice been given the advertising award of the year, The Moving Finger, for her brilliant texts.

Jason found Pearl bright, neurotic, skillfully dressed to hide her too skinny legs, yet a figure of chic and sophistication with a heavy chignon of teased hair.

Esme Lowell didn't like Pearl Adams. "I admit, Jason, it's only partly because she is smarter than I am, and she's a beauty with that new nose, and those goddamn great Nina Ricci clothes. *Um!*"

"She's studying Paul."

"Maybe she can get him to do a Seltzotak commercial?"

They were seated on the terrace of Potomac House. Jason was hoping Austin Barraclough could be talked into attending some of the sessions preparing for the convention. It was one of those clear pleasant days, rather rare in the early fall, and the green was already turning into tobacco-brown in certain parts of the river bank. There had been reports of Canadian geese and V formations of wild ducks moving south, but it was too early for any great migration. Washington offices still had their air conditioning on; the humidity was often unbearable without it. The flood of tourists had fallen off, as had the tacky school kids led by banner-bearing guides, the busloads of blacks coming to visit the homes of heroes of the past with names like Douglass and Scott. Muggings were down, but data showed they would pick up by Thanksgiving.

The group trying to recover the city from the control of Congress was again presenting petitions, holding meetings, aware they'd get nowhere. Minor student groups—very few compared to the great marches of the early 1970—were badgering the police, but most had departed with their backpacks, sleeping bags, beads and beards. "The last of the true idealists," wrote a columnist. There were pickets around the White House protesting the FBI, the CIA and the Indian massacres at Wounded Knee (nineteenth *and* twentieth centuries). One man had chained himself to a White House railing, but was in the city jail for spitting on an undercover agent. Another individual, Jason read in the *Post*, had climbed the White House fence with a petition to pardon the Watergate criminals still out on appeal; he had been shot in the ass, and was set (he claimed) to tour the John Birch locals as a speaker.

Jason wondered if life in Washington was a comedy or a tragedy. It was all, Esme said, how one stood to the angle of vision.

Austin Barraclough came out on the terrace wearing a planter's straw hat. He was smoking a pipe, or rather trying to keep it alight wth a flaming kitchen match. He was supposed to be drinking only wine. He looked over the river below the terrace.

"The dying season, the maple leaf turns red. Now the damn Greeks, they gave the fall a reality with their legend. We just prepare to put antifreeze in the car."

Esme crossed her legs and nodded indulgently, looking at her uncle closely. "How goes it, Uncle Austin?"

"Take that imbecile smile off your face. I'm self-sufficient, if you must know. Well Jason, how moves the kingmaking?"

"It goes, but who's to know for sure which way?"

The older man sat down, gave up on the pipe and laid it aside. "Too early, much too early. A year and a half, isn't it, before the convention? Self-indulgence by the fat cats. Could be heading for a fiasco."

"That's why, Senator, we'd like to have you at some of the meetings. Well, not meetings, just talking things over."

"They don't want a busted crock like me. Besides, I don't feel up to the talk and arm waving and sandbagging. Anyway, it's still all superficial. I'm a burst pistol to them."

Esme stood up and seemed to reform herself into her clothes. It was a gesture Jason had noticed on most attractive women, but Esme had a way of doing it all her own, a ballet-like movement that seemed to adjust undergarments, take care of the breast areas and place the legs properly in position for walking.

"You don't try, you just don't try. Hell, you're the party's *chef de protocole*, or should be, when they talk of the next national candidate."

Austin was amused, slapped a thigh in glee. "You think me psychopathic, say it, girl—I'm not conscious of my responsibility? Well, I just want to grow moss, be a ruin. It's in a way an enviable position, I feel, to observe and not be part of anything. Yes, I remain unsympathetic and free of treacherous dealing." He was trying to light the pipe again, and did puff it into life. "Jason, you understand more than most. I hope you never come to thinking privacy ludicrous. Anyway [puff, puff on the pipe] there is truth and there is justice and others fight for it, for me, them. And [puff, puff] I don't object to Paul Ormsbee, but maybe like me he's been too long in harness; the horse *can* feel the excitement of pulling the cart has gone . . ."

They left him there, striking matches from a batch he had in a jacket pocket, an incipient tremor of his head. Esme said to Jason on the front steps, "He's full of the grape today. Sorry we couldn't get him to come to a meeting. But maybe in this shape it's all to the good."

"I had hoped he was improving. If I could get to the core of his—"

"Don't meddle. Maybe some day you'll get a hint of something."

Jason as a politician had to get along well with men, but he was at his best with women. Not sexually; he had been loyal (faithful?) to Sheila, with but some few lapses while out gathering votes and an affair of two weeks with a woman author who wrote books about old historic houses, ghost towns and old tombstones. But it had amounted to merely an interest in a woman who turned out to be very neurotic and wept after lovemaking and called him her "uncouth Lincoln."

He enjoyed talking to Clair, who told him she was delighted with Washington and partied with a set of rather wild young people in civil service who owned Hondas, danced in Virginia and Maryland dives weekends or went on country picnics, swam in mountain lakes. Clair was brisk, bright and had changed her shade of lipstick, wore more padded bras. He sensed she'd marry some government department head, even a young congressman, in a year or two. Miss Munday—she had a sister who worked in the American Embassy in Rome, read Henry James and Simenon, knew a lot of the town gossip, the past histories of certain key figures. She was rather shy of men and rarely went out with them unless interested in causes. Her little VW had a bumper sticker: *I Brake for Animals.*

Jason was a man at ease with women; the dreadful Snow Williams would call him and he'd chat pleasantly for ten to twenty minutes and she'd end up asking for information on some topic she was going to discuss on her noon broadcast. ("Like to get things wight.")

His relationship with Esme Lowell gave him some sense of belonging to the scene. She was the niece of Austin Barraclough, she had the opaque surface of a woman who had been through hard times and carried her tall, slim body with grace; didn't stoop or wear ballet slippers as if ashamed of her height. He took her to lunch twice a week—she asking how Uncle Austin was progressing.

"I try, Jason, not to see him too often. A crusty old bastard, my uncle, with an old-fashioned romantic thorn stuck in his heart."

"Fill me in. To me he's as romantic as a bear trap."

"That's the remains of the public facade."

They were standing by the plush rope of the Red Hen, it was noon and the place was crowded. Esme signalled Henri over with a gesture of one index finger. "Don't go shaking your head, Henri. Give us a good table and not one where you hide the tourists who order sandwiches . . . Yes, *that* will do, and get us Waldo, to start us off with two *very* dry Martinis. The senator prefers Beefeater . . . Damn maître d's in this town act like Herr Doktor Kissinger did when his katzenjammer face was directing traffic in this town . . . So you're a grandfather? Well, I suppose in ten, twelve years, I'll be explaining the pill to Bianca. She's in school, Miss Clapterris's in Charleston. Wouldn't raise a kid in Washington . . . You and Uncle Austin really think the party has a chance in the next national election? . . . Waldo dear, this martini isn't cold enough or dry enough. Tell Andre *not* from the bottle of the already mixed. And whomp us up a batch from the vermouth up . . . Wait, I'll order . . . the broiled short ribs good today? Eh, Jason? Short ribs it is, a tossed salad, blue cheese dressing . . . Black coffee for me, you too? . . . You're getting talked about. Saw you on the ABC show with that million-dollar babe; always looks as if she dared you to pinch her ass while on the air. You really believe the Chinese see a war with the Soviets? . . . Ah, much better, Waldo . . . God, I love to eat. When I came back from Europe I felt America was killing itself with that dreadful white bread and fried chicken . . . Listen, I agree Uncle Austin has these periods when he makes great sense. He wants to train you, steer you right. You're a dreadful yokel, you know, Jason. You still do things, say things, the way they do them in the tall timber where you come from."

He liked to listen to her while they enjoyed their food. They were both good feeders, and they had the second Beefeaters. She made hard sense and he felt there was something vital and perhaps cruel beneath the glassy surface. She had no respect for authority, for the power brokers, the kingpin lobbyists. She felt the nation would survive and very little would change but the slogans, the budgets, the senators and congressmen getting into trouble with women. She believed survival was all. In her handsomeness, her skill of dressing to suggest good taste and yet a daring use of design and material, she seemed to Jason a kind of woman that he had never in his pre-Washington life suspected existed.

At times he wondered whom she was sleeping with; she looked damn well taken care of. But he had no deep desire to probe her emotional and physical life. She was the kind of woman, too direct, too worldly, that would naturally frighten him away from any intimacy. So very much the clever female, not inspiring any move on his part, for all her looking such a ready woman.

Yes, he was a rube, and he had ideals, and visions that were backwoodsy, tall timber, country lane stuff; trout wriggling against a pebbled bottom, a sudden explosion of wild flowers. But damn it, he was also an ex-governor, a man gaining a place for himself. Yet somehow Esme Lowell still treated him like a Gary Cooper kicking a ball of horseshit on Main Street with his boot tip, while playing shy with the new schoolmarm.

Jason valued her most as a sort of hoped-for pipeline into the secret life of Austin Barraclough; he hoped someday she would begin to talk of what had destroyed the man. Jason felt himself truly to be a decent man, with values, a code of conduct; he didn't feel he was using Esme. Yes, true, there were times when he wondered how far he would go in using people to advance himself. At such times he'd think: I'm like most people. All people, he felt, who had done some shameful things—things that could be called dishonorable. Nothing world-shaking, of course, but little items, petty events, scenes that left no remorse, but did at times produce regret.

He enjoyed the lunch at the Red Hen. They ate the short ribs with relish, avoided the mounds of mashed potatoes (both being "sensible eaters"), waved off the idea of a third Beefeater. They talked seriously about an international Arab terrorist problem the State Department had muffed, the latest exposure of the skulduggery of the FBI and CIA, and of Paul Ormsbee as the party's best hope for possessing the White House.

"Of course, Jay, some barefooted flannelmouth can come out of the bayous, or riding a Western saddle, rattling his spurs and spoiling the party's hopes. The great innocent lemmings, the voters, could fall en masse for the sweet talk of some political Billy Graham or Elton John who promises to castrate Washington and serve up the balls as mountain oysters to the simple folk in the boondocks . . . More coffee? Waldo . . . and the check for the senator . . . Got to run. I'm showing the Soviet commercial attaché a house by Burning Creek. They live real high, these lovers of the workers. House must have a pool, bidet, hi-fi, Roman bath. Jesu, I think of Lenin and Trotsky in their Salvation Army hand-out suits and plumber's caps, and see the swank of the ruling class today in Russia with their three-thousand-dollar Swiss watches and Bond Street shoes, and wonder why any guy in the streets doesn't start a revolution? . . . Yes, yes, Sheila called and I'll come to dinner Friday night. Not that I care for Courtney Wunder as a dinner partner, he's even to the right of Bill Buckley and Butch Goldwasser. Yes, I know, the Immerton-Welsh Power Bill needs every vote, you're wising up. 'Eat with the devil but use a long spoon,' Uncle Austin used to say . . . Lunch Tuesday? If I'm free. In exchange I want you to appear at some historic festival to save some wreck of a house at Harpers Ferry. I know these ruins are nostalgia crap . . . Yes, sorry you're having trouble with your own place, but it's Georgetown, Buster, and any time you want to sell it, I'll get you more, lots more loot than you paid. Well, true, repairs are running high, but hold on for another year or so. Look, if something happens to Paul Ormsbee's chances, I'll help you and Sheila refurnish the White House. Don't laugh, Uncle Austin said he'd have given you a thousand to one the stumbler wouldn't have ever made it to sleeping in Lincoln's bed from his record and . . . Waldo, I know my wreck of a car is being hidden from view, have the parking man get it out front . . . *Bye.*"

And Esme was gone, moving with that grace and speed, waving to someone, shaking a hand with a smile at someone else—an operator. He still felt the pressure of her gloved hand as she had risen and touched him, the whiff of that faint scent of hers, a garden flower perfume and a suggestion of healthy body sweat. He signed for the meal as Waldo returned his credit card. Esme was a bit of too much; smart, witty and, he supposed, to some men very desirable. Somehow he couldn't see himself in her bed, that long body with the rather prominent breasts exposed. A game of images he had played with most desirable women—as most men do.

"I've added the tip to the total, Waldo."

"Thank you, Senator. Have a good day."

"You, too, Waldo."

Miss Munday had several telegrams waiting for him to answer, and Clair produced a secret report on the WDU. A senatorial committee was investigating (again?) union fund frauds. The committee was having trouble with the Justice Department, getting certain union leaders to appear before the committee. Who in Justice was covering for the unions?

"Good lunch?" asked Clair.

He said not bad and called the Number Three man he knew at Justice.

BOOK IV

Temptation
and Concupiscence

Chapter 19

J. Willard arrived in Washington, looking to Jason much older; yet he had seen his father just a few months before. But he seemed as chipper as ever, no signs of lassitude or fatigue and, as usual, not too sure there were too many people to trust in Washington. "Not too many I'd trust with a female dog in heat. Well, Senator, you run a nice set of offices."

They were seated in Jason's private office, which was taking on more the character of things personal to Jason. Some children's paintings, the result of a contest in the Vista County's school system; theme, "My State." A stuffed mallard had been sent in by the oldest man in Pioneer County. Over the bookcases hung a map of the state made entirely of wheat, beans and corn seeds—shown at the last Farm Fair. Jason himself was represented by a set of golf clubs, files of the *Congressional Record*, various government publications, a wall of photographs of various people—notorious, famous or related.

"Yes," said J. Willard, reclining in an overstuffed chair. "Nice; no goddamn modern art, like a sixteen-foot stuffed enema bag or a crumpled auto fender; that's the Emperor's New Clothes crap the Vista City Museum shows. You want a moose head? I have one in the attic."

"No thanks, Pop. I've got enough junk. You're staying with us at the house, a 'genuine' falling-apart Colonial."

"Not on your tintype. Buster and Bascom Rice are due in tomorrow and we're staying in town. Going to do a little elbow bending, town painting and get together a quorum to solidly set Paul Ormsbee for the next national nomination. Anyway, test the way the foul eastern wind blows."

"You think Paul can get the presidential nomination? Isn't it too early to start the thing?"

"Hit the bell early and hit it hard." J. Willard got up from his chair and wandered over to the bookcases. "You can't start too early." He picked up the ticking alarm clock. "Hell, haven't seen one of these big tin babies since I was bucking barley in my youth in the Red River country. Yep, this is Paul's last chance, maybe he is too old as it is. You like him, don't you?"

"Of course I do. A wise old bird. And he'd make a good president."

Jason's father smiled and cocked his head to one side, "Good, *not* a great one, eh?"

"Good is better than most we've been getting."

"You ever think of yourself, Jayboy?"

"What kid doesn't?"

"Alright, in a year or so we push Paul for the nomination—and four years later Jason Crockett—if you don't fall on your face or get caught buggering a Chinaman in a YMCA locker room."

Jason studied his father's expression. It had been lightly said, but there was a serious look in the old boy's eyes. Pop was in one of his special moods, what some called "Ol' J. W.'s hand in the jam jar," others just "shit-his-pants." Jason stood up, took the alarm clock from his father's hand. "Things move fast these days. And if Paul makes it, he'd do eight years of getting his mail at the White House."

"Damn it, Jay, you'd only be fifty-two even then."

Jason put the clock carefully back in its place on top of the bookcase. "Where are all the really great men for public office? The Jeffersons, the Lincolns we used to produce?"

"I'm tired of *that* cockeyed song. The remark is a cop-out. They weren't treated as great men when they were alive or ran for office. Abe was called an ape, Jefferson crazy for black quiff. And we've had some great, or near great, men in our own time. I always thought Barraclough could have been up there with FDR as to class and political savvy."

"Maybe so."

"You're chummy with him, I gather from your letters."

"I'm learning a lot from him. But he's, well—"

"We know, he hasn't a snowball's chance in July, no more."

"I want you to meet him."

"Happy to. Once I settle in with Buster and Bascom. There is no committee, not official anyway in Washington. We're here to put muscle into any plans there may be for Paul. We represent a good solid block of western clout with money behind us from the right places. Your old buddy, Wallace Klamath, is playing host for a couple of nights. Top man in the National WDU; he heads it now, doesn't he? Has a suite in the new WDU buildings. Runs the whole megilla, I hear, with a real kick in each fist."

"He's the same bastard he always was, and he's still thick with shady people."

"Just remember, Son, labor has the country by the balls, it's their turn. Twenty million members in the WDU, and a war chest as big as General Motors or Exxon. Paul will need Wally, the party too, him and his boys."

"Austin doesn't think labor, a solid union labor bloc, the asset it used to be."

"Don't you believe it, Jayboy. We may say we play down the blacks and union voters, the Catholics, Hebes, the WASPs, but enough of them *are* groups worth going after. Paul never offended any of them. Goddamit, he's eaten more chitlins, watermelon, knishes and bagels, tacos, tortillas, turnip tops and pot likker, rice and red beans, egg roll, than any man his size and girth. You have to have a brass stomach besides a set of good teeth that look great on television, these days, to run for office . . . be seeing you."

Jason sat at his desk after his father had left, promising to show for dinner in Georgetown. J. Willard, he decided, was still the role player, the character actor; the wise rube, the sly backwoods party worker; at least to the eastern establishment, the Washington mucka-mucks. National columnists, when they were in need of a subject, described the J. Willard Crockett type of political state chairman boss as passé; like hell. The chairmen might ride in air-conditioned Caddies now and not chew tobacco, or drop their *g* endings, but the party was solidly serviced by the county chairman, the city boss, the state's powerhouse. The backwoods delegate, the woman on the make, the lawyer who helped his practice by being chairman—all made votes. Also the boys who cozied up to the lobbyists from the oil, airplane, lumber, co-op setups, and who handed you fifty to a hundred thousand in bills in brown paper bags, were vital links even if they didn't want anything but "a little friendship."

J. Willard was a good man, a decent man, more so than some.

There were many like him in politics who felt the party was best for the nation, and who didn't skim anything off the top for themselves. Such men, if they knew where the smell was bad and who made it, retained the philosophy "You can't cross a meadow and not come across cow shit."

Perhaps there weren't as many like J. Willard around as there used to be. More of the slick young men from Harvard Law, the early refugees' children who were professors in the Ivy League schools or serving the big foundations. Also coming forward were the shaved and housebroken Texans who no longer wore the Stetson and the two-hundred-dollar boots. Perhaps the media were responsible; the TV announcers and newscasters turned stars, seers, messiahs of journalism, replacing the older newspapermen who could drink raw whiskey without ice, didn't label a whore a call girl. Perhaps Pop belonged with the past, like a derby—or did he?

Jason called Sheila and told her to be sure the table was set with the linen napkins, the old man didn't like paper ones at supper; he still called the noonday meal *dinner*, as they had done when he was a boy.

Sheila said she'd have a couple of lobsters, even at $14 a pound. Jason said not to tell Pop the cost of *anything* in Washington, he would yell bloody murder; the country was going to hell in a hack, and he would repeat how he used to peddle cooked lobster along the West Coast waterfront at 20¢ a pound when he was young.

That was one thing J. Willard did that riled some people. His habit of relating how hard people really worked when he was a young rip— how they accepted hardships as part of learning of life, and how 20¢-a-pound sweet country butter, a half-dollar chicken tasted better than the damn chemically fed nitrate-loaded stuff they put in their gut today. "Hell, there isn't a tasty old-fashioned tomato grown anymore for public sale. Where are those big red beef tomatoes? No, it's all those tasteless little hard things that are picked by a machine invented by some endowed loafer at a cow college; stuff tastes like chewing caterpillars."

Maybe, Jason thought, J. Willard, Buster and Bascom Rice and all the western people would find out they didn't fit into the way the party now put forward a candidate, someone to build up for the next national convention. The alarm clock's loud ticking seemed to sound skeptical in its steady separating of time into second by second by second.

The meeting of those of the party's top people who were inclined for Paul Ormsbee to head the national ticket was to be on the yacht *Seastar,* anchored on the Potomac off Fowler Landing past Fort Belvoir. "To run a man for the presidency," as Judge Fowler put it, "you have to get him the nomination. And that's no slouch of a horse to ride."

Judge Amos Fowler still held the title of the party's Wise Old Man, or as some of the opposition called him, "that venomous, foxy sonofabitch." He was eighty-two, small and thin, mischievous, with a prognathous jaw, a wise ferret-shaped face, a head of heavy white hair, and moved with a kind of skipping grace that belied his years. He had been a famous lawyer in his youth, defending corporations (and also citizens against insurance companies), had been a U.S. Senator, head of the Justice Department during an ill-fated crisis in the party, where the audacity of his cynical wit served him well. He had written the Fowler-Resnick amendment to the States Rights Utility Bill, and been involved at seventy-two in a paternity case, which he found, as he told the reporters, "Very flattering but, alas, impossible; moral indignation is a waste of time."

For the meeting on the yacht there would be J. Willard, Buster Miller, Jason, Tom Pedlock, Senator Redmond, Sam Montjoy of Worldwide Motors, Tony Gucca of the WDU. As Judge Fowler suspected the CIA, the FBI and certain agents of perhaps bugging his house, he had suggested the meeting be held on the boat. "Besides," he had told Jason, "I like things done on water. I have fornicated on six of the seven seas. You feel the world under you like a mattress. It's going to be a great night for a cruise."

Everyone had arrived by nine o'clock of a starry night, the moon in a net of clouds. First there were drinks at the Fowler mansion, in the oak-lined library under framed engravings from Audubon's *Birds of America.*

Jason was impressed by the Fowler mansion. It stood easy and old on its gardened acres on the river; too much house, tradition and antiques for one man. Judge Amos Fowler had inherited more than house, acres, stocks, bonds, and a few boards-of-directors seatings. He had only to look at the paintings of his ancestors, the solid merchants in blue-and-gold Continental uniform in which they had fought the American Revolution. There was a model under glass, Jason saw, of *Seastar*, the yacht his father had built. On blue-grass meadows were the descendants of the trotting horse that his grandfather had raced into the first mile under 2.17. There were the branched chandeliers that the British had fired at in the War of 1812 on their way to burn Washington. And Civil War portraits and World War I plane models.

Jason knew that the Fowlers, full of toughness and with little compassion, had come to the Virginias soon after Jamestown. Younger sons with no fortunes and with a hunger, they were not real to their descendants—even in their blackened portraits. They became cotton and tobacco growers with an eye for the right chance, spread out to planters' clubs, the House of Burgesses, horse races and cockfights. They achieved a respectability and a dignity by virtue of their money. They lost their wealth, until they were nothing but cold pride and a seedy gentry. But they were still very much respected, and in time were rich again.

They married French-Flemish stock crossed with Scottish and late Colonial blood. They were important and remained so. Some were readers of Plutarch, members of the imported Anglican Church mixed with solid Scottish-Irish Presbyterianism. A few had the Presbyterian belief in predestination. Yet none wanted the presidency. It puzzled Jason. Vestrymen, church wardens, a hardworking aristocracy, unlike the Tidewater grandees of the Rappahannock and the James. They had a keen taste for business. Ships, tea importing, grain, cotton exports. Timber, pitch, Jamaica sugar for rum, indigo for dyes; and they always had a good head for figures. By the time of Judge Fowler's father, their incomes had been converted mostly into stock issues and bonds. The old account books could be put away and the weighing scales sent to a dismal fraud of a museum-converted Williamsburg.

"My grandfather," Judge Fowler said, "suspected the twentieth century would smell bad. He backed Douglas against Lincoln, yet was for the Union—disliked the southern hotheads—served as Cleveland's Secretary of State. I remember my father sitting in front of his ivy-covered brick columns with his law degree from Harvard and an ancestral cherry-wood cradle in the attic; not a happy man. There was talk of a youthful love affair gone sour, of my mother dying young when I was ten. He attended balls and cotillions and always carried a thousand dollars in gold when he traveled. He was fully aware of his responsibilities. While the planters and the wild Virginians and crossroads squires drank away their estates and broke their necks on frisky horses taking impossible jumps, my father planted fruit trees, trimmed the hemlock hedges, set out chrysanthemums, improved the dairy herds, cut timber, smoked an H. Upmann cigar and went every other year to Europe. Where he spent a lot of time doing what he called 'scraping off the bad taste growing stronger in America.' He was vice-president of the Panhandle Southern and Great Gulf Railroad, and a friend of Henry Adams, Mark Hanna, John Singer Sargent, Thomas Huxley and a lot of expensive and disrespectable women in Paris, London and Rome. He expected me to fill the place with children. No luck, Jason, my wives were barren. Well, when I'm gone it will become a public park."

J. Willard smiled at the gathering and sipped his drink of Tennessee mash. He had always, for all his distrust, secretly admired the eastern men who had so much power in the party, and now it looked as if they would back a man far to the west of here. Should he trust the felicity of Judge Fowler's expression?

Tom Pedlock was sipping soda water. He said to J. Willard, "I like your son. He's a doer."

"Always was. And he'll help Paul Ormsbee carry the Northwest, the coast. Why isn't Paul here? And Senator Silverthorn?"

The young man smiled, shrugged: "Judge Fowler thought we could talk more freely if we didn't have to soft-pedal anything. Something anyone could bring up against him. And I'm the token Jew here tonight."

"Bullshit," said J. Willard. "Jews are *in*—like Lennie Bernstein."

Senator Redmond held up a glass of Scotch and waved it in the direction of their host. The judge was wearing a blue jacket with gold buttons, suggesting a ship's officer. "We'll have one more round," the judge said. "Then to ship, and a cruise down the river. Ever see St. Catherine's Island in moonlight?"

Sam Montjoy, 265 pounds of Detroit auto power, set down his glass of sherry. "A calm night and no wind."

Jason was surprised to see Esme Lowell enter the room, dressed in a dark-blue knit suit. "Sorry, Amos. Traffic."

"Not at all, my dear girl." Judge Fowler kissed her cheek, giving a proper hardy smack and just a touch of her rump. "Gentlemen,

Miss Lowell is the niece of Austin Barraclough, and represents him. She's a damn good sailor too."

Jason said, "How is your uncle?"

"Feeling pretty good. But he said he'd be damned if he'd go out just to see a lot of nasty lecherous men get sloshed on an old boat."

"Never mind," said Senator Redmond. "He's keeping an eye on us, I can see that. He's for Paul, isn't he?"

"Didn't say—just said he's showing an interest in whom the party thinks it can elect. For God's sakes, somebody give me a drink."

They left the house, crossed a sweep of lawn, great trees hovering over the fringes of the estate. They walked in scattered groups, the night balmy, a dog barking someplace, the river laid out ahead beyond a gentle slope. Jason and Esme walked hand in hand, a faint breeze coming up from Maryland Point. Their shoes made crunching sounds when they felt their way near the pier. At the end of it the yacht seemed attached by cobwebs; it stirred, Jason thought, as if wondering why it was not moving. There was activity aboard, sound of engines below and some smoke from the racked funnel. A Chinese steward or sailor at the open section of railing bowed to greet the party.

The judge had produced a yachting cap with some faded gold braid on it, and he cocked it over his alert features as he took the salute of the man waiting for them, and called him Charlie.

"Charlie, chop chop, have Captain Ames cast off."

Jason helped Esme over the cork and brass plank that led to the yacht's deck.

"She's a beauty," Esme said, "a real beaut."

The bearded captain appeared, nodded, didn't speak and disappeared.

The lights from across the river on the Chesapeake and Ohio Canal burned in the background of the night. Across a bridge cars were moving with timidity, one after the other, their headlights spying through a fog rising in ribbons from the river.

The yacht was 147 feet at the water line. She was painted white, contained much polished brass and was 261 gross tons, according to Lloyd's, Judge Fowler told them. She was pretty to look at, all white and golden shine and teakwood doors and walnut panels, with leaded glass casements and yellow deck and a row of oak and canvas lifeboats swinging on their davits, with bare booms and natty rigging; all in order.

Two sailors cast off and the party stood on deck as the yacht moved from the shore, or as Esme suggested, "Did the shore just move away?"

Chapter 20

The cruise downriver was remembered by Jason with a sense of unreality as they passed Mason's Neck, the night smelling of shore grass and marsh, of crops; the river ripples all silver coins as the yacht moved down the Potomac under a veiled moon. Esme and J. Willard were telling each other boating jokes under the lee of the chart house. Charlie the bar boy passing with trays of drinks and some kind of food on small crackers; pungent, cheesy stuff Jason found it, touched with curry and some exotic spice he couldn't name. He also felt the metaphysics of night change—a dark world over water. Later, after they passed Pope's Creek, Senator Redmond took over in the big red and gold cabin, Judge Fowler standing by him, swaying on his feet as if he had his sea legs and the river was stormy, which it was not.

Jason remembered some of the remarks of Senator Redmond: ". . . with this we want to elect a good man, a man who can please the people and can collect the wherewithal to run. This is no public meeting so we can all speak our minds. Now I like Paul Ormsbee as a great guy, as a politico: gutsy, wise, but I want to hear from the rest of you in order, or out of order. So speak up. We want to go on. This group and what it represents, anyway, is for Paul. But the floor, gents and lady, is yours. Or is it called a deck, Amos?"

Montjoy, large, lardy, wide, moonfaced, very intelligent, chairman of the board of the largest, or nearly the largest, corporation in the world, made a wry grimace by reforming his face, aided by a set of flexed lips. "Industry, and I think I can speak for a lot of it; steel, glass, etcetera, isn't going to put its ass in a sling again, pardon me, Miss Lowell, as it did with that bum from California. We were blackmailed for funds and did nasty things. We were over a barrel, threatened with investigations, trust busting, tax investigation. It was pure paranoia. I guess you know how anyone at 1600 Pennsylvania can tighten the screws. But let me say this, we like Paul Ormsbee, and we'll do what can be done legally, by the right people. As this isn't an official meeting, just a talkfest, eh Judge? I'll leave it at this; for all of the party's ramifications, Paul doesn't rile industry."

Judge Fowler smiled. "And will not. There will be no inconstancies. As you say, he doesn't rile industry."

Tom Pedlock asked, "And labor?"

Tony Gucca rubbed his chin, still showing at forty-two some old acne scars. Tony was second-generation stock; out of Wharton School of Business, held a degree in industrial management from Cornell, and had been cleared of any Mafia connections when he headed the Seafishers and Dockers Union in New England. He abhorred violence and had a flair for working liaisons.

"I'm sure you are all aware that organized labor is just as interested as anyone in supporting a man who sees to both sides of American well-being and full production—both by boards of directors and the rank and file. We need a man with sympathy for all our dilemmas. I can say that the WDU and the Seafishers and Dockers Union have locals that understand who their friends are and who their foes are. Of course, unlike other unions, we don't twist the arms of our locals. *But* they listen, listen good, and we are holding friendship meetings since joining with Wally Klamath and the WDU upper ranks here in Washington for a united front against cheap imports of foods and products, and a need for a greater freedom of exporting our surpluses."

J. Willard said, "Wally is one of our own state-raised boys. He has backed Paul with his union locals all along the line."

Tony nodded and looked reflectively at Esme's legs. She was seated deep in an easy chair, mouthing an unlit cigarette. "Yes, well, it will depend on the outcome of the pension funds investigations. And," he added, "how the fink right-to-work bill, the newest gimmick, the Weston-Bronkin No. 564-A, gets bounced out. I'll say more about our pledges when things get moving."

Esme tried to pull down her skirt a bit more. Jason stood up. "Tony, of course Paul Ormsbee is a man that the workingman has always had faith in. All we hope, all I hope, speaking only for myself, is that the unions keep their bookkeeping a bit better. Right now I'm against the Weston-Bronkin bill, and will continue to be. But because I dislike it—not as a favor."

"Now, Senator, sometimes you press us working stiffs a little hard. Wally Klamath doesn't say bad things about you, but he doesn't smile either when he talks about you."

"We have known each other for a long time. There is no subtle psychology between Wally and myself. We manage."

Tom Pedlock went into a long talk, speaking while examining bits of paper with figures on them. It was about the cold cash, the tenacious techniques it would take to gain funds to run Paul through major primaries; what large funds would be needed for television, radio spots, what could be spent on printing. "And the cost of certain items such as gatherings of cheering crowds, meetings at airports, flags for little children to wave, and the taking of certain professional trend polls from time to time to see how the wind blows."

Judge Fowler adjusted his yachting cap. "I don't really trust polls; they are damn costly, and the organizations that run them hedge like hell. But we must have them, I suppose."

J. Willard looked through a porthole off toward the shoreline. "How much would we need, Tom, to get Paul off to the races?"

"Twenty million."

Esme said, "To start."

The meeting began to go off into tangents, fantasies. Senator Redmond brought up hard facts from the past, and certain stories were repeated of the snafus of the last ten presidential runnings—some old, some new, some not at all true. J. Willard, Esme and Jason went up on deck. They were passing Mattox Creek, the yacht moving at a slow pace past clusters of trees, past a yacht club strung with yellow and pink lights. The notes of Noel Coward's "Someday I'll Find You" came low and insinuatingly across the water, mixed with the crackle of night insects—making that mellifluous mood of nostalgia that music heard from a distance carries with it.

"Jaysus," J. Willard beamed benevolently, "I didn't know anyone played *that* one anymore. I danced to that with Jay's mother someplace."

"Moonlight behind you," sang Esme. "It's a good solid bit of romantic corn. I like good corn. There are times I like things sentimental. I used to cry at old Bette Davis movies on television."

Jason leaned on the rail as the yacht slid past the orange windows across the water and the music turned to "Papa Won't You Dance with Me." These good moments, he decided, are doled out to us like a miser's allowance.

"It's a hell of a night to be thinking of politics."

Esme said, "That's what Washington is built on, politics. I don't think your man Paul is good enough."

J. Willard turned toward her, laughed, put a hand on her shoulder. "Oh, come now gal, you've been around. You're close to Austin Barraclough. You know no one is good enough *until* he's tried, until he's in office taking his whacks and emerging bloody and maybe unbowed."

Esme tapped fingers on the teak rail. "It's too late usually, isn't it, if he turns out to be a stinker? Well, we're turning back; past those red and green lights are Cobb Island and St. Cat."

"You have your car?" Jason asked.

"No. The Heap has burned out a bearing, is in sick bay. Came by cab."

J. Willard leaned over as the yacht turned toward the opposite shore, tilted. Somehow the sound of the engines came clearer from below. Jason studied the half-moon of their white hissing wake.

J. Willard turned up his coat collar. "Jay has his car at Fowler Mansion. We'll drive you home unless you live in Baltimore."

"I don't."

From the big red and gold cabin came voices, laughter, the sound of glasses clicking on a tray and as the yacht made a tighter turn, breakage was heard from below.

"The lions and the lambs," said Esme. "But who are the lions, who the lambs? Labor or Capital?"

J. Willard said, "Ever hear the definition of *capitalism* and *communism*? Capitalism, some say, is man exploiting man."

"And communism?"

"Communism is the same statement, but backward."

Esme laughed and kissed J. Willard's cheek. The yacht was now moving upriver and increasing its speed, engines sounding louder, the single funnel giving off a thicker, darker climbing plume of smoke. There seemed to Jason to be more stars overhead in the night sky than he had ever seen before.

After the car ride back from Judge Amos Fowler's yacht, J. Willard asked to be dropped off at the big bronze soldier statue, to walk to his motel. "Hell, I don't fear muggers, and it's well lit and patrolled."

J. Willard liked to walk in Washington; night might be dangerous, but it was also exciting, mysterious. Passing the big hotels, the mansions, the apartments, embassy lights going out, servants wheeling out empty bottles, greasy papers, broken bits of cake to trash cans; for the early pickup, he imagined. Security everyplace; locks, time clocks, tapped wires, bugged walls, intimate reports, secret drops, hand-to-hand. Sadists in uniform with hard clubs, MP, SP armbands, deadly steel in holsters. Someplace in the town some mutterfucking, muggings or a drunken sailor; white boys gangbanging a yellow girl, a group mainlining under a red lightbulb, and in a lonely room, a suicide waiting, carp-mouthed, listless, for the sixteen pills to bring release . . . Yes, but J. Willard felt children slept and dreamed, young Washington girls recited old poems in their sleep. The reprieved ancient houses creaked a bit, settled a fragment of an inch deeper into history.

Someone had pushed an advertising folder under J. Willard's motel door. A colored picture of an impossibly endowed woman:

LIFELIKE INFLATABLE WASHINGTON PLAYGIRL
IN BRA, BIKINI & WIG
(SHE'S 40-20-40, A HONEY)

Just think of the fun you can have with this instant babe! You don't have to buy her perfume, flowers, or even a cup of coffee. 5'5" tall, instantly inflatable, and ready for laughs as you stick her in the guest closet, boss's office, car trunk, on boat deck, under your arm, etc. Her knees bend, and arms flex for many riotous positions. Molded of sturdy, fleshlike heavy vinyl, with lovely soft skin finish. Great decoration for a bachelor flat, more fun than a pimp. Simple vinyl patch repairs any wound suffered in the line of duty. Guaranteed: you'll never be bored with this broad!

Your Instant Inflatable Washington Hostess
With Wig, Bra, Bikini—$69.95

Chapter 21

The meeting on the yacht had left Jason with a delayed reaction; soon he was in one of those states of needing release. He had come home to Georgetown, found the house dark. Hurrying upstairs he had pressed on the lights in the hall and in the bedroom.

"I tell you, that was some meeting," he called out as he shucked his jacket. What he wanted was some active bedtime with Sheila, their usual animated lovemaking that would release him from his tensions. He was making sympathetic sounds when he became aware the bed was made, untouched, no Sheila waking slowly, no wife in her flimsy alluring nightgown. No musky sleeping shape to welcome him. It came to him Sheila was away; of course, with that damn daughter of theirs, with Libby the grandchild in some infant crisis. Of course he had forgotten, been filled by the excitement of talk of making a candidate, talk of strategy, votes, primaries. A hell of a note. He gave a plaintive whistle.

The drinks had evaporated; he felt wound up like a clock spring; his physical needs were activated. He undressed, got into his pajamas, looked around him, up at the rain-streak made by a new leak in the roof, at Sheila's slippers like puppies at rest by the bed, heels slightly worn down on one side.

Jason went downstairs and got himself a glass of milk, nibbled on a section of some kind of seedcake.

Upstairs again, he lay on the lonely bed on his back, the night table lamp on, an arm over his eyes. He thought of an adolescent form of release from tension, but decided against it. He took up a book he had borrowed from Austin Barraclough's library. *Democracy, A Novel.* No author. But Austin had written on the title page: *1st ed. Henry Adams.*

Jason tried to read—between indignant moans of desire—but Adams had little skill as a novelist. Witty, sardonic, yes, but the irony seemed stale, malicious—the sour little snob. He turned the pages hoping to find something that would hold his interest. A half-sheet of pale blue notepaper fell out. He recognized Austin's slashing handwriting. It seemed to be a poem. Another facet of the old boy?

> I am like the king of a rainy country.
> Rich—and impotent.
> Young—and very old.
> He despises the kowtowing
> Or his court, and is bored
> By his dogs as with
> All his creatures.
> > For nothing now can
> > Cheer him. Prey
> > Nor falcon. Not even those
> > Of his people who come
> > To die beneath his window.

Wow! Jason read it over and saw the name *Baudelaire*. The old man had amused himself by translating this from the French. Yes, Baudelaire, a French poet (2nd year Lit). Amused to find Austin out; the wrong word, *amused*. Austin in some time of dark thoughts had most likely felt the poem's mood as his own. Jason put back the half-sheet between the yellowing pages of the book and set it on the night table. Switched off the lamp, felt a heaving of his diaphragm.

The poem turned his mind from his own tensions to thoughts of Austin Barraclough, to the old house on the historic river, to the men —an almost clairvoyant view of many men who had once on these banks thought bitterly of their own hopes, their destinies and their defeats. Lincoln in the dark years of slaughter and very slim results for all the casualty lists; Jefferson in his conflicts with Hamilton. And forward to the Calvinist mists that enveloped Wilson as he sat paralyzed in his wheelchair, his hopes for the League of Nations turned to bile by Senator Lodge. FDR?—banks closing, the unemployed shivering on street corners, *apples five cents* . . . and Jason slept.

Before waking he had a dream, or a wisp of a dream, of rain slashing into the river banks and the waters humping themselves like muscled animals. He was walking under historic trees, bedeviled, anxiety driving him through the mist moving along the ground. A woman appeared, floating rather than walking toward him, with a deer-eyed look. He let her come to him and he felt her arms, damp yet warm, go around him. He was a crowned king behind fragile balustrades in a huge bed, silk-covered, making love to the woman, a fierce love, a heroic fornication. The woman lifted her head, mouth open showing regular and powerful teeth, and he saw it was Esme Lowell. He said, "How now? How now?" and fell away, skidding along a hall of the Capitol Building, past a stern marble Washington, a full figure done up in a toga as a Roman . . . and behind him Jason heard the laughter of the woman . . . and he came awake.

It had been a shock, that fragmented dream, and in a way a pleasure. But Esme? Esme Lowell? Goddamn! It was morning—no more sleep. He got up, showered, decided not to shave, and in robe and slippers went downstairs. The maid Fran was up, smoking her morning cigarette, setting out the cream pitcher, the sugar bowl, the morning newspapers delivered to the front door.

"You had yourself a night. Overslept?"

"Politicians never stop talking."

"The missus called last night."

"Any message?"

"Baby's better. She's staying on a few days. Moving them all to a place in town."

"About time. I'll just have some rolls and jam, coffee."

He looked at the headlines in the *Post*, in the *Star*, compared them with the *New York Times*. The usual anthology of disasters, betrayals, Nature on a tear with earthquakes, floods, and too much rain *here* and no rain *there*. The market was off four points, the cheerful news from federal figures showed that unemployment would not rise more than 6 percent, inflation 8 percent; both figures, the administration proudly stated, would be less than expected. Obstinate imbeciles with the Big Lie. He'd go through the papers later.

He sippped his coffee and recalled the dream. He knew as much as most educated people about the misinterpreted popular Freudian mythology and meanings to sense that his dream was the speaking of his unconscious, subconscious (same thing), about the Libido and the Id. He was as superficially ill-informed as most as to the deep meanings and signs of what he was thinking about. Triggered by the fact he had had a hot dream about Esme, and that it was a signal about something, he moaned out loud at the incoherent rambling of shrinks and finished his coffee.

Truth was he knew he had been thinking of her as sexual and desirable, but always with wonder about her past male friendships, and what reaction a man would get from such a strong-willed, self-sufficient type. There had been scabrous gossip . . . He put the newspapers into his attaché case and had Dolf drive him to his office on the Hill. Even with the House and the Senate not in session the Hill was still active. Many representatives, he saw, had stayed to catch up on their work, their projects. Not all took junkets, cheated on their mileage allowances, added phantom staff members, or faked trips home for the costs.

The tension was still with Jason, but half tamed, resting fitfully just under the surface. He met with some union people, listened, and made the kind of promises that are vague enough to be satisfying without promising anything and strong enough to show what side he was on. He called the old house they still kept in Vista City, but no one answered the ringing phone. He began a letter to Sheila and gave it up. He had a bad lunch sent up and finished off with two Di-Gel tablets. He wound the alarm clock and overwound it and tinkered with it, probing it with a letter opener till it began its loud tick of confidence.

At 3:22 Esme called.

"You busy this PM?"

"Some text on highway regulation I have to prepare for the hometown newspaper."

"Drop by around five for a drink. I found that book Uncle Austin wrote years ago."

"*The Ruined Republic: The Age of Grant?*"

"That's it. You can have it. See you."

"See you."

He sat listening to the friendly old clock tick, heard the buzz of traffic, the boom of a far-off plane a mile or so above the city. He was not a man indiscreet or irresponsible. He preferred acumen and tact. He studied, disconcerted, the picture of the Blue River country on his wall. He had no idea of what Esme thought about him in the field of personal physical attraction. Jason felt caught, certainly caught in a cleft stick, or rather his genitalia were, his emotions. He might convince himself he could be in love with Esme. (Or was he again fooling himself; as J. Willard used to say, "You want a thing to be so, Jayboy, and you imagine it's so. You lie to yourself a lot.") He couldn't, no, he couldn't really be attracted to Esme just because she was Austin's niece and could be one more strand in some pattern he was weaving to reach high political power. Christ, if it had to be, it was because she was certainly a desirable woman and he was a functioning man. Sensual enough, but not a voluptuary, just a normal guy. He left a note for Miss Munday, who was checking records someplace, that he'd be gone for the day. Clair was away, moving Laura and the baby.

He had a shave, bought a tie, drove with care, listening to Debussy on the car radio. But once seated in Esme's sun-room in the back of her little run-down house, drinking her martinis, he just stared at the neglected garden with its long uncut grass, its one surviving apple tree hung with cocoons of the tent moth, noticed the pile of old coal ashes by the wild-grown hollyhocks, ashes he thought must have been there since before the house was converted to oil-burning.

"You ought to get a torch of some kind and burn off those cocoons."

She smiled, patted his arm. "Oh hell, I'm going to do this house over real *House and Garden* and sell it for a profit. I do over two to four of these run-down wrecks a year. Pull out the old wiring and plumbing, give them a new roof. Then I gussie up the front, do a cute planting and put out a For Sale sign."

"There's always a shortage?"

Esme was in a lounging outfit, apple green, loose, soft; and she was very relaxed, but he held back, felt a muddled oaf. The tension was directing him to spring, his more collected self—wary, worried—insisting if he made the pass and was coldly rebuffed, slapped down, there would perhaps go his closeness to Austin Barraclough. But the tension whispered *if* you make it, just think—in like Flynn—how much closer it would all be, like a member of the family.

Esme was talking, perfectly at ease, sipping gin, reclining on a wickerwork sofa of pale yellow with cushions of burnt orange and green. He tried to follow her talk, his hand uneasily fingering a tall vase of pampas grass.

"... I add a fancy kitchen and a fancy bathroom to these remodeling jobs, but the real trick is the day you're showing the house for sale you keep a pot of coffee brewing on the stove, see, and you dampen a loaf of bread, cut off the crusts, and put it into the oven at a very low temperature. The prospect comes into a house smelling delightfully of coffee brewing and bread baking. I've sold more houses with a half pound of coffee and a stale loaf of bread than by pointing out original rafters and the advantage of a good WASP neighborhood."

He reached for her hand, rubbed her wrist, and stood up. "Thanks for the drink. Must go work on a talk I'm giving tonight at a dinner for some Four-H kids in town visiting the Smithsonian."

"Sheila still away? Why not come to dinner tomorrow night? I've got some frozen lobster tails Bread O'Rahilly sent me, and you can bring the wine."

"I can take you out to—"

"Come on, never fear—I'm a good cook."

So it was the next night that Esme took Jason to bed, after the candlelight, the fairly good bottle of rosé, the lobster tails in a black bean sauce. It was very simple and very direct. They had been sitting on the wicker sofa with after-dinner cognac in small pale amber glasses.

She sipped and said, "You do want to go to bed with me, don't you?"

Jason frowned and twirled his glass with two fingers.

"Christ, I've hardly been able to keep my hands off you."

"I certainly felt that last night, but you chickened out. Morals? A sense of sinning?"

"No, I guess I just had this fear of being slapped down. I didn't want to lose your friendship in a burst of rejection, hilarity . . . Christ, Esme, I'm very fond of you and you're a hell of a woman."

She said, "I'm a hell of a lot of woman. And I've been chasing you in my own way. Pulling back—saying whoa there, Esme, *easy* girl. I didn't want to get kicked in the teeth again . . ."

She had her arm around him and he reached too, and kissed her with an incoherent mutter of words that came from him without thinking. A phone rang on a Chinese-decorated ceramic barrel-stand. Esme flung off her shoes and kicked a long naked leg in the direction of the instrument, a kick that removed the phone from its cradle.

*   *   *

An hour later, after furious delightful lovemaking, they were in the big brass bed of the pale blue bedroom, Esme smoking a cigarette, both of them jaybird naked, resting after the deep-felt, earnest sexual pleasure of lovemaking. The first encounter had been on the wicker-work couch; they having removed in blind haste most of their garments. Nothing is as ridiculous, Jason had felt, as a man with a hard-on trying to get out of his trousers. It had been exhilarating, almost a storm of released emotions, gorged desires, by two healthy people encountering each other after groping for weeks in a capricious vexation of a wary courtship. In the first expenditure of energy and passion on the wickerwork sofa they had realized they were of the same bedeviled nature in seeking the fulfillment of their natural needs. Sensibilities satisfied—his once muffled by his position on the Hill and the pattern of a long marriage, and hers by the social conditions of a city of quickies, one-night stands, where she took too many looks of appraisal and did not find the strength and earnestness she wanted in a relationship.

They had made love and looked into each other's eyes, feeling no need after the first climax for words, and also they had little breath for them.

Jason was surprised to find Esme not at all the cold bitch, the withdrawn cynic about the relationship, the intimate, most intimate reactions of men and women to each other. She was almost, he felt, an adolescent, almost waiting for his moves, gestures, before following through. But strong and almost cruel in the way she held him, directing his thrusts by her hips and rolling torso, the long legs kicking out.

Going upstairs, naked to naked, arms around each other, the covers tossed off the brass bed, they came to each other again, and he heard her sucking-in of breath as she became tender yet demanding; such a surprise this night. Unexpected—like a conjuror's pigeon that seems to appear from noplace. The second bout of lovemaking was more of a pleasure than the first. They were more at their ease; they made love in intimate detail, with leisure, but for those racing periods when the hearts beat faster and the mouths wet and open found each other, in moaning words, neither profound nor recalled.

He noticed, as they rested and touched here and there, that her ears were large with long lobes, her pubic bush was like fuzz. Her voice after lovemaking had a light delicacy, but there was no shyness. After a while she rose and stepped over him in the bed.

"Got to pee, Darling."

She had a deliberate walk, like a cat, a neat instep, a fine ankle, and she seemed not so tall but wider-hipped when naked. The breasts were a little too large, had a slight droop.

As the plumbing gave off its obscene sounds from the bathroom, Jason felt at rest in a deep personal privacy, a baroque nest of emotions among the rusty brocade window hangings, the two little bed lamps tinting the atmosphere, Dufy's racehorses and Matisse's table life on the walls.

He was, he told himself, not to think of the future, of regret, gravity, adultery, extracurricular sex, cheating. These were *just* words, semantics. He hadn't felt like this since sex in his highschool days with one of his first girls, Boots Condon the pom-pom girl and cheerleader—*Vista! Vista! Hit that line! Score! Score! Fine! Fine! Fine!* and a somersault showing Boots Condon's silk-and-lace-covered crotch. Loving in a Dodge roadster J. Willard had given him on his sixteenth birthday. Crazy, crazy, he had thought later, twisting with Boots Condon on the imitation pale-brown leather of the Dodge car seat, carried under the old oak trees of Bison Park. He shook off the past—it's the *now* that matters. This *now, here,* the emotions of a mature man he had calmed into a smooth and narcotic state.

Esme was back, still naked, taking up a cigarette and activating it with a brass lighter with a caduceus, the emblem of healing, he knew, of the medical profession, engraved on it. (A former lover? A doctor surgeon from Walter Reed, or Bethesda?)

She slid across him. "I like, Darling, always the right side of a bed." She inhaled, exhaled, blew rings toward the ceiling, then kissed his cheek and leaned her head against his. "If you want this to continue, we will have to be discreet, if you—"

"Of course, I want us to be like this, to go on being like this."

"You don't feel at all wrong, guilty?"

Jason said, "Of course I feel guilty, guilty as hell. Oh, I'm no goddamn saint, but pretty much I've been a faithful husband. I feel men are polygamous, and that our society is two-faced, for it knows this when it insists on monogamy."

"Oh shit." She kissed his shoulder and laughed. "You *macho* bastard. You're thirty years out of date. Positively medieval in your thinking about the sexes."

"You said I was a yokel. Downstairs you said it—"

"Listen, I know about yokels making it with the calf, and cornholing their buddies in rustic fun. I grew up on a Virginia farm." She beat out the cigarette on a tarnished silver ashtray. "Look, now we've calmed down enough to breathe without using our mouths, let me explain. I'm sensual, and a long time between men, maybe too long. You see, Jay, I'm sexual but I'm not promiscuous. I believe in true, long, solid relationships."

"Tonight, here, sure, I'm like that myself."

"I held off, I was thinking you were making it with that Miss Clair on the senatorial couch in your office. It's no secret a lot of office girls on the Hill are dropping their panties at the call of the intercom buzzer."

"I never saw Clair in that light; my father used to say, 'Never screw your secretary, for you then have a shrew in the office and a shrew at home when the wife finds out.' "

"Good thinking."

They slept then, arms around each other, he open-mouthed, Esme snoring softly.

He got up at five, searching to identify the setting, the dawn just pinking the eastern sky and peeping through one of the drapes. He showered after the natural morning indecencies, found a Japanese Kabuki robe. (Another memory of some past male, in possession and back from Asia with gifts?) He put it on and went down and made coffee, toasted some bread, found a pale purple jam and a battered tray with some ruins of Rome painted on it.

Esme was just stretching when he came upstairs with the tray. She smelled of sleep and of Esme, the faint odor of their lovemaking in the room.

"I wake hard," she said. "Don't talk to me till I get some coffee in me." She sat up in bed sipping the coffee and he put jam on toast and fed it to her in small sections. After the second cup of coffee she bunched back her hair away from her forehead and smiled.

"I can now face the day, but I snarl and bite without a first cup of coffee . . . You're getting a bit of a tummy, darling. Watch it."

"Had it since college. It's all muscle. *Feel*."

"I'd like to, but it would get me horny, and I've got to bathe, dress and be in Alexandria by eight-thirty on a deal. Unless you need a quickie?"

He said no Honey, he'd be able to hold off until nightfall. He kissed her, getting jam in return and an ardent tight hug, with the words, "Darling, Darling. You'll find me self-sufficient but *not* reserved. Fair warning."

He reached for his shorts. "That's my girl."

Chapter 22

J. Willard earnestly wanted to visit Austin Barraclough, he had known him years ago at conventions. Jason just phoned Champ he was bringing his father out, and that was all there was to it. They sat on the terrace at Potomac House and encouraged Austin to talk.

Said Austin, "The danger of Washington, J. W., is really the narrowness of its life. It may look large and important, but the longer one stays there, the more the outer world seems to shrink and lose its values. Life here becomes a sort of substitute existence. Everything changes here, even the conception of time. There are crises; we live from sensation to sensation, scandal to scandal, and the old normal tick of time withers away. Only Washington time matters."

J. Willard said, "Yes, I've noticed so many defeated congressmen become completely incapable of life back in their hometowns. They have lost the capacity to take up ideas that aren't dominated by Washington thinking. So they stay on."

"It's a city that reads the public polls, not Hume or Burke or De Tocqueville. You win elections by figuring out the discontent of the voters. Ideals aren't really what the citizen wants; he desires a promise, a resolution of his uncertainty. For the voter is always nursing a grievance."

"Yet," said Jason, "I suppose he doesn't really believe promises."

"Why should he, Jason? Government as it's handed to him is often infantile, incompetent, irresponsible and a grandstanding folly. Hell, disillusionment is inevitable. So he puts some old fart out of office and turns to some snake oil salesman with a loud voice."

"Senator," said J. Willard, "I find skepticism the worst sin of the political scene. My son insists we have to believe in a moral order, loyalty to sense and reason."

"He still manages to win elections: by morality *or* deals and favors?"

Jason laughed. "There are times, there are times, yes, when Pop says he gets the grue about how things are done."

"Well," Austin said, "the do-gooders and bleeding hearts all sound so damn honest, and their ideas so natural and humanist. But study both kinds, liberal or conservative. You can't even depend on optimistic rationalists bedded down in their illusions; both are in flagrant contradiction of the facts. Some half-hatched messiah out of the Ivy League with his ideas of how things should be done is just as whacked out as a slum kid who's misread Marx and asks you to start a new world, say Tuesday, at two o'clock."

J. Willard frowned. "The radicals' dreamy ideas I understand, but see no validity in dispensing the guarantees of our society's continued existence."

"We set up rules we hope will serve," said Austin smiling. "Sure, rules of authority to keep the nation in order. It's rough, maybe, but we've had no four-star general taking over, no Pentagon coup d'état. Sure, under the surface we had the FBI and CIA operating in some ways as if they were in Russia or Hitler's Germany. But that's all part of us being asleep when that SOB yelped *I am not a crook*. It came pretty close, with his court of hoodlums, to destroying a lot of what is basic."

"You think he—" began J. Willard.

"How do I know how close he was to declaring a state of emergency some Friday night and putting the nation under a military alert? Or was there a bigger 'enemy list' and the concentration camps? Anyway, somebody got their senses back in time to chip out the rot."

J. Willard said seriously, "I still feel the best of politics calls for an intuitive perception, a sense of reality. And how to get the folks back home to feel you mean it."

"Yes," said Jason.

"Do we have to have messiahs?" asked J. Willard.

"We are all fallible. Never put too much trust in any man. *Only* in the country, J. W., even whatever mess we've made of the ideals that founded it. Christ, J. W., how did this talk get so far up God's asshole?"

Austin Barraclough seemed to grimace at whatever thought he was having. He said to Jason, "How's the new granddaughter?"

"Gaining, I gather. Sheila keeps the records she gets over the phone."

"You have a son?"

"Teddy. J. Willard here insisted he be named after Teddy Roosevelt. My grandfather was a Bull Moose man. Backed T. R. for a third term."

"Sheer nonsense, J. W. No third party can survive our two-party setup. They have the money, the city wards, the backing of the unions and the corporations . . . I used to think of what my son would be like, but—"

"You had a—" Jason asked.

"Oh, by my first wife. We had a boy, lived three weeks. Didn't know that, did you? Well, I'd have been a rotten father anyway. My father, *he* was a good old man to me. A horse lover, a cunt-crazy sportsman, they said when he died, but added 'a credit to his family.' Raised me fine, outdoors, didn't understand why I liked Princeton, or writing essays, why I went to England and did not shoot grouse or screw milkmaids, but as a Rhodes Scholar spent a winter in a dig on the Tigris hunting up old pots and stones. My old man said, 'Austie, you're an overeducated young bastard. All that is not going to do you any good when you have to go out and kick the world's behind before it kicks yours.' He was right, of course."

J. Willard asked, "How did you come to politics, Austin?"

"My father insisted I do something practical. His version was to run the Barraclough Tidewater breeding farms, the tobacco and cotton holdings, our fish canneries on the eastern shore. That is, make more money than he spent on buying prize horses, keeping some floozie in sables or designing a new yacht to race for the America's Cup. I had to work with lobbies, Washington bureaucrats, departments, IRS, and as a businessman—so I joined them, ran for public office. No Barraclough ever lost an election in our county or in Virginia."

"You liked it?"

"Like a duck likes water. I wasn't shocked. I had been exposed to Washington's best society since I was a kid, and had known the big-shot office holders, the megalomaniac committee heads, drunk or sober, and heard them with their hair down telling how it was. Yes." He gave a sigh that seemed to end in a growl. "And I could of, yes, had the whole shebang, just by a nod. Only I didn't give a shit when it was offered. I had gone off the bend. I just, just saw it was all less than nothing.

> "I find my zenith doth depend upon
> A most auspicious star, whose influence
> If now I court not but omit, my fortunes
> Will ever after droop."

J. Willard thought, remarked, "Sounds like Shakespeare."

Austin grinned and slapped J. Willard's back. "Give the man a cigar, Jason. *The Tempest,* that's where it's from . . .

> "Yes . . . all shall dissolve,
> And like this insubstantial pageant fade,
> Leave not a rack behind."

Later J. Willard said to his son, "What a great afternoon. Too bad I couldn't buy Austin a drink."

Jason discovered he did have a small sense of guilt about Esme, a hovering sensation of sinning. When Sheila returned home he was very attentive, tried to make things easier for her around the house, as if atoning in some small way for his unfaithfulness.

"Lord, Jay, stop worrying about the air conditioning—it's getting into fall. And you don't have to leap forward to help me with the bundles . . . You and J. Willard been taking care of yourselves?"

"He's busy with the old guard. Laura and family all settled in?"

"Yes, I got them a three-room apartment on Pine Drive, and Sam is working at the television station sorting tape reels of music or something. Once you get to know Sam, he's fairly nice. I took a lot of Kodak Instants of the baby. Darling little thing. Bright. Her eyes follow you when you come into the room."

Jason inspected the two dozen color photos, agreed their granddaughter was a prime and special child, and had J. Willard's brow, but Sheila's family's nose and mouth. Jason said he wasn't so sure about the nose.

He went to the Hill. Miss Munday came in and put the morning mail he was to look at in his In tray.

"Got a card from Clair. She got dunked going down the Colorado River on one of those rubber rafts, but she's having a ball."

"Yes, I had a card from her, she and Ed. Who's Ed?"

Miss Munday pursed her lips as if to blow up a balloon. "Ed? He works in Printing and Engraving at Treasury. I suppose I'm not modern enough in my outlook. Love is a fine thing, natural, don't you think so, Senator?"

"I was taught that, Miss Munday."

"But the way people now just shack up, as they call it—and with no intent to marry. I mean Washington—nearly everybody is making out with everybody, even church folk. It's what brought down the Roman Empire, wasn't it? Immorality, raw sex?"

"I'm no authority on the fall of Rome, Miss Munday, and what raw sex is I have not defined . . . Get me figures of junkets by Congress this year. Not the public figures, but the stuff they hide. And the Pentagon has spent illegally one hundred million in Iran, getting the Shah's military hardware in order, *and*, as usual, has buried the facts. See if Jack Anderson can fill me in."

"My sister is in Rome, at the Embassy, says it's even worse there."

"Costs hidden?"

"The immorality."

"Thank you, Miss Munday." (Does she have a first name?)

Jason had spent the nights for two weeks with Esme, while Sheila was settling Laura in, back home in Vista City. Now, since his wife's return, he could only at the most manage two nights a week, by leaving some special meeting early and getting home by one o'clock. If his bit of guilt feeling hung on, there was also the sense of being young again and tomcatting, and also the romantic atmosphere of furtive, secret lovemaking to a remarkably handsome body and with a woman with a crisp attitude, almost a male mind. But female enough, and desirable. Even call it love, yes.

Why not, he'd think driving back to Georgetown late at night. I want to be honest; a man could love two women—could share himself with two creatures that made life happier. There are examples in the Old Testament; all the great Hebrew studs, King David to King Solomon, begetting and begetting, and beyond them, men with more than one woman to love. Look at the feisty Mormons, the most well-behaved, hardworking folk you could find; polygamy part of their creed. Maybe in public now they have only one woman in view, but there are colonies of them in New Mexico, in Arizona —breakaway Mormons, Jack Mormons, and others who have their eight to twelve wives—and the federal government has stopped harassing them.

Not that he wanted more than he had. It wasn't an effort rightly, but a couple of nights a week with Esme, and once or twice, at least every seven days with Sheila; it was alright, but it kept a man on his toes, or rather prone (joke). Good thing Sheila was not as interested in sex as she had been. The Change of Life? Or all this moving of her interests to the new grandchild?

Esme, even if spontaneously activated, had been practical. Lying side by side with him, her cigarette glowing in the semidark, she spoke in that deliberate voice of hers, so different from the tones when she cried out in their lovemaking and said plaintive, exciting things, endearing sometimes, erotic, usually unbridled and husky. Now she said:

"I don't want any mess. I don't care to hear about Sheila. I can face her, talk to her, even have a drink or a meal with you both."

"Of course you can."

"I have my daytime life, my daughter, my position in Washington. So have you, Darling. We must be careful. I don't mean we have to be sneaky and slink around, coat collars up. I'm not ashamed of us."

"I should hope not. Hell, we're doing no harm to anyone. I respect you. I don't see us enigmatic or paradoxical. There has never been anyone like you in my life and I like it, love it."

"It or me?"

(They always, he thought, ask such questions after awhile: there comes that time when they want an answer. "Do you love me, really?")

"Words are just words, Esme. It's all told in the way we act, feel. That's the truth of it, isn't it?"

"Do you really love me?"

(There it was, right on time!)

He faced her and kissed her cheek, made sympathetic sounds. "I love you, of course I love you. Your mind, your handsome body, all our anticipatory pleasures. I wouldn't be here if I didn't have such feelings."

"Maybe I'm just convenient."

(The second gambit—the I'm-just-convenient ploy.)

"Look, Honey, you're *not* convenient. You're damn inconvenient. Setting up times to meet, arranging so I'll not be missed or paged. And I don't know what your uncle would think if he knew."

"You find him helpful, don't you?"

"I admire him, and of course I find him helpful. Hell, you think I'm here to cozy closer to him? Maybe I think I'm helpful to him. He is better, much better. So no more of this convenient shit. There are plenty of convenient girls around on the Hill whose pants come down faster than the flag at Taps. Or the convenient women boozing at the Burning Tree, or the English birds at the convenient Limey embassy, and—"

"Please, no more inventory. I'm sorry, I'm sorry I said it. I'm sorry." She moved over to him and whispered in his ear, "It's just I have to be sure. I wasn't for the first few times. I held myself mentally a bit in check. I wanted to stand off, sort of, to one side and watch us."

"That's a mean trick. For me your pier glass is enough."

"It's all or not at all for me. Now, just remember I'm not going to make trouble, I'm not neurotic. You know that, Darling, don't you?"

"I wasn't sure of that from the start. I'd run from a neurotic. Jesus, look at the time. Gotta go."

"Just a few minutes more. Hold me. Ever read the journal by Lady Murasaki, that Japanese noblewoman a long time ago? She wrote that the gentleman must not act after lovemaking as if he has to hurry; she should never have to feel he's had his fun and is leaping into his trousers. No, he should instead say how much he regrets leaving, how he'd want to stay . . . Did samurai wear pants?"

Jason laughed and slowly, carefully got out of the bed. "Ah-so. I am sorry I must hurry away. I would want to stay. Ah-so, your presence, it's intoxicating." He bowed. "So sorry."

She threw a pillow at him.

Driving home through the city in the cool chill of a night drizzle, he imagined the things this city had seen: the British in polite red-coated parade order to set it on fire; the assassinated presidents on their gun carriages, preceded by a riderless horse held firmly to a walk; the times of Watergate and the sinister fool thrashing about in a net of tapes, hemmed in by his Prussian-sounding gang of ruffians. And as he neared home he thought of a great-grandfather who had marched into the city with the rebel General Early, who had crossed over and looked around and then pulled back, and of Sheila's grandfather who had come with Coxey's Army and Jack London, and been arrested for walking on the Capitol grass.

Jason, saturated in a mood of the city's past, put the car into the coachhouse done over as a garage. He sniffed his hands and clothes; Esme had promised not to use perfume or scented soaps. He inspected his two handkerchiefs for lipstick stains, automatically felt his jock (on the left side as proper). For him it was the most humiliating moment of the affair—this entry and inspection, this checking. Then a progress on tiptoes into the house. He had showered and scrubbed at Esme's, being careful to keep his hair dry (there was, he remembered, this prig in State who was having a thing with a gay at the West German Embassy, and one night late his wife felt his damp hair as he got into the kip with her, and she didn't accept the story of handball and a shower at the Y; she'd called her lawyer in the morning, the Y had been closed a week for repairs).

Sheila was asleep, the night table lamps on, an Agatha Christie, *Twelve for Dinner,* open on the bedcovers. She came awake blinking, moved her head to view the little traveling clock.

"Late. Couldn't sleep. Worried. Laura isn't taking care of herself, so underweight."

He undressed, managing some small talk. Sheila, if her sleep was too long interrupted, would have a problem going back. He had thought of moving into the guest room, but such a sudden decision would raise up suspicions. He was finding he was suspecting things for no reason at all; that was the bit of guilt harassing him. Jason got into his pajamas and into the bed. Sheila moved about, hunting the best position for a return to sleep. She stirred against him, a probing of breasts, knees, and he felt one of her arms go around him. She made little moaning sounds of pleasure, then rubbed her face against his shoulder.

"I just *can't* seem to go back to sleep."

"Don't think of sleep, just rest, recite something."

"Sheep don't work, um, um . . ." nibbling at his throat.

"Recite the titles of books of some author. Dickens—you'll be sleeping half way through."

"Um, David Copperfield, Oliver Twist . . .? Tale of Two Cities
. . . Christmas Carol? No, that's a short story . . . I don't know
any more titles right now. Jay. Jay? I want sex. That always calms
me, you know . . ."

He tried to protest the hour, his hard day, but he knew he
couldn't carry on too much of those excuses; it would bring Sheila
wider awake. He kicked off his pajama pants, reached and hiked
up her nightgown. He took the position they used to call, when
first married, Ma and Pa fucking . . . At first he had a sickening
terror of failing, of not being able to rouse himself. Sheila sighed
and wriggled and he managed a fairly good rigid condition. Pro-
ceeding to his task, he told himself it was just as pleasantly satisfactory for him as for his wife. Just as.

J. Willard was going through Jason's library and was touched
to see some of the volumes he had given his son as a boy were
there on the shelves. *The White Company, The Mysterious Island,
Twenty Years After,* and the battered red-covered favorite of J.
Willard that kids didn't seem to like. He took the book down and
opened it just any place.

"Well, in our country," said Alice, still panting a little, "you'd gen-
erally get to somewhere else—if you ran very fast for a long time, as
we have been doing."

"A slow sort of country!" said the Queen. "Now, here, you see, it
takes all the running you can do to keep in the same place. If you want
to get somewhere else, you must run at least twice as fast as that!"

Strange—it was too pat to think that what was once fantasy
seemed to become reality in another era. He was going to reread
the book, but Sheila came in and said to him, "You know more of
this city than people who live here."

"Oh, I like to poke and roam about. And I've been coming
here for over forty years."

"I hear Saturday night, tonight, it's the wildest kind of town.
Look, Jay is talking to some club. Take me out on the town. The
wilder the better."

"You're not fooling? Well, I'll take a heavy cane and you carry
your valuables in your girdle."

"You mean it, J. W.?"

He said he did. He hadn't seen much of the hell-raising of a Saturday night in Washington since the days of the Vietnam War at its most deceitful; "When Lyndon B. was screwing himself more than the nation."

J. Willard insisted there was an analogy between the habits of individuals and nations. Saturday night in Washington after dark proved his point. The jails are full, he said, drunk tank, fish tank, security cells. The hospitals are laying stretchers in the halls, the bail bondsmen are busy as beavers building dams. He insisted, "Saturday night, it's the winner as the drunkenest town in the world at the weekend."

"Prove it."

J. W. said, "Honey, it's a mad idea. Every clerk, every section secretary, pool typist, State Department janitor or code clerk on the GS-4 scale up to GS-6 is breaking free of his dull routine, his files, bad breath, his miserable office time-clock life. Boy *or* girl. She wants action, too, and she's trying to lap it up in one night. It's a feeling of the illusion of living that makes Saturday night so macabre."

Washington: loneliness, despair, boredom, lost hopes, old age; all merge on Saturday night in dreams, J. W. told Sheila, "Dreams never to be fully fulfilled." The young studs hunting high yellows on the Negro Broadway. The dank, urine-smelling bars full of sad girls, young and not so young, buying Chivas Regal Scotch for pickups, garage hands, soldiers, small-time spies. "The Air Force fly boys, the cadets moving about, rolling John Wayne buttocks with contraceptive kits in their jeans. The belly dancers, stripteasers beginning to whirl in cafes and places of entertainment. The MP's Shore Patrol, husky sadists, helmeted goons, grinning, tenderly rubbing their oak clubs as if worshiping phallic objects. The hoarded money of gone-without-lunches appears. It is at first a happy wild night town before the amiability dies, deodorants fail."

Sheila said, "Show me." So they did the dark bars on G Street, where if you bought Courvoisier you were eyed with respect. Went arm in arm past the grass island of Thomas Circle, where the fags parade for a mark, stood under the bronze statue of George H. Thomas (Major General), beloved by his comrades, his nation and the capital pigeons. Sheila accepted Trader Vic's, where they had lobster Cantonese among the Tiki gods and an Afro-Asian mission feasting in long white robes. After fortune cookies (*Your character is made up of contradictions*), Latin jazz was good at the Ring Ding Club on Fourteenth Street; the air was thick there and the bongo heads jumping. A man from War Surplus Sales said it was moldy fig and took them both to a private party in an old house on Massachusetts Avenue. Sheila noticed lots of Chinese lacquers, Duncan Phyfe and Sheraton, an oil painting shiny in brown gravy of a former chief justice long dead; his wife welcomed all to the party. It was going full blast with GS-10 to GS-12 people from the Smithsonian, National Museum, State and National Archives, the better-tailored, better-fed bureaucracy—high GSs. (That's how one judges people on government pay in Washington, J. Willard explained, by their GS ratings.) It was all laid out for them by a long-toothed girl with stone knees she kept stabbing with as she sipped her booze. She said she was GS-10 and took care of the pornographic section of the Library of Congress. Sheila must come.

Sheila said, "I'll make a note of it."

"Had enough?" J. Willard asked.

"No, no. It's a Washington I never knew of."

They moved on as part of some close group of government workers (GS-4s) to a professor's Connecticut Avenue apartment where a lot of Jesus freaks and bearded Zen students were smoking pot and the professor was playing Eskimo fertility chants on his tape recorder. It was here it happened; a fellow fell down on a broken beer bottle and gashed himself deeply in a leg. They couldn't get an ambulance on the phone or a doctor either—not on Saturday night. And the poor bastard (he was GS-6 in the Civil Service Commission) was terrified at the sight of his own gore. J. Willard and Sheila put him in a taxi and took him to General Hospital.

It was a madhouse scene there—finale to a Saturday night. Ambulances clanging coming and going, drunks, amateur hara-kiris, raped girls, busted arms and legs, bruised and bone-shattered victims of muggers, aborting women with labor pains, damaged perverts and casuals of way-out parties; all merged here massed in the hospital's lobbies, waiting repairs, beds, emergency treatment, stitching, injections, stomach pumps.

Sheila wondered if there was any kind of mad logic present in this species, indigenous to an incompatible Saturday night, making the hospital scene.

"A suicide," J. Willard said, "has the right of way over a knife wound unless the weapon is still in the body."

The fellow they had brought from the party was whimpering, his gashed leg wrapped in a tablecloth. Sheila forced her way into the crush of the maimed and moaning and came back at last with a fat little man with Spanish skin and Cuban features.

"Damn, damn *el río pasado*," he said. "Missus Senator Crockhead, you see how mad everything is. It is the Hell Night. Everybody wants to get drunk Saturday—get laid, get doped, eat bad food, begin to abort, bugger a pet, walk in dangerous places, think of jumping in the Potomac—all on Saturday night. Yes, your *amigo*, he fell on a broken glass? Dark blood—may have nipped an artery. Not a bed here, not a ward."

"Do something."

"Yes, Missus Senator, but we are filled *hup*. Well, there may be a bed in maternity. But I have to *hust* sew up that gash and hope we have his blood type for a transfusion. What is his blood type? That's right, get his wallet, look it *hup*. Wheel him this way, boys. Blood type B? *Cual el cuervo tal su huevo*. He isn't a southern one, eh? Not mind if it's a transfusion of nigrah blood? We're very short just now; the white college boys don' sell their blood to us for twenty dollar a quart till after Easter, unless *hust* real short of cash. Ah, he's puking—good. Well, goodbye Missus Crockhead, Señor. My love to Senator, the Grand Corregidor. It's crazy in there. LSD acid heads coming out of it—don't come in—and soldier boys with Mickey Finns. Well, I would kiss your hand, only I'm a mess of piss and blood."

The stink was strong of Lysol, blood, wounds, floor buckets, the starch of tired nurses, stale breath; it was too much for Sheila. J. Willard got her out of the hospital hall where new damned and bloodied were arriving still; some fighting, some moaning, some not caring at all. The duty officer at the desk was smoking a short cigar. He looked at the wall clock. "It tapers off about four in the morning. Place smells like an early High Mass by then. No, we don't get the top White House or State boys. They go to Bethesda, Walter Reed, where they have real care. Hell, we run out of X-ray plates by nine o'clock on Saturdays."

Sheila said, "I'm glad I saw it. But once *is* enough."

For J. Willard, the streets away from the hospital had a special mood, still a sense of the antebellum plantation owner about the old Washington. The newer part suggested a movie shot. There remained a flair about the city that made one a victim of its special allure, J. Willard said.

"It is, of course, in part Gomorrah-on-the-Potomac in the picture and newsweek features, but they are always looking for the offbeat. They holler there is more crime, more drinking, more unmarried misery; but there are also as many eager workers, lovers of order and law, packed tight with national pride. It's the dullness of the jobs, the hopelessness of being racked in a system where the road from GS-4 to GS-14 is twenty years long and ends with a pension of money printed on snowflakes. The lowly clerks and professors in the service, the scientists, mostly take to moonlighting. They tend bar, play banjo in little dives."

Sheila took a very hot bath when she got home. And a strong cocktail.

Chapter 23

It was J. Willard's last night in Washington. Jason and Sheila took him to a restaurant with a real fireplace, a nostalgic pianist noodling Jerome Kern, and outside a parking lot with mostly older cared-for American cars, no Mercedes 220s.

"It isn't that I'm one of those old creeps who thinks the horse and buggy was the best form of transportation, or that the randy old family doctor who made house calls really was better without a knowledge of modern medical science; it's just we're creating more history than we can consume."

J. Willard was drinking bourbon and enjoying pork chops well done with red-eye gravy as he liked them. "Now we hope to get Paul Ormsbee off and running, I want to get out of Washington. It's still the same city of homogeneous Greek-Roman buildings and monuments of spirals and parabolas. But now it's really out of touch with the rest of the nation. It's milking the country and spending like mad. Ten million federal employees! I know I sound like a sockless populist fearing the city slickers entrenched in the corridors of power. Truth is, the Texans are in and the big corporations are run by snake oil salesmen who came off the farms. Not that I buy the naiveté of noble ideas made of snowflakes; I really feel we're not prepared to face the next twenty-five years of this damn crazy century . . . Waiter, another Old Forester and less branch water."

"I think, Pop, we're aware of your fears. But you heard Austin Barraclough; since the Grant Administration there has been both erosion and evolution. The changes since Gettysburg haven't been properly evaluated. I hate to say the spiritual qualities we may have once had have been ignored. But I think I know, hell, I'm sure, we can survive. Unless some crackpot Russian or Arab presses the button on the doomsday machine."

Sheila looked up from her *cordon bleu escalopes.* "Dessert?"

"A blueberry pie here that isn't full of cornstarch?"

They didn't have blueberry pie, but there was a fairly good apple pie, piping hot and a good chunk of country cheddar to go with it.

"We used to call it rat cheese, Jay, or store cheese when I was young. Isn't that the goddamnest saddest line in the language? *'When I was young.'* Yes, let's go walking tonight. Washington has all the good shapes right out of a fifth-grade civics schoolbook. I suppose they don't have those old civics books anymore in the classrooms?"

"It's not safe," said Jason, motioning to the waiter for the check. "I mean some of the streets."

But they did walk (in the more lighted places) where the prowl cars passed every few minutes. Walked where the lemony neon flickered with red patterns, past the stealthy whisper of fountains sounding like night beasts drinking. Walked by, hearing warm voices disappearing into the darkness, past trees fighting gasoline fumes, chemical dusts, beige and almond-green in the little parks hiding forgotten bronzes. Many of the public buildings were outlined in skillfully placed lighting.

J. Willard said, "No, *not* the Lincoln Memorial; too many cheap bastards have used it, sentimentalized it. Just let's walk on the old slate slabs, those that are left. The Willard Hotel I hear has gone down before progress. When I was a small boy, would you believe it, you could still find a bit of horseshit in the streets. My father stayed at the Willard, backed Teddy Roosevelt when he ran as Bull Moose."

"We know," said Jason, "and we're keeping it quiet."

"Let's walk. I remember when me and Buster Miller were here as young punks, and one morning we ran into Charles Evans Hughes out walking, beard and cane and, so help me, spats; yes, spats. And we ran after him yelling 'Beaver, beaver,' and to get away from us he jumped into a cab. Charlie Hughes was a good old coot, you know. Went to bed one night thinking he had been elected President of the United States, and woke up to find out California's vote had put him in the ashcan. Let's walk."

But they had walked too far. J. Willard's legs, or the effects of the bourbon he had taken on, affected him and they, like Charles Evans Hughes, took a cab, were driven back to the eating place and Jason's car.

They delivered J. Willard to Dulles Airport for his midnight flight back to Vista City—meeting Buster Miller and Bascom Rice, who seemed also to have been celebrating in Washington. There were exchanges of greetings, farewells, and J. Willard not only kissed Sheila, but also his son, a real old-fashioned cheek kiss which Jason felt sentimental about, was really touched.

"Now, Pop, you and those two old rips just take it easy, and not more than two drinks each from the hostess."

The airport lights blinked ruby and emerald, the sound of jets made a background; the sky was moonlit and the heavy steel birds seemed batlike to Jason, who had had more to drink than he usually did. The effect was not wearing off. Walking arm in arm with Sheila to the parking lot, it seemed to him he was again in the mood of the young hopeful trying for the governorship and the life in Washington seemed alien and unreal, even untrue. Esme was right, he *was* a yokel. Thinking of Esme, with his wife clinging to his arm, Jason felt the feline cruelty of life sometimes, its illusions. He lost the intuitive perception, his feeling that the last months were vital; all melted away in the dark. So close to the physical presence of someone to whom he was being unfaithful. Was life all flagrant contradiction? Did one do good, press one's hopes by dispensing with so much one had been taught? Disillusionment is inevitable for a politician if he thinks. (Amos Fowler had said that casually, thrown it out.)

He felt Sheila shaking his arm. "Two dollars for your thoughts?"

"Two dollars?"

"Used to be two cents. Inflation."

He unlocked the car. "My thoughts? Just windy daydreams. Or rather night thoughts. Pop looks so old, still a bit raucous, but you get the sense of time passing too fast. That sort of banal thinking."

"Liar. You were moon-gazing on a different level."

She slid into the car seat and he got behind the wheel. "I was really thinking of the two dancing girls I'm keeping in the Shoreham. Gift of the Shah. These honey buns know every secret of the Kama Kura. One hundred and fifty pounds of animated amorous butter, each of course."

"I ate too much," Sheila said, turning on the car radio to a whine of Nashville sound.

Jason drove carefully at a good clip. Esme had somehow intruded into his thoughts. His gob of guilt was flitting there in the roadway just ahead of him.

"You don't believe in my dancing girls?"

"Of course I do. You really have bad taste in women." She laughed and hung on one of his arms. "I'm the only good taste in dames you ever showed, Mr. Crockett."

He let it go at that. What the devil was he doing? Trying to be found out? Be punished, humiliated? Jason was sweating and he lowered the car window on his side. The night air smelled of wet earth, of traffic and that odd scent, was it the world revolving on its axis? He brooded on what event the day would bring beyond country music on car radios.

For a week Jason was the faithful husband. He even convinced himself, almost, that he had been attracted to Esme Lowell because she was related to Austin Barraclough, that part of his motive in going to bed with her was to come closer to his scheme. Well, not a scheme, but a plan, a pattern. It wasn't all that clear to him and he was aware he didn't fully know himself. He was, he knew, motivated by various emotions, driven to know, to find out, to test; yes, he convinced himself, to test himself against someone like Austin, who had been so close to what every politician worth his salt wanted, top position in the running of the party.

But as the week passed and he remembered Esme—the bedroom, their romps; *romps* seemed such a harmless word—he was astonished to discover the physical urge, the drive in him to see her again, to carry on as they had begun. I am not an evil man, he assured himself. I am human, much too human, and I may be trapped by my body, my sensual side. And so further reassuring himself as so many men, and some women, have in a like situation; I, she, we are harming no one.

He was busy. Congress would soon reconvene, there were bills to prepare and meetings to be held, and the publicity work to be done to project Senator Paul Ormsbee as one of the possibles, the one best possibility, as the man to nominate at the next national convention.

Then, almost without thinking much about it, as if driven by certain deep-seated impulses that he could not control, Jason phoned Esme. Not from his office (yes, I am becoming furtive). He called her from a public phone off the Senate Dining Room.

"Well, how's the busy man?" The sound of her voice sent a spur along his spine.

"Damn busy. Up to my navel in getting ready for the coming session."

"Been busy myself—have this ten-acre farm in Virginia on my listings, and the buyer, one of those television stars, has been playing the Arab rug peddler game, making small rising offers. Tonight?"

He thought, and heard her say, "Huh?"

"Tonight. I'll be tied up till seven." To his surprise he added, "Missed you."

"That's what I like to hear. Seven. I'll whomp up something. Like soft-shell crabs?"

"Like *everything* you serve up."

Goddamn the Noel Coward dialogue. But he walked away from the bank of phone booths feeling younger, elated, at least the eager part of him; there was, as always, that lump of guilt, small but there.

They made love in the sun-room before the dinner—on the wickerwork sofa, knocking over the vase of pampas grass. Then later again upstairs in the big brass bed. There was no hint from Esme of why he had not called her for a week, and he wondered if she had accepted his excuse, or if this silence on the subject was part of the nature of women that he would never understand. The female instinct to gloss over what would displease—as he had heard—at least at this stage of an intimacy. Also when they had pleasured each other and were sated, resting side by side, the smoke of the post-sexual cigarette weaving its way slowly toward the ceiling, there was in Jason just the small thought that she had been perhaps involved with another man. The television star? Some small adventure on the Virginia side, with the careful buyer? He didn't feel he was being fair to her, and besides they had no binding agreement as to their faithfulness to each other. In fact, the subject had never come up. Had been carefully avoided.

For the next two months he managed at least two visits a week to Esme's small house. They began to talk somewhat of trivial things in their pasts. Exchanged small confidences.

With the opening of the new session of the Senate and the House, Jason found himself no longer a freshman, a man serving for the first time on the Hill. He was a second-year man, and clearly much above the freshman senators and congressmen whom he helped with advice, locating apartments and flats, aided by Esme. He taught the new men the ropes; the tradition, political rules. He held long talks on the party's policies for the coming session.

People began to see Jason Crockett not just as some backwoods ex-governor from someplace west of the Mississippi where they cut tall timber, canned fish and backpacked into the high country. He did good work on the Appropriations Committee.

He and Sheila were on the White House grounds when Prince Ali Bedur Youseff and some of his harem were welcomed by the President and the heads of State; the marine band tooting after a twelve-gun salute to the prince, who was in syphilitic progressive paralysis; he controlled so much Middle East oil and approved of a potential U.S. naval base in the Indian Ocean.

The Crocketts danced at the British Embassy on Commonwealth Day, and a week later drank Rhine wine with the Germans, a few of the staff (when too deep in drink) regretting, they told Jason, the failure of the Thousand Year Reich. As one of the attachés said to Sheila, whirling her around the dance floor, "Not enough of the *Juden* went up the chimney." But she was not aware of this Teutonic jest about concentration camp ovens. She and Jason didn't care for the self-aggrandizement of Germans.

They liked best the English, the Italian Embassy parties. The French served a fine bouillabaisse at their parties, and Jason grew wiser about the Machiavellian, masonic ways of life in Washington. He felt he had lost any provincialism he might have brought with him. He now saw the social scene as part of the political launching pad one must use.

Lunching at the Capitol Hill Club with Paul Ormsbee, Senator Silverthorn and Tom Pedlock of Pedlock & Sons, Fifth Avenue (as Paul whispered, "the largest and most exclusive chain of department stores"), Jason was able to sense that Paul Orsmbee would indeed be able to collect funds to run a good solid primary campaign for delegates to the national convention, now just a little over a year away.

Joel Silverthorn sat solid, handsome and amused. "There is no eastern establishment, Jason, that you folks among the low plains and high mountains fear. And Wall Street doesn't control anything much but the forty to sixty corporations that own the country. Am I being frank, Tommy?"

Tom Pedlock seemed overpolite. "Now, Joel, that kind of talk only imbeds the idea we are still ruled by the old-line political systems. That's all over, Senator, believe me. The country is being split apart by conservative forces of both parties joining together and by the liberal forces of both parties beginning to think alike."

Paul Ormsbee looked up from his crab à la Maryland. "You think the old-line parties are going down the drain?"

"Not likely," said Jason, "unless we act like the Whigs and the Federalists did. Fight a civil war inside the party and one day wake up and there are no Federalist or Whig parties. Now, Paul, Joel, myself and others on committees of the next convention have been jockeying—they see you as the standard-bearer, have also been meeting to see what's needed."

"Money," said Joel Silverthorn.

"Lots of it," said Tom Pedlock. "Friendly bureaucrats, as Judge Fowler said, who pat you on the back, are not enough."

"I've loyal good friends. They like me," said Paul. "Why, I can phone two hundred people in any state in the union and they'd be glad to help me. Two hundred in *any* state—well, maybe not in Maine or Hawaii."

Jason signaled for a refill of their coffee cups. "Now, Paul, with new laws, regulations, and memories soured by the Nixon look, illegal corporation washing of money in Mexico and Switzerland— anyway, the party isn't playing with any of *that*. Here's a list of contacts Tom has made of those who will raise funds for your primaries. Legitimate. Laramie Scudder has his hands on the moneybags in New York state. Senator Dudley Giron of Louisiana will get the gas and oil personnel to help. Jim Houston will handle the lawyers, corporation attorneys who want to help the party."

"Isn't Big Jim the lawyer for the big protected crooks and bribers?" asked Tom Pedlock.

Jason said smoothly, "Big Jim is the keenest legal mind in Washington, and *our* legal adviser. Every man is entitled to the best lawyer he can buy."

"Congressman Cheu Chin Lee helping?" asked Paul. "We gave Hawaii a lot of defense sites, navy yards, ship repair docks."

"Congressman Lee will see the big sugar and pineapple, hotel and tourist people support us."

"And the unions," asked Paul. "We could have put Wally Klamath and some of his union buddies in the Atlanta slammer and some of the others too, and a few of the dock unions."

Jason smiled, "We still may, Paul, but I think we can count on certain of the unions supporting us, also the farm co-ops, the milk, the dairy people and fruit combines. We've done as much, and more, as the opposition to raise their prices. How much, Tom, do you think we can raise for a solid primary setup for Paul?"

"Figure ten million before the nomination and a matching federal fund if it isn't screwed up by some changes."

Joel Silverthorn shook his head. "That's a lot of money before the nominating convention, Senator Crockett."

"A hell of a lot, Senator Silverthorn, and it's going to get bigger. Television, the media, airing some dislikes of politicians by the people since Watergate, sidestepping questions of the FBI and CIA spying and break-ins. All of this calls for a new way of humanizing the candidate."

"Jesus," said Paul Ormsbee, stirring his coffee, "most presidential candidates once used to sit on the front porch whittling on a bit of soft pine with a jackknife and drinking lemonade, and the voters didn't even know FDR couldn't walk. Too much exposure these days, and eating of gefilte fish and bagels in public. No offense, Tom."

Tom Pedlock smiled. "That's alright, Senator, some of my best friends are Christians. It's going to be a mean campaign. You can't depend anymore on the party loyalties of the voter. He's crossing lines. He wants sweet, satisfying answers."

Joel Silverthorn agreed. "Washington has fucked the public once too often. Austin Barraclough used to say they'll catch on we only love them once every four years. They no longer will accept the orthodox schisms, the distortions, evasions of old-time politics."

Jason said, "Our problem is not to let some hairy messiah from the tall grass muddle the real issues. Or some rock-hard reactionaries raise up their indignation at paying taxes."

Paul Ormsbee smiled. "I'm as grass roots as they come, I've been talking to the voters for a long time. I know them. Let's put the show on the road."

Jason, at that remark, felt that perhaps Paul, for all his self-righteous, shrewd knowledge, had talked to the voters much *too* long.

Chapter 24

The huge corporations and the unions were wary of contributions, even through legal methods. But in answer to Judge Amos Fowler's phone calls, some of them did pony up. Not as in the past, when both parties' financial directors had demanded millions, very much like blackmail, from defense contractors, oil companies that serviced the armed forces, motor companies that made tanks and ammo carriers. And from suppliers of beef and foodstuffs, corporations that needed favors from Internal Revenue, Justice, State, or other branches of government where a word from a senator or congressman would be of some help.

As Judge Fowler put it to Jason while they played a slow round of golf at Burning Tree, "You're going to get it, big money help. But don't expect it like it's been since the Civil War. Empire builders, or call them robber barons, steel and transport, food processing, drug and auto industry—you just winked at them in those days for handing out. Old Mark Hanna made it a perfect system, remember Mark Hanna? Ask Austin Barraclough about him. The front for coal and steel, ice and gas, at the turn of the century. He made a science out of scaring the shit out of big industry, the moneybags, and collecting millions to beat William Jennings Bryan for the presidency a few times. Put in McKinley and got really screwed when down went McKinley with a bullet in his gut and up popped Teddy Roosevelt. But Hanna started the whole political big-time money going to the party that played footsie with big business. Austin Barraclough's grandfather investigated it—nothing came of it."

"But that's over since Watergate."

Judge Fowler addressed his ball with a very old man's care,

stopped his swing in midair. "Bullshit and you know it, Jason. You just find out how it can be done next year. Say, how much of a handicap you going to give me?"

"Twelve."

"Want to bet five thousand dollars on our personal game?"

Jason smiled. "If you were a lobbyist you'd let me win, a legal bet between two sporting gentlemen. I'll bet you two dollars."

The judge swung and got off a fairly good drive. "Of course it isn't done this baldly anymore by any lobbyist. All the corporations have millions in secret and not-so-secret funds in Switzerland. But Uncle Sam is watchful. Tell me no bushwa—can Paul Ormsbee win the primaries?"

"You tell me, Judge. You take polls."

"He might *just* do it. How about dinner tonight with some of the Continental Food Products and National Metallic boys in town?"

"I want to talk to them, with the WDU and the AFL-CIO boys, but I have a dinner date, can't break it."

The fox face of Judge Amos Fowler remained questioning. He just said "Huh," as Jason sliced into high grass. Did the "huh" mean he knew it was Esme Lowell with whom he was having dinner? Christalmighty, there is no really well-kept secret in Washington. Snow Williams had called Jason twice to appear again on her noon-hour national broadcast. And her tone seemed to suggest he better *not* say no. Somehow he didn't seem to care; he wasn't careless and he didn't flaunt his mistress (he shivered a bit at the word *mistress—* it had the sound of decadent French kings in bed between lace sheets; also of French political officials knocking off early to visit some scented flat out of Colette, a granddaughter of Mata Hari waiting to have a nation betrayed).

Technically Esme *was* his mistress. They dined, not too often, in little out-of-the-way places in Virginia. They took walks along country lanes safe from muggers. They even at times went on the river after dark on a forty-foot launch owned by Jack Klein, a building contractor whom Esme knew and often worked with in land deals. It was fine on the water, even when a scud of clouds turned to tea-colored rain and the moon hid. They would come damply back to Esme's house, moist and amused, take showers together, several times bathe in the large tub and reenact scenes Esme claimed were from a Roman villa's wall paintings. They were still ardent after three months and liked to listen after lovemaking to mushy, sad recordings on the hi-fi, a gift to Esme from the firm that had her work out a way of getting their product—mar-proof tabletops—into a new motel in Virginia. Esme had a dozen items that had been given her by companies whose products she helped get into public view. Jason never questioned her too much about this taking of gifts. It was common in Washington, not at all considered payola, even if Jason couldn't see how it differed.

"Oh, it isn't done for money, Darling. It's advertising really. Better me than that fat CBS or *Time* magazine, plugging something."

Esme had become rather indiscreet; sharing with him some of the secrets of the town, the deadly gossip, the hanky-panky going on. He, like most people in Washington, was interested in gossip and enjoyed the often sordid games of the important people, the plaintive, ordinary desires of men, and a few women, who imposed their will on so many.

One night as they lay in the brass bed, the music—Scriabin's *Piano Preludes*—very, very low, Esme talked of something she had avoided so far in their intimate relationship. Jason had not brought up the subject, but suddenly, mashing out her cigarette in the semi-dark of the bedroom, Esme began to talk of Austin Barraclough. She had been rather sad that day, feeling the pathos of life, she said, and he suspected her period was near, the nipples of her breasts swelling and being very tender. She spoke softly, addressing the ceiling.

"You're getting to know Austin pretty well now, aren't you?"

"Not really. I hear stories from Amos Fowler, and compare them to what I know of my contact with your uncle, and well—"

"Amos is a clever man—he fears Austin Barraclough."

"I sense that."

"There are a lot of stories they tell about my uncle."

"It's as if there is a great secret they don't all know, but talk about."

"Everybody thinks they know some of it."

"But strong enough, I mean something big enough to keep him from the last national convention?"

"Look, it was being offered, it was Uncle Austin who refused."

"All right, you tell me why?"

"Oh hell, that means backtracking into family history. Uncle Austin liked women, needed women, I mean he was a man who enjoyed being married. When he was a widower you could sense he was uncomfortable at Potomac House. Just him, a housekeeper and Champ as his valet, butler *and* stooge. It was six months after he buried the first Mrs. Barraclough that he met Mona at a horse show in Westchester. She was a crazy rider and looked wonderful on a horse. Reckless—she once won a jumping event after a fall, went on with a broken wrist. Did he fall in love? Was he infatuated with the way she rode or looked? Who knows. He decided to marry her."

"She was much younger?"

"Twelve years. Been divorced. Was a Randolf, which means something in certain circles. Anyway, Uncle Austin, he's a hell of a charmer—'charm the hands off a clock' someone once said—he got a new tailor, gave up heavy Havana cigars, Mona didn't like them. And in six weeks it was all settled. Champ was sent away to the stock farms in South Carolina, decorators came in to change the color scheme at Potomac House, the best furniture was recovered. Historians of furniture moaned over what was done to Regency and Chippendale. Never mind. There was an English butler, Mona's Irish maid and a chef who had papers showing he had been in the kitchens of the George Cinq in Paris. The couple moved in after a short honeymoon, attending an international conference in Rome. It was the only happy period of the marriage."

Esme picked up the glass from the night table and took a sip. Jason lay back in the bed and studied the ceiling, its cast shadows created by the one lamp lit in the bedroom.

"It didn't work, the marriage?"

"Never had a chance. Once moved in at Potomac House, it was clear Mona couldn't settle in anyplace, that there was a wide neurotic streak in her; that she lived on adrenalin, always on the go, always seeking excitement, wanting something different. A sickness. One doctor explained it by irregular brain waves, inherited nerves. The Randolfs were all a bit nutty, and some violent. I think she had this Hemingway thing, a fear of natural death and always looking for the other; on horseback, sailing or fast driving. Okay, maybe I'm making *too* much of her induced accidents."

"No, there are such people."

"Well, Uncle Austin is no rose, he has a temper and has got enough *macho* built in him to yell back and shake a fist, point a finger. He tried to bring Mona to heel. He knew her soon enough for the bitch she was. But he loved her. Maybe all those crazy ways

of hers intrigued him, I don't know. I was close to them then and
I didn't like Mona, so you're getting pretty lousy values of her
from me."

"At least I'm getting something."

"Pour me another drink . . . Yes, I saw, heard slanging matches,
and Mona lifting a riding crop to Uncle Austin—just lifting. Also
times when they were really loving each other and howling with
laughter, up to their asses in hunting dogs and smelling of the best
horses. Trouble was, Uncle Austin was the party whip in the Senate,
and being mentioned more and more for the presidency. And he had
to entertain the uncouth congressmen, the slobs and the party bosses.
Mona hated all this stuff of practical politics. Never tried to understand there was a side to Austin Barraclough that belonged to, loved
the game of politics. She made a rotten hostess and put the verbal
knife into the big mick who owned Chicago. Also she tried her wit,
she had a cruel barbed tongue, tried it on the lump of meannesses
who controlled the unions. It got so Uncle Austin entertained in
hotels . . . It looked good, damn good for him the year before the
national convention, to get the nomination."

"It sure did, Esme. I had the whole state ready to have its delegates committed to him."

"Yes. Then something happened, several things happened that you,
none of the delegates, knew about. First off, of all the irritations,
there was no Barraclough heir. Uncle Austin wanted one, had for
years, and the first Mrs. Barraclough never could give him a surviving kid. Mona got pregnant, and you never saw anyone carry on like
Uncle Austin; you'd think some shepherds had seen a star in the
sky and three wise men were on their camels hunting for the stable
of an inn."

Jason touched her naked shoulder, kissed it. "You really don't like
the second Mrs. Barraclough."

"I don't hide the things I like or dislike, do I?"

"Not with me. But there was a child, or—"

"Mona used the pregnancy to try and push the senator around.
And he made her cut down on her social habits, her parties, the
booze hounds and horse set, the kooks in their Porsches, the weekend
cross-country picnics. At first she gave in. I think she was a coward
about having that baby being made inside her. Really, this new experience of being with child, it scared her. The only time I ever got
really close to Mona was those first few months. She wanted me near

her to talk of how I had felt carrying my daughter, how I survived, all of my morning sickness, the whole megilla of being pregnant. What did I crave, did I feel? As if I had a cannonball in my belly all the time? I had a rather easy time of it, but I made it out to Mona to be a risky, mean business. I'm a bitch at times, aren't I, Darling?"

"No comment. So—?"

"Although her pregnancy was a secret, there were a few people who knew she lost the child. Only they believed she had defied Uncle Austin and entered a horse show, fallen at a jump and miscarried. Truth is when Uncle Austin was away in San Francisco at a meeting of western governors, she got so bored at Potomac House reading Balzac, uncle's favorite author, she got pie-eyed on one of the oldest bottles of Barraclough brandy and fell down the main staircase—right from the top. That ended Uncle Austin's hopes for an heir. Mona said no, never, to trying it again when she came back from the hospital."

"I don't see how that turned the senator off from accepting a nomination he could have had hands down."

"Oh, *that* happened two months later, the kiss-off to the nomination. Mona, to recover her health, insisted they stay for a month at some island off the Bermuda group. Some rich English sportsman had an estate down there and Mona had known him from her prize-winning jumping days. And he offered it to them. So they went there. One morning after a violent battle, according to Champ, who had been reinstated and taken along to valet the senator, Uncle Austin left the place in a rage. He walked the beaches till darkness. Came back late at night. Mona met him at the door, shot him with one of the rifles taken from a case of weapons her sporting friend kept to hunt wild goats on the island. Shot him through the right lung."

Jason made a whistling sound and stared at Esme. She was leaning on an elbow in the bed facing him, amused at the expression on his face. "Gotcha there, didn't I?"

"If I were standing, you'd have knocked me right on my duff. I mean, none of this—there hasn't been any hint of—"

"You're damn right. It took a bit of effort, bypassing law and order. But the sporting friend was a power on the islands. It wasn't even listed unofficially as an accident while cleaning a rifle. There was a French surgeon nearby on an island. He took out the bullet and it was touch and go for a week. You remember the story, the senator was off deepsea fishing with some scientific hush-hush purpose? Well, he was on the island with drainage tubes in him and two nurses restraining Mona. No, she wasn't violent all the time—just sat smoking cigarettes and talking to a fox terrier in residence. She was mildly sedated."

"But the senator did appear at rallies, made party speeches."

"Sure he did. But by then two Frenchmen and a Viennese set of Herr Doktors had flown out to treat and evaluate Mona. Their verdict; she was of unsound mind and could sink into dangerous dementia at any time. Uncle Austin was not going to take *that* kind of First Lady into the White House. He blew his hopes at the convention."

Jason found he was staring at the opposite wall, his mouth open. He heard Esme say, "It busted him for a long time. It was like a bad cut; you don't feel the pain for a while, then it begins. I felt so sorry for that poor bastard, my uncle. And Mona with a nurse or two, getting away with it . . ." There was entreaty in Esme's voice as she turned to Jason. "I need a little loving."

The building up of Senator Paul Ormsbee's image began with a presenting of the man as being all good things to all sections of the country. He took on the task of appearing in many places. At country fairs to the whine of country music, where he admired the fine points of the rumps of cattle, tasted pickled watermelon rind and assured the farmers (as he ran some soil through his fingers) that he had as a youth been at home behind a tractor plow and that he loved the taste of well water (both true.) He also donned his Perregaux watch and was entertained at Grosse Pointe in Regency rooms with ormolu mirrors and tables of detailed marquetry, where he agreed with auto magnates and executives that the auto transportation of the nation—the heart of the national economy—was best left in American hands and that he was considering higher taxes against imports from Japan and Germany.

Jason laid out the master plan with aid from the most costly minds on Madison Avenue and among those in the party who were backing Senator Ormsbee for the highest office. Paul was a tenacious talker, a bit past his prime perhaps as a speaker, his notions of appealing prose just a bit out of style. But six young men and women recruited from newsmagazines and Hollywood were kept busy writing Paul's speeches—which he insisted on editing, as he told Jason, "to my way of talk. I don't want to quote Whitehead or Proust or throw them into a catatonic state of doubt by wit, like poor old Stevenson. They don't want a smart aleck."

"Just don't say too much about how things were better in the old days or of the hardships of the pioneers against the Indians. The majority of the voters, their early folks came over steerage or were slaves, and the good old days were sharecropping, sweatshopping and getting beaten by the police when they tried to strike."

"Jay, I *know* the people."

"Nobody knows the people anymore. J. Willard says the old days of lifelong party loyalties are gone. The people now change sides like in Red Rover, and there are younger generations that scare me at times."

"It's the same good old country, Jay, underneath."

Paul Ormsbee did well with his good old country style, and certainly he was ahead of two of his rivals in popularity in the six months before the primaries, as some private polls showed. He was solidly impressive, a bit too bulky, but clever tailoring and a strict diet fixed that. And he could answer questions as to the financial fiddling in some departments. Nefarious payoffs by big business got its lumps from him in the farmlands, while the meanness and narrowness of the backward sections of the nation toward social progress was pointed out to liberal gatherings. He talked out to blacks and chicanos, claiming bigotry was as out-of-date as stoning sinners, and was against busing to fight segregation.

Paul Ormsbee was a good man, Jason knew, a man perhaps too eager to please, but with a good record, at least in his early years in the Senate. He looked fine, Austin agreed. "He sounds good, even if a bit pompous. He doesn't rub the liberals the wrong way, and the damn reactionaries may scowl, but they'll support him if he wins the first primaries. They know the side their dividends are buttered on."

Jason kept himself from clashing with the advocates of Paul's two rivals in the party. They were also going to enter most of the state primaries. Zack Boone was the latest of the southern populists, the pride of piney woods, the redneck folks. He really had come down barefooted from the hills to attend law school, made speeches in Baptist gatherings, sold Bibles and sewing machines, and was bright, mean-eyed, with a hatred of all who had exploited his kin in the mill towns, or driven them off their acres by foreclosures and tax sales. Zack Boone was not a drinking man, but a good, clever speaker in the country language and crossroads jargon of solid privy words. Some northern reporter wrote he was like William Faulkner's Snopes, a mean-mouthed, greedy primitive who "would shoot his mother, some say, and bet you which way she would fall." But Zack Boone won elections—county clerk, state senator, lieutenant governor, state's attorney—and he had twice been governor of his state, handling its financial affairs skillfully. Allowing only those things no political wise man would do away with; letting the sheriffs control the permitting of gambling, and a lot of bootlegging. "They handle their own affairs as long as they get the voters together on election days." Zack Boone was a good governor, beating down the railroads' rip-offs, the oil companies' cozy tax setups, even if his own brother-in-law did a lot of the state trucking and his wife's father had the biggest insurance business in that whole section of the South.

Zack himself didn't care for much but handling a crowd with his fervid preacher style, gave up the corn whiskey that used to keep him mellow after hours. He was faithful to his wife, who was part Cherokee, loved his four children and had the idea that the common people had "had a hoe handle up their ass so long they were afraid to shit—or see who was stealing them blind. I like the nigrahs and they get their share of the state jobs. They know and trust me, and they have been as bad off as sharecroppers as any pore white. I don't give a good goddamn about the Klan or the American Legion. They support me and I yell on 'em if they get too randy or scare booger. I got support all through the Middle West, and the big-city folk in them stinking, sick ghettos are beginning to see I can do something about making their streets safe. And taxes—I can cut down taxes by cleaning out at least five million loafing bastards taking coffee breaks on the federal payroll. The State Department now has got twenty thousand people on its payroll pushing cookies and serving tea. Whatever for? We don't need anybody in the State Department but some Harvard dude to tell the Russians to fuck off and a staff of office boys to be polite. Hell, we appoint most of our ambassadors because they pony up cash for elections, don't we? I'd castrate federal power like we do our hogs back home."

Crude stuff, a lot of Washington said. Jason's polls showed Zack Boone could do a lot of damage to Paul Ormsbee.

He told Austin, "Zack Boone, he's a spoiler. He's mean, but he's smart. He reminds some people of Huey Long and George Wallace, only on a lower, more honest level. He's closer to the dissatisfaction of the poor, black and white, than the others ever were. He likes blacks, he's a very smart Okie, a hillbilly who has some majority of the anti-big-city people seeing him as a hope."

Austin lit a pipe, puffed it into smoking and drawing well. "People forget Faulkner's Snopeses were also smart enough to grab off a lot of what they wanted from the fat and greedy. They never gave a damn about the glories of the days *before* the 'War between the States.' And they were smelling the good life in the windows of Sears and J. C. Penney's and beyond. If Zack Boone starts rolling, he can cut into the party's hopes so far he'll ruin Paul's chances."

"What's to be done, Austin?"

"Invite him *in* to sit at *our* table. Ask what he'd like for his people. But not just yet—wait until the primaries show what strength he has. But go talk to him."

The other candidate who would carry some weight in the primaries was Grover Asa Bremont. Third-generation money, inherited, not earned, in shipping and natural gas, multimillions of it. And dozens of Bremonts; a natural solid family. Papal Knights, Knights of St. John, publishers of a string of conservative weekly newspapers. Loud, handsome people with far too many teeth and rather small eyes; pious breeders, with estates at Grosse Pointe, Santa Barbara, the West Indies, in the Carolinas. All aggressive, reactionary, respectful of the status of money and social position, even if here they never had cracked the top exclusive ranks of Protestant society at its highest levels. Having to make do with the Murrays, the McDonalds, the Butlers, the Kennedys, the Buckleys and the Kellys ("with their princess of a crap table"—J. Willard).

The Bremonts, as with most of the newly rich, were always reminded by their enemies of their early rise from pork butchers, paddies, gandy dancers, lace curtain Irish, peasant French; who, through luck and certain debatable pasts, had made it big.

Grover Asa Bremont was stiff, slow of movement, well mannered and low-spoken. Some felt him a snob, others thought him dull. But no one ignored his steady drive, his persistent awareness of his money, his aggressive family; all the brothers and sisters, uncles, aunts, nieces and nephews who were also aggressive and bright. The female Bremonts seemed even sharper and more abusive than the males. All moved in solid rank behind Grover Asa Bremont. He had handled the family business from youth to maturity, had joined the family law firm, been elected to the state assembly out of Chicago (with the help of a solid political machine and the great industries behind him), as attorney general of the state, Ambassador to Ireland (he wanted Paris, got Dublin.)

Now he was a congressman, the party whip in the House, and was rallying his forces to make a run for the presidency.

Jason feared him more than Zack Boone. "Grover lacks the warmth of John Kennedy, he's got no humor, no ability to bend down to people, but he gives off the glow of wealth, and the middle class can be fooled that everybody against a Bremont is a no-good radical, that Grover stands for good solid values we've lost and a return to tough law and order, capital punishment, abolishing the rights of every woman to a legal abortion, and no equal women's rights. Two-thirds of the women of this country seem to hate women in power, *other* women having rights. The bastard also has the money and all those newspapers behind him. The French peasant side of him is crafty."

"There's no solid Catholic block of voters," replied Austin. "That's a myth. A poll shows half of them don't even go to church regularly."

"Not a solid block maybe, but he could grab off enough to ruin Paul. Anyway, it's the blind conservatives, the reactionaries I fear."

"If Paul makes a really big showing in the primaries, he'll be getting a majority of the far-right voters Grover has been hoping for. That and the rest, the liberals, the middle-roaders, can show Paul's strength."

Jason hoped so. Six months before the primaries things looked very good. The polls, both public and private, showed Paul ahead, for what the polls were worth. ("If you polled Heaven you might find a majority for the Devil by people who wanted a change"— Austin Barraclough.)

Paul Ormsbee was set to address the International Policy Association in Philadelphia. It would be a keynote speech before the convention, and would get the attention of the nation. It would be televised. Jason and the writers worked on the speech with Paul. Expert legal advisers were called in to vet it; prominent members of State, of Justice, offered hints as to content—in conversations in private clubs, of course.

Paul was confident, continued on his diet, took advice on the writing of the speech. A retired screen star coached him on delivery, two gag writers submitted six pages of jokes, of which two were accepted. Paul radiated energy, felt confident. "It's the biggest thing since I came out of the Blue River bottoms to run for county controller."

Chapter 25

"Let it ring."

"We forgot to take the phone off the cradle."

"Pay it no mind."

"*Why* do they keep ringing?"

"Most likely wrong number."

"What time is it?"

Jason looked at the little clock on the cluttered night table, set between a pack of Winstons and an ashtray in the shape of a water-lily, lettered *Atlantic City*.

"Eleven-twenty, damnit." Jason was feeling in need of sleep. He was visiting Esme for the first time in five days; there had been so much to do, with editing speeches to be given, okaying copy for newspaper ads in small towns when the primaries started, approving TV spots. So tonight he had felt he had to get away to Esme. And with Paul Ormsbee on his way to give that speech tomorrow in Philadelphia, Jason felt he had earned a night, or at least some part of a night, of love.

He had just been dozing off, and Esme was reciting to him the success of a shopping area, a plan that she and that contractor client of hers, Klein, had put over; Jason wasn't paying much attention, dozing in the relaxed therapeutic atmosphere that followed his sexual activities, when the goddamn phone had begun ringing.

It continued ringing, almost in spurts of a nasty ding tone. Esme got out of bed. "I'll take it off the hook." She picked up the phone and hesitated about putting it down, listening for just a hint from the caller. She listened for a moment and glanced at Jason, sitting up in bed rubbing his naked chest.

She said, "What? . . . yes . . . wait . . . hold it."

"What kind of a fool call is it?" asked Jason. "The hell with it."

Esme reached for a robe draped across a chair with her free hand, as if someone on the phone could see her in her nudity. She faced Jason. "It's Clair Brooks, says she wouldn't have called but this is of the most vital importance."

"Clair? How did she—never mind."

He got out of bed, scowling. How did Clair ever trace him here? How did she ever know? What did she know? He took the phone from Esme's hand as she began getting into the robe's sleeves.

"Hello—what is this all about?"

Clair's voice came through to him, pitched a bit too high. "Sorry. I'm sorry to call you at—never mind, I *had* to reach you. The Associated Press has just announced that Paul—Senator Ormsbee— was early tonight removed from the club car section of the Amtrak special train *The Senator* when taken ill. At first it was thought to be an attack of indigestion. He died a half hour ago at the Cape May County Hospital of a massive coronary."

"Senator Ormsbee, Paul dead?" It didn't seem the right thing to say or the proper reaction. He stared at Esme who was fully covered, tying the belt of the robe, her eyes were wide open, her lips parted in surprise at the news. Jason felt suddenly very ashamed of being naked. "Look, Clair, round up, oh—Joel Silverthorn, India Kingston, Judge Fowler, Shirley Lippman, Jim Houston, contact any of the Ormsbee campaign committee. And Sarah Pearl Adams if she's in town. They're to meet me at the Protocol Club in half an hour. Alert the club manager."

"Yes. We've been trying to get you, at the Hill, Georgetown. The *Washington Post* got me at home. I'm sorry, but the *Post,* the *Star* all want statements as to—"

"Yes, yes. No statements until after we meet. Call my home and tell Mrs. Crockett you've found—contacted—me. I've been discussing sites to rent for election headquarters all through the Tidewater and eastern shore."

"Yes." He didn't know if Clair sounded sarcastic, or cold, or was just upset by the bad news, this turn of affairs.

Jason hung up and found his shorts. He put them on, hunted his socks. Esme stood facing him. He looked up at her, aware of the smell of cigarette smoke from her last cigarette, the scent of their bodies in the room, fresh from lovemaking; it seemed obscene suddenly.

"Paul Ormsbee dead," he said slowly. "He was really in good shape. Had a physical last week, and was passed kay-okay."

"That's how heart failures seem to run, according to tradition. *After* a good checkup. What will you do?"

"Decide if we have someone else strong enough to put into the primaries. I'd hate to think Grover or Boone are going to gain by this death. Paul was a good man. Not a great man, but a fine human being."

"Well, tuck your shirt into your pants and let me get you a drink. We need it."

He began to tie his shoelaces. "How did that girl know to get me here?"

"Oh, come on, mister," said Esme, returning from the bathroom with a bottle and glasses. "Sometimes I need a morning snort; it's a help sometimes." She poured and he drank a strong brandy. Esme was wryly smiling. "A secretary who doesn't know all her boss's secrets isn't worth having. She'll be discreet. They all usually have little dreams about the men they work for. Seriously, tragically, you Ormsbee people are now high and dry. Beached."

"We haven't really prepared a second-string man. Senator Dudley Giron?—nineteenth-century mossback. Joel Silverthorn, he's too Jewish; as a Jew you have to be an Episcopalian named Goldwater, and he didn't make it."

"So?"

"Roland Redmond is too old. There must be somebody. If only your uncle didn't have that tragic situation hanging over him. He's been very active. Really, almost the way he was in his prime."

"Well, Uncle Austin, he's out, with Mona talking to imaginary butterflies in Latin. Look, Darling." She came to him, buttoned his shirt, held him close, said, "Esme is a wise girl and knows a lot. *Don't* let them hang it on you. You're the brightest, the most popular young senator in the public eye. But—"

"But?" There had been that thought in his own mind. Who could take on the primaries, replace Paul—who, who . . . would it be him? Now he put an edge to his voice. "But *what?*"

"You're not ready. You're not ripe enough yet."

He turned away to zip up his fly. "Ripe? What the devil am I, a banana?"

"Now you're angry, Jay. I've fingered your ego."

"Still a yokel to you?"

She released him, stepped back, put one hand on her hip. "No, you're not any longer a hick from the tall timber. You're a smart operator—know all the ropes, even where some of the bodies are buried. But you're not ready at forty-four. You need more solid bills passed in your bag. More exposure nationally. And a little more knowledge of regional politics; in the South, up Maine way, the Mississippi basin. They're not like your own home grounds."

"Wait till I'm say near fifty, eh?" He seized his tie (like a strangling cord), flung it around his neck. "I'm more ready than those bastards Boone or Grover. I'm not in training to be Oliver Wendell Holmes or Thomas Jefferson. And, lady, I'm more than just a good lay!"

He shouldn't have said that, made that outrageous superficial crack. He could see Esme's features go taut, her stance become stiff-kneed. He could sense he had wounded her, and he hadn't meant it really. He let the tie ends flap as he turned to her. "That was a rotten thing to say. You know how I really feel about you. I'm deeply, deeply beholden to you. It isn't just for a—"

"A good fuck?" She hadn't relaxed her face. He bit on his lower lip as he knotted the tie.

"Esme, you're bright enough to understand this news socked me cold right on the end of the chin. I said anything that came out without thinking."

"Yes," she said, slapping one hand on his shoulder and with the other adjusting the tie knot. "Something certainly came out. You threw up the fact you think I'm just a sex maniac and I'd jump between the sheets with *any* well-hung stud."

He reached for his jacket and she continued to look at him, disconcerted, as she refilled her glass and took a gulp. "Damn, damn, damn. What are we fighting about? It's a crisis in the party, and we've both been lousy to each other facing it. We've failed each other this time. Call me when you've had the meeting."

Jason adjusted his jacket, shrugged the collar into place. He then held her and kissed her. "What's happened between us?"

She shrugged and leaned against him, moaned, "Oh, Jay, Jay, don't you ever leave here angry. Promise?"

"Promise."

In the deserted street he had trouble starting his car; the starter grinding, the battery losing power. But at last the motor sputtered, roared into life and he drove off toward the club. He spoke out loud, unaware of it, *"Who* isn't ready?"

The Liberty Bell Room at the club had been opened, lights turned on, ashtrays laid out on a scarred mahogany table. The place smelled of unvacuumed rugs, long dead cigars, also of decaying paper from bound volumes of old newspapers kept behind diamond-shaped glass doors. Joel Silverthorn was already there with extras of the *Post* and *Star*. He looked as if he'd dressed in a hurry: tieless, his vest unbuttoned. India Kingston was fiddling with an old-fashioned radio, getting mostly static. The old club steward, Mac Morris, shuffled around setting down on a rickety side table a tray of glasses, two pitchers of water, as if taking a calculated risk.

Joel Silverthorn said, "Right between the eyes. Hard. Paul Ormsbee!"

Jason nodded, sat down. "Jim Houston coming?"

"If Big Jim is in town he'll be here. Judge Fowler is in Palm Beach. The media been bothering you?"

"Not so far. Haven't reached me. Been busy on details."

"Yeah," said Silverthorn too sympathetically. Jason wondered did he, too, know of Esme? Jim Houston came in. He had on a camel's hair coat over his pajamas. He looked even larger in undress. "A hell of a note, a hell of a note. Sandbagged our plans."

India Kingston gave up on the radio, opened a portable typewriter. 'We must issue a statement. I'll draw up a release and you all go over it. Christ, it shakes you up. It's all that damn dieting. Paul was taking thyroid pills and other stuff, you know."

"No," said Jason, "I didn't know."

"Losing weight too fast," said Big Jim. "They had me at some freak health farm couple years ago, I got so weak from the pills and no food and the exercise I couldn't sign my name. Incredible."

"Oh," said Jason. "It was most likely a heart attack, like so many men Paul's age."

"Please, no mention of age."

Congressman Roland Redmond, in evening dress, entered speaking. He had been an actor in his youth, and a good one.

> "O when degree is shaken
> Which is the ladder of all high designs,
> The enterprise is sick!"

"It is," said Jason.

"Well, first of all we'll bury Paul honorably and then pick someone as worthy to carry on."

"Not tonight," said Jason. "India is getting ready a statement. How do we do it, India, heavy specific or simply a good man gone? Let's not be corny."

"Destiny," said Redmond, "contemptuous of consequences."

"Thanks, Roland," said India, looking up from some sheets of paper she had been typing on, correcting with a ballpoint. "Here's an opening anyway, see how you like it."

Big Jim scratched his ribs. "Maybe Sarah Pearl Adams should handle this."

"No! Paul isn't a detergent or armpit spray." She put on her Churchillian half-glasses. "Hmm . . . Paul Ormsbee's death removes not only the most promising candidate of his party for the presidency, but a longtime public servant, ardent, hardworking, fair to all segments of our society. Never a special pleader for any special interests of our nation, but rather a man honorably dedicated to seeing justice done. He fathered, co-authored, supported many bills; the original fair wage laws, the Monson-Ormsbee Water Rights Bill, the amended civil rights legislation, the Ormsbee Railroad Bill that did so much to keep the surviving rail lines open, even in certain sectors, to proper and—"

Silverthorn tapped fingers on the table. "A little more human, Indy. I mean the kind of jolly square shooter he was, his happy family life, his visit to the miners' families with funds, food and clothing in the big strikes—know what I mean? Consequential human contacts."

"*You* write it, Senator. I don't mind if you think my prose isn't—"

Jason waved a hand. "Come on, no huffy infighting tonight. It's fine, India, just right. I'm going to alert Vista City to prepare a return of the body home. He was decorated a major, was with Patton's tank division, the Second Armored. I'll get J. Willard on the phone, he'll take care of that end."

The old steward was back. "There's reporters downstairs. Wanta talk to somebody, anybody."

"You go, Jay," said Silverthorn. "Just something simple, sorrowful. Christ, we do feel sad. Say we'll have a written statement—India, in half an hour?"

"About. I'll keep it to eight, nine hundred words. An official statement can come from the party tomorrow."

Jason, downstairs in the bar, felt the reporters gathered there were a bit heartless, wanting details, offering clinical information that had come in over the wires. Jason seemed to satisfy them and he avoided any statement as to whom the Ormsbee section of the party would replace him with. Jason parried off several names, including his own. It was three in the morning when he got through to J. Willard.

"Yeah, yeah, Jay—a good man gone. It's going to be a mighty sad city here. We're arranging everything—Legion marching band, muffled drums, half-mast flags in all the state. How's Alice taking it? When you see her, well, you know, tell her how we all feel. Oh, he did so much for the railroads, the K and P is getting out its pet historic locomotive from storage and is going to bring Paul home in style. By rail all the way, the parlor car that everybody from Woodrow Wilson to Harry Truman campaigned in."

Also, Jason on hanging up remembered, Warren G. Harding and Richard M. Nixon.

Chapter 26

On board the Special Train en route to Vista City

Dear Esme,

It is a strange journey taking Paul home. The shock of death still vibrating along my nerve ends. I was surprised when your uncle showed up at Union Station to join us as the train was about to leave for its run to Vista City. He looked good and he said, "Don't look so damn surprised. I know you didn't plan on me to go along with the body, but I respected the man and was ready to help him. Someone once said 'The world is an arena which friendship alone makes tolerable.'"

I don't suppose Austin and Judge Fowler were ever really friends after they parted. They are such different types. But Amos shook your uncle's hand cheerfully and added, "As we get older we lose more of those we knew. There's bourbon and Scotch aboard."

"No thanks," Austin replied, and added they *were* getting older. In the private car, an ornate monster, are Senators Redmond and

Silverthorn, Big Jim Houston, the Vice-President, subdued by a series of cocktails, Bread O'Rahilly, an old friend of Paul's for a long time, and Wally Klamath, the union boss with whom I once locked horns. Honor guards of the dead. Wally seems very much at his ease now as a power on the national scene. We are polite to each other. Austin, as the train began its slow start from the station, sat with us listening to Judge Fowler tell of other dead men he had escorted to their graves. At times the judge is saturnine and inscrutable.

I'll keep writing you details as we slide through a day of vivid butterfly colors into night, going *click, click* past station platforms with people waiting to watch us pass. And we roll into the darkness past signal lights turning red to green on lonely platforms, jerkwater whistle-stops lit by a few hanging lights. There are often people waiting, we not stopping, just moving on to the sound of the train bell and the spine-clutching train whistle. It's all like a kid's dream of railroading—somehow the steam train whistles sound different from those on modern trains . . . I had no idea Paul Ormsbee would arouse such interest.

The train carrying Senator Ormsbee home, where bells and black-draped buildings wait. "A great, fine man is dead," said the train conductor come out of retirement. A senator going home on a train that he admired. In honor of a famous railroad bill of his, an engine from the past was polished up to bring him home. The locomotive is a 2-3765 series Northern, with black flags and silvered cylinder heads scorching the ballast, the carbon steel pistons pumping, the valve gear of molybdenum, the side rods flashing in the cold night air, the wind tearing at the trailing black ribbons outside the club car where party members escort the dead man.

Home is the Vista City that saw him born, helped make him again and again Senator to Washington. And "almost," Big Jim recalls, "President of the United States."

We sat in the private club car and tried to remain mournful, but I was aware of a tension among the other men in the car. Who would be appointed to fill Senator Ormsbee's unfinished term of office? Did every man in the car dream of himself as candidate for the presidency?

The friends and guests in the club lounge and observation car sat up late in the man's honor. A porter mixed drinks. The men were telling each other what a great guy he was. "And he was," said Senator Silverthorn, "a great guy."

The locals and milk trains and the freights waited to let us pass. The engines, called yard hogs, blew whistles in sadness. The flanged stacks belched black plumes in his honor; reefers, gondolas, cabooses and cupolas saw us pass, the 4-8-4 wheels of the engine grinding into the landscape.

The train moved past the sleeping land, and then the next day it was roaring down the river valley, past the white farms, the rolling furrows and the patches of green plants. Past the river mills sprouting, past birchwoods. I stood up and looked back at the receding tracks.

The senator's nephew, Andy Richter, red of face and getting fat in middle age, sat in his chair drinking good whiskey with Bread O. In the next car the editor of the Vista City *Herald* mused on the obit he had written and wired ahead. Judge Fowler asked me, as he pulled on his trim gray moustache, "Have a drink?"

"I've had several."

Austin, shaved, chin powdered, in a fresh, neat pinstripe suit, still stood watching the earth leap by. I went up to him. The train was slowing, spinning by slopes of green land, blowing at crossings and slipping over the rails past signal arms and way stations, the engine snorting in its strength.

Bread O'Rahilly, in his chair, nodded. "I never thought I would ride with his body."

"You are morbid," said your uncle.

The train whistle welled up to haunt the right of way. Oooohhhhwahoooooo. The whistle repeated Oooohooooawahoooooo. Austin motioned to me and we went toward the front of the train, past the flower-decked private car. The huge bronze coffin rested heavily on its oak supports. There was a gagging odor of dying flowers. An undertaker's assistant sat reading a detective story.

We were entering Vista City after an all-night run. Church bells had been ringing since before dawn, the bells of St. Mary's copper dome and the Unitarian spires answering. The boats in the river had taken up the dirge. The city waited for its dead man.

I stood watching the city come nearer as we ran across an iron bridge, the water smooth as oil below us.

Later we sat recalling the dead of fifty years past.

"Any liquor here?" asked Bread. "I feel ghosts about me."

The undertaker's helper snickered as he hoisted a great floral wreath alongside the casket. "Got some fine embalming fluid."

"Go to hell," said Big Jim. "You have some respect for the dead." The judge came in with a handful of yellow forms.

"Who are the wires from?"

"Senators, ambassadors, and just folks who knew him. Here he has been away from this town for years, always traveling around or busy in Washington, yet, you know, it's still his town—just like it's still his state."

Austin said, "Whatever the party left him of it."

"He could get out of the casket right now," said Silverthorn, "and make the eagle scream and he'd carry the town, the state and the whole land by a bigger majority than ever."

Someone handed out pairs of new black gloves. The town and the land and the factories all along the river had gathered, a circling ring of mourners, while the bronze casket stood on the trestles and the voice of some minister spoke the cold comfort of ritual.

Writing this long letter to you keeps me calm. I'll mail it to you first chance I get. Besides Paul's loss, this trip reminds me a lot of when I was nine years old and J. Willard took me to Chicago to have my infected ear treated. He didn't trust anyone, he said, to know ears in Vista City. For all the pain, I ate a lunch of cheese omelette and caramel custard pudding.

(I have time to write more as the train is being held up just outside the city while I suppose dignitaries will come aboard in East Vista; the mayor, the governor, local stuffed shirts and deep-feeling mourners, the local Episcopalian bishop, whose favorite sermon begins "Each day is a threshhold.")

Anyway, while we wait, puffing out steam, let me tell you about that painful journey of a kid with an infected ear, a temperature of 102 and a feeling that someone was pouring hot lead into my ear, burning out my brain. And worried I'd die and miss the summer fishing with Pop on the Blue River.

J. Willard all the time on the train kept telling me funny stories and I kept swallowing aspirin like it was salted peanuts. Pop was wonderful. He was worried and I could see he was holding himself in . . . and what brought this all back was not just riding a steam train again, but memory of my ear aching when we got to Carbontown where the mines are, and a termite-eaten, lopsided depot all gray dust and weathered timbers and not enough paint on them. I still recall they wheeled out the depot cart holding a dozen crates of turkeys, six battered milk containers, some burlap-wrapped bits of farm machinery and a long crate made of raw pine planks, cheap wood, badly jointed with big knots and a cardboard tag tacked to it.

I was feverish but I seemed to see clearly.

I asked Pop what it was and he said some miner was dead and being shipped home. I was not scared of death in others, I knew I would never die—but all my family and friends would and I had this 102 temperature. Sam Orley was the conductor, been with the K & P as he said, "since Christ was a cowboy." I asked him as he came by, brushing gray mine dust off his shiny blue serge jacket with the brass K & P buttons, "Who they loading into the freight express car?"

"Oh, that there? Some Bohunk what got careless and fell into mine-hoist gears. No sense, them Hunkies, about machines. The company is burying him in Watsonville. He goes as fast freight . . . and all for free." Sam Orley, people said, was a card.

I was two weeks in the hospital with the infected ear after they lanced it and treated it. Christ, I screamed nights, and J. Willard, as the fever remained high, stayed with me, sleeping in the visitors' room on the couch. And for the first time I knew someday I'd die. I suppose it's too obvious I'm thinking of Paul Ormsbee's homecoming compared with the poor Bohunk who fell into the mine-hoist gears. But there it is—and the mayor and governor are on board at last and we've just begun to move toward the station. With all the understanding, all good thoughts and shared deeds.

THAT FELLER

The burial services for Senator Paul Ormsbee were more like a jolly celebration for the state's most honored son who had somehow managed to die in so conspicuous a manner. The train had been met at the K & P station (still referred to by older citizens as the depot) and the remains escorted to the First Presbyterian Church of Vista City, where services were held in the great nave. The bishop himself, Homer K. Mullberry, was assisted in the rituals by three local ministers. With Sister Superior Mary Beatrice and Father Bromley Volonsky, S.J., seated in the front pew with rabbis Abner Rosenweig (Reformed) and Avrom Essrick (Conservative).

Alice, the widow, was protected by a group of grown children, married, and their various offspring.

It was a solemn event, with the television cameras of two major networks present. Hector Mallsbeck, the governor, spoke, the leader of the Senate said the proper things. Jason was the final speaker and he hardly remembered what he said, although he had made notes the night before ("Honor and wisdom can be more potent than beauty").

When the giant organ pealed out (was it Bach or Chopin? he never did remember which), Jason had gone up to the widow and looked into Alice's drawn, unteared face and pressed the black lace arm she offered him, as if to pass on the message of the unexpected calamities of life.

Burial was in the Drood Park's Eternal Rest, where all the town's pioneers (who had died well-off) were buried. It was still a splendid olive-green slope, well cared for, but it was no longer out in the country. Developments of ranch houses were creeping nearer, as was a great auto court of a new motel. The river, a bit polluted by paper mills, ran below the stone wall of Drood Park's planned squares of marble and granite, stone angels and urns, some showing weeds.

The Ormsbee burial plot held great-grandparents; an embezzler Jason had known, also a benefactor who gave the college a gym and a library; two dead from World War I, one from the second major war of the century. Also Wilbur Ormsbee, a nephew, a homosexual marine who was killed in the Tet Offensive destroying two Russian-made tanks.

Jason, standing with Sheila and J. Willard, looked off toward the Crockett plot, a little lower down, seeing just the tip of his mother's tall gravestone. All these buried streets, he thought, six to eight feet underground. Neighbors or strangers, the evil and the good, the greedy and the lonely. I'll be carried here myself to be planted some day.

He was aware Sheila was giving him the elbow to turn respectfully toward the liberal minister, Charles Munnell, who was standing over the casket set on overgreen Astro-turf.

*   *   *

"I see men's judgments are
A parcel of their fortunes, and things outward
Do draw the inward quality after them,
To suffer all alike . . ."

(The Vista City *Times* gave the quotation to Longfellow.)
The casket was slowly lowered by mechanical means and the American Legion honorary firing squad, rifles lifted, got off a properly regular volume.

Jason and Sheila had a late lunch at J. Willard's. The dining room wallpaper looked older, the hallway beams had been painted shiny white, hiding the fine graining of the wood Jason had so admired as a child.

Sheila said she needed a nap and went upstairs. J. Willard and Jason smoked cigars in the room his father refused to call a den or study.

The raccoon over the fireplace that Jason had stuffed at age twelve seemed to need more sawdust. The big photograph of himself and J. Willard fishing on the Roaring Fork River in Colorado had turned yellow (how thin I was at seventeen, and worried over pimples).

J. Willard caught him studying the picture. "Eh, that was a fine fishing trip, wasn't it? And visiting Leadville, and Cripple Creek, where the whorehouses and the gambling places were selling cokes and dreadful hamburgers . . . Well, Jay, you've got some fast thinking to do."

"I'd rather not."

"God rest Paul's soul, or whatever deity there be, but you've been handed the chance to grab the gold ring on the merry-go-round. At least you can reach out and grab it."

"You think I should enter the primaries?"

"You're darn tootin' you should. You have to. Hell, you want that mackerel-snapper Bremont with the silver spoon in his mouth to take over, or Boone, that graduate from Tobacco Road?"

"There are other, better men. Senator Redmond, Judge Rowse."

"They couldn't catch snowflakes in a blizzard. Inadequate compared to you. You're not shy? Or modest?"

"No, Pop, I'm not. But to most of Washington's entrenched people I'm still a hick. They pal around with the majestic ghosts of the great dead."

"Well, screw Washington. Anybody who thinks they're an asset to public office doesn't understand what's happened in the last twenty years. The country doesn't trust Washington, or the Congress, or the FBI or the CIA, or the State Department. And you can add Agriculture and Internal Revenue. Maybe they're still having a liking for the Secret Service, and Abe Lincoln in a stone seat, but that's it."

Jason slowly puffed on the cigar. "I want to talk to Austin Barraclough."

J. Willard gave a hollow laugh. "I respect him. He's got savvy, or had, and he's class. But he's not going to approve of some kid from the western rivers and fisheries running for this high office. Fundamental principles my ass—they're all snobs along the Potomac."

"He's not a snob."

"Doesn't have to be, maybe. He's got a built-in sniffer that says a lot of us smell bad. Sure he likes you, and you've helped straighten him out. But that he'll resent, without knowing it even. Oh yes, you want somebody to dislike the way you walk, talk, eat, or kiss the girls—you just do someone a *big* favor they can't return."

"No, you're wrong about Austin. I admit he's a bit against what he calls the commonness of the common man, and he doesn't think a really honest government can ever exist. Unless some men from Mars take over."

"Forget Mars, Son, the scientific loafers don't think there's much there but cosmic spit. All right, you talk to Barraclough. I'm starting the boys building you up, Jayboy. And I'd do it even if you weren't my son and smart as all get-out. And honorable. I'd do it if you were black, green or a headhunter with a bone in your nose. Goddamn it, Jay, you act as if you're doing the country a favor. The job—Number One—may kill you, overwork you, ruin your health, drive you down dark alleys with the rage of the people setting their dogs on you to tear you apart, like that moral cripple Nixon. No, it's no gift, the White House, no three wise men getting off their camels to offer you spices."

J. Willard went over to Jason and put his hand on his son's head. "I may lose you. By tragedy, not just personal. Maybe an atomic war. I dream my fears of utter devastation, and men fighting in the end with stones and sticks, living in caves, using each other as food supplies . . . God, I have these bad dreams, these thoughts that man is Nature's greatest mistake. I suppose I'm getting ready to shuffle off this mortal coil, eh?"

"I never knew you to talk, to feel like this. You always were such a wily optimist with a light and ironic touch."

"It's gone, I suppose, and seeing your mother's grave today . . . Do what you want, Son. Decide. And let me know. You're a precise, taciturn man. I'm not. I make waves."

After dinner Sheila stayed in bed with a headache, J. Willard went to sit with Paul Ormsbee's widow and her brood. Jason found an old raincoat in the hall closet. It might rain. He went out into the street in pensive agitation, walked past the old houses with their marvelous solid detail: the weathered brick, the great porches, the spacious lawns (one still with an iron deer) and all with TV aerials on Victorian-Edwardian roofs. The business district had its window lights on, the New Vista Hilton looked precariously sterile and too tall. The city was becoming so much like every other city; standardized, computerized, chain-stored. He noticed the same smart shoddy, the same Detroit tin with too much chrome aberration and unneeded streamlining.

The Old Indian Warrior Hotel had survived, but as the sign now noted, RESIDENCE BY WEEK OR MONTH. The town's best-smelling whores used to parade its lobby of blue-green marble and beveled ornate mirrors. Buster Miller's father had run the cigar stand, and taken horse bets; he also knew a local abortionist who was safe.

Jason entered the lobby of the Warrior. Some attempt had been made to modernize it, make it pay its way. A corner held a photocopying shop, Roger's Rapid Printing; a side wall was taken over by Nat's Bargain Overstock Shoe Store with the SALE sign showing its age. The cigar counter was gone, replaced by Hasty Tasty; coffeepots stood in the reek of stale grease burning, the sharp bite of Lysol suggesting bugs. The old Swiss watch repairman—Moses Weener, a little hunchback who chewed Sen-Sen—was gone, as was the bar with the nude oil paintings of Indian maidens; it was now the John Wayne Lounge and Grill.

But the row of teak phone booths were still against the back wall. Only the instruments were more battered.

Jason got into a booth, took out bills and change and called Esme. There was some delay. He let the phone ring. An echoing sound in a void and he was about to hang up when Esme's voice, sleepy as if interrupted, came on.

"Huh, *who*? Oh, Jay . . . Yes?"

"It's been a hard day. Whole town, state, seemed to turn out."

"Yes, I can understand. I didn't think you'd call."

"I interrupt anything? I mean you going out or something?"

"When will you be back?"

"In a day or so. I want to have an earnest talk with you, with Austin."

A silence, a muffled effect as if she were covering the phone with a hand and talking to someone—or was she pondering what he would ask of her?

"I can guess," she said serenely.

"That's right. Some people think I should enter the primaries. You don't. I'm too much the hick?" He failed to give the line the light touch he intended.

"I said what was on the top of my mind, Jay. We'll kick it around. I must get dressed, going out with some people. Need to put on a face . . . Goodbye and don't brood."

"Goodbye, Esme. Honey, I'm more dependent on your opinion than you know."

"Are you . . . ?" A goodbye, a kissy sound, and the dead phone.

BOOK V

The Apprentice Tested

Chapter 27

Jason dreaded his meeting with Austin Barraclough at Potomac House. Austin had not stayed on in Vista City with Judge Fowler and the rest beyond the church services for Paul Ormsbee. He had taken a plane back home right after the services, not gone to the old cemetery for the formal burial scene. Austin had said very little, except to express himself to a local Vista City reporter: "Many good men die before their time. And others, some men who would have wrecked their destinies, pass on at the proper moment. Paul Ormsbee was a good public servant, had the supreme sanity, the simple heart. That's all I have to say, young man. Get out of my way."

Back in Georgetown Jason felt restless, keyed up. Some noisy masons were repointing the bricks in the old chimney; it had developed leakage in the seasonal rains. Jason's mind turned often to thoughts of Austin—he wondered if he should wait for an invitation, or just appear at Potomac House. Austin had certainly shown new vigor—had snapped at Judge Fowler's ironic remarks at times—and he was clearly following the crisis of events in the party. The Barraclough office on the Hill had been done over (new drapes, fresh paint), two new secretaries were on duty. Yes, Jason had to admit while he had attached himself to Austin Barraclough for a political education, he had also revitalized the older man. Was it only a temporary improvement? Time would show; Austin might go on improving, or tomorrow slide back to the drunken fuddy-wreck. Or, invigorated back to his audacities and skills, that aura of substantiality? Do I see Austin as a rival suddenly? No, of course not. He would never run for high office, not with his family secret.

The Senate Cloakroom was no place to talk. Invade the Barraclough offices? Esme was out of town. The old gal who answered the phone at Esme of Washington, Real Estate said Miss Lowell was in Maryland, Baltimore—on some zoning problem with the shopping center lease she was involved in with the Jack Klein people. Miss Charney, the old gal, was very polite, but she had been used at times to relay Esme's messages to Jason and it was clear she didn't much approve of the relationship of her boss and the senator. Jason put it down to the old bull dike's jealousy.

On the Hill he had started to work out something that called for delicate handling. The AP carried a notice of it in its Washington service:

Senate Chiefs Urge Office Building Be Named for Sen. Ormsbee

Washington. Senate leaders introduced a resolution Friday to name a Senate office building now under construction for the late Senator Paul Ormsbee.

Democratic and Republican leaders said they hoped all 100 senators would join in sponsoring the resolution (offered by Senator Jason Crockett).

The structure is an addition to a Senate office building named for the late Sen. Everett M. Dirksen (R-Ill.). Another Senate office building is named for the late Sen. Richard B. Russell (D-Ga.). Also one for Sen. Philip A. Hart (D-Mich.).

Jason wished he could talk to Esme on a very vital topic. In some way he wondered what her reaction would be to his running in the primaries. It was true one didn't rule one's public life by the women one took to bed. Lord, he was sounding like Judge Amos Fowler. The judge had shared a seat with Jason on the plane back to Washington, an Air Force plane that someone in the Pentagon had arranged to pick up the Washington party in Vista City. Amos Fowler had patted Jason's knee at 40,000 feet with obvious joviality (there was a rumor that in his youth Amos had been a switch-hitter).

"Boldness, boldness, Jason, *always* boldness. Step in and announce that your state still wants a favorite son in the race for the nomination and that's it, a quick, clean decision and no dark night of the soul, eh?"

"Hardly that easy, Judge. There's the party leaders, city chairmen, the poll-takers, the funds to find to run in primaries in twelve to twenty states."

"You leave that mundane stuff to me and the gentlemen known as the boys."

And the judge had closed his eyes, put a smile on his neat, handsome, angular face and dozed off—a man aware, as he had said, that small irrelevances spoil enormous meanings.

Now that Jason had decided to announce—after a respectful wait, say a week after Paul's burial—he had to find out how he stood with Austin Barraclough, who had some obscure dislike of Judge Fowler. Jason, dressing at home, heard Sheila humming something below in the kitchen between explaining to Fran just how the senator liked his roast beef for dinner. "Not spurting blood, but pink as a baby's bottom." Jason went to his den and dialed Potomac House. He waited for six rings and was about to hang up when Champ's voice came on, throaty, raspy.

"Who that?"

"Senator Crockett. How's the chief? Not been on the Hill the last few days. How are things?"

"Hasn't kicked my ass today, not yet."

"I'm going to drop in before noon."

"Well, now . . . huh . . ."

"Be seeing you, Champ."

He hung up. He'd hate to call a black man uppity, but—if there was a call returned from Potomac House *not* to come, it could be a sign he was up shit creek and no paddle, as far as Austin backing him. But no call came in the next hours. He told Sheila he'd be back for dinner unless there was some special meeting planned (he still hoped to contact Esme; damn it how a man could be led by the nose, or rather his genitalia, that deep-seated region of natural response—in his prime, anyway).

Sheila was looking over the department store ads. "I'm not going to overbake the roast. Be on time."

"Let you know in plenty of time if I get tied up."

"These night sessions, I bet you all just sit around telling dirty stories."

"Sure. If I hear any good ones, I'll bring them home."

She looked at him with an ironic twist to her mouth, or was she just wondering about spoiling an expensive roast? Women; if not devious, they were hostile. And some had that charm of fragility that could change to treat a little indiscretion like the vices of Caligula. Guilt was always such a damn presence if you'd had a moral upbringing.

All the way to Potomac House Jason groped for some sign from Austin in the recent past that he was doing right. Jason had an aversion for open conflict. In politics, J. Willard had once said to him, "Son, there are no fixed orders of truth. One bases one's career on a system of rituals old as a witch doctor's grunts. And on observations. It would be better if there were rigid principles in politics, sure. But men are not built that way. And no nations run on unvariable judgments. You file that information away. Took me fifty years to figure it out."

Jason drove up the winding drive of Potomac House. The landscaping looked better cared for. Some trimming of hedges and rebuilding a stone wall around a meadow had taken place. The grass lay apple-green and flat, the turned, dark earth smelled good.

Champ let him in, expressionless, and pointed in the direction of the terrace overlooking the river.

Jason walked past yellow flowers in brass jardinieres toward Austin Barraclough in a tweed hunting jacket, with a Panama hat, a bit yellowed with age, on his head. He sat smoking a pipe, staring at a wedge of trees reflected in the river on the other side.

"Hello, Jason."

The tone indicated nothing; it was not unfriendly but the speaker hadn't turned his head to greet him. Just continued his interest in the landscape, puffing on his pipe. At least the old drunken, raucous moroseness wasn't present.

"You're looking well, Austin."

The head turned, the expression remained poker-faced. "You're looking a bit flushed. How's Sheila, the grandchild?"

It wasn't like Austin to care for domestic details; he hadn't ever before asked, well hardly ever, about the family.

"They seem okay, Austin. You must have suspected I'm going to announce I'm taking on the primaries in the key states."

Austin laughed, showed expensive dentistry. "I could smell that desire, mister, in you before we buried Ormsbee."

"I wasn't that sure—and it's not going to be easy. Zack Boone and the society snob, Grover Bremont, and—"

"And you want me to endorse you? That's about it?"

"That's about it, yes."

Austin stood up, lifted one foot and knocked out the dottle of his pipe against a leather heel. There were live sparks in the pipe and they fell to the stone floor of the terrace and died.

The older man straightened up and blew through the stem of the empty pipe. "You used me, Jason, and you helped me. But mostly you've used me like a ubiquitous Jesuit. I became aware of it when I was able to reevaluate my experiences of late, and—"

"Oh, come on, Austin. I was maybe like a new kid learning the ropes from an upperclassman, but—"

"Very neatly, nicely put. You have a way with you, Jason. A charm. Yes, a goddamn charm. And I didn't mind being used. That's right, I didn't mind. I was, I suppose, in no condition to mind."

"I never intended you to feel like that."

"I don't give a damn what you thought. You did give me a shoulder when I needed it in my imbecile behavior. You humored me, gave me the old friendly buildup to get me to . . . never mind. And while in time I saw through you, with my resistance atrophied—I was that low, I was that much sunk in self-pity, yes, quivering jelly—"

He stopped talking and went back to examining the opposite riverbank as if turned off by the shameless intimacy of the moment.

Jason shook his head. "I've always admired you. I've felt some greatness tight wound up in you. If I seemed to have taken advantage of you, well—"

"Let's cut out the Dostoevskian anguish, huh? You're good political stuff. You're solid; you're a driving man. You're smart, too, and don't make enemies, only a few friends dangerous to the country. Just dangerous ones like Amos Fowler. So I don't want you as president."

Jason frowned, grimaced and kicked at a bit of dropped pipe ash with the toe of his shoe (Lord, just as John Wayne would push on a bit of cowshit with his boot to show deep thought). He looked into Austin's dark, derisive eyes. What the devil was the brain behind them processing?

"You think some traits I have overbalance my good points, *if* they are good points?"

"Never mind what's not triple AAA in your character. We've had real moral cripples, near morons and golf players in the White House.

No, it's your connection with the Judge and his gang. Big Jim, Bread O'Rahilly."

Jason showed his doubts. He spoke with a mouth too open for just words. "Why, why, you were one of Fowler's bright young men. He made you the Senate's party leader."

"That was a long time ago. I broke with him before—forgive the old-fashioned expression—before I lost my soul to the demonic old bastard."

"He's still a power in the party, he can marshal resources, win elections for people he backs."

Austin rubbed the bowl of his pipe against one side of his nose and laid it down on a small glass-and-metal table.

"He's cynical, he really loathes the democratic principles. He doesn't mind that the just are sacrificed and the unjust prosper while he sees to their interests. Is that enough to show the kind of man you seek, take, expect support from?"

Jason waved off Austin's words. "How many men, Austin, like him, have felt they could control the men they elect to high office and find they haven't bought a man's integrity?"

"Any means to an end, as the old bromide put it? Well, Senator Crockett, it's a risk I don't take. That you'll come out of the pitch barrel pure and white as snow. Gaseous moral values tend to evaporate when power is held in the hand. Christ, you know the power that is in the White House. I was scared stiff that Nixon, when he was caught in his own rattrap, would some Friday night declare the republic in danger, and order a military alert and put the country under martial law 'to save and protect it,' of course. What president dropped two atom bombs on men, women and children after the enemy had for months been asking for peace terms through Switzerland—and became a folk hero! And Lady Bird's husband killed fifty thousand young men because his damn pride couldn't let him admit he could get mired down in jungles. Hell, we almost got into a jam in Korea when some officers got killed. Over what? Cutting down a tree."

"I know it's a world of harried compromises."

"You're too dangerous, mister, for me. You've got the appearance, you do have a sense of honor, of purpose. You really feel for this country, its virtues, its hopes. But you're beginning to accept gambles, odd friends, to put you over. You're making contacts with all I fear and hate. Somewhere along the line, in some room at the convention, in a conference with four or six men who think they own this country, lies the real danger for an eager man. Manhattan-Hudson Bank and Trust, Nu-World Motors, Delongjah Chemical, the big three unions. And maybe you'll knuckle under and nod to what you're told is the price."

Jason held himself under control, didn't shout. "Damn, damn it. You have no right to talk that way to me. I've never betrayed a trust; I've never wavered or made dishonorable deals."

"As the artist Whistler said to a certain writer on another subject, 'You will, Oscar, you will.' "

"You've become lugubrious. I'm sorry. I feel I've as good a moral sense as you have. Good, solid Christian values I believe in, follow."

Jason knew he had said too much, been inane. Austin Barraclough gave a small smile. "Like fucking my niece, is that part of your marriage vows made in a church ceremony?"

Jason lifted his hands head high, flexed his fingers, almost spoke, but what tangled rationalization could he make? He just turned and walked away quickly, not hurrying, just at a good pace. He had wanted to shout that more than half of the men on the Hill in high office were adultery prone. That from Harding to Kennedy marriage vows hadn't been kept. But what was the use? He felt as if an anvil had fallen on his chest. What had put a wild hair up Austin Barraclough's prat was Amos Fowler. Well, Amos Fowler could make a president and Austin Barraclough couldn't.

Chapter 28

"My, aren't we jumpy this morning."

"I've a lot on my mind."

"Isn't that *all* settled?"

Jason poured himself another cup of breakfast coffee. He didn't want to appear irascible or supercilious. "Settled?"

Sheila laughed. "I'm already picking curtains for the White House's private rooms. Oh, come on, Jay, I'm making a joke. Cheer up."

Jason felt a wave of acute anxiety come over him, a feeling of alienation. How now to maintain a conscientious calmness, how to face his wife with any self-deprecating humor?

"Truth is, I'm not sure. I feel like a damn circle with no center."

"Oh dear, that bad." She was still amused and tenacious. "Tell me."

"Austin will not support me."

"Why ever not? Weren't you two buddies?"

"There's this thing between him and Amos Fowler, some singular crazy ramifications. He sees Amos as, quote, a ferret-faced bastard pickled in political vices, unquote."

Sheila decided there was no use trying to laugh Jason out of his querulous mood. What she called the Crockett ass-drag was gripping Jason. J. Willard also had it at times; that Crockett sense, at certain times, of a painful perplexity over something other people wouldn't even give thinking time to. And when—in Crockett ass-drag—you got down to pulling an answer from them, you'd get something cockeyed like J. Willard saying, "Dilemmas exist because we make excuses."

*   *   *

Sheila felt to cheer herself up she'd go call Laura from the upstairs phone. She rose from the breakfast table taking a final sip of coffee. "Your Miss Lowell should be able to bring Barraclough around."

"*My* Miss Lowell? What the hell kind of remark is that?"

He saw at once his overreaction to her remark.

Sheila put the breakfast dishes on a tray. Fran was attending some black congress on minority rights ("What the devil are we housewives whose servants didn't do their job *but* minorities ourselves?").

"Well now, Jay, don't bite my head off. I'm not accusing you of getting in the kip with her. It's just that you said she's smarter than most of the women of intolerable inadequacy around Washington."

Jason sighed. Christ, this was no morning to be a repentant adulterer. But Sheila wasn't the kind to jest if she really felt he and Esme had—well. To duty first—there was a lot to do and think about without setting up an antagonist at home. "I'll go see Judge Fowler and decide once and for all."

He'd like to go see Esme; maybe she'd be back from her damn shopping center planning. Yet in a way he dreaded seeing Esme. Was it Joseph facing Mrs. Potiphar (wrong setup, *he* was the married one) or was he now fearful of the involvement in an inextricable drama that could, yes could, end messily? Become something that might wreck his big chance? As they said back home in Vista City, he sure had a scoop shovel full of problems. And yet with Esme it had just started as the best of life-affirming impulses.

He phoned Fowler's mansion and the judge sounded chipper; an old man so cheerful so early in the day? What the hell did he have to be so cheerful about? He, so near the grave and yet so raffish and sardonic. But soon, on the phone, he got down to the business at hand.

"Of course, Jay. Of course, problems, problems. I'm always open house to you. How about lunch? Some friends in Colorado have sent me some marvelous trout. You like trout? Good. I'll have the cook grill us a couple each."

"Thanks, Amos. I've got to talk over some problems. Crank up my self-sufficiency. I'm getting doubts, as the man said when the dogs dragged him under the house."

"Ha ha. Just remember every pope began as a doubting seminary student, at least once. If I can only teach you young men to see it all as a comprehension of one's duty."

The old fox, Jason thought as he put down the phone; he always had the right word, even if the wrong reason, to feed one's appetites and ambitions. In politics, Amos Fowler preached, one does the greatest good when one doesn't brood over scruples and deficiencies. It was a code that had put the old bastard into high places, had certainly given him power in the past. And the judge still controlled a large segment of the party, its philosophy. Most of all, people said, he knew how to win. For all his jesting, Amos Fowler was a tough, wise old boy.

I want to be nominated, Jason thought, and if nominated I can win. And in high office I'll be a good man, with the abilities to get things done. I shall not sink to the dishonorable extremities of other men who have held the office—the greedy, the dishonest, the nondescript goof-offs.

Amos was in his small dining room, the one overlooking the glass flats in which he grew vegetables out of season. It was a room with a cheerful yellow wallpaper and old, polished copperwear used only as wall decor. The judge was in a well-cut Edwardian jacket, suggesting horses and the best-bred dogs. In fact, a goldenhaired retriever bitch nursed four puppies in a padded basket by the bay window. The judge petted the bitch with a hand sprinkled with ecchymotic brown spots.

Amos Fowler was at his best as they sat down to the trout served by a Puerto Rican youth with blue-black hair. There was a fine sauterne in crystal glasses. The judge, as they ate, recalled other meetings with men who went on to high office, told a charming story of a Kennedy escapade. They drank the good wine, and Amos Fowler told the history of its vineyard.

"Good trout, cooked just right," said Jason.

"It's all in knowing how to treat what you cook with respect, even with love."

After the boy had brought in a cheese board and some golden pippin apples, Jason took the plunge. "I've been to see Austin Barraclough."

Amos was skillfully, slowly cutting a slice of cheddar. "Ah, my old pupil. One of the most remarkable disciples I ever had."

"He doesn't speak that highly of you, Amos."

"No." The old man chewed thoughtfully on cheese and apple. "No, Austin always had this pretentious self-satisfaction that the Barracloughs, like Caesar's wife, were above suspicion. He found me immoral because I felt one went into politics to win and that the men who win are the best of the litter. Losers are people of low vitality, of inconsistency. I don't say he's wrong, but he's handicapped by ill fortune. Yes, Jay, luck is important in politics. A good man yet unlucky. Well, scratch him out."

"Austin has not only been unlucky, there are personal disorders."

"Stiff-necked, too. I like Austin; I admire him. And, damnit, the party is spacious enough for both of us. He told you, I'm sure, I was a liar, a cheat, dishonest, dishonorable, that my motto is *homo homini lupus*. Man is wolf to man."

"He wouldn't go that far, or use such language."

"Ah, that's his weakness—gentlemen's rhetoric. I can guess how he must have worded it in his superior tranquility now that he's recovered. He has recovered, hasn't he?"

Jason tapped an apple, recalling as a boy the raids he used to make on orchards, satisfying his sense of guilt by thinking it's not really stealing; shucks, thousands of apples are never picked and why let them fall to rot? In a way, listening to Amos Fowler he was involved with the soothing philosophy of orchard "borrowing" again.

"Jay, let me tell you about myself. Men wear masks, men turn away satisfied with half-truths, turn their backs on reality."

"What is reality, Judge?"

"What we *think* we see of life. I can't do any better than that. *What is truth*? a Roman once asked, washing his hands. My reality is that I see us as a great nation which I love, you love, Austin also loves. The world today is a time bomb, ticking, burning at the edges, and in our corporations' greed for profit, we've given every half-assed nation the wherewithall to make atomic missiles. That suicidal game keeps this nation great. Waste, conspicuous waste, keeps us great, keeps the miserable middle-class taxpayer on his toes. I admire middle-class morality—in others. Shocked?"

"Not really. Few people have much faith left in politics."

"Maybe, maybe so—but it's the only game in town. Anyway we stay afloat. We have powerful enemies in the new Ivans the Terrible, the Arab scum with billions and billions of dollars, the Chinese, the rising tide of black Africa which has to win. So, Jay, there are no moral niceties in politics. You play to win, you win because you have to win. So you may have to give a kick in the balls to those you have to beat. You lift that knee, hard *and* fast."

"Austin sees it as going back to Watergate methods."

Amos laughed. "That set of slobs were only after personal power. They didn't give a shit about national honor or the welfare of the American Century that Harry Luce used to talk about. The Watergate crowd were small vermin. No, no, you're an hombre with principles, ideals, and you're clever. You'd never cop out, make personal enemy lists, or pay off greedy Cubans."

"I hope not. I know not."

The judge sat back, chewed apple and cheese slowly, with relish. "If you don't see what is your duty, if you fail to understand that we must save this country, if you go wishy-washy, then step down and let Senator Redmond take over. Or do you want that clod of a rich boy, or Zack Boone, a Faulkner character, in Lincoln's bed in the White House?"

Jason laughed. "You've the devil's persuasiveness, Amos. You know we can't have Bremont, rich boy, or the hillbilly go on to tear the country apart. Redmond, well, I like him—"

"So do I. But he's an actor, putty in the hands of whoever tosses him a compliment or asked for his autograph . . . Stay for dinner."

"I must get back. Really must."

"All right, join me for cocktails after my nap. I hate to see the sun go down without a glass in hand, or alone. Go take a walk, make phone calls—I've a lot more to tell you."

Amos Fowler always napped after lunch. He rose at three, with glowing cheeks, took up an ivory-headed cane and walked with Jason along the riverbanks. Jason thought of Austin, of Amos Fowler; here they are, these two men, twenty miles apart on the same river. One the solid believer in values, a student of the tragicomedy of humanity's hopes and transgressions. The other activated as if by springs, the realist, the practical man. The advocate of complicity, the caustic, ironic, with a sophistication that suggests history was always made by direct actions and not by any deep philosophy. And by placating a volatile society for their own good.

Amos had martinis made just right by the boy, and served in a gazebo, an open structure with eight sides set among shrubs, overlooking the yacht tugging at its mooring lines below them. Across the river, larch and hickory grew in graceful patterns.

"I love Washington," said the old man, pursing his mouth over a swallow of martini. "For what it is, not for what people imagine. We rule the world from here. Our inventions, our corporations, our scientists. Oh yes, we keep the old globe spinning. Faulted as we are. Too, too human. Yes, it's true the dreamers who don't know politics say we could have made the twentieth century the greatest, happiest of all. We gave it over, some say, to Lenin, to Hitler, to Franco, Mao, to the Japanese. Never mind the past. Now, today, Jay, it's all slipping from us, the world. Orwell my be right. Oh damn, the setting sun makes me morbid. Forgive me. It's like a gaudy Turner, the sunset, isn't it?"

Jason looked at the bloodshot sky, the dying day expiring to the west; low on the horizon flew a flight of shoveler and cinnamon teal. "I haven't seen many Turners. We have one at home in the Vista City museum. A shipwreck."

Amos refilled their glasses. "Washington, Jay, isn't easy to take. The hundreds of thousands of office workers servicing it, the pretty girls sitting at those IBM machines dreaming of a better life. Yes, I too sense the whole secret life of the city, its underground existence —not just the phone wires and sewers. What's really going on in the FBI, the CIA."

"We don't seem to want to control them."

"Not too easy with Washington's far-rightists wrapped in nylon Old Glory. New Left protest rallies on the steps of the Jefferson Memorial. The citizens baffled by those who invent the news and send it on to *Aufbau, El Diario, La Prensa, Paris Match.* All journalists have in common is the desire for free booze and food, the testing of air pressure in a pair of tits. They swallow whole anything State spokesmen leak to them while they zip their flies among gold fixtures."

Jason, on his third martini, said, "I enjoy the old houses on N Street; they retain a flavor of Grant's Washington, Teddy Roosevelt's boy's-life view of things. I like the black leather sofas of the Woodrow Wilson era, the fumed oak of FDR, the air conditioning smelling of the Kennedy charm. Old ladies with blue-white hair, often leaning on a gold-headed cane, telling the new one about Alice Longworth or Eleanor, the vulgar love life of Harding. And how fine it was when Henry Adams and Justice Oliver Wendell Holmes said all that was needed to be said about the nation and the world. Or the General, who never could finish a sentence in proper English, and never read anything over a page long."

"You're a goddamn poet, Jay."

"To function at the full of one's potential is dangerous. There is, I've observed, very efficient service in some departments, for all the talk of waste, boodle and private interests. The admirals who sit behind desks demand clean sweeps of paper work, fore and aft, and in the officers' clubs in the humid afternoons drink Scotch, cursing civilian-socialist welfare-state thinking. Damn the rocket components, atom warheads; full speed ahead! The world, they swear, is getting too clogged up with triplicate multinumber inventories, cursed coffee breaks, sick leaves, disappearing bond paper, pencils and paper clips. Bureaucracy cries in the press for economy *and* adds sixty thousand people a year to Civil Service. Internal Revenue acquires miles of machines to discover who forgot to list a dollar."

Jesus, was it the third *or* fourth double martini? Jason Crockett knew he was drunk. Really sloshed, slopped drunk. And it had not been just the martinis. Somehow he focused on Amos Fowler's amused face looking up at him. He said in slurred tones, "All politicians are guilty until proved innocent."

"You're too tight to drive, my friend. I'll have Chico drive you home. He'll take a taxi back."

Somehow he let himself be led. "I can, I can drive." He was seated on the right-hand side of his car and the Puerto Rican boy was behind the driver's wheel. There was cool air on his face and he was riding toward the city, the car radio playing something with that sadomasochistic Latin American sound. It was night, somehow he has stayed later than he had intended. (With alcohol you get consolation maybe—never thought.) His head was clearing, the thoughts were confused. I am to save the party, the nation; no, the world. Somehow it isn't at all clear how.

All of Amos Fowler's talk has left is the sound of pizzicato fiddles in my head. I'll have to think over what I've been told, what we discussed.

He said to Chico. "Want to make one stop. *Gracias.*"

"What you say? Yes. I stop."

He gave the boy the name of Esme's street. Yes, that would clear his mind, drain his feeling of being pulled in several directions. A good boff, an hour or so of lying in her arms. Some good solid talk of lovemaking, and of his problems.

He stopped Chico half a block from Esme's house, around the corner from its facade. You never know; it's best to be wary. Prepare always for something that doesn't happen.

"Chico, you go find yourself some dinner. I may be a couple of hours."

Chico took the ten dollars from Jason's fingers. "Like you say, I bee bock in two hours, hokay?"

"Okay." Still too shaky to drive myself, he figured.

Jason found he could walk properly, walk a straight line, good as any man taking a police drunk test. He felt a rising tide of desire, of hope. He turned the corner, walked past two houses, one with a porch light on, a swing hanging from rusting chains, the other had rubber plants in a bay window. Esme's house was in need of paint, the lawn carelessly mowed. He felt it was like coming home from boys' camp, seeing something familiar again, solid reality where one was always welcome. There were no lights on. The drapes were drawn. Damn. If she was still away . . . His groin ached in protest at the disappointing thought. He moved down the worn brick path toward the front door.

He didn't see the muggers. There was no intuitive warning. Didn't hear anything, just felt a smelly cloth sleeve and arm go around his throat, something from behind him hit his right temple. His legs dissolved, went away from under him. He roared in protest as he twisted around and saw two black faces and one white. Jason struggled, kicking at shins. He was hit again and again. He fell shouting, blood ran down his nose, entered his mouth and they kicked him, rifled his pockets, took his watch, a ring, credit cards, an old gold football award.

"Mutterfucking honkey."

And followed this with another kick in the ribs. That seemed by the pain to revive Jason and he had a glimpse of a face intolerant, casual, a kind of expression that has no connection with anything but a miserable gratifying of personal needs (could he really catch all that in one glance, Jason wondered?). He suddenly kicked out and up with both of his legs and connected—heard a jawbone crack and a scream of agony. Then he was rolling to one side to avoid the full force of an army surplus boot aimed at his head.

He half-rose as he maneuvered a pained body and something hit him hard on the back of his shoulders and again he avoided a blow on the head.

"Cut him, cut the ofay!" someone shouted.

The screams of the youth with the shattered jaw were louder. Jason almost managed to get to his feet but could not, for now his head was being battered. He fell back into a blackness scarred across by lightning flashes. Then he failed to sense anything at all.

In the next ten minutes several cars passed, their drivers saw a body lying on the sidewalk and moved on with an increase of speed. A small boy on a skateboard, hurrying home from a movie, stopped by the prone man.

"Hey, mister."

Chapter 29

There was a feeling of diverting untrustfulness, of alienation in a void, an abyss of nothingness and the sound of electric guitarists playing. He had always enjoyed guitar music but now every note seemed to be a spike plunging at his brain. He thought of the unprofundity of the superficial and wondered what he meant. He was being lifted at the speed of light; in this way he was aware one could outpace one's anxieties and he was on a snowy road on the outskirts of a large city where he had never been and yet somehow knew so well. He was asking people Where am I? What is this place called? and no one would answer and when he tried to stop a taxi or some car they drove past him as if he wasn't there at all. He had an impression it was as if he were pushing on a heavy door he feared would close on him, and the French for orgasm was *la mort douce*. There were lights and he was flat in a bed, all his aches seemed numb.

Sheila and Clair were bending over him and he felt the stitches on his scalp itch and then hurt.

He asked, "What's it all?"

"Oh, Jay," said Sheila.

"What's it all about?" He blinked myopically.

"They caught them," said Clair.

"What?" But as he asked, it was all back, the attack, the shock, and he shivered and felt sweat seep from his armpits. The mugging was being replayed, the blows fell, he heard a jawbone crack under his kicks and he cried out to try for another level of consciousness, "No, *no!*"

"It's all right, dear. You're in Walter Reed."

Clair said, "They picked up this black goon with a broken jaw when he tried to get medical aid and he named the other two. They're all junkies with records."

Junkies? He was thinking better, connecting events, conversations. And his voice was getting over just uttering strangled monosyllables.

"You were lucky," said Sheila.

"Yes."

"The scalp wound took ten stitches and you have sore ribs, nothing broken, and well—we're happy we didn't lose you." She wept.

He tried to find an arm to cheer her up. Failed. Jason did touch his right cheek, felt pain. "Must be a beaut of a mouse. Don't feel much."

"You've been sedated."

Clair held up the front page of the *Washington Post*. There was his picture, an old one, and a headline: "Muggers Attack, Injure Senator Crockett on Washington Street." His eyes didn't focus enough to read the story that went with it.

A nurse came and adjusted his pillow. "Dr. Norris is coming soon. Will we have some juice through a straw?"

"I think so. I'm thirsty."

It tasted chalky through a glass tube. Sheila readjusted the pillow as if demonstrating property rights. She was controlling her agitation very well.

The nurse said, "Soon, tomorrow, two soft-boiled eggs, toast . . ."

A heavy man in a pale-green hospital gown came in, white hands looking as if he boiled them. Behind him was a plump, short man with a hard, black face, a gray moustache.

"Hello," said the large man. "I'm Dr. Norris, Senator, in case you don't remember. A tough skull—very. You took some exquisite stitching last night. How's the temperature, O'Hara?"

The nurse held up the bed chart. The doctor grimaced. "Hmm, yes, a bit of a concussion. We'll X-ray the ribs later, may be cracked. Yes, well, Senator, you're the third official this month got worked over in the streets of our fair city. Oh, this is Sergeant Curtis of the Detective Division."

"Good morning, Senator. Happy to see you're recovering."

God, thought Jason, it's like a goddamn play, even the dialogue. Sheila frowned at the detective.

"It's a disgrace. These young punks own the streets after dark."

The detective nodded cheerfully, "Daytime, too. It's a problem. Now, Senator, soon we'd like you to look at mug shots. You think you could identify the suspects we hold? You get a good look?"

"One at least, two maybe. They were, well—"

"Blacks? Yes," said the black officer. "One has a badly shattered jaw and the other suspects we collared, one is black, the other white. However, all have juvenile records long as my arm. You know: hub-caps, car radios, looting a candy store."

Clair said, "You'll press charges?"

The detective looked into a small notebook. "Two are under six-teen and—"

"The usual crap," Sheila said. "Broken homes, no fathers, mothers work. I've heard that recording before."

The sergeant appeared amused. "No, ma'am, actually one of the boy's family are very successful undertakers, the other black boy's folks are post office workers. The Caucasian is a runaway from a re-formatory in New Jersey."

The doctor was sniffing the bandage on the scalp. "I think we can let the senator rest now. He's running a slight fever and there has been a loss of blood."

Jason had an idea he blacked out, not all the way; he could still hear voices: Sheila and the doctor and Clair and the nurse. And he was in a tight, soft chrysalis, like a butterfly. Sleep was good. He wanted to ask where was Esme? Where was Austin? Where was Amos Fowler? Why should they be here? And he fell into dreamless sleep.

The mugging and slugging of Senator Jason Crockett made the national press and there was television footage of the three suspects being arraigned, their public defenders smiling. A suspect, the one with a cocoon of bandages around his head, smiled too. An assault on a member of Congress in the streets of Washington was no longer shocking news. The media did point out that Jason was expected to go out in the coming primaries as a contender for delegates for the presidential nomination. Enough people who until the attack on him had not heard of him (or only vaguely) now took notice.

As J. Willard put it when he flew to Washington, "Crack on the head and a couple of ribs stove in and you get as much attention in the press as Miss America or a new Cola drink."

Jason was sitting up in the hospital bed—feeling stiff, but better. "I've about decided to go after the primaries."

"Well, why not? You're the best man they have and they're not all flagrant mediocrities."

"Austin isn't happy. In fact, he's against it. Me running."

"Well, Judge Fowler is happy as a grig. Had a talk with him."

"Yes, he's coming over to see me this afternoon. What do you think of the judge? I know he's flamboyantly assertive."

J. Willard took a pear from a gift basket of overpolished fruit by the bed. "I think he can get you nominated and most likely elected. No questions, please."

Jason tried to laugh. It hurt. There was still a dim hovering of dreams. "You don't like him? Austin doesn't."

"Don't go do my thinking for me. Don't go bumping with disembodied gossip. You're electable. He, Fowler, is the man who can do the most for you. Total perfection is achieved only by the dead."

"I'm going home tomorrow. We'll talk, but not now."

J. Willard took a hefty bite of the pear. He ate it slowly with relish, smiling at his son. Yes, Jason thought, Pop *is* getting old, and now he doesn't care how it's done; he wants his son a president. "What about Judge Fowler?"

"Too small for a man; too big for a shoat."

When J. Willard had left with the fruit basket (Jason had insisted —it was from Snow Williams), Jason looked at the list of people who had called the hospital and left messages of *Get Well* and *Cheers.* Esme's name was not on the list. He missed the special sensibility that contact with her gave him.

He wondered if he should call. But he didn't want the hospital switchboard to have any record of such a call or someone to listen in. Why not call anyway, he asked himself. He was just dozing, at 2:22, when the call came.

The floor nurse's voice simpered on his phone. Would the Senator take a call from a Miss Lowell?

He said yes, he would. "Christ, Esme, how are you?"

"Better still, Buster, *how* are you?"

"Aching but okay. I was wondering where the hell—"

"I'm here, right now, up at Green Springs, near Cumberland, you know in the Allegheny plateau; dogwood in bloom, redbud and poplar. Beautiful. You all right?"

"I'm all right. What are you doing up there?"

"In the big woods? Looking over a site for one of those Disney-type parks, and so was out of touch."

"Want to see you. And soon."

"Heard on the radio up here of your damn mugging. You sure you're all right?"

"Going home tomorrow, in good repair. All systems go."

"Well, don't strain anything. I'll see you as soon as I get back in two days. Listen, what's this talk of replacing Ormsbee in the primaries? I thought you hadn't made up your mind."

"Press talk. You know reporters. I'll tell you all about it when we get together."

"Yes, well this is some kind of local party line phone setup, a dozen people all ears. Call you soon as I get back. Heal quick."

"Yes, Esme. Yes."

It was a most satisfactory phone call, he thought. Then as he looked at the baskets of gladiolas he decided no, it wasn't. But what did he expect? Esme to rent some old flying crate and come flying back, or tear up the dirt roads out of the mountains to get to his sickbed? After all, he wasn't dying, wasn't even badly hurt. He'd taken a tougher beating, a real clobbering, in some football games. There is no way of figuring out one's life with a ruler and pencil. It's all wild lines, scribblings, and he slept again, after phoning the nurse to get the damn flowers out of the room.

At home he was babied, though he insisted *no* nurse. He walked in the garden, gave two press interviews and did a broadcast with Snow Williams and her television crew in his living room, seated in his best dressing gown and a bandage over his sewed-up scalp.

Neither the reporters nor the television personality spent much time on his scars of the street attack. But would he enter the primaries?

He said several times he was certainly giving it a lot of thought. He was sure the party chiefs were too. No, there was no final decision as yet. Yes, he had given it much really deep, searching thought. Yes, he would decide within the next two weeks. Give it real comprehensive judgment.

Snow Williams pressed him hard. "Of course, if you should go into the wegular primaries your policies would be against what your two most prominent wivals stand for, their weasons for wunning. Do you feel your political morality is above theirs?"

(Oh you bitch, he thought—hinting at Esme and me? But he smiled.) "I am ready to measure political moralities with anyone running, and I shall face my conscience, *if*, Snow, I decide to take on the major primaries, *when* I take them on."

Judge Fowler sent over galantine of capon and a tin of pâté de foie gras in aspic.

When Jason returned to work, he got a cheer on the Chamber floor and he spoke for the Ocean Rights law. He looked over in private with Andy Wolensky, his administrative assistant, the test polls in six states that were the most important ones to carry in the primary races.

"New Hampshire, J. C., is just a sentimental starter, where a yes or no, well it's a news item but no more. But New York, Ohio, Florida, California, you've got to take three out of four to mean anything at the national convention. Committed delegates from the majority of these states and you've got a big advantage."

"What do you think, Andy?"

"It's no lead-pipe cinch, but it's all in your favor."

"You really think so, Andy?"

"Amos Fowler does, too. Any chance of Austin Barraclough issuing some nice fat statement?"

"Don't bank on it. I've got to pick between him or the judge."

Andy folded his reports. "Amos Fowler can do things and Barraclough can't: money-wise, lobby-wise, delegate-wise."

"Wise the hell out of here. I've a four o'clock appointment."

He was going out to Esme's house at four o'clock. Somehow he felt both a bit shaky and elated—as it had been when J. Willard let him borrow the car and he had a date with some high school hotsy-totsy (what dated talk), a pom-pom girl, and knew it was going to be really good necking—and making it, making out, were the expressions then in use, or was that later?

He went down to the Senate barbershop, had a shave, got his shoes shined. He drove to the Van Der Hoff flower shop and bought a long box of roses and other flowers he had read of in a study of Shakespeare's plays (poor Will and his Dark Lady, a man was never sure of the true equilibrium of love).

Christ, if he kept thinking like that he'd spoil the afternoon. It was not at all as in the novels of Irving Wallace or that Susann broad, where everybody just shucked for mindless debauchery and leapt on each other in hot prose copulations never enacted by man, woman or beast. No, in reality there was a subtle complexity, a perplexity, even a complicity about making love.

He carried the florist box under one arm and inserted the key she had given him some time ago into Esme's front door lock.

"Hello there," he said from inside the hallway, pocketing the key. From upstairs came a reply, "Hello."

His scalp itched, he reached to scratch it and remembered his hat and the stitches under the pink strips of adhesive tape.

Chapter 30

Esme was fully dressed: gray slacks, dark-brown turtleneck sweater, tobacco-colored buckled shoes. Jason also noticed tiny green stones on each of her earlobes. Not at all her usual costume when she'd meet him in an open robe and little else, her long naked legs animated and her hair twisted back in no attempt to look stylish. But now—almost a fashion model on display.

"Come in, come in."

"I'm in."

He was wearing the hat on his injured head rather high and he took it off. The adhesive tape covering the stitching seemed shameful to him.

"At least," she said, "they haven't shaved your head."

"No. Just a loss of a little hair. You didn't come to see me." (In spite of everything his tone, he felt, was too petulant.)

"No, I didn't."

(He felt a taut serenity in her answer.) Esme led him to the sunporch, and to the familiar wicker furniture. The pampas grass, he noticed, had been replaced by a stunted Japanese maple in a rust-and-gold-colored ceramic tray.

She said, as he seized one of her hands, "I was worried you were seriously hurt."

"Sure enough," he said sitting down, pulling her to his side. "I'm still groggy, you know, the world tipping at times." He reached an arm around her. "Esme, the damn thing happened right in front of this house."

"I know, I was away." She was studying his face as she lit a cigarette. "Been hell to pay if I were here. Be identified by reporters, the whole mess."

His head ached, not from the stitches. He thought, she fears for her privacy, a scandal. She had sent to the hospital a pot of blue flowers wrapped in silver paper and just a card, "Esme L." But she hadn't come to visit him the six days he was in the hospital under observation, and getting X-rayed, thumped, having his kidneys checked. Lord, he had felt like a ten-year-old Ford car getting a 10,000-mile checkup.

Esme had called twice, he remembered, and they had had short conversations, small talk, and as the calls had come through the main hospital switchboard and the floor nurse's desk, it was very unsatisfactory talk. Like nibbling around words.

Now with her so close at his side, he felt something very wrong. He took her in his arms and kissed her. She didn't resist, didn't really participate. In moving away from him she accidentally banged an elbow into his ribs. He cried out *Oh ouch!* and she said *Sorry* and his confidence began disintegrating. Jason's impulsive exhilaration at entering the house was gone.

"What the hell is the matter?" he asked.

"I'll tell you what's the matter." She studied him with pensive, eloquent eyes as if searching out visible deficiencies. "It's all about you seeking the nomination."

"I'm inclined that way, yes. What's that to do with us?" He had expected commiserating over his hurt; not *this*.

"With us it means a damn lot. A very damn lot."

"How?"

"Ever think how you'll sneak me into the White House? Like Warren Harding did his girl, in a clothes closet? Or are you planning little nude romps on a rocking chair à la Kennedy?"

"That's a long way off."

"Not so long. Primaries in a couple months, then whooping for the convention."

He felt his stomach in his anger get a jolt of adrenalin. "You're seeing everything, Esme, from the wrong angle."

"Nuts to that, Buster." She stood up and ground out the cigarette in a pearl-clam shell. She glared at him, suddenly inaccessible, inviolate. "You've used me. You've used Uncle Austin. Oh, you bastard, how we've been had. And all to get yourself set on top of the heap."

"That's damn unfair. Up till now we understood each other. You're crazy," he said. "How can you talk this way? We haven't been playing games, we've been serious. I've been damn serious. We, we—"

"*We* is no more. Maybe I'm stupid. It came to me slowly. I'm not too bright emotionally. Once a man is in my pants I lose all sense of outside awareness, of purpose—of thinking on a bouncing bed."

He tried to wrench from her a residue of sympathy. "It's not the way you make it sound; a common affair."

"That's it—just *cazzo* and *potta*. A little slap-and-tickle adultery to advance yourself, to get close in—grab information about Austin Barraclough. Damn it, I said once you're no candidate. I felt I'd convinced you you're a fine leader in the Senate, an important man in Washington. But this flying to the top of the tree, really—"

He stood up, found himself holding his hat. He ran his fingers in frustration, self-commiseration, around its brim as he rotated the headgear. He was also feeling a deeper anger, a kind of rising rage. And also some guilt. Maybe a bit of what she had said was true. But even if a lot of it were true, it wasn't as if he were using her like a whore or a corporation call girl. Lord knows he'd desired her, even this minute it could maybe all dissolve if they got into bed.

"You don't understand me, Esme. I'm what I am, a man with purpose, hope. But—I'm not laying a line on you—my attraction to you was nothing I planned. In fact—"

She said very quietly, "In fact, Senator Crockett, you can save all this for your speeches. I feel you've never been truthful with me. I liked you, wanted you, needed you, okay? How's that for a confession? I didn't ever want to be Mrs. Senator Crockett, maybe I didn't even want to be in love. But damn, damn it—it came around to that."

He stopped rotating the hat in his hands. "Yes, I think we were mature enough, sure of ourselves, we both fought it, didn't realize its drive, its turning to more than just a good time together."

"Uncle Austin knows you now. Knows how you studied him, worked on him." She laughed. "But you see, wise guy—you did too much, were too effective with Austin Barraclough. You resuscitated a drowning man, you recreated the Austin Barraclough that was."

"Thank you. I don't regret that."

"But you overdid it. Now he's seen through you, as I have. Now he's discarded you. He isn't going to support you. He's going to fight you."

Jason sat down and put a hand to his aching head. "I don't right now care about any of that. I want to hold on to you, grab hold again. I want to be as we were."

"You want to go to bed, get between my legs? Well, no dice, Senator. I'm not putting out for you."

"It wasn't just—I came to be with you."

"Yes, but there is no equilibrium in lechery. You're up, I'm down. I'm forgetting the amenities of the past in my bed."

He sighed, relinquishing hope. "You had me come here to give it to me, the big brush? I thought you had more class."

She covered her face with her hands and suddenly began to weep. "Get the hell out, you conniving bastard."

"Jesus, Esme—let's not tear it up like this."

He tried to reach her, but she twisted away and then beat off his arms with hard fists when he tried to seize her. He stopped to observe her. It was all unreal drama—involving him.

Esme let tears run down her face; her voice was plaintive. The voice of a woman regaining control, outrage gone from its tone. "I don't want any more, Jason. I want just *not* to be with you ever again. That's all."

He winced and made a futile gesture (Laurel waving to Hardy?). "I'll call you tomorrow."

"No, no sham or pretension. It can't be as it was. I'm going away, I'm going to Bicca Island on the Keys. Going to set up a summer hotel, a development, there."

He asked, "With Jack Klein?"

"Oh, think what you want. I don't have to answer to you." She walked away from him, an animated swaying of her body.

He watched those magnificent flanks, the haunches rippling, that torso that he worked over so ardently, those legs that had been so often amorously entangled with his own. He was near to an erection. Now all this talk, this deed of parting done in daylight was also giving him a paralyzing despair. The best solution would be with a prone woman talking in the dark (scrub that image).

Esme was on the stairs sobbing, and he knew this was not at all the way she had planned it. It was a failed masquerade, this meeting. He panicked as he thought: *this* is the last meeting. And he caught the all-pervasive scent of her: body powder, sweat, that personal odor of only Esme.

He said, "Don't plan anything, please; don't judge me too hard. Let's just think. Yes, think for a few days."

She continued up the stairs, her sobs turning into a kind of bleat. She rubbed the wet end of her nose with a finger.

He said, "I'll call tomorrow."

She continued silently up the stairs. Jason let himself out into the strong lime-colored day, put on his hat and stood looking about him. There was a dark stain on the sidewalk; could be the remains of his own blood (*There is a fountain filled with blood. Drawn from Emmanuel's veins*). A woman nearby, holding the leash of a large dog, was looking away while the animal, straining desperately, bent in a half circle, deposited a turd on a carefully cultivated lawn. Two little girls went by on roller skates, giggling . . . The day whirled before his eyes, his head ached, his ribs hurt. The dog finished his task; the dog woman looked at Jason with disdain and he discovered he'd locked the car doors with the keys inside. (*Jack and Jill went up the hill and Alice said jam yesterday, jam tomorrow, but never jam today . . .*) He held onto a young tree and the world, inane and incomprehensible, went swirling past.

A half hour later Jason was sitting in the Falstaff Olde English Pub, a bar done up to look like a London public house, drinking a second vodka gibson and waiting for the auto club to come and open his locked car. "Proud and truculent," he said to the black barman, thinking of Esme; the barman gave an ambivalent grunt and added, "Right man, right." No one said "right on" anymore, Jason thought. Too bad.

He looked up into the face of Edward the Seventh, yes Seventh. The punk with Mrs. Simpson, he had been Eighth? The head of the old hedonist set in an opulent green velvet frame, looking across at a picture of Lillie Langtry in tight stays, maybe eighty years ago, holding a little stuffed bird for a photographer. The old lecher and his fancy woman. Did they suffer too—did they weep over their *chateaubriand grillé, saumon fumé* and all that bubbly?

The man from the auto club, in soiled white coveralls, came in, wiping his fingers on his loins.

"All oke, Senator." He held up the key ring.

"Have a beer," Jason said, handing over a five dollar bill.

"Sure-mike, Senator. What you need is an extra set of keys, see, you know, in a little magnetic metal gizmo, and you know, you just stick them under a back fender, never be locked out again."

"Easy as that?"

Jason drove slowly to Georgetown and he had such a petulant, repellent expression that when he saw himself in the rearview mirror he had to shake his head. It would never do to face Sheila with a desolate mug like that. Maybe a bit of Uriah Heep would be more in the right mood. Hell, damn Esme—Gloomy Gussie—he'd win the primaries, he'd dance with Esme, yeah, with her yet, the night of the Inaugural Ball. Yes, damnit, she'd be sorry she thought him a hick. Joseph whirling Mrs. Potiphar around in the White House ballroom. That amused Jason and he laughed so his ribs ached.

There was no one at home, the girl Fran was off—seemed she had more days off than working periods. Sheila was playing in a bridge tournament someplace. Her note on the dinette table read *Be back late—if hungry lob-tail with may. in fridg—or cold rosbif Lov, Sheil.*

He didn't need a drink, he told himself . . . I'm fine. I'm the luckiest man in the world. Got it all. Friends, family, high hopes, great office promising. Yes, only I'm too *macho* to give myself a good cry like some woman I know.

If in the next two weeks Jason Crockett had personal problems, or waited for a phone call that never came, if Sheila eyed him with a frown and he wondered in his vulnerability if she suspected anything with Esme, and his son Teddy had to be bailed out for reckless driving of a borrowed car, also his granddaughter, Libby, was having a hard time teething—for all that his public image shone. In the Senate Chamber he was a hero pointed out from the visitors' gallery as one lawmaker who had not meekly submitted to muggers and had a head wound to prove it. In the newsmagazines his picture took on a sculptured solidity.

It was clear that the majority of the party in the Senate and in the House favored him at the coming national convention if he made a good showing in the primaries.

Clearly, with senators Silverthorn and Redmond, Big Jim Houston, Judge Amos Fowler, the party chairmen in New York, Boston, Chicago and Los Angeles smiling at him, Jason could put up a good fight against his two rivals in the coming tests ahead. For Zack

Boone had not yet made up his mind to defer his own running and move over to aid Jason.

Austin Barraclough was now present at most Senate sessions. Nodding coolly to Jason if their paths crossed—yes, the old closeness was gone. Austin led the Old Guard, the elderly men of integrity. And they were few in number, but solid and entrenched in the position of presenting their own candidate in the coming primaries. Would it be Senator Dudley Giron from Louisiana, an old war-horse with a silver cloud of hair and a courtly manner, a deadly watchdog against wrongdoers with federal expenditures? There was also talk of James Jerome Leadbeater, a major magazine publisher, party fund collector, art patron, former Ambassador to the Court of St. James's as presidential material (mostly in his own publications). He and Giron were good, solid party men with no major scandals attached to them. But getting on in years, the two of them, and neither brilliant speakers nor crowd-exciters. Judge Fowler insisted, "They pulverize audiences to boredom."

When Jason spoke in the Senate Chamber he would become aware of Austin Barraclough watching him, his features bent into an ironic smile. It did not upset Jason; he had been too long in politics, been faced by too many hecklers, doubters and psychopaths to let anything upset his public performance.

He avoided direct mesmerizing glances aimed at him. He gazed just above Austin's baronial nose and thought not of political wounds given or received, but of how much he admired the bastard and how amazing his recovery had been. There was no use resenting Austin's reaction to him, it would be purposeless perversity. Better just to call the older man inconsistent and temperamental, and never for long gaze into his basilisk eyes.

After a hard debate as to what to do with the always degenerating postal service and the matter of another billion dollars to prop it up for another year, Jason walked into the Senate Cloakroom, where a group of senators were taking their ease in the comfortable chairs, unbuttoning and in some cases unzipping. Austin Barraclough was talking to two younger senators about the transitory moods the Senate was usually in before a national election, and of the embittered frustrations that came into the open when some high office was up for grabs. As the younger men drifted away with some new apprehensions, Austin took a filled pipe from a pocket and hunted for a match. Jason held out a pack of matches with the Burning Tree Club crest on the cover. The momentary gaiety of several nearby senators stopped as they watched the two men.

"Thank you," said Austin, puffing his pipe into drawing well. He held up the matches.

Jason shook his head. "I have others."

Austin looked at Jason, expressionless. Jason wondered at the subtle complexities of the man. He said, "It was a hassle today. The post office matter."

"Yes. The language of Job, Jeremiah and Ezekiel, all over getting a letter of no importance from here to there."

"How are you these days, Austin?"

The older man seemed to think it over as he puffed on his pipe, his demeanor showing no trace of wonder at the question. "I suppose I'm fine. You're bouncing around like a demented golf ball."

Jason sat down facing the pipe smoker. "I haven't had much chance to talk to you since we—anyway, I didn't feel it right to try to see you at Potomac House."

"Correct. I never severed a friendship so completely in my life. It was a distressful termination of the affection between us, a thing in some ways not at all superficial or flippant."

Jason leaned forward. "No, it wasn't. You might, no, I suppose not—"

"Thank you for plucking me out of the pit of despondency. [A puffing of smoke from the pipe.] *Pilgrim's Progress,* isn't it? The slough of despair, the path of frustration? But that does not forgive your outrageous use of me to help you try to seize power."

"Power?"

"Yes, you've taken over the strongest section of party power, have on your side the big men in the Senate—or at least they see eye to eye with you. Even the old mossbacks and turtles of some of the major committees, the senile party dodos look to you as the man to back."

"I hope to help the party to have a bigger say in the welfare of the country."

"Hope is a soft mattress, Senator Crockett, but, goddamn it, you need honest springs under it."

Jason saw there was no chance of amiability. "I'm sorry you feel that way. I'm no fraud, no man with his hands in any federal pockets. I should think you'd know me whatever my nature, or as you see my character as someone who isn't ludicrous. And who has learned, yes, and used a lot of your own way of once doing things."

Austin looked into his glowing pipe bowl. "Go away, man. Go away. You make me think I'm a goddamn parody of a public official. You see me only in a distorted sideshow mirror."

Jason stood up. "That's unfair, and you were always a fair man, even at your worst moments. What the hell do you want, a rite of purification?"

Austin smiled. "They were bad moments, weren't they? Yes, I musn't overlook that you were there and you offered whatever it was that kept a man who was pathetic from becoming pathological. All right, I thank you. This once, never again."

"I'm going to run hard in the primaries. You support Giron or Leadbeater and you'll just open the door for Boone or the rich boy to wedge their way to the top."

"Please, no lobbying in the Senate Cloakroom. And let's not stare at each other as the thwarted and the fallen. We're amusing the *other* zoo animals."

Jason glanced at the senators observing them. There was still a wide streak of misanthropy in the old bastard. And always there had been that unctuous morality, that acid lash of flippant Calvinism. Like Esme (don't think in that direction), Austin, too, saw him as a kind of sly yokel from the tall timber. These goddamn Tidewater aristocrats. Fuck them—and he thought of the one he had.

Chapter 31

As Jason after his encounter with Austin Barraclough hurried from the cloakroom in a mean mood, with a disgruntled truculence, Senator Joel Silverthorn seized his arm. "Temper, temper, Jay. The quality been telling you off?"

"You mean Barraclough? Yes, I guess he did rattle me. Just for a minute."

"A grand man, once. He's out of an old play, his tunes don't carry. Nobody whistles them anymore. Hell, I like him. I respect him. But we have primaries to win. And, Jay, Judge Fowler had word from Zack Boone."

"What's his attitude?"

Senator Silverthorn tilted his handsome head to one side. "He spoke to Amos about taking the last big rate freeze off the interstate natural gas producers."

"It could mean increases in gas costs to the consumers."

Senator Silverthorn bowed to a New England senator, a collector of Han and T'ang pottery (and secret funds). "Jay, not many of us are call girls in a hotel lobby. But staying in politics costs something. Costs a lot. Nobody is after your cherry, just a little smile in the right direction."

"Boone isn't a phony."

"He's fighting to stay on top. Like so many of us. He's now weighing how much leg he'll have to show and still not be considered a tart."

"It's true, Joel, without certain big-shot support he'll not be able to get roads built, or get federal funds to improve community services. He's in a bind."

"I like Boone. He's not simple. God-fearing, yes, but, Jay, God the paternal deity is not a God for democracy, is he? He's only dealt with kings."

Jason left the Hill in a fairly good mood. He had talked to Austin, not for any satisfactory return to their old standing, but the older man hadn't just turned away silently. Austin had managed to get a few barbs in; well, okay, it made him more human. Driving to Georgetown, Jay thought of the Blue River country, of Pop much younger and when they fished there. The sweet serenity of desiring nothing but a well-cast fly and a three-pound salmon trout giving you a nice fight. Why would any man want more, seek power through public office?

There had been no more contact with Esme since their last parting. It was an ache, a deep pain, but he knew it was over. He saw Esme as in a quiescent outrage, gorged with pride, like her damn uncle. Gone, gone like incomplete dreams we chase on awakening. He thought of Sheila; he had done her no harm, even if he was a bit ashamed of his passion away from her bed, *their* bed. He'd watch himself in the future. It could become a habit. He hadn't been reprehensible, no, just lonely and horny. The car radio was playing *Till Eulenspiegel*; Teddy and Laura had liked it when they were young; holding hands, dancing to its gay, fey mood. Maybe that was all his potential was—producing children for the future.

He must make an effort to like his children more. He'd been a good father, but not a great one like J. Willard. He switched off the music. Truth was, is, he'd been a lousy father. So busy, so driven by political hopes—yes, he admitted, I never got down into the playpen.

Amos Fowler decided he and Jason should go see Zack Boone.

"He's still talking big, Jason, but the country has seen too many of these firemouths, and been let down by them. They put on shoes, get dollar cigars lit and love up girls with clean feet for a change."

"Boone's not like that," Jason said.

"He's having trouble getting money. He's lost a lot of the support of southwestern newspapers."

"Why should we visit him? Let him wither away if that's the way things are going with him."

"We are all walking wounded—and should help each other."

"Boone still wants power, wants to be a top hound dog."

"Maybe we could convince him he'd remain a national figure if he threw his followers to us."

"You fooled me, Amos, with that 'walking wounded' line. For a minute you believe that's possible, he is linking up with us?"

Judge Fowler gave his foxy grin. "Now, now, anything is possible, even the impossible if you trust your heightened perceptions. Boone is smart. Very. If he sees he's on the deck of the *Titanic*, he might like to be rescued by say a comfortable yacht. He'd be doing his followers a good deed if he saw you as the man who *can* win. He can't. Besides, those natural gas boys would be grateful too."

"Boone likes being a spoiler."

"It's a sterile role. Goldwater, Wallace, McCarthy—all of them found that out. Anyway, he's staying with the big cotton converter out at Mill Dam Creek. Billy-Tom Howie's place. Damn the names these people have."

"It's folklore," Jason said, laughing.

"So. I've gotten us an appointment with Zack Boone for three this afternoon, to chew the fat, as they say down there."

"I'll be damned."

"First get nominated and elected. You'll be damned fifty times a day. Come on."

Billy-Tom Howie's place was a replica of Mount Vernon—twice enlarged—with old millstones for a walk, an eight-hole golf course, a ten-horse corral, and two Rolls Royces out front. Jason felt it was an old MGM film set, not real.

Zack Boone met them in the parlor, which had an organ built into one wall. (The house *was* real, Jason saw, not just a film facade). Boone was a man a bit too tall, and seemed all tanned, weathered skin and bones, but for a potbelly. Most of his growth seemed to have gone into his large feet and hands.

He sat well back in a rocking chair, dressed neatly in a pinstripe business suit, a soft yellow shirt with a silver longhorn-steer tieclip on a narrow shoestring tie.

"You gents comfortable, Judge? Senator?" It was a good, clear voice and lacked the twang and folksy nasal drawl Boone used in public at hoedowns, barbecues, camp meetings, football rallies.

"We are," said Judge Fowler. "You can't talk right if you aren't comfortable."

"That's true," said Jason, adjusting himself to a Victorian sofa. The judge smiled. "Now this is a little talk we've wanted to have with you for a long time."

"I like good talk. You'll have something, hard or soft? I don't drink, no more, that is. I'll just ring up one of the help."

"No thanks, Zack," said the judge. "If I could have a clear line —to talk."

"You got it." Boone didn't seem unfriendly. But he twirled one big foot in a big shoe, clockwise.

Amos Fowler spoke well and spoke with earnestness. But never heavily, Jason noted, not leaning on his words. Spoke with tranquility and no urgency. He put it to Zack Boone as he had to Jason, leaving out the more prickly parts of his idea of Boone's supporting Jason and not seeking delegates himself.

Boone took it casually, nodding, shaking his head at times as Amos Fowler delineated and dissected the plan. At the end he held his hands palms out, fingers spread. "That's about it, Zack. We want you, we need you. You don't diminish, you grow—retain your place in the public view."

"That's clear—that you want me, need me. You think I've got my licks in and it's futile. I'm just behind the barn beating my meat?"

"That's hardly," Jason said, "the way we'd put it."

"You haven't promised me a thing."

"And aren't going to," said Jason. "Promises, my old man said, in politics are last year's fleas."

"But," added Amos Fowler, "you can ask for our clout."

Boone thought, rocked. "You know what I stand for, who I'm for—the poor sonofabitch and his worn-down missus. I've gotten a lot done for some back home. But, as the judge says, the fat money boys aren't coming running with mitts full of cash. I scare 'em." He laughed. "I scare the cocksuckers shitless. Maybe I've been too close to the dirt for them."

"It isn't that," said Jason, "it's the ideology of success. They want to win, to back winners. And they want to be sure. Real sure."

"I'm a risk, I know it. But when I get up to talk things up, the folk are listening good. They know ol' Boone isn't talking for big oil and big auto car or big steel or waltzing around to get Wall Street to frig 'em. And now you think I can turn my mudsills and shantyboat people pledged as delegates over to you?"

"Yes, sir. Frankly," said Judge Fowler, "a lot of the South and much of the Southwest looks to you to point out the weather."

"Or which way to piss. Sure, I'm not modest. Yes, I suppose I have their confidence." He pulled a bell cord and a little old black woman came, wearing a white frilly apron. "Lacey Belle, some lemonade for the gents and myself." When she was gone he said, "I used to be a drinking fool. No more. See that little ol' nigrah? She don't like me, but she trusts me. I don't favor whites over blacks—only in bed."

When they were all gripping icy glasses sweating moisture, Boone rocked himself a bit and cleared his throat. "Truth is, I'm too genteel. If I did what I'd like to do, I'd pick up something real heavy and smash one of these Washington big shots in the head and then burn the courthouse right to the ground. But I'm too genteel. We need in this country some big men that used to work in the steel mills with about a tenth-grade education. A fella like that wouldn't be so genteel. But most folk are like me. Got too much education. They're too genteel. You genteel, Senator?"

"You're talking off the record, of course," said Jason.

"I'm talking grammar like we all do. Ain't-got, no-he-don't, and all that—I know better but it's comfortable. I went on television with this big sissy. I talked like I always do, and he was with that grammar and big words. And they quoted me, made it look like I don't know anything, don't know the origins of the Anglo-Saxon-Scotch-English language."

"You're smart," said Amos Fowler.

"Had a hard life, dealt with a lot of juries. Just *know* people. Then I'm dauntless, never give up, got more persistence than anybody else in my neck of the woods."

Jason remained poker-faced and sat back in his chair. "Zack, I know you love your country your way. Can we count on you—never mind how we disagree on details?"

"You call liberals, civil-righters, details? The intellectual liberals came to power and think they know what's good for folk. Any hotel clerk—and I don't mean to throw off on them, used to be one myself—knows more about why we're for tradition than a Yale professor sitting up there in his ivy tower. We got to get all this theory out of our lives."

"We can't, Zack, overlook everybody's rights."

"The problem, real problem is intellectual liberals in power to oppress people. Insist they vote, and won't let them run their affairs when they do. They insist the people don't have morality and integrity to run their own affairs. They got to be run for them, guidelines and all. There's more feeling against the nigrah in Chicago and New York than in the South. All this talk about bigots—all the bigots I know hang around the public square and you can't help know them. But they'll fight for this country. They're just old-fashioned romantics, most of 'em, with their dander up."

"You haven't been saying any of this to the newspapers?"

"Now, I do down home—and interviewers come down from the North to try to make a monkey of me."

"The anti-Communist line is safe."

"I don't see a Communist under every bed. Don't believe all this talk about poor folks turning to welfare bums. The damn rich turn to loopholes, I tell you. You ever seen a poor tax-cheater? Just tell me where."

"Zack, how do you see yourself in this coming election?"

"Just a little ol' country political leader who has facts people can't get every day. So I has to educate them. Can't just say, what will be popular today. They'd think I'm just a demagogue. They'd say about me: 'He's just blown up with wind.' No, they come miles, they shake my hand near off when I explain the truth. The people have the facts on encroachment on the rights of the states. They know the score. They're tired. I couldn't change anybody's mind if I wasn't in God's sight doing right."

"You've supported rich ranchers, wheeler-dealers," said Judge Fowler.

"I've had to stay afloat."

"Understandable."

"The rich ain't got enough votes—or voters who trust 'em. The national parties pay too much attention to rich folk. Shoot, all they care for is money."

"Our party is aware of that."

"These national parties recognize people are fed up with crime, stealing, mugging, raping ol' ladies in the streets. But they just talk about it election time. I mean, people of all races are fed up with courts and politicians coddling criminals. Too, we're tired of handing out foreign aid every which way while nobody helps us. Tired of Germans, or helping France when they don't help us, tired of folks raising money and blood for them nigrahs in Asia, Africa, Israel, for academic freedom, freedom of speech while our ambassadors get shot at. And we've got to differentiate between what's dissent, academic freedom, and what's treason. The two parties continue along this path, attacking property rights, free enterprise, a lot of people will be out of a choice and I'll give them one, maybe."

"Maybe."

"No, I ain't one of these fellers with a wild hair up his ass. A fellow like that couldn't get elected to office. Couldn't get elected on a hate-big-business platform. People everywhere are tired of the government telling them to sit down, get up, go to bed. The people need to be enlightened about this and I'm going to do that inside the party. Or, if not, outside the party."

"That's hopeless," said Jason.

"I speak easy—my way. Once at Chapel Hill I was getting an honorary degree and it was the most cultured, polite, well-dressed crowd I ever saw in my life. Gave 'em a real cultured talk until I started getting a head of steam. I forgot, called the Supreme Court a sorry, no-'count outfit full of poison. That cultured crowd just stood up to cheer. People are about the same everywhere. I'm a vote-getter—don't go counting my teeth like I was a tom-mule up for sale."

"We'd like you to pass the word around the senator is a winner."

"Kill the hog, fry the chickens, use a hot sauce." Zack rocked a bit and smiled sadly. "You-all kind of think I'm a freak. I know that. None of you ever think the trash has a hell of a problem. Our pore whites are in many cases pore as any nigrah cotton chopper. You collecting funds for him? You don't see us as a well-established society at all. With ways, habits, good thoughts, old burying grounds, kissing kin. All you care 'bout is forcing us to change to your candidate because you suddenly got morals. Where were you the last hundred years?"

Zack, sitting there, rocking, Jason felt, had power. The ideal of human perfectibility seemed a deadly game.

Zack stood up. "You're the most unmoral people up north we ever had. Go look at your goddamn records in union busting, racketeering, Tammany, the big-city machines, the folks with accents, the Rosenbergs, the Dagos you put in the 'lectric chair up Boston way. How you talk biggity *and* crowd the pore nigrah and Porto Ricans in them smelly slums owned by rich landlords; the way your lobby boys in gas and stocks and bonds and motorcars have things their own way. Your price-fixing corporations, income tax lying. *Shoot*, man, we may be narrow, we may be ready to fight, but we're closer than you bleeding hearts with your rotten Mafia as the second government, your whores in society." He spit on the clean floor. "You make me sick—all cant and sales charts. But . . . right now I'll think over what you said, all cozy under your wing. Yes, ol' Crockett may not git the sixteen-jewel drum-majorette magnolia-blossoms welcome."

He went out, his shoulders sagging.

Jason said, "A lot of what he just said sticks like barbs to our hide. We've always been very moral about *other* people's duties."

Driving back from Billy-Tom Howie's spread, Jason felt depressed. For all the irrational images Boone had suggested by talk or appearance, the man was no primitive. There were no confusing inconsistencies about him. He'd go down to defeat holding to basic ideas that were too simple, too direct, but they were ideas. The sad ferocity of the man was that of a trapped animal who knew it was out of place, ignored in a world of computers, space travel, moon rocks, and whose reliance on God was weakening under the inexorable urgency of the time's senseless pace.

"Well, Amos, we got nowhere today."

The judge chuckled. "You didn't use your eyes, you didn't listen. You expected elegies and panegyrics? Boone is smart enough to know he's outdated, knows the deficiency of his backers, the hopelessness of going against the monolithic powerhouses of both political parties. Hell, I could smell the farts of defeat in his pants."

"You sensed defeat?"

"What else, Jay? The long, bitter speech spilling out the hot mush of his feelings. He's a man in painful agitation. He's ready to be given a big title by us, to be glad-handed, interviewed. Happy to speak up for you with his people."

"Easy as that?"

"No, he's not taken the hook all the way yet. The nice thing about politics"—Amos Fowler slapped Jason's knee with glee—"is that chaos prevails as usual."

"And that's good?"

"Good? If you use that chaos to step yourself between the raindrops and keep your eye on the main chance. You know, in Boone's part of the country they hunt raccoons by torchlight. Now, will he want to be the treed coon? Or the braying hound dog about to be fed?"

BOOK VI

The Day of Battle

Chapter 32

Extracts of transcripts from various television political interview shows out of Washington, D.C.:

MEET THE PRESS
MC CLOUD (NEW YORK TIMES)

There is much talk that there is a personal vendetta, a mutual antipathy between you and Senator Jason Crockett, and your backing of Senator Dudley Giron in the upcoming primaries is not merely a political choice.

SENATOR AUSTIN AMES BARRACLOUGH

I have never paid too much attention to rumor or gossip that drains through Washington like muck through a stagnant swamp. Senator Crockett and myself are members of the same party and I'm certain we will both work to elect whoever is nominated. It is the choice of all free men and women to back with support, vocal and in other ways, those whom they would want to see as best representing the desires of the voters. Is this statement pompous enough?

MC CLOUD

Thank you, Senator. Now in this matter of funding these elections, isn't there in the process of raising large sums of money an identification of the special interests who provide it? Senator Crockett has great resources from unions, the people in the lumber and fishing and cannery interests. Is that a burden to his principles?

SENATOR BARRACLOUGH

Money is no burden to a politician, Mr. McCloud. It's the only load lots of people will be happy to take off your hands.

WOLSKINKY (CHICAGO TRIBUNE)

You're a practiced political hand of old standing, Senator Barra-clough. Isn't it just possible that if your backing of Dudley Giron shows failure at the primaries, you could—alienated or not—switch your support to Senator Crockett?

SENATOR BARRACLOUGH

As the girl says in that Bernard Shaw play: "Not bloody likely."

BURTIN (NEWSWEEK)

There has been talk you are the true dark horse candidate yourself. Wouldn't Senator Crockett support you if it seemed you were the man to beat the opposition? What's your reaction to that idea?

SENATOR BARRACLOUGH

Ha!

FACE THE NATION

MODERATOR

Zachary Thomas Boone is a name that has more and more been focused in the nation's attention due to his wide and popular support at the grass roots level in the South and the Southwest. Senator, Governor Boone, how shall I call you?

ZACK BOONE

Right now, I'm attorney general of my glorious state and my support is national, not just regional.

MODERATOR

Fine. Mr. Boone, before we open the discussion with the full panel, Jack Anderson yesterday in his column stated you might pay attention to your standing in the polls showing you lacking support in the northwestern and central states and might at the convention throw your delegates to Senator Jason Crockett.

BOONE

I don't throw nothin'. Only my Stetson into the New England primaries where some of the people—not the majority—are stiff-necked [blipped] frozen pilgrims and busted farmers who haven't laughed since John Alden, he courted the wrong girl up thataway.

MODERATOR

About Senator Crockett. You said, on the Johnny Carson show, that you "watch his antics with rambunctious amusement."

BOONE

I apologize in six different positions for being so mild.

SALLY BEENINSTOCK (READERS SYNDICATE)

You said of Grover Asa Bremont's candidacy, and I quote you in the *Pine Hill Daily Herald*, "He's a flower blooming through cracks in a coffin."

BOONE

Now *that* sounds more like me. Fact is, I'm the only candidate someone doesn't wind up like a toy and push around.

THE TODAY SHOW
ANNOUNCER

And now back to this morning's guest.

GROVER ASA BREMONT

I would like to say I am flattered by Mr. Boone's describing me as a blossom rising from a casket. He has the native wit of the region he comes from, a small place and so a small wit. But I would like to point out that the nation is walking in pathological somnolence following him, or Senator Giron, or Senator Crockett. They are all three dedicated to the gradual, inexorable decline of this nation. By seeking the support and making promises to the lowest segments of our society, those who neither pay much in taxes, nor seek any higher level of life than the welfare state. The other candidates are for the destroying of honest labor that seeks the right to work, free from gangster-controlled unions, and they are in league with those who would destroy the effectiveness of the Pentagon to keep us fully armed. They would also strangle the CIA, the FBI, and keep prayers from little schoolchildren. My rivals sneer with sanctimonious obscenity at those among the church faithful who would outlaw abortion, while *they* favor homosexual degeneracy. Boone, Giron, Crockett, I am sure, are the kind of men the Soviets would rather see in the White House than myself.

THE SNOW WILLIAMS SHOW
SNOW WILLIAMS

I've managed to pry Senator Jason Crockett away from his busy day while in the middle of his preparing for the trip north to show himself to the weally solid New Englanders in the first primaries of the year. Senator, is it weasonable to see the fine Italian hand of Austin Barraclough in your losing two percent in the last three polls? I mean his speaking out for Senator Giron on various talk shows? Oh, the power some of us television folk have.

SENATOR CROCKETT

First of all, Senator Dudley Giron is a very good man and a close friend of mine. As for polls, have you ever been polled, have any of your friends ever been polled? Have you ever had a phone call from people representing a polling organization? What of the millions who don't have phones? And how many people answer truthfully? So much for polls. All polls that try hardest hedge their figures by wide spreads. So, what of Senator Austin Barraclough? I think he's a fine man, intricate, wise, and who has again brought himself back into the national picture with his old wit and vigor. He's an exuberant presence. In fact, I admire *everything* about him but his not backing me. The function of a politician, he once said, is like a function of the criminal in society: to provide employment for policemen.

SNOW WILLIAMS

I don't get it.

SENATOR CROCKETT

The function of the politician is often to take the voters' mind off the real issues, as Senator Barraclough is doing.

SNOW WILLIAMS

I know from knowing you so well that you very much want to be president, wather than have control of the Senate.

SENATOR CROCKETT

Of course I want the people to see me as presidential timber. Would I be sitting here with you when I would rather be fishing with my father than expose myself as a candidate?

SNOW WILLIAMS

Naughty man. I'll be wight back after the next message from our sponsor, and—

Judge Amos Fowler and Bread O'Rahilly were in the Protocol Club on H Street, in the Henry Kissinger bar—so called because it contained several framed photographs of Kissinger caught in various parts of the world, all autographed to the club in slightly old-fashioned penmanship.

Amos smiled and waved some fingers at the cocktail waitress. "Honey, will you mind turning off the television . . . Thank you." He set down his empty glass. "And two more of the same."

They had been drinking Scotch and watching the Sunday afternoon political news shows. "The human psyche on these shows seem to be made of some gummy plastic. Are they popular, Bread?"

"Hell, who knows who watches what on these Sunday TV ghettos? That Boone I like—a funny fellow. The rest, well, Bremont is still scraping a Yale education from his shoe like dog shit. Austin comes on strong but with too sharp teeth. And Jay? He's doing fine, who else could fight off the bitchery of Snow Williams mauling her r's?"

Amos lifted the fresh drink, gave the waitress a pat. "Thank you, my dear . . . Grover Asa Bremont doesn't bother me; outside of his restricted wards and the skirts of the cardinals, he doesn't count. It's Boone's endeavor I fear. He'll do badly in the Northeast, sure, but he's cut into Jay's sweep of the Middle West. And the kooks on the West Coast? Who knows what they'll do? The Southwest, maybe, and always the South are Boone's. He's a prickly porcupine of a guy, that bastard. Moral, honest, simple."

"The South's waking up, Judge."

"Only one eye is open, Bread. A native boy with a hog caller's voice never fails to raise their hackles for a time anyway. I'm going to talk to Boone again—alone. My figures show he can't really get near the nomination. But he can hurt Jason. What would he like in a horse trade besides no freeze on interstate natural gas?"

The lobbyist shook his head, sipped his drink. "Doesn't want to be ambassador to anything. His state has all the Pentagon defense plants they can eat. He doesn't shtup call girls or take on movie stars in the kip, doesn't booze. The country would scream if he became Secretary of State. How about head of the Justice Department? Running American jurisprudence."

"Would Boone take the Vice-Presidency?"

"Not in a million years. Agnew and Ford's Fang have pretty much made that Dracula Hall."

"Head of the Justice Department? Attorney general?"

"After the shmucks, the chair polishers we've had there, he'd be a change. But don't say anything to Jason. He's a bit contemptuous of men whose only principles are rewards."

"Bread, I think he's changed."

"One more, Judge, to travel on?"

"My liver says no. Jesus, the first thing I always teach a young political hopeful is that it isn't as easy to slip into the bigger national scene like into a warm bath."

Bread O'Rahilly signed for the bar chits and waved off the judge's attempt to seize them. "No, no. What the hell good is an unlimited expense account if you can't flash it? That bitch gossip columnist who kisses ass for an item, she's been hinting Jay has been making it with Esme Lowell. Opening art shows together, inspecting a new armored tank, eating and sipping aperitifs in out-of-the-way joints, that sort of privy sweepings."

The judge pinched the bar girl's cheek, handed her five dollars. "You're like a tonic, my dear."

"Thank you, Judge."

The judge took his topcoat and homburg hat from the hat check opening, pinched another cheek and left a dollar.

Small, graceful, neat, the judge almost skipped through the door the lobbyist held open for him.

"Bread, that affair is all over. Kaput. Miss Lowell is a marvelous-looking woman, isn't she? Twenty years younger myself and— However, she's Barraclough's niece and is herself politically wise. It's all right to roll in the linen with a senator. You can subvert reality at that stage, when politics is all games and status striving. But she isn't seeing herself replaying that old movie *Back Street* with anyone in the White House."

*   *   *

The two men parted cheerfully in the russet gold of a late afternoon. The judge, being driven back to his house, sat in the corner of his Rolls Royce, a travel rug skillfully wrapped around his thin legs, his lean hips. Chico, his houseboy and chauffeur, was separated from him by the thick glass behind the front seat. The new Rollses didn't all have the private roll-up window between the driver and owner. Only on special order. Amos Fowler didn't mind change; he didn't protest against what was called progress. He didn't even mind old age. He had survived. Total serenity is achieved only by the dead. He had done many things, with women, with boys. He had accepted from either sex the fidelity of love and its disastrous games. He had also accepted the failure of love to last at its highest pitch. Only politics satisfied his full sensibilities.

He had done good, he had done what some might call evil. Enjoyed them, been bored by strange divertissements. He had held high office and had sunk at times within the range of mean men marinated in money, who thought to use his knowledge. But he had despised them.

He dozed as the car sped on . . . and he thought of this last national adventure. He believed in nothing anymore but the fun, the excitement of the game. He would make Jason Crockett President of the United States. Goddamn Austin, curse Boone, a plague on all bureaucrats and eggheads. But it was all there was. Sex was gone, most sensory impulses; milk and crackers and pills were increasingly his diet. God, no longer a classmate, had faded out. Mankind? A dangerous species bred without taste. He was aware of his own decline—all appetites and ambitions blunted, but for this one last twitch of his ego. How wise was that Roman emperor who wished the world had one collective head so he could cut it off with a sword.

Chapter 33

Two events that spring (that always surprising Washington spring) impressed themselves on Jason Crockett. It was not the usual twenty-four-hour watch the newspapers had set on the Japanese cherry trees to overwhelm the first blossoms with attention; nor the fact the placid tourists were arriving in greater numbers than before, without any raucous protest marchers, or that the usual hanky-panky in the Pentagon bookkeeping was exposed (and forgiven) or the newly revealed (what again?) sexual adventures of another aging senator, or was it a congressman?

No, the first item that jolted Jason was the marriage of Esme Lowell to Jack Klein in Miami. "They were involved in setting up a new community for retired senior citizens in Florida," Big Eyes, the columnist of the *Washington Post*, noted:

> The new Mrs. Klein is the niece of Senator Austin Barraclough. She is aged twenty-four [sic], has served in some vital tasks coordinating American-Italian film interests, and has a daughter by *what* Italian film director? No, *not* Fellini. Jack Klein is thirty-two, one of the famous Klein Brothers of Yonkers who built just masses and masses of middle-class housing in northern New Jersey, communities known as Kleinvilles. Jack is a graduate of the City College of New York, served in Vietnam as a Hughy helicopter gunner. He is the grandson of Rabbi Emanuel Katzenelenbogen of Boston. The couple will make their home in Bog-gla-Tan, the new development they are designing south of Miami on Mangrove Inlet.

At breakfast, Sheila, reading the item, observed to Jason, "I always thought the Barracloughs were anti-Semitic."

"Why would you think that?" Jason asked, waving off a favorite dish, Canadian bacon and eggs, that Fran was bringing in from the kitchen. "No, no, I'll just have toast and coffee."

Jason wondered why people thought the seat of the emotions was in the heart. They sat in the stomach; he could feel that sickening feeling in the gut as if his stomach had shriveled up into a tight fist and was punching its way out. He could taste the bile in his throat. Somehow he had held on to the foolish idea that he and Esme would make it up, somehow; deliberately contrived, be together again, radiant and urgent. He had fooled himself, deceived himself that her mood was only a fluctuating female gambit. What a monumental tactlessness since they had last faced each other. Not a word from her. He several times had found himself lifting the phone to call, once even dialing her number and yet hanging up in panic. Other times in some imbecile cheerfulness he had the thought in a few days all would be as it had been. Two grown people pouting like precocious adolescents. And now the blow between the eyes. Esme married to some flashy Jew latching on to a shiksa.

"I like her," said Sheila. "Never had any personal antipathy to Miss Lowell. She was not really snotty high society like so many of those Virginia people."

Jason looked up. Sheila was chewing toast, her eyes on him. *Good Lord*! It was clear to him suddenly by his wife's voice, by the way her mouth was set on the toast as she spoke, then as she folded the newspaper with a snapping to the op-editorial page, that Sheila knew of his affair. And somehow here and now she was having her moment of victory. The wife over the mistress, decency over immoral depravity.

She looked at him over her Churchill half-glasses. "I suppose we should send at least a telegram."

"To whom?"

"The newlyweds."

He looked at the no longer naive, credulous Sheila he had imagined. How wrong he had been to think that. Look at her; she sitting there with a feline satisfaction on her face—the fidelity of the marriage bed.

Outside he found a hint of rain. Dolf was polishing the hood of the car and looking up at the mackerel sky in its various tones of silver-gray. A black kid caromed out of a driveway on his skateboard.

"Might rain, Senator," said Dolf.

"Might."

The skateboard rider went past, yelling "Geronimo!"

Washington from the moving car seemed depressive: the delicate tracery of trees soon to die of auto fumes, the big church where the television cameramen had waited Sundays to catch presidents coming out after an unhinged, quotable sermon. The large sign on the church lawn read *The World the Flesh and the Devil. Here Sunday. 10:30 a.m. The Reverend Montross H. Rinehart, D.D.*

The world, the flesh and the devil. Jason thought: men desire them more than they usually admit. It was good to get to Capitol Hill to find he had a full day's work. He was on the committee dealing with the problem of the money to support the United Nations ("that damn Third World Club," as J. Willard called it, "of terrorists, pederasts, and loafers, just simple paranoids *and* conspirators"). Jason in his office watched the noon television broadcast of Snow Williams: a high-binding coffee klatch by that wily manipulator of trivia and spite. He went to an afternoon meeting with Big Jim and Tom Pedlock on funds for the coming primaries; should they spend for the newspaper media or for radio and TV? Or for sending out teams of young people to ring doorbells? Somehow he kept thinking of wicker furniture, pampas grass, cigarette smoke in semidarkness.

Clair reported that the polls were good, but not really strikingly in his favor. Grover Asa Bremont was within four points of him, Zack Boone was not making a fight of it. Amos Fowler dropped in. He wasn't impressed by polls. "They are like illusory ear noises, you know, they only seem to exist. Jason, think of *homo impoliticus,* man's stupidity, and how easy it turns to *homo ferox,* man's ferocity. It's the fact that the mass is so changeable that keeps a politician full of hope."

"I keep feeling the average man and woman, Amos, has real good sense, a benevolence. Yes, always a hope things will get better."

"You sound like a mountain patiently waiting for the sunrise."

"Austin once said something like that to me . . . His niece got married."

"Oh? Large girl. Cold as a witch's tit, I heard." Amos Fowler continued to speak of the fluctuations of popular appeal, and the elusive quality of judging the public's choice in picking favorites.

Three days later the second event occurred, or rather was reported two days after its occurrence. It came from David Brinkley over

NBC: "Condolences are being offered tonight to Senator Austin Barraclough on the death of his wife, Mona, which occurred Wednesday but was not discovered until her body was found in the wreck of a car in a ravine of Raleigh Creek, a branch of the Santee River near Millard, South Carolina. Mrs. Barraclough, a noted horsewoman and society beauty, had been resting at Kingtree Farms, an exclusive, very posh cosmetic and body slimming establishment for the beautiful people."

What the brief news items did not reveal was that Mona had taken the place's hairdresser's car without permission at the "posh establishment"—actually a sanitarium, a strict one. Later she had been observed acting strange at the Saddle Club Inn, drinking Jameson's Irish whisky. Later still she had been stopped for driving eighty miles an hour. Unable to produce a driver's license, she had sped off before she could be issued a ticket, and sight of her was lost in the heavy growths along the Santee River. She had plunged off into the ravine at what must have been an excessive rate of speed. The car had plunged, turned over and Mona had died instantly of a broken neck; a fey smile on her face when found two days later by two muskrat trappers. There were some hints that the death was a devised catastrophe. There were in the newspapers old photographs of her riding her horse, Red King, at the Piping Rock Horse Show. Also her greeting the Queen and Prince Philip at the Piedmont Ball; a dim view of her standing with a younger Austin Barraclough on the terrace of Potomac House during a Fourth of July celebration.

Clair had cut out all the press stories, pictures and items and placed them on Jason's desk, with no note. It was a sad collection of the directlessness of mortality, Jason thought. A foot on the gas backed by three drinks: curtains. He read some of it to J. Willard over the long-distance telephone. "People are dying who never died before," J. Willard said.

"Not funny, Pop. Not funny at all."

That was the sour sediment of life, J. Willard said; the fact that God "or whatever" was indifferent to beauty, wealth, to corporation mergers, dividends, the hope that our life has meaning.

Jason began to compose a telegram to Austin. No, better a handwritten note delivered by Andy Wolensky at Potomac House. As for attending the church services, he would see. Yes, at least the services anyway.

He and Sheila in dark attire at the big church? He worked over the note to Austin with tenacity and three cups of coffee.

Dear Austin,

Nothing ever said or written about death has ever seemed satisfactory. I offer, with Sheila, condolences at your loss. At such a time I hope a word from me will recall our friendship and that I offer this letter as part of my great affection for you, with an added wish to express a sense of oneness with you at this time. I know this that I write is most unsatisfactory, clumsy, and perhaps will not be received with the intent I want to convey. It doesn't matter—I have released how I feel for you at your loss.

Always,
JASON

It wasn't a superficial letter, but it didn't fully suggest what he wanted to say in the way it should be said. It was the best he could do, and not feel phony. Not dressed up with great quotations. Jason sealed it, addressed it and got Andy into his office. Andy had gained weight, even a wisdom of sorts as Jason's administrative assistant. He wore better clothes and his hair was styled now, at fifteen dollars a shot. But Andy was still the wary, busy Number Two of the senator's office, and he had no ambitions beyond that, just yet.

"She was kind of kinky, wasn't she?"

"I don't know the clinical details, Andy. Just leave this envelope with Champ."

"I better hustle you and the Mrs. two seats at the church. People really turn out for burials in this burg. You'd think they got their jollies that way."

It was a very good turnout for a burial. Crowded wide streets and people very respectful. Pop, Jason recalled, was here long ago for FDR's march past on a gun carriage. ("Everybody was crying like a baby," J. Willard said.)

Sheila had said over the phone, "Arrange for a wreath for Mrs. Barraclough as proper. Not too fancy. Taste, you know."

"I know, Sheila, not too colorful, not too weedy, *lots* of oak leaves. Just a card attached: *Senator and Mrs. Crockett.*"

Jason, after he ordered the wreath, walked about in his office, wound the old alarm clock. It was ticking like a heart in a horror movie. He decided to calm down. Austin would be polite to him in the church, maybe Esme, Mrs. Jack Klein, present (had it been a Jewish wedding, under the chuppa, with the circumcised groom breaking the wineglass set on the floor to signify the destruction of the Temple, or, as some insisted, the breaking of the bride's maidenhead? No luck there, Jackie, I didn't get it either).

J. Willard insisted it was important to evaluate in what condition this left the Barraclough forces backing Dudley Giron for the nomination. If the tragedy sent Austin back to the booze, if the old rummy appeared again, it could blow up the Giron surge. If the Giron forces, left headless by a backsliding Austin, were practical men—and they were, these old tough-skinned fat cats, *and* wise timeservers—they'd see Jason was the best man to switch to. How to get them to see this would take skill, Jason felt.

J. Willard agreed. "Elections, Jason, are won by fate, error, frailty. By sorrow and commiseration. Genius in public office is partly an acute sense of self-preservation."

Jason had Clair try to hunt up Judge Fowler. He was not at home, a servant said—just galavanting around town. The Burning Tree steward remembered he had been in earlier for lunch, "drank a half bottle of Perrier-Jouet Brut." Clair at last found the judge at the Protocol Club.

"The balloon's gone up, eh, Jason?" Amos said over the phone.

"It's tragic, damn tragic, of course."

"This sort of thing was bound to happen. Mona's mother leapt into the Gulf of Mexico off a cruise ship, and her grandfather, Monte, he was crackers; collected six hundred clocks and they'd all go off at once in his house. It's a flawed family."

"It may appear heartless, Amos, but with Austin broken up about this . . ."

"Yes, we should begin to contact the Giron people and try and bring them over to us."

"Well . . ."

There was a pause. Jason could just see the little wily, cold bastard sucking on a thin cigar, inhaling, exhaling. "Jason, he may not be broken up. Austin may now run for it himself."

"What!"

"You heard me. I've known Austin since he was a lanky halfback at Groton, or was it—never mind. He's a man you can't predict things about, except his integrity. And he can cold-cock you with that."

"But this tragic event."

"Not tragic. Expected. I'm sure Austin knew something outré would happen to Mona, had to—Destiny's prey—everything pointed to it. Now he's a man with no secret in any closet. Like Cleveland, he can go to the White House as a bachelor. Even have a White House wedding to some young chick, as they say."

Jason, over the phone, could hear Amos Fowler chuckling. "Judge, you are serious, aren't you?"

"Serious as a dog sitting on a burr. But not sure. If the Giron backing goes over to him, suppose Boone does too, eh? eh?"

"I think we could interest Boone, if we make it sweet enough."

Again the chuckle, and a grunt as if from pyloric pressure. "Ah, you're pliable. Good. Let's just wait and hold our cards close to the chest. You play poker, don't you, Jason?"

Jason said he did. He found he was sweating as he hung up the phone. He still often used the expression "hang up" the phone, from the days when Vista County still had wall phones out on the farms.

Chapter 34

At first there was a story out of the AP that Mona Barraclough would be buried in South Carolina, she having so desired it in a letter found in her effects. Then there was a following story that Senator Austin Barraclough would bring the body of his wife north to be interred in the old Barraclough burial ground near Potomac House, after services at St. John's Episcopal Church at 16th and H Streets. Pew 54, the White House press noted, would be occupied by the President and his family.

On the morning of the services, no one ever was sure if the demonstrations of grief and respect for widower were planned, or just happened. But the church was packed and the lists of people permitted inside were checked by stern men in swallow-tailed coats from the most fashionable undertaking parlors in town. Some there were attracted by the history of the violent life-defying impulses of the dead woman.

There were cameramen and reporters. Snow Williams was there and had her wide hat knocked off. Senator Redmond lost a gold and ruby cufflink shaking hands in the crowd outside the church. Jason with Sheila and Andy Wolensky sensed a popular surge of interest in Austin Barraclough. What should have been a service for the dead was somehow turning into a demonstration for the senator.

Sheila in a hat, with a short veil just barely reaching her nose, said, "It's got everything, this turnout, but pickets."

And as they moved toward the great doors, Andy looked about him, avoided the elbows of an old lady pushing hard. "You think, J. C., this is organized?"

"It's a sacred service that the media has shown a lot of interest in."

"No, I mean, you know, along political lines. Headlines like *Grieving husband buries beautiful wife before turning to seek nomination as his party's candidate.*"

Jason didn't answer. He studied the crowd as they entered the church, aware of the low moan of an organ containing itself within the lower register of its many silver pipes. There was the odor of flowers, and from the upper-class people the scent of clean bodies, perfumes and after-shave lotions.

Sheila nodded to several people. "It's become a social event. You think Judge Fowler will show up?"

"Don't think so," said Jason. "He's so damn old he says he'll only attend his own burial. Besides he and Austin . . ."

Sheila gave him an elbow nudge. "There's Austin."

He sat in a front pew just below a bank of dying flowers sending off too sweet smells. He was seated between Champ and Esme. Beside Esme sat a handsome, sun-tanned man with curly brown hair—that, Jason decided, yes, that would be Jack Klein. Jason wished the man had looked cunning, with a huge nose, little mean beady eyes. Hell, he didn't look any more Semitic than Paul Newman.

The great, shiny, overpolished casket was closed and banked with more flowers. Seated, Jason felt a shiver, a quivering in his stomach, his knees. Was it the sight of the new Mrs. Klein? And the resulting images that printed themselves in fast succession on his mind; their naked bodies, candid camera angles of cavorting upstairs and down, the final zooming in to sweet agonies of climaxes. Also, *also*, there was now the sense of being a loser, of having excruciatingly not just lost love, yes, of a hurt vanity. The old ego is chipped, raw edges grind, he thought, as Bishop Hamilton Watterley came forward. Yes, Jason thought, as they all rose, the ego felt she preferred *him* to *you*. She could have had you and she picked him.

He heard little of the bishop's discreet intonation—with an added bronchial tribute to the Barracloughs. The President hadn't come, but had sent the Vice-President. There were present the Chief Justice of the Supreme Court, the whips of both houses, the attorney general.

Andy studied the packed pews. "If somebody dropped a bomb on this church, you'd have to elect a new government right down the line."

"The flowers," said Sheila, "they're giving me a headache."

A young minister, rosy-cheeked, in longish hair, was reciting something not a prayer. The man rolled his vowels like an actor:

"Beauty is but a flower
Which wrinkles will devour;
Brightness falls from the air;
Queens have died young and fair . . ."

The young minister bobbed his head. "These lines are read at the request of Senator Barraclough."

Jason looked over at Austin. He was sitting straight and expressionless. The organ welled up, cut free to reach for its most mournful notes. The air was thick, the shuffle of feet, the movement of bodies was louder. An announcement was made that the rest of the service would be private; would the people please leave. It was a reluctant mass of people that followed the secret service men escorting the Vice-President and his family out. The last sight Jason had of Austin was of him seated still straight and expressionless in the front pew between Champ and Esme. Was he numb to events, or excruciatingly unhappy?

Sheila took Jason's arm, "Perhaps we should stay."

Andy shook his head. "No, there's a private list, just about two dozen people. Her doctor, the shrinks, some Barraclough cousins, servants, and Mrs. Klein."

Sheila seemed about to say something, but changed her mind. Jason remained silent. They pushed their way through the crowd to where a tangle of fine cars were trying to approach the curb. Snow Williams in the too-large hat grabbed Jason's arm. "What a crowd, a wegular circus."

Sheila said, "They were a popular couple, Miss Williams."

"They were, they were *au courant*. Senator, have you heard there is a group wanting Austin Barraclough to wun in the primaries himself?"

"The town is full of rumor and gossip all the time, isn't it, Snow?"

"I mean, how would that affect your own plans?"

"Not at all," Andy answered.

"Senator, there's your car," said Andy, and he pulled Jason down to where the car was at the curb. "The bitch, no respect." Andy added, "At a funeral looking for a story."

There was a milling crowd turning raucous that had to be faced, and Sheila was sure someone had pinched her before they were safely in the car. Police tried to direct traffic away from the church, but the streets around the structure seemed to be packed fuller than before. Some young blacks were larking across the street and in a park. A car with a crushed-in side was being led away by a tow truck flashing red lights. Someone was igniting fires in corner trash cans. Jason's car was held up ten minutes before it was free of the tight grip of the traffic and what appeared to be street fighting.

Jason looked back over his shoulder. "Andy, get Judge Fowler to meet me at the club, also as many of our committee as you can raise up. There is something in the wind."

"I feel it too—this turnout. But what?" asked Andy. "The Giron people may not even back him if he declares, and drops Giron. Who else is for Barraclough? Some bleeding hearts, a few old crocks who once backed a general?"

"No guessing now—just call the meeting, Andy."

Jason was feeling the way he had felt his second year in college when he was so damn sure of a halfback position on the football team, and then—he recalled it vividly—that damn Polish steel-worker's son had appeared, Biff Jablonski, and shown spectacular skill in catching impossible forward passes, and line-bucking. Jason had despaired and given up, slackened his training, ass-dragging low. Only Jablonski's failure to get good passing grades, and the affair of the waitress and the keg of beer sent Jablonski on his way to play pro football with the Green Bay Packers—and Jason became an All-American. Now that same icy feeling was all along his spine, and just as fearful, foolish, a state of fear. Foolish because Austin Barraclough was a million light-years from having the organization, the money to run a successful campaign, *if* he actually was planning to. It could all be a planted rumor started by some enterprising reporter building a story out of very little. He muttered, "It's paranoia time."

The meeting at the Protocol Club had a too-cheerful tone. Said Amos Fowler, "Well, I hear the quaver of violins in this room, playing for some volatile weeping drama. What's really happened? The crowd just loves a good funeral. They always turn out en masse for an important death—any buggy psychiatrist will tell you that. So they view Austin Barraclough because his wife, the late Mrs. Barraclough, was always worth a sensational feature story. She looked splendid falling off a horse, and it was no secret she had gone off the deep end mentally. That's all cake and caviar for nosy people."

Jason took up a list. "Tom Pedlock and myself have been analyzing the polls, public and private, here about town."

"Put it away," said Fowler, smiling. "You'd do better burning chicken feathers with a witch doctor, or reading the entrails of a hen."

There was light laughter from the dozen people present.

"That's whistling in the dark, Amos. The way it reads, I have a good chance of beating Grover Asa Bremont if we make an arrangement with Zack Boone."

Big Jim nodded. "Booney, he's seeing the light; the secret word is natural gas." Big Jim laughed. "We've got the Indian sign on him there."

Tom Pedlock said, "That could give us a fairly good majority in almost thirty-two states, even if even only forty percent of Boone's people follow him into supporting Jason Crockett. We can handle Barraclough."

India Kingston adjusted an earring. "This ground swell for Barraclough is big. The UPI, the AP are getting a lot of calls for information on him from newspapers coast to coast. I've seen these things no bigger than a man's hand grow into a huge cloud and then fade out. As a young gal I remember there was Stevenson, MacArthur's paper dragon. So . . ."

"You think," asked Jason, "this Barraclough surge will fade too?"

"Has to. He hasn't the big money, and he'll sure as shooting not get the southern delegates, or the wild men of the coast."

The meeting at the Protocol Club ended with a few ribald stories going the rounds, details of a homosexual scandal in the German Embassy, and much reassurance to Jason he had nothing at all to worry about. A good solid showing in the primaries, a piling-up of locked-in delegates, and the nomination was his at the national convention.

Jason went home feeling the weight of loyalties helpful. After all, the majority of the party's policy makers, fund raisers were with him. Even if to some, Austin might appear the better man, the wiser, older politician. But as Amos Fowler said: "A man with so much experience behind him, he is also a monument. And we plant monuments in public squares, not elect them."

And with that, Jason agreed. It was Austin's problem, he being a monument. Too long around, too many ties going back to the bad,

bad days in the party. Austin had been eccentric too long, a misfit drunk, sitting in darkness when he should have been building his political strength. Integrity, sincerity never won elections even if people try to think they do. It was an image, Amos Fowler insisted. "Identification, and socking away, keeping up the pace."

Jason undressed, drank a glass of milk, got into bed. He turned to Sheila and put an arm around her. There was in him that tension that needed release, the kind of nervous potency that only making love could calm, reinforcing and bolstering his self-relevance.

Sheila half opened her eyes. "Oh, it's you." She was smiling and Jason said yes, it was him.

For a moment there was the quenchless fear in him that she would bring up Esme. But not Sheila, not wise, ol' Sheila (pat pat) who knew he loved her, still did, always would, and was too wise to go extracting certain confidences from him (lift the nightgown). All their married life, the small wounds given and received had created no prolonged intentness between them (kick back the covers), and if she carried any grief, any rage at what she suspected of his unfaithfulness, she would not bring it up now at this crisis in his life (roll on), their life too, he thought . . . They made love and for sure it was clear she would create no calamity. Sheila climaxed in a slurry of outcries of agonized pleasure and he followed. He prided himself then that he had not a moment during the act thought of the *other* one. Never felt a comparison was there to be tested. He decided he would make no more tactical errors in sex. He was not adaptable to cheating like so many men.

Jason could sleep and he had no fears of any rival. Amos Fowler's last words had been "Fame, Jason, is the total sum of the damn misconceptions gathered around a name. Sleep easy."

Sleep easy, sleep. And he did.

He rose early, gathered the morning newspapers from the front steps while the coffee boiled. He read that the latest Gallup and Harris polls put him way ahead. He filled coffee cups and took them upstairs on a tray to share with a wife in a society heterosexual and monogamous.

Jason was aware he differed from Austin Barraclough in the matter of what some called the tragic awe of life. One had to be born with an awareness of it, he supposed, to sense fully the great outer darkness of the unconscious universe, so indifferent; the smallness of the planet and the dust motes that were the short-lived items called people. Even experience didn't help to make one feel gloomy over the heavy burden of the strangeness, the sadness of much of living and the misery of so many.

He could pity, he could feel, he was perceptive. But deeply tragic, locked in hopelessness, he could not be. For there were always the pleasures of living as he had since a very young man—a period he missed now—had no time for. Remembering riding the drift fences and saving strays, working his way into the confidence of a fractious ranch horse. Living unbathed for two weeks with everything you needed to survive rolled in a saddle tarp in some national forest.

He was far from all that youth's past—and the present was full of great promise. J. Willard said he got enough of the tragic awe of life, the ironic proclivities of existence by reading Thomas Hardy. And he'd also quote somebody called Wittgenstein: *I am committed, but I do not know to what.*

No, Jason felt he'd have to work things out as he felt and sensed them. For a purpose, for a reason, even for a morality. Do what he felt he had to, and if now he was not sleeping as well as he liked— he'd have to get used to it. The convention seemed so far away, and also so very close. He'd wake up shivering, worrying.

Chapter 35

His old dreams returned. He'd get to sleep, sleep soundly for an hour or two, then wake up with the images of the recalled dream that had occurred still someplace in the room, but not making much sense. It had all the elements of his dream syndromes. Of being lost, asking for directions, and no one answering. Lost, ignored in a strange place, but also somehow it was a familiar, distant city. He'd come into an old house, a marvelous Edwardian house from the days when they built them solid. But a house now in decay, with a pit yawning beneath its foundation. And the time element would shift from his childhood, mixing with people long dead. Again it was the present, everyone was watching him, laughing, hinting at something foolish, shameful. There was no solid dramatic line or plot; events made little sense when he came awake.

He got up so as not to wake Sheila and went downstairs and heard Fran snoring in the maid's room. It was just before dawn. He made himself strong tea—coffee was bad at this hour—and sat sipping it in the living room, in the dark but for the seepage from the corner street light. Any lamp lit in the house, and the police car would stop and knock to see if everything was all right.

In a week or so he would have four secret service men when he went out to the first of the primaries: that would be a pain in the butt with no real privacy, and adding to a sense of danger. Now, as he sat in darkness, a sliver of thought came to him between sips of the tea. Could he go out to address fairgrounds, impress a state of strangers that he was the man for them to instruct their delegates for? He sat wondering. His mind was tired or perhaps his mood grew careless; he thought, *was* he the man to run for the nomination?

Was it the time to surge ahead, to boldly follow those sensory impulses, give victory to his long-held desires? So why now was he beginning to think he was not the best man? What irrational guilt sat on his conscience?

No! He sat finishing the tea, now cold. Austin Barraclough the best man? But the best men didn't get elected these days. Austin didn't have a chance. He could not be a true participant with the organization he had. Senator Jason Crockett had the inside track, he told himself in the dark. Also good fund raisers, and that old fox, Amos Fowler, on his side. Austin with his contempt for compromise (yet with the same appetites and ambitions as other men), resolute, striving, was not any more or less the egocentric manipulator of the way the game was played now.

Lord! Jason rose, the teacup clattering in its saucer dropped to the floor, shattered. Why am I thinking I could hand him the nomination. If I was crazy enough to do it, it would most likely make him president. Watch it, boy, watch it! It's a sick night thought. The dark silent hours bring up painful silly perplexities, shove moral dilemmas into your face to make one wonder if one can fulfill one's potential. Go back to bed (let the shattered fragments stay till morning) in the late hour, house silent but for the creak of dry rot in the timbers shifting, the fridg motor coming to life. (Sheila gave me that cup on our fifteenth wedding anniversary.) In the morning you'll be free of night thoughts, busy on the Hill in the attenuated web of Senate politics, in the smell of Cloakroom cigars, the wax polish on his desk in the Senate chamber.

He moved through the Capitol, and the smell of the bean soup in the Senate Dining Room, the marble statues (old friends now), riding the private subway to a meeting of a committee in the Capitol building—all were pleasant, familiar. All fitted together and his skill, his drive made him an important man. He was applauded from the visitors' gallery, he met constituents and listened to their versions of crop reports, the tearing down of a historic bridge, the hopes of better prices for potatoes and heifers.

He ate a late lunch, went to his office to look at the mail, listening to the old alarm clock ticking. The sound was soothing, safe, familiar, and to its ticking, he dozed off into incomplete dreams to awake to the intercom buzzing.

Clair's voice was loud and clear, tearing him free from the last fragment of sleep. "You want to set up a press conference for the media tomorrow? Andy called, he can bring the wire services together at the Press Club tomorrow at two."

"Could he?" Jason tried to clear his brain, to focus, and he missed the tick of the tin alarm clock. "Any conflicts?"

"No. Oh, you promised to appear before the Western Pioneer Society, in front of the Washington Monument, at two. Lots of folks from our state are in town."

"Yes, yes. I want to make an important statement before the monument, and to that kind of group. Tell Andy the press can get it there."

"There will be television coverage."

He looked over at the silent alarm clock. "Fine. Oh, anyone been overwinding my clock?"

"The clocks, J. C., are all electric. Oh, you mean that antique?"

"I mean the clock on the bookcase."

"No, no one touched it."

"It's stopped ticking. I wound it myself this morning. Never mind."

He went over and took up the old clock and looked at its face, compared it with his watch. Been dead for one and a half hours, he noticed. The opening lines of the speech for tomorrow began to take shape. He began to wind the clock, but the key just turned loosely with no spring pressure. What had happened to its innards? He shook the old clock, there was some odd metallic rattle inside. He needed that old loud tick; the reasons were amorphous vagaries. It seemed silly to feel that way over an object, and he put the old clock away in his desk. He'd have it repaired if they still could find parts for the relic. Christ, the trifles we clutter our lives with.

It was like him, he felt, to be inconsistent and temperamental like this over an object. An old clock, suddenly feeling its age, dies of metal fatigue, or a broken spring. He needed to talk to someone alive, *not* an object. Sheila was too good a listener; loyal, loving, smart, but when he tried to talk out something deep with her, she tuned out. Just smiled and nodded. Esme, now there was a listener. Mrs. Jack Klein, and so that was all incredibly now the past, sealed off. Not Amos Fowler. Joel Silverthorn? No. Someone closer. He decided to call J. Willard. Pop was always a good listener, and able to nod to unrestrained speculation, clever old coot. Jason picked up the phone to have Clair get Vista City, and then shook his head.

Never use your office phones; not just that your staff could overhear; the FBI, the CIA were as shitty as ever about respect for their non-bugging orders.

He went down the elevator to the Senate gym, a place smelling of old socks and forgotten laundry. A flabby lame-duck senator was flexing a springed muscle builder, and a lean, narrow-hipped black was elegantly punching a bag, his butter-yellow skin shining with effort, muscles rippling like little busy animals under the hairless skin.

Jason waved to both men and went to a bank of phones just off the locker room, where someone had very recently spilled Brut. Some clown had also shot darts into the ceiling.

Jason got J. Willard at home.

"Hello, Son. Was just making a checklist of the polls. The goose hangs way up there."

"But as yet out of range, Pop."

"Christ, reminds me, we haven't been out at the duck blinds at Wattow Marsh in years. Mallard and teal, remember the goddamn sky just wallpapered with them in great big Vs? Buster Miller and me, we'd go, as young bucks, loaded on illegitimate hooch."

"Pop, I've had some strange thoughts the last few days, and nights."

"Sure, sure, why not."

"I've been think—yes." The damn phone was greasy to the touch and smelled of peppermint. "Tell me . . . what makes me think I'm ready to be president?"

There was a pause at the other end, a kind of whistle. Jason wiped the mouth section of the phone with his handkerchief. "Jay-boy, you sometimes don't follow patterns. I remember you thought your voice was too sissy to join the high school debating society. Hell, you swamped every speaker you debated. And first year of college football. You kept saying that big Polack fullback, that packinghouse lug, had the position solid. I had to practically hog-tie you to get you to fight for the job."

"I made halfback that year."

"I thought, no bullshit, you always in the end did justice to your potentialities."

"Pop, Austin Barraclough is the best man for the White House since FDR."

"Oh, is he now?" A long pause. "You've got buck fever, Jay.

That tremor in the limbs, like that quake in the voice before facing the other debating team. You used to vomit up your supper days before you ran for governor."

"J. Willard, I'm very serious. There's a discrepancy between mind and desire. Maybe I'm just a yokel, a smart country talent. A politically wise one, sure. But this thing is so big and the right man is here, available. And he can't win."

J. Willard's voice became lower, clear. "Look, that's not *your* problem. A man plays, knowing the averages at dice, at poker, and he takes advantages of his run of luck *and* card wisdom. Hell, you say Barraclough he can't win, so it's a load off your back. It's not like you were a spoiler. So don't get any butterflies in your gut."

"That's just it, he could win, if . . ."

There was some coughing on the other end of the phone line. "Swallowed the wrong way. I get it, you've decided—no, you're thinking of tossing your organization, your backers, the funds behind Barraclough?" J. Willard didn't sound sad, just hollow, raspy.

"I hadn't decided, Pop, just thought about it. Now I've talked to you, yes, I'm going to announce tomorrow at the Western Pioneers rally at the Washington Monument that Austin is the man to support, and I'm withdrawing my own candidacy and throwing everything behind me that will switch to him."

"What are you smoking, son? What makes you think the organization so carefully built up for you is going to change horse asses in midstream?"

"Now, you're angry, J. Willard. You're getting sardonic."

"I'm getting tired, I guess."

"It's my job to convince my backers. I'm strong enough, good enough to get him our backing. Yes, and I think Zack Boone's backing too."

J. Willard made meaningless sounds, then went on: "If politics weren't such a crazy, salacious racket, I'd say you were blowing your cork. Elections are built on frailties and catastrophes. All we Crocketts are lacerated idealists. Yes, I see it. I infected you. We want what's best for the nation. We see the vulnerability of this country to disaster through stupid, sick or dishonest leaders. Yes, it scares me nights. I had hoped . . ."

"I know what a sock on the jaw this is to you."

"Well, you play your chips as you see it, handle the cards that lie on your side of the table."

"You're hurt, Pop."

"No, just disappointed. A permanent state of mind when you get old."

"You think I'm a fool?"

"Yes, if your pipe dream for Barraclough is just wind. Oh, hell, there's some stubborn intricacy in you I don't savvy. Never did, truth is. But God, or whoever is moving the universe around, bless you."

Jason knew he had hurt the old man. "I can't explain in detail, Pop, my state of mind or reasons. I just keep telling myself as I talk to you it's the right thing to do. I've been made greedy by my possibilities, and J. Willard, I've been tainted, too."

"Well, as no one will ever thank you, I'll just say maybe you know your own mind in the end. So anyway, I'm the first to know."

"Yes."

After common goodbyes and J. Willard's tenacity keeping him from shouting, Jason hung up. Somehow he hadn't really been as decided as he had told his father. Yet it was good to have come around to saying it, getting it out. A sort of final exorcism of his doubts. He had sweated profusely, and showered when he got home. He slept well that night, after making violent love to Sheila who insisted they'd have to get new springs in Lincoln's bed in the White House at this rate. He did not tell her of his plans.

Next morning he typed out a statement on an old Underwood, ending with the words ". . . so I have picked this historic spot to announce that the only man of stature, integrity, of size and wisdom to lead this nation in this world of crisis and growing tensions, a world of revolutions, with new untried nations rising out of terror and bloodshed, with weapons of the most deadly kind distributed to them by us and others—the man to see us through is Senator Austin Barraclough. I shall put all the resources of my own backers and all those who will follow me to support Austin Barraclough for the Presidency of the United States. If I should fail in this endeavor, I shall never have regrets that I didn't try for what was best for all of us, and for the world."

Well, it wasn't Gibbon, or FDR or Churchill. But it would do. He took the statement down to the Senate library and made thirty photocopies of it, fairly clear ones. He wished he were a better stylist, wrote in more poignant rhythms.

Back in his office, Jason had Clair come in. He handed her a photocopy. "Read this. No comment. You're to release six copies I'll give you to the major wire services. And the *Washington Post*, the *New York Times*."

She looked up from reading, bug-eyed. "When?"

"At two o'clock. Also here are copies for Judge Fowler and Tom Pedlock and Silverthorn."

He saw the color of Clair's face change as she read. When she finished she said, "I think, I think I understand. It's just—Oh, J. C., you can underestimate yourself."

"Now, now, *no* comment."

"It's a shock. I think I'm going to toss my breakfast."

"No you're not. Get a copy to Andy. Where is he?"

"Lunching with the fund committee." The naive, credulous tone was gone from her. She had J. Willard's sardonic twang.

"I don't know how this will turn out. But if it does, Clair, what do you think?"

"Maybe there will be a miracle."

Jason shook his head, smiled as if begging understanding. "Anyway, you're being honest. Maybe it will take a miracle to pull this off. Get Dolf to have the car ready at one-thirty to take me to the rally. What happened to the old clock?"

"I took it from your desk—and down to that Swiss watch repairman near the Smithsonian. I know you liked to hear its ticking." She shook her head. "He said not a chance. It's all worn out and he'd have to make too many parts by hand."

"Throw it out." The old alarm clock seemed suddenly peculiarly irrelevant, absurd.

Chapter 36

They had come from far places, these people with badges and slogans who cherished perhaps a too simple idea of a past. They relished memories of log cabins, or sod huts, talked of great blizzards and flights of plaguing grasshoppers. They recalled great-grandparents' talk of bears killed in clearings and fighting the railroads to retain land, of tree stumps still scarring the hardscrabble farm, now sites for Exxon stations. They were "nostalgia hounds," as Snow Williams said in a broadcast. "Some think they are also people who take pride in the past."

The members of the Western Pioneer Society in Washington were mostly elderly, as Jason saw when Dolf drove the car as close as he could to the crowd packed around the Washington Monument. Dolf said, "The young don't seem to have any interest in any pioneer past."

"Unless it's a rodeo."

There was cheering as Jason left the car, Dolf pushing clear an engulfing path for him. Hands were offered and Jason recognized badges from counties he knew well: Reedflats, Blue River, Clangmore, High Sky, Killamook. Even some of the faces were familiar, and they would take umbrage if he didn't greet them.

"Well, how's it going, Wilbur?"

"That's right, Wilbur Stanish."

"And you're Fred Moore of Clangmore."

"Sure am. My wife, Maria, Senator."

There were, of course, reporters, cameramen. Jason suspected there must have been a leak of his plan. A news service perhaps, or the grapevine that spread secrets off the Hill, out of the Senate buildings.

Val Burton of the AP was at his elbow. "Senator, what's with this story you're withdrawing and handing over your organization to Senator Barraclough?"

"Your service has a statement."

"Can you just . . ."

"No, not now. Just listen to what I say here."

Jason, standing by the banner of the Pioneer Society, was shaking hands, looking out at a thousand people, all expectant of something. A microphone was set before him. He took a last look at his notes, folded small in the palm of his right hand. He thought for a moment of the fallibility of human beings under stress. He began, and after a formal greeting, "A man who has come from equalitarian surroundings, Austin Barraclough may appear an agrarian spirit in an industrial age . . . is still a defender of all that remains vital and honorable in an overwhelmingly materialistic century . . . and as a president who . . ."

Jason looked up in that significant pause he always practiced when addressing a group, searching for that *one* face, that one person he would focus his attention on while he spoke. Long practice had perfected for him this way of making what he said seem more personal, more direct and earnest. He broke off, searching—and found himself staring into the ugly shock of the barrel of a pistol. The surprise, with adrenalin-sharpened perception, registered the image of the youthful face of a rather plump man who held Jason's attention. The weapon pointed its one small black eye directly at him. *What the hell!*

He felt his scrotum tighten. Someone screamed as people either withdrew or moved forward. There was a kind of pileup of bodies thrashing about as if a football play had gone wrong. Jason was aware of Dolf pulling him down as the flash of flame came darting at him. Jason felt a searing blow someplace on his body. Heard the herd cry of fear, rage, a sound that seemed like the roar of the falls on Killamook Slope . . . He had a sense of falling; while near comatose he muttered *No, No, No,* the earth opening, support being offered, limbs propping him up . . . sky spinning, a woman's face bent over him, she sobbing, "Oh oh why, why. Poor man . . ."

NBC News Special

This is Martin McNarney, Washington D.C. At 2:07 this afternoon, Senator Jason Crockett, about to make a startling unexpected
political announcement, was shot at close range by a man identified
as Eugene Bromley, who from four feet fired a Colt 45 into the
chest of the Senator. Senator Crockett is still in surgery at this
moment at Walter Reed, and there have been rumors he may not
survive. No reason has been given by the assailant—a white Caucasian aged 34—for the assassination attempt, beyond shouting,
"Exorcise me! Exorcise me. Get me a priest. The devil is in me!"
From papers found on him, Bromley appears to have been at one
time a book salesman for the publishing firm of Abbot & Sandell,
but is now unemployed and living in the Washington YMCA, a
member of the Other Earth Society, dedicated to a revival of a
form of Druidism and the Farmers' Grange movement of the nineteenth century.

There is as yet no connection between the assassination attempt
and Senator Crockett's startling, even amazing press statement, issued in his name, that he will not run in any of the state primaries
seeking delegates for himself at the national convention. Also that
he is withdrawing in favor of Senator Austin Barraclough, and ex-
pects to bring over all the fervor, assets, and committees to make
possible the nomination of the man whom he calls "the American
most capable and honorable enough to run this nation in the present world crisis."

We shall report all bulletins issued of Senator Crockett's critical
condition. He is still in surgery. This is Martin McNarney with the
NBC news special from Washington, D.C.

At first it was dark, then it was light and after some time one
could not measure time for it kept slowing up and then speeding
up, as one broke through in splintered consciousness into sweet air
to the sound of the world again and all cold incoherent images subdued. One was prone on one's back and wore across one's chest
armor, but no helmet, and he had died at Agincourt and lay now
among the broken knights. Or it could be he had been lifted from
earthly mortality and was in that limbo between those who still
lived and ghosts by the billions that moved among the woodcut

clouds—Christ, I feel like a cat's dinner—Doré engravings for the *Paradiso* on the parlor table of one's grandfather. And someone reciting from a book read in college: *Our doubt is our passion and our passion is our task.*

"Darling," said Sheila, standing over the bed. "Dammit, Son," said J. Willard. He was so old and so concerned and he was very frightened: I have destroyed him. Done him great damage.

Sheila gripped Jason's free hand and for the first time he was aware of the tubes up his nose and a cast on his right shoulder. The encased shoulder did not seem to belong, not to him.

A voice of authority from someplace spoke. "Now *just* five minutes."

Sheila was fighting back tears and Jason saw for the first time his daughter and son Teddy, with their expressions of a communicable fear one finds in hospital rooms. Jason smiled at his children. Laura was getting too plump. Teddy had a guilty look for some reason. Adolescent boys usually do. I did. Sheila patted his brow. It was not easy to smile with the tubes in his nose, the drainage pipes in his ribs.

"Well, old girl, I'm still here."

"You're alright. Doctor Ringel says it's a miracle it missed all vital parts, just some bone and tissue damage. The press reports were all wrong."

"Hurts. Was it anybody from home?"

"What?"

"Who shot me . . . was it . . .?"

J. Willard pushed his head forward over the bed. "No, no, just some addled young nut. Like in the movies; wanted to pistol down some important gunslinger to get himself a reputation, attract attention."

"So, I'm John Wayne in Dodge City?"

"You're more this . . ."

And then everything faded out for Jason under sedation, and it was all dreams that couldn't be remembered and for a long time he didn't want to open his eyes.

It was evening, the blue-green light came from a lamp on a small white table. The shades were drawn, there was only a suggestion of the sound of wheeled traffic someplace near. J. Willard was seated by the lamp reading a newspaper. A stack of other papers was on

the table. Jason noticed flowers in the room for the first time. A
dozen overgarish baskets set all round the place, their odors too
sickening sweet. Fruit, too, he thought. Somehow he had always
felt a hospital room should have a basket or two of at least hot-
house pears, grapes, big red apples. He became aware the tubes
were no longer up his nostrils. And his mind had a quickness of
perception lacking till now.

J. Willard looked up. "Sleep good, Son?"

"I guess so. I really corked off. I was asking for someone?"

"Sure were. That boy you used to pal around with—Hank Wales
—he's the one got drowned. Your best friend as a boy."

"Yes, Hank Wales. How am I doing?"

"As a human being you're recovering. Not much damage, really.
The media built it up too much. Like you were dying."

"Did they?"

"Want me to read you the news?"

"Doesn't matter."

"The hell it doesn't matter. I'll save these papers for you. You
know what you've done?"

"Got drilled."

"You're a damn hero for your pushing Barraclough forward, and
I guess by getting shot maybe for doing it. You'll make both *Newsweek* and *Time* covers, I hear."

"Two cheers for me, Pop."

J. Willard got out a cigar and carefully lit it. "I promised not to
smoke up the place, but just a few puffs, what's the harm. It was
a long shot, your turning to Barraclough, and I don't think it would
have worked. But getting gunned down—why the party could hardly
wait long enough to spit before coming over behind you to back
you up. They figure what kind of a bunch of jackasses would they
seem, eh, if with you lying in heroic gore, they didn't back something noble you nearly gave your life for? Anyway, that's the tune
they're singing."

"What does it matter how it happened, Pop; most of the party,
I gather, is now behind Austin."

J. Willard grinned, "Even that sad-eyed hound dog, Zack Boone.
I guess he wanted to gather in a hunk of your glory and press headlines."

"You said on the phone, didn't you, it would take a miracle for
my idea to work?"

"Well, get down off the cross and forget politics for awhile. Heal first."

"Did . . ."

J. Willard cocked his head to one side, exhaled a plume of cigar smoke. "Austin Barraclough? Well, two calls . . . so far."

"I hope Austin doesn't think I got shot on purpose. Too damn painful." Jason tried to grin; he'd have to practice more; there is no more delicate deceit than a grin given in pain.

J. Willard fumbled among papers. "There are lots of messages. Amos Fowler—every hour. Oh, some woman from Florida . . ."

"Yes?"

"She insisted I deliver a message. Said, quote, You're my favorite yokel, and I'm sure you're also the fastest healer in the West, unquote. Said, Just E., you'd know."

It didn't matter, Jason thought. Nothing really matters but surviving. All good deeds must be punished: J. Willard used to say that, whenever Jason was feeling too chipper, too proud of something in the past. Now he had given up a great deal of himself, had been entangled in moral alternatives, even the power of delusion. The striving was in cold storage right now. Appetites and ambitions seemed such foolishment from a hospital bed. Enough, enough of scruples and renunciations.

I feel neither heroic nor significantly changed. It's like the year in camp, aged seven, and I jumped into the Roaring Bend River when the camp leader said, "Everybody in for a swim." I hadn't dared say I can't swim good in a river, have never been in one. And I had gone down, down, time and time again, holding my breath, coming up for air, and ashamed to yell help, help. Nothing at all had flashed through my mind, no movie of my entire young life as popular tradition said, no biography at all. Then someone noticed me bobbing about like a cast-off cork, and pulled me out.

There was a sharp tap on the door. J. Willard grinned. "I think you have a special visitor."

The door opened and Austin Barraclough in a well-cut dark suit entered, followed by Champ carrying a bottle and tray of glasses. Austin seemed amused as if at some private, embellished jest, as he advanced toward the bed.

"What the . . ." Jason said.

Austin motioned Champ forward with a baronial gesture. "I dug up *this*, my last bottle of so-called Napoleon brandy. I have shocking news for you, sir. Champ, pour a round."

Champ was already pouring amber brandy into two of the glasses, a few drops into a third.

"You see, Jason," he said, leaning over the bed, "your plan has failed. Men must in politics act out their past—there is no alternative."

"What the devil is this all about?" Jason took the glass handed him. J. Willard held his drink under his nose, sniffing. Austin Barraclough took the glass with the few drops of brandy in it and lifted it toward the ceiling.

"Gentlemen, to the next President of the United States, Jason Crockett."

"Wait a minute!" Jason wondered at just what stage of reality he was functioning.

"Drink, you lucky bastard." Austin seemed in a mood vicarious, yet heavily serious. Jason allowed himself a sip. It was certainly prime old stuff. Austin merely held his glass against his lips. "It's like *this*. I never had any real intention of running for the nomination. Shut up, don't talk. Listen. If nominated, I would not accept, as General Sherman once said, and if elected, would not serve."

Jason found more strength to his voice. "But damnit, Austin, it's a clear track."

Champ brought up a chair and Austin sat down. "Jason, you never come back all the way at my stage of the game, no, never all the way. I'm a burnt-out case."

J. Willard felt some protest was due. "That's a little strong, Barraclough."

"No. I'm a charred facade, a pretty good one, once, I admit. But the inner world no longer matches the outer one for me." He looked into the glass and then handed it to Champ. "I couldn't face a long, dirty political tour again. And the opposition, they'd dig up, somehow, records of my trips to the 'drying-out' farms, and something about Mona. But most of all, I'd never stand the pace; somewhere along the line I'd sag, take to the drink for support and *then* . . ." He waved a hand in the air.

Jason took another sip of the brandy, his hand trembled. "I really meant for you to have it all the way. It wasn't a grandstand play. I didn't feel, well, worthy."

"Hell, a good man rarely does. But don't you see that you're now a national hero and they love heroes—for a time. You, with your arm in a fine black silk sling, facing the people and all the support you'll have, why you're a shoo-in."

J. Willard motioned to Champ to pour again. "But Barraclough, you've already been announced. I mean, Jay has publicly issued a statement."

"Forget it. I've just issued one of my own. Champ, my eyeglasses." Champ handed them over. Austin swung them across his nose and took out a sheet of paper from an inner pocket.

"Ah . . . As of noon today . . . this release is to announce that for reasons that seem valid and clear . . . and while I am grateful for the gesture of Senator Jason Crockett in making me a gallant offer to step aside in my favor, I cannot, will not accept it. For he is the younger, the more ready man for the great office he will fill so well. I am old, and after so many years in public office I am tired. And I have earned my time to go to pasture. Jason Crockett is ready, alert, wise to public need, public service, and has those qualities of strength and determination I no longer feel I possess. So I shall remain in public life only long enough to speak out for him, back him, and ask all my friends and colleagues to do the same. Then . . ." He grinned. "I shall retire to write my memoirs. So friends and enemies, beware."

Jason wanted to shout *I refuse*, wanted to protest, but the shoulder hurt and he also was aware of the principles of political necessity that ruled one's life. Austin Barraclough seemed to read Jason's mind.

"You can't refuse and you know it! The public would damn you as a yellow-bellied coward when the country needs you. Oh, Jason, you *have* trapped yourself, haven't you?"

J. Willard said, "Looks that way, doesn't it, Son?"

Austin Barraclough nodded. "Champ, pour me just a little one, a libation, as we used to say in the Senate."

He took the glass and sipped, rolled it in his mouth, swallowed, sighed.

"I'd have been a damn good president, too."

"Yes," said Jason.